THE ALPHABET KILLER

OTHER BOOKS BY
JEFF VANOUDENHOVE

DARK PLACE

DARK LANE

DARK QUEEN

DARK CHILD

THE FINAL DARK

SCREAMS IN THE DARK AND OTHER TWISTED TALES

THE ALPHABET KILLER

JEFF VANOUDENHOVE

JAVO PUBLICATION

Westfield, MA

JAVO Publication
Westfield, Massachusetts 01085

This is a work of fiction. The characters, places, and events portrayed in this book are either the product of the author's imagination or are used fictitiously. Any similarity to real persons, living or dead, business establishments, or events is coincidental and not intended by the author.

ISBN
979-8-9865975-3-9

Library of Congress Control Number: 2023902301

Cover design by Joseph Weymouth

Acknowledgments

I would like to give a huge shout-out to Captain John Cartledge of the Northampton Police Department for working with me on some of the details in the writing of this book. When a moment struck, and I needed help sorting through some of the finer points of police work, I didn't hesitate to reach out to him, and he always graciously accepted my frantic requests for factual information. Thank you, my friend.

I'd also like to thank my editor, Elizabeth Kelly, who never disappoints in her daunting efforts of making my story better than it would have been without her valuable input.

I'd like to thank my cover designer extraordinaire, Joe Weymouth for the fantastic job he did on the cover design. His imaginative flair is a wonder to behold.

And finally, too numerous to name, I'd like to thank those who have supported me and encouraged me to continue writing the thoughts that are swirling in my head. It's been a wild, exciting, and sometimes trying time, and I couldn't have done it without your help. Thank you all. And on to the next.

IT BEGINS

This had always been a rough city, with its dark, towering spires looming far above the dregs who crawled in the dank, rat-infested bowels. It had a way of chewing people up and spitting them out as if their lives were meaningless, leaving them to scatter among the lowest of the low like the rest of the city's vermin. The fading light of the sun as it sank behind the artificial skyline of metal and glass cast the threatening shadows of those that lurked behind every corner of every building. They presented themselves boldly, cautioning random, hapless passersby of the impending dangers that awaited them should the shadowy distortions be taken too lightly or ignored. Whatever was once good in this conurbation was slowly receding into the sewers like the rest of the fecal matter after a hard rain. It was getting harder and harder to clean up the mess.

In my eighteen years on the force, I'd seen it all. I'd had to deal with domestic disputes (and not only where the man was the aggressor, though I'd rather it. It's uncomfortable and awkward taking a woman to the pavement without being able to show a hint of remorse). I'd dealt with my fair share of shoplifters, robberies, smash-and-grabs, home invasions, and carjackings. I'd even investigated a bank heist gone sideways (who would have thought the two masterminds involved would have gotten into an argument and shot each other right there in the bank?). I'd raided crack houses, busted prostitutes and their Johns, and rid the streets of three rapists. I had even tracked down the arsonist responsible for burning down half a city block a few years back. I'd had to deal with the aftermath of a mass shooting (one of the most difficult ordeals of my career, consoling those poor families who needlessly lost loved ones). I'd had to talk a few miserable souls down from a ledge; one from a bridge. Hell, I'd once delivered a baby in the hallway of an abandoned tenement. I've saved lives, and I've taken a life (I wasn't proud of that, but it was him or me, and I'd be damned if I was going to let my son become fatherless). As I said, I'd seen it all. Or at least, I thought I had.

Maybe I'd just been lucky to that point, though the thought alone was enough to make me question my sanity. For many people, the idea of being lucky was finding a quarter in the parking lot of their local grocery store or scratching a winning lottery ticket that offered them half their money back. I didn't believe in those things, so I'd never be *that* lucky. My kind of luck had always been more about facing impossible situations and learning to maintain some semblance of control over my emotions. I trained for it, I accepted it, and I lived it every day and have since I first swore an oath to protect the good people of this city (though it had gotten harder each day to sort through the garbage and smell of the festering turds to find those "good people").

Keeping one's emotions in check was a necessary skill, especially in my line of work. If I was unable, if I lacked control, I would have lost my job after only two weeks out of the academy, when Charlie and I, he was my partner at the time, had been called in on a possible child-abuse case. By the time we had gained access to that apartment, the situation had far exceeded abuse and teetered on sick and twisted.

The twelve-year-old's name was Sabrina. I can still picture her to this day, the way she was tied to the bedpost, her left arm distended and broken for disobeying an order by her disgusting, uncaring parents. It was clear she hadn't been allowed to use the bathroom for days, forced to roll around in her own excrement and urine-soaked sheets each night. Her wrists and ankles were raw and cut right to the bone from her struggling to free herself from the copper wire they used to restrain her. The girl's face was battered and swollen so badly that all her features blended into a ball of unrecognizable flesh. She had burn marks along her legs where her sorry-excuse-for-parents had used her as a human ashtray to snub their cigarettes. And her breathing was so shallow and labored that I didn't think she was going to survive long enough for the paramedics to arrive.

The sick individuals who did that to their poor daughter were present when we busted in but acted like they hadn't done anything wrong. After seeing the awful condition Sabrina had been left in, and what they had put her through, my thoughts immediately jumped to my son, Ben, who was seven months old at the time. My mind kept flashing snapshots of him being in this little girl's place, and I felt like I was going to lose it. Had I not kept my cool, I would have beaten both parents with my stick until they were a bloody pulp, and not even Charlie would have been able to subdue my rage.

Both parents were brought up on charges of child abuse, child endangerment, neglect, and several other things that the boys back at the station and I scraped together and threw at them to see what would stick. Sadly, a week later, murder was added to the growing list, when Sabrina died in the hospital from her injuries.

Charlie had already been a veteran of twenty-two years when he was paired with my rookie ass, so he had seen it all before. He'd seen the worst in people; he knew all the dark crevices of the city where light refused to shine. He was numb to all the atrocities people committed against one another. I was quickly learning.

As I stated, this had always been a rough city, the way it dug its claws into you and took its fill of blood without giving anything in return. But tonight, it gave something back.

A body turned up behind the old mill on 42nd and Main, stashed beside a dumpster amongst some used tires and weathered pallets. She'd been on the missing persons' watchlist for two weeks, her file ready to be relegated to a cardboard box in a dark corner of the basement like all the other unsolved cold cases. Instead, it was her rotting corpse that was found cold. I hadn't known it, but my worst nightmare was about to begin.

Chapter 1

D

It was situations like these that made me miss Charlie that much more. He had a calmness about him that defied logical response. It was almost as if he was dead inside after having lived through all the shit this city piled on top of him. It was just as well; if the kidney failure hadn't taken him when it had, today's horrific scene might have done the trick.

I got the call at 6:12 this morning. I knew it had to be serious, otherwise, it would have been Richie that was here instead of me. Don't get me wrong; Richie was a decent enough detective when he first joined the force. He knew his shit, and he knew these streets, but somewhere along the way, Richie's decency faltered, and he lacked that extra something you needed for this job. Sometimes you needed to listen to that feeling you'd get in the pit of your gut. You couldn't do that if you were a "strictly by the book" kind of guy, which was what

5

he was. I was more of a "fly by the seat of my pants" kind of guy. It sounded somewhat unprofessional, or at least unconventional, but it had always worked for me. It was why I was promoted to head detective at the precinct. It sure as hell wasn't my charm.

"What do we got here, Mick?" I asked the uniformed officer standing at the police tape, holding back the massive crowd of four onlookers. We didn't usually make a habit of calling the rookie beat cops by name ("rook" being the standard until they got some experience under their belt), but I knew Mick pretty well; he was like a kid brother to me.

"It's not pretty, Jimmy" he returned. "I hope you haven't eaten breakfast yet."

"I haven't eaten breakfast since you were a kid in Boy Scouts," I replied as I lifted the tape to slip under it. "I learned that a long time ago."

"Yeah, well, it's a good thing; you're in for quite a shock."

"Sad to say, kid," I responded over my shoulder as I walked toward the scene, "but nothing in this godforsaken city shocks me anymore."

Two other uniformed officers were standing by the dumpster as I approached. One had his arm outstretched, his hand clutching the rim of the dumpster as if trying to prevent himself from falling over. The other had his hat in his hand while scratching the top of his head, staring down at the victim's body. I was sure he was getting his jollies off of gawking at the woman's naked form, except, when I arrived, she wasn't naked at all.

"Step aside, gentlemen," I said as I tapped the head-scratching officer on the shoulder. He squeezed closer to his dumpster-leaning partner to let me pass.

I wasn't the first official on sight who had the authority to properly investigate the crime scene. That distinction went to

Mort from the city morgue. He was squatting beside the body and taking pictures, documenting every inch of the corpse and the immediate surroundings. He was blocking my view of the victim while he leaned over her, snapping away.

"Don't you have people to do this for you, Mort?" I asked, half-jokingly.

"When are you going to stop calling me that?" he asked, sounding annoyed as he stood erect.

Mort wasn't his real name; it was something we started calling him because he worked in forensics at the mortuary.

"Hey, sorry about that, Lenny," I replied, putting my hands up in front of my chest apologetically. Lenny Shurek was a geeky-looking fella who looked perfectly suited for the career path he chose, with his oily-slicked hair and the masking tape-repaired, horn-rimmed glasses he wore. At thirty-three, he was the youngest appointed Chief Medical Examiner this city had known, but the best we'd had in years. It was after my apology that he stepped aside, and I caught a full glimpse of the victim.

"She's a real mess, Jim," Lenny said as I stepped in closer to the body.

"I can see that." And she *was*, too. Lenny wasn't exaggerating. Her body lay crooked across the top of some disorderly stacked pallets as if she had been discarded like the rest of the garbage. She had large, blackened bruises up and down both arms, and her hands were covered in blood. Her pinky and ring finger on her left hand were snapped backward, as were her feet at the ankles. Her legs had scratches in all directions, indicating a possible struggle, maybe while kicking at her assailant. But the most appalling sight was the woman's face (or at least, what was left of it). The killer had taken a blade and cut around the perimeter of her face, then he peeled the skin down from her forehead to her mouth, revealing her skeletal structure beneath. I'd have hoped she was already dead before the killer disfigured her in such a way, but her bloody palms were a clear indication that she probably used them to feel that her face was missing.

"Fuck, Lenny. Warn me next time." I wiped my hand across my forehead to remove some sweat that seemed to have immediately formed while Lenny continued to snap pictures. "What can you tell me about her?"

Lenny snapped another picture and then turned to me. "I can tell you her name is Denise Flemming, she's thirty-seven years old, and she's been missing for two weeks."

"You got all of that from snapping some pictures?" I questioned. Lenny was good, but I didn't think he was *that* good.

"Her I.D. was left on the ground by her head," he said, pointing in the direction of her bloody skull.

I walked over to the opposite side of the pallet and sure enough, a blood-stained driver's license lay conveniently beside her. "This could be anyone's; how do you know it belongs to our vic?"

Without a word, Lenny walked to where I was standing, and with his gloved hand, he pulled the woman's flap of facial skin back over her bare skeleton.

"Jesus Christ, Lenny. Isn't there some kind of rule about doing stuff like that?" I glanced over at the two officers, one of which looked as if he was about to lose his breakfast.

"She's already dead, Jim," he replied. "And it's part of my job."

"Okay, fine," I said as he released her face, and I found myself averting my eyes. The sound as it flopped back down to her chin was enough; I didn't need to see it too. "But how do you know she's been missing for two weeks?" I asked.

"I get John and Jane Does in all the time," he answered. "I keep a binder of all the missing persons' notices in my bag for reference. Well, six months' worth anyway. It comes in handy. She's in there. Third page."

As messed up as that sounded, it actually made sense. We weren't always given the luxury of a victim's identification, and pulling prints only worked if the person had had a prior arrest or if they'd been through a CORI check that also required fingerprinting. Lenny's logic for keeping a binder was sound, if not a bit distasteful.

"So, you got anything else for me yet?" I inquired just as a familiar vehicle pulled up behind mine, followed by a news van. "Aw, shit. Here we go. Like I need this before 7:30 in the morning." I looked at my watch and saw that it was actually 7:48, but I got the feeling Lenny understood what I was implying.

"Don't like talking to the media hounds?" Lenny offered quizzically, turning his stare to the parking lot.

"I could care less about those idiots," I returned. "I was referring to my Lieutenant." I nodded my head politely in acknowledgment to the man as he stepped from his car, even though every part of me wanted to turn away and ignore that he was there.

"You two still having a lover's spat?"

I gave Lenny my best-annoyed look, though it wasn't real. I couldn't be annoyed with him about that; I'd never known him to have a sense of humor before. It was more refreshing than anything else. Maybe he *was* normal, after all.

The Lieutenant marched up past the two watchful officers, pointing at the dead woman and waving his finger from side to side, while Mick did his job keeping the camera crew subdued behind the police tape. "You want to fill me in on what this shit is?"

"Glad you could make it, Frank," I said sarcastically. I couldn't help myself. "What we have here is a genu-ine dead body. Did you forget what one of those was, or does your brain stop working after sitting behind that desk all day?"

"Watch your mouth, asshole," he responded angrily. "I'll have you pushing paper all week. I was talking to Mort."

Without batting an eye, Lenny stepped forward, pointing at the vic, ready to spill what he'd found. I wasn't sure if I should have been insulted that he didn't call Frank out about calling him Mort, as he had done with me. I understood it, though; Frank held rank over me.

"Woman in her late thirties," Lenny started, "obviously murdered. We know her name is Denise Flemming, according to her I.D., and that she was reported missing two weeks ago. That's about all we know right now, except, as I was about to tell Jim as you pulled up, I found something interesting on her leg."

He leaned in at her right side and pulled up the fabric of her shorts, exposing more cuts on her upper thigh.

"Jesus," Frank stated. "What the hell is that?"

"It's the letter 'D' cut into her."

"It looks more like a sideways triangle to me," I added.

Lenny nodded. "One would think so, yes, but if you look closely here at the front point, you can see where the killer tried to make a round cut but was unsuccessful."

I squinted to focus on the cut but had a hard time seeing what Lenny was pointing out. I wasn't buying it, but I thought I'd humor him. "So, why a D? What's it supposed to mean?"

"You're the detective, Jim," he answered, "you tell me."

"She's dead," Frank chimed in. "Maybe that's what the D is for. 'Dead.'"

"When I send out for a tox-screen, we'll see if she has any drugs in her system," Lenny added. "It could be for 'Drugs.' Maybe 'Dirty?'"

"Or maybe for 'Dumb,'" Frank jibed, rolling his eyes.

He wasn't wrong. Lenny was good at telling us how a vic died, but he was awful at deducing any reasoning why. Frank wasn't much better. I had to jump in.

"It's her name," I said. "The D is for 'Denise.'"

"Now, we don't know that, Jim," Frank stated argumentatively. "Don't be jumping to conclusions. It could be anything."

This is where my skills were best put to use. Or perhaps, it was that gut feeling I had mentioned. Either way, let the education begin.

"The killer carved a D into the victim's leg. He wanted it to be found, and he's telling us there's some significance to it. He also placed her I.D. right out in the open by her head. He wanted us to know her name, something he also felt was significant. He's showing us two matching pieces of the puzzle. D, Denise. The letter is for her name."

"What the hell are we supposed to get from that?" Frank asked, shrugging his shoulders.

"There's the question of the day, Lieutenant," I replied. "What the hell *are* we supposed to get from that? I just can't help wondering, do we really want to know the answer?" I walked away toward the camera crew that was scrambling to set up, even as I heard Frank say, *"What the fuck's his problem?"* My problem was, it was only 8 a.m., and I had already seen enough for one day. I didn't want to think about what Denise Flemming's death could mean. If it *was* a D cut into that woman's leg, then the killer was trying to send a message, and I suspected there was more to that message than only the letter D. I kept running different scenarios in my head, and I kept coming up with only one conclusion.

I sure as hell hoped it was only a triangle.

Chapter 2

STREET CHATTER

Word got out quickly once the media hounds sank their teeth into a story, and, in this one, the teeth sank deep. They were just doing their job; I got that all too well. And as this city continued its descent into the grime, the press became more demanding. We hadn't given them any pertinent information about the crime scene, only enough to satisfy their morbid sense of information-sharing like they were performing some kind of goddamn community service by reporting all of the gory details to the public. As if the community hadn't already known about the twisted shit that went on in the underbelly of this city. It shouldn't bother me; as I said, they were only doing their job. But I also had a job to do, and they needed to give me space. It wasn't up to me to force-feed them information. As such, the reporters who often stuffed their microphones in my face always received my standard response: "No comment."

Depending on my mood, or their dogged insistence, they might've occasionally gotten "Call 555-eat shit." That was my favorite, though, for some reason, the soundbite never made it onto the nightly newscast.

It was never an easy thing, especially in a homicide case, to break the unfortunate news to the family of the deceased. It was the worst part of the job. We learned that the victim was married and had two daughters, ages five and seven. According to the husband's statement, he had taken the kids on a road trip to visit his parents in Rhode Island a few weeks earlier. Denise couldn't make it because she had to pull a double shift at the hospital where she worked as a nurse. When the family returned, Denise was gone. A day later, after having had no communication from his wife, the husband filed a missing person's report, which wasn't taken seriously at first, since any person over the age of sixteen wasn't considered "missing" until after the first forty-eight hours. It only became serious after three days had passed, and the husband persisted in reporting her absence. What we didn't know, and may never know, is how or why the victim went missing. Had she been kidnapped? Had her marriage become too much for her that she felt the only way out was to run away? Maybe she was having an affair and planned to stay with her secret lover. I could speculate all day, but it wouldn't change the fact that the woman ended up dead.

After the first news reports of Denise's death aired, I took to the streets. You'd be amazed at what you can learn if you were willing to listen hard enough. I'd always been good at that. Somebody knew something, and contrary to popular belief, people *wanted* to talk. Unfortunately, not many of them knew what they were talking *about*; they just wanted their fifteen minutes of fame. But now and again, you'd hit the jackpot: an eyewitness, a secret conversation, a would-be suspect, an unintentional confession. If that were to happen, it would certainly make my job easier.

Even when I was a beat cop, I was out there talking with the ones who lived in the grime every day. They heard it all; they saw it all. I had to become friendly with them if I wanted them to talk. I needed to earn their trust, which wasn't always easy to do while wearing a badge. We called it a shield, and it acted like one too, shielding us from the people like we were above all of them. That was a bunch of horseshit, though most of my colleagues didn't share my view. They would rather stay at their desks researching on the computer than get their hands dirty on the streets. Maybe they thought they would catch something from somebody just by asking a few questions.

I'd say things used to be different, but they weren't. Nothing had changed. It was the same old filth no matter how much you tried to dress it up. Once you got used to it, it became a part of you, and you couldn't wash it off. So, the only thing you could do was roll with it. So, roll with it was what I did.

I started at Marty's Bar, a seedy joint down by the industrial park. It was close enough to the crime scene that some of the late-night or early-morning patrons could have seen something or someone unusual. I was familiar with most of the shady clientele that frequented the establishment. Hell, I'd busted half of them at one time or another. None of the regulars would have done something like what we saw by the dumpster; not even in an intoxicated state. They weren't violent drunks, only stupid ones, trying to drink away the misery that life had dumped upon them. They didn't realize that their excessive drinking was helping to contribute to it. No, I wasn't looking for one of the regulars, which was why I thought it would've been easier for one of them to rat on someone who wasn't. It would have given them an excuse to remind me I "owed them one" should they get picked up for something at a later date.

The hardest part of the questioning process was expecting results where there were none to be had. As optimistic as I was walking into Marty's, I was as equally disappointed, if not more, when walking out without so much as a contact buzz. Though the customers were cooperative, even remorseful about the woman's death, nobody had seen or heard anything. They *did* tell me that if they should learn something, I'd be the first one they'd contact. Right, like I believed that. Marty's turned out to be a dead end, so I was quickly off to my next destination.

The Ruby Room was a singles rave located three blocks from where the body was found. I wouldn't expect it to be a place that the victim frequented, nor would I expect any of the ravers to know anything about what had happened. I didn't go there for them; I went there for Papa Rio. He was the man in charge, holed up in the back room of the club, supposedly because he was agoraphobic. I couldn't confirm that, but whatever he lacked in public appearances, he made up for in knowledge of everything that went on in his little territory.

Papa Rio was one of three crime bosses this city called its own, and the only one who'd never been charged with anything more serious than serving alcohol to a minor (and even that was only once, and the kid he served had one of the better fake I.D.s I had seen). The lower west district was his slice of heaven, and he knew everything that went on behind those pearly gates. If there was anyone in this city with information about the murder, it would be Papa Rio. The trick was going to be trying to pull it out of him. The man only ever gave up enough information to keep the police off his back, and only if it suited his agenda.

It was early afternoon when I walked in, so there was no crowd to speak of. Things didn't pick up in this place until the sun went down. Papa Rio was expecting me; his goon at the front door radioed ahead to ask if he was available. I humored the call instead of just busting in; it was cleaner that way. I didn't want to get my hands dirty before even meeting with the man. It all worked out. Papa must have known why I was there, and he knew I wouldn't take no for an answer. He understood the game as much as I did.

The interior of the Ruby Room was quite large, with a stage along the left wall and a bar that spanned the entire right wall in a semi-circle. But once you got past the main room, the building became secluded and small. A couple more of Papa's men guarded the entrance to a series of pale hallways that led to a singular stairwell up to the second floor. They let me pass without incident like good little pets obeying their master. I suppose I should be thankful that Papa Rio had such obedient men (except when it was a detriment to my case); any one of them would have posed a significant snag if they chose to stand in my way.

The second floor consisted of a single, long hallway with only two doors adorning its plain walls. The door at the end was the man's living quarters, easily identified by the hired grunt standing out front. The other door, located halfway along the left wall was padlocked, probably housing an arsenal of weapons or a stash of illegal drugs. It didn't concern me, I was here for another reason, which, by the surly look on his face as I approached, was not conveyed to the bruiser guarding Papa's door.

"You're gonna turn around and walk away," the burly man said as he extended his arm and jabbed two fingers into my chest. He was a big man, maybe six foot four, easily two hundred eighty pounds, all muscle. Too much for me to even attempt to handle on my own. Perhaps his boss had changed his mind about seeing me?

"I'm here to see Papa Rio," I said in a calm, smooth voice, hoping I could reason with the mass of muscle. "He knows I'm here. How else do you think I made it this far?"

He looked at me with unflinching eyes as he folded his arms about his chest, a clear indication he was unwilling to budge.

"Come on man," I continued, "why don't you check with your boss? Don't make me call in the rest of the boys; I'm sure he wouldn't like that kind of heat."

The big man's eyes narrowed with annoyance, but before he could express how much, either verbally or physically, a faint buzzing noise sounded, and the door behind him clicked open. The large behemoth of a man took a slight glance over his shoulder, saw the door ajar, and stepped aside to offer me entrance. As I mentioned, I respected their obedience, as long as it didn't hinder my investigation.

I stepped past the human guard dog into the crime lord's loft, making sure to look up at the mountainous man with a victorious stare, a sort of "I told you so." He probably didn't appreciate it much, but I didn't care. Once inside, I turned to close the door, but the hired heavy beat me to it, pulling it shut. They knew their roles well; I'd give them that.

It wasn't my first time within those walls, but it had been a while since my previous visit. It was nice to see everything was as I remembered; it left little in the way of surprises. The massive space, one that had all the comforts of a luxurious suite in the finest hotel, with its freshly polished hardwood floors, extravagant artwork, and overly-priced furnishings, was in direct contrast to the gray world outside its walls. The same could be said of the man who sat behind the large cherry-wood desk at the far side of the room.

Papa Rio looked more like a pimp than a major player in a criminal cartel, wearing his trademarked white fedora, feather boa, and zebra-striped smoking jacket. In front of him, lying on the desk, was a cane with an exquisitely carved hand grip in the shape of a lion's head. I heard he had shaped the masterful walking stick himself, carved from a piece of 4x4 lumber after he had used the scrap wood to beat a man to death. He simply cut away all the blood and brain matter to get rid of the incriminating evidence.

The man stared me down for a few minutes before picking up the cane and using it to point at the leather chair across from him.

"Sit down, mon," he ordered. "Then we talk."

The poorly-delivered Jamaican accent was for effect, as were the dreadlocks draping down from under his hat. Papa Rio was born in this city. His real name was Alvin Todsen. I guess he felt having been named after a cartoon chipmunk and being just another kid from the hood wouldn't exactly strike fear into his enemies. Hence was born Papa Rio, along with the Jamaican persona he adopted.

"If it's all the same to you," I responded, "I'll stand."

"Suit yourself, mon."

"You know why I'm here?" I asked, standing firmly centered in front of the desk.

He smirked. "The dead always bring someone calling. You t'ink I got somet'ing to do wit' dat, mon?"

"No," I replied, "but I think you might know something about it."

"Let me tell you what I know," he offered. "You got the stench on you. You can't escape it; it's followin' you. Dat girl be dead, but her life was taken as a lesson. You don' want not'ing to do wit' dat, mon. It be coming for you, the learning. And you'd best learn quick, or death be coming for you too."

"What kind of voodoo philosophy bullshit is that? You *do* realize I'm not one of your cronies, right? I didn't come here for you to spew your nonsense."

"You t'ink what I speak be nonsense, mon?" His tone became harsher.

"Listen, you either know something about the murder, or you don't. If you've got nothing for me, then I'm just wasting my time, and I'll be on my way. But if you do, I'd appreciate a little cooperation. Otherwise, I've got no problem with my men coming back here and hauling your ass in for obstruction."

I don't think he took my threat kindly as he squeezed the lion's head in his palm and glared at me with fire in his eyes. Then, after a tense, silent minute, I saw his grip relax, and a forced smile came to his face.

"You do what you must, detective. But know dis; coming into my house and threatening me will get you not'ing but misery."

"Yeah, well, misery loves company."

"Death do too, mon."

His blank stare sent a chill through me. Then he continued.

"I told you, detective; it's all about the learning. School is in session. The girl you ask about was not the beginning of your lesson, nor will she be the end. The assignment's been handed out, and the teacher is just getting started."

"What the hell does that mean," I questioned.

"It means death lingers about you, mon, and it will continue to do so, just as it will deliver more death to your door. The question is, will you be ready for it when it comes knocking?"

I had nothing to say after those foreboding words. I couldn't tell if that was a warning or an observation. As a homicide detective, dealing with death was part of the job. He knew that. Still, I couldn't help but think he was alluding to something far more disturbing. Or, he could just be fucking with me and didn't know anything.

"If there is not'ing more, detective," Papa Rio pointed his cane toward the door, "I've got a club to run."

I nodded but continued staring into the man's cold eyes for a moment, mostly to let him know I wasn't one to quickly jump at his commands. It wouldn't last though; he knew that. I had no game here, no cards to play.

"All right, Papa Rio," I submitted. "I'll go. But if I find out you know something more than what you're leading on, I won't hesitate to come back here and nail your ass to the wall."

"I would expect not'ing less, mon," he replied with no hint of anger in his voice. "Now go."

I turned and walked away. There was nothing to gain by sticking around. I wasn't getting anything more from him even if I pushed the subject. But as I reached for the doorknob to let myself out, Papa Rio's voice rang out again, only it had no hint of the familiar Jamaican accent. It was Alvin Todsen who was now speaking.

"Oh, detective; good luck out there. I truly hope you catch your man."

I couldn't tell if it was sarcasm or sincerity.

"As if you give two shits," I replied.

He stood from his chair and spread his arms out to his sides. "I'm Papa Rio, mon." His accent had returned. "I give many shits. Death be bad for business."

I gave a final nod, then opened the door and walked out without closing it behind me. Let his hired help take care of that. It's what he gets paid for.

I went to Papa Rio, searching for answers I thought he could provide. I left there feeling more frustrated, and perhaps, slightly less intelligent. All he fed me was a bunch of gibberish about schooling and learning a lesson. What lesson was I supposed to learn? And why did it seem more menacing just then coming from my thoughts than when the words had first left his lips? I kind of wish I hadn't gone there to talk with the man at all. Now I knew this job was beginning to get to me. I was starting to second-guess the decisions I had been making. Shit. Thanks a lot, Papa Rio. Thanks for nothing.

I didn't suspect Papa Rio had anything to do with Denise's murder; it didn't fit his style. Just the same, if he did, or if it was part of some "boss war," he'd try to clean things up before his empire crumbled around him. I'd request a patrol unit keep a loose eye on his and his men's movements. Maybe we could finally catch him with his pants down.

Chapter 3

E

Receiving a wake-up call from Mort was never a good thing. Did that guy ever sleep? I knew he liked his job, maybe a little too much, but 5:45 in the morning was a bit uncalled for. He said he found something else on Denise's body. Whatever it was, it could have waited. She's dead, for crying out loud; it's not like she's going anywhere.

Since I was awake, I figured I might as well do my fatherly duties and make my kid some breakfast. I was surprised Ben wanted to stay with me for a little while when I asked. Now that he was older, he didn't usually choose me. I wasn't offended by that; he didn't usually choose his mother either. He'd gotten to that age where his friends mattered more. Still, it was nice to have him here, if only until he went back to school. I just wished it wasn't during this messed-up shit I was dealing with. I'm either working too many hours or trying to get a few hours of solid sleep. That's probably why Ben was eager to stay here; he had the place to himself most of the time.

I'd never been good at juggling the two halves of my life: the responsible husband and father, caretaker of his family, and the dutiful cop, protector of the innocent. If I had been better at multitasking, maybe Karen would have found an excuse to stick it out with me. Instead, I heard she'd been seeing some guy named Phil. Good for her. She deserved someone who could give her more attention than I ever had.

With that pitiful, lingering thought on my mind, I dragged myself out of bed, shaking my head in frustration at the early hour. Would it have been too much to ask for a decent night's sleep? It was bad enough I had Papa Rio's gibberish rantings in my head, keeping me up half the night, now I had Mort thinking he could keep me on speed dial like I was suddenly his best goddamn friend. The first chance I had, I'd be confiscating his phone and deleting my number.

As I wandered past Ben's bedroom on my way to the kitchen, I heard him stirring. My conversation on the phone must have woken him. I'd never been one to keep my voice down when aggravated. It was just as well; if I was going to cook the kid breakfast, he might as well be present to eat it.

I opened up the fridge and saw I was out of eggs, then recalled I had used up the last of them a month earlier when Ben stayed the weekend. I'd been meaning to pick up more but, you know, the job. The freezer was just as unkind, offering no bacon or sausage. I'd have to make do with what it *did* have: two frozen waffles and a half-eaten box of toaster strudels. I pulled out the two items just as Ben walked around the corner, rubbing his eyes and yawning as he spoke.

"Don't bother, Dad; I'll grab something a little later when I meet up with David."

"Sorry if I was a little loud in there," I nodded toward my bedroom. "It was work, you know?"

"Yeah, I figured," Ben responded. "It's okay. I was already awake anyway."

"At this hour?" I questioned. I felt obligated. Ben had never been one to wake up earlier than expected. And don't even get me started about how long he slept on weekends.

"I didn't sleep well," he answered. "And, before you question it, no, I'm not uncomfortable being here."

Smart kid. It *had* run through my mind.

"I think I'm just getting nervous about college in the fall," he continued as he slid a chair out from under the kitchen table and heavily plopped himself into it.

"Your mother's not still pressuring you about your classes, is she?"

"No, she's too busy with her new boyfriend to make a stink about it anymore."

"Hey," I said while placing a frozen pastry in the toaster, "don't be too harsh on your mom. She's allowed to date other people, you know. It's been over a year."

He reached up and rubbed the back of his neck while staring at me. "So, what's the case you're working on?" Ben asked, immediately switching the subject. I could tell he was upset about his mother's new dating habits. I was never there enough for the kid, but Karen was always present to play both parental roles in my absence. If she was suddenly spending more time with this Phil guy, Ben was probably feeling neglected. I wasn't going to harp on it.

"It's a serious one," I alluded. "I can't get into the details of it."

"Does it have to do with that dead woman? The one on the news last night?"

I sighed heavily while nodding my head. I'd always tried my best to shield him from that side of my job, but it'd gotten harder as he'd gotten older. "That's the one, kid. But that's all I can say right now." I watched his shoulders drop in disappointment. He probably felt this was a bonding moment between us, at least, until I cut it short. But I'd be damned if I was going to discuss the awful shit I had to deal with on the job. It was enough to give some people nightmares for life. I wouldn't do that to Ben. Suddenly, it was *my* turn to switch subjects.

"So, you're meeting up with David today, huh?" The toaster popped, and I quickly grabbed the strudel, threw it on a plate, and placed it on the table, sliding it toward Ben. "How is he doing these days?"

"He's all right," Ben replied. "He just moved out of his parents' house. I told him I'd help him arrange stuff in his new apartment." He looked at the pastry, deciding if he was going to give in to it, then shook his head as he couldn't resist. "I told you not to bother," he said just before biting into it.

"Let me feel like I'm doing something Dad-like, would you?" I shrugged my shoulders and gave him a little smirk. "I'm going to take a shower. Have another one if you want; put the rest back in the freezer." I patted him on the shoulder as I walked past him. He smiled.

"Thanks, Dad."

It wasn't the easiest thing, leaving my kid to go to work as if work was somehow more important. I imagined that feeling wouldn't change no matter how old he got. Kids didn't always understand that we did these things for *them*, to make their lives better. And as I walked into the morgue and saw Lenny studying the victim's body, I was reminded that my work *was* important. There was a killer out there who needed to be caught.

There were two other tables on the opposite side of the room that had bodies on them as well, both uncovered enough to see that Lenny already had his work cut out for him.

"You ever turn the heat up in here, or what?" I asked, feeling the chill through my clothes.

"Can't do it, Jim," Lenny replied. "These bodies would decompose too quickly. It's bad enough I had to drop the temperature a few degrees more than usual so that those two could be stored out here."

"What're their stories, anyway?" I asked, pointing at the far tables.

"Nothing exciting there," Lenny replied. "They're just a couple of holdovers from the funeral home that got delivered to me the other night. I've got a couple more of theirs in the coolers too. They've been so backed up with funerals since the start of the pandemic, they still haven't caught up. *They're* out of space; *I'm* out of space. The whole situation's a mess. Anyway, one's an eighteen-year-old kid who couldn't handle the stresses of life, I guess. He closed himself off in his garage while his parents were at work, fed a hose from his tailpipe into the rear window of his car, and sat there choking to death on carbon monoxide."

"Jesus. And the other?"

"That guy needed a lot of work when he first came in. Half of his body had been severely burned. He was working in his basement using an acetylene torch, when a large metal shelving unit fell over onto him, pinning him beneath it. Poor bastard had dropped the lit torch by his side and then couldn't free his hands to keep it from burning him. Even after his clothes caught fire, the torch was still directed at his side. It burned a hole clear into his gut. His wife found him when she returned from grocery shopping."

"Fuck, I'm sorry I asked, Lenny. Damn hobbyists. I don't know how you do it, dealing with death all the time the way you do. I see enough of it in *my* line of work. I can't imagine being around it day after day. I don't envy you with the stuff you must see."

"After the life leaves the body, Jim," Lenny began to explain, "it's no longer something to be troubled about. It takes on a new form. It becomes a mysterious shell, a tool we can learn from. And each body tells a remarkable tale."

"Sounds a little weird, Lenny, but whatever floats your boat. So then, tell me what tales you've learned from Denise's 'mysterious shell' here. What's so important that it couldn't wait?"

"Sorry about that, Jim," he apologized. "I had no idea of the time. There's a reason why I work in a morgue, you know. I have no clue about the social rules of people. But anyway, check this out; I found something you might be interested in."

He walked over to the far side of the table where Denise's head lay. Lenny had done a fine job stitching her face back together so that she looked more presentable - more at peace. Unfortunately, it did nothing to ease what I was feeling.

"I almost didn't catch this since everything else was so out there and in your face." He brushed aside some of her hair just above her ear to expose a small glimpse of her scalp. "Take a look."

I bent over and squinted to focus my eyes. There appeared to be some barely visible cuts or scratches.

"What am I looking at?" I asked, still trying to determine the importance of his discovery.

"You don't see it?" he questioned, sounding somewhat judgmental.

"Humor me," I said.

"It's another D cut into her flesh," he answered.

"Another D?" I questioned, still trying to make out the shape of the letter. "Why another one? What's *this* one stand for?"

"Well, if you're honestly asking my opinion," Lenny stated, unsure if my question was rhetorical, "I'd tell you it's for the same thing as the one on her leg."

"Then, why a second one?" I asked.

"Actually, *this* is the first one," he replied. "The one on her thigh came second. I found a strand of her hair in the lower wound, suggesting the killer cut this D first, then immediately cut the second one into her leg, leaving a trace of her hair. As for why.., I imagine it's because of the reason you're having such a hard time seeing it now, and the reason I almost missed it. I think the killer wanted it to be found, and whoever it was thought the first attempt at it wasn't clear enough."

"So, the person cut a second one just to make it more noticeable?" I questioned. "Sick bastard."

"It's just a theory," Lenny added.

It was as good a one as anything *I* had at the moment, and it was all I had to go with. Just then, my phone rang, startling me. I wasn't usually jumpy like that, but something about being around all these dead people got to me. I glanced at my phone and saw it was my Lieutenant.

"Yeah, it's Jim," I answered in an annoyed tone. I was hoping he heard it in my voice. If he had, he made no remarks about it while he delivered the unpleasant news. "What? You're shitting me. Yeah, I know, I know. I'll be there. Yeah, he's standing right beside me; I'll bring him along."

I hung up the phone and shook my head as I tucked it back into my pocket. "Looks like we're going for a ride. We've got another body just found behind Alfred's Appliances. Fuck, how bad can this city get?"

"I'll grab my things," Lenny accepted. "You're driving."

This city was going to the dogs. This latest body made eight already this month. I should be thankful they hadn't all been homicides, but only one of the deaths was from natural causes. One addict overdosed on heroin, one man had a heart attack at his work just two weeks before he was set to retire, and one individual crashed his motorcycle into a tree after he'd lost control from excessive speed. It hadn't been a good month. If the pace kept up, this city would be among the worst in the country. Hell, we might've already been there.

We arrived at Alfred's Appliances even before the news vans, which was surprising since they could sniff out a story before it even happened. One of the lab's staff was already on the scene snapping pictures. Frank was there too, standing at the rear corner of the appliance store, smoking a cigarette and giving the photographer some room to do his work. Next to him, looking distraught, with one arm folded about his chest and the other hand pressed firmly against his forehead, was Alfred, longtime proprietor of the appliance store. From the look of it, I'd wager he was the person who stumbled upon the body. He was pale, sweaty, and looked like he had become close and personal with the porcelain god a few times.

I walked past Alfred, giving him a slight, understanding nod. He'd been an upstanding member of this community since I was a kid, always friendly. He didn't need to be subjected to the darker side of what went on in this city.

"Hey, Frank, what do we..,"

"Goddammit, Jim! How many times do I have to tell you to address me as Lieutenant?"

And just like that, we were off to a rocky start. Someone had a stick up his ass this morning. Couldn't say as I blamed him. He'd been catching a lot of heat from the Captain about the number of unsolved murders piling up in our district. The cases weren't always cut and dried (wouldn't that be something), but lately, with the last handful, it seemed like we kept running into dead ends. We just had to stay diligent and remain hopeful we'd eventually catch a break in one of them. Still, asking me to call him "Lieutenant" was a big jump. Most others in the station called him "Lieu" or "L.T." He was always just "Frank" to me.

"Sorry, *Lieutenant*." I gritted my teeth when I said it. I was sure he understood my tone. He took a drag from his cigarette, then dropped it at his feet and tamped it out with the front of his shoe, all the while keeping his eyes fixed on the victim.

"You see this shit?" the Lieutenant said, pointing two fingers at the body as if he still had the cigarette wedged between his digits. "I need this like I need a hole in my head. Another day, another fucking corpse. I'm telling you right now, Jim, you'd better start getting me results on these homicides. I've got the Captain crawling up my ass, and the Chief is up his. And it's for damn sure the Mayor's gonna want answers."

"I'm already on the previous murder case, Lieutenant," I reminded him. "And I can give a rat's ass what the Mayor wants. I can only juggle so much. Why didn't you call Richie in on this one?"

"Christ, Richie couldn't solve a jigsaw puzzle if he had only three pieces left. I need *you* on this, Jim."

I drew in a heavy breath and let it out as I turned my stare to the victim. It was times like these I wished I wasn't as good at my job as I was. No rest for the weary.

"So, what do we have? What's her story?" I inquired as I picked up the Lieutenant's crushed cigarette and handed it to him, giving Alfred a nod. Frank didn't look as pleased but placed the cigarette's remains in his jacket pocket anyway. I was probably going to pay for that later.

We both walked forward to get a closer look at the victim while the lab photographer continued to circle the body, taking pictures from all angles. Lenny trailed behind us a few steps, showing how intimidated he was whenever the Lieutenant was around. Then, Frank began.

"Alfred said, after he arrived this morning, he went out his back door to toss the trash out, and there she was, lying in front of his dumpster. That was just after 8:00. And for Christ's sake," he yelled to the photographer, "will you stop taking pictures for a minute? Jesus, I can't think with all that clicking."

Lenny, the mouse that he was, sprang forward at Frank's angry demand and shuffled the worker aside while I tried to lessen Frank's temper.

"Take it easy, Lieutenant," I said calmly (believe me, I had to work hard at that). "Let Lenny have a look. We'll get you some answers." I nodded to Lenny, who was already squatting over the woman's body. She was lying face up, her head tilted to one side. Her legs were straight, and her arms were extended over her head, suggesting someone had dragged her there by her arms and then dumped her. Other than that, the body looked clean. If it wasn't for my theory about the body being dragged to this location, I'd wonder if this was even a homicide at all. "What can you tell us, Lenny?"

"Besides the obvious?" he started. Not a good line to begin with if the goal was to keep the Lieutenant's blood pressure in check. "Well, for starters, there's some scuffing at the back of her shoes. I'd say she was dragged here, most likely by a man, given her size."

It was good to hear I still had what it took to be a decent detective.

"Her body is stiff but not from the effects of rigor mortis," he continued. "The skin is still warm, but her muscles are stuck in a contracted state. Judging by how rigid her body is and how her hands are in clenched fists, I think she was electrocuted."

"Electrocuted?" I questioned. "Sounds more like an accidental death than a homicide."

"It's just a guess," Lenny continued, "until I can open her up."

"Wouldn't there be burns on her if she was electrocuted?" Frank asked.

"Not necessarily," Lenny answered. "It would depend on how easily the current passed through the body. And also for how long. She could have died instantly if her heart stopped, or she could have lasted a bit to where her insides had fried."

"Jesus, Mort," Frank raised his voice.

"Sorry, Lieutenant," Lenny offered. "What I can tell you, with at least 80% certainty, is that her time of death was within the last two hours."

I immediately looked at my watch and, from the corner of my eye, saw Frank look at his. It was 9:12.

"Right now, Lieutenant" I began, "with what we know, I think we can all agree the body was dragged here, but that doesn't mean she was murdered." I glanced toward Lenny, "You got anything conclusive that tells us this was a homicide?"

Lenny shook his head and shrugged his shoulders. "I'll know more when I can get her back to the morgue."

"Does she have a name?" Frank chimed in. "Something? Anything? I have to get someone to alert her next of kin."

I pointed beyond the woman's body, closer to the dumpster. "Is that a purse over there? Check if that's hers, would you, Lenny?"

Lenny stayed low to the ground and crawled a few feet to the leather bag. He ruffled through it for a minute before giving up and dumping the contents on the pavement. He brushed a few things aside, but I could tell even before he looked back at us, shaking his head, that he hadn't found anything.

"Fran..," I stumbled a bit. "I mean, Lieutenant," I really was trying to be more vigilant about that. "I'm going to speak with Alfred for a minute." I nodded my head sideways toward the elderly man. "Let me know if Lenny finds anything else."

Alfred hadn't moved from his position since Lenny and I had arrived. Who knew how long he'd been there before we showed up? Poor guy; I could tell he was taking it hard. I stood in front of him for a moment, silent, peering at his tormented expression as he stared at the woman's lifeless form. The man wouldn't even look at me, his face showing pure dread as if he'd never seen a dead body before.

"Alfred," I said softly, "you know me. My father used to come in here all the time. Talk to me. What do you know?"

He looked at me and shook his head. "I don't know anything," he said in his heavily-accented Italian voice. "I told your boss already; I came out here to dump my trash, and that woman was just lying there. I thought she had maybe passed out or that she was homeless and sleeping back here. I called to her to wake her up, but she didn't respond, so I reached down to shake her shoulder, and that's when I felt she was stiff as a board. I jumped away and immediately called 911."

I nodded my response while looking up along the roofline at the rear of his store.

"You have any cameras out here, Alfred?" I couldn't see any obvious ones.

"No, sir."

"Was there anyone else here when you first walked out?"

"I didn't see anyone, no."

Just then, Lenny shouted, taking my attention away.

"I got an I.D."

I looked back at Alfred, who continued to look flustered. "You're not in any trouble, Alfred, but I will have to ask you for a formal statement. Try and collect your thoughts. I'll be back."

I walked back to Frank's side and saw Lenny on his knees, waving a driver's license over his head to get my attention.

"Yeah, Lenny, I see. Do you mind filling us in?"

"Her name is Eva Henry; she's twenty-seven years old. She lives just a couple of blocks from here over on Stanton."

"Thanks, Lenny." I turned to Frank, shaking my head. "We don't know if this is a murder investigation. Do you need me to go to her residence to deliver the bad news? Maybe get some background?"

Frank sighed. "No, I'll send over a uniform to take care of that." Then, his voice raised to almost a shout, making sure Lenny could hear him. "But I want to know all the details on this one by tomorrow morning; you hear me? I have to let the Captain know what the hell is going on around here."

I nodded as Frank walked away, and although I didn't see it, I could tell Lenny was nodding along with me. Another cruiser showed up just as Frank made it to his car. He stopped to fill them in on the situation.

I turned back to Lenny, "All right, call it in. Have your boys come and get the body. Can you get a ride back with the van? I can't be around this anymore."

"Yeah, I'll take care of it," he responded.

"Oh, hey; where'd you locate the woman's I.D. anyway?"

"It was in her shirt breast pocket. Why?"

"Nothing."

Only, it *wasn't* 'nothing.' Why wouldn't her license be in her purse? Why would she have placed it in her shirt pocket? Was it so that it would easily be found? I didn't like where my thoughts were leading me.

It wasn't as if her license was in plain sight for all to see like Denise's was; it was tucked into her pocket. It didn't mean anything. I couldn't let one case affect my judgment about the other, and I couldn't let Papa Rio's words influence my thoughts. Hell, we didn't even know if this was a homicide yet. I needed to keep my focus on the woman we *knew* was a murder victim, which wasn't an easy task, considering I didn't have a lot to go on. I only knew I had to get away from *this* scene if I were to concentrate on the other. I knew I had told Alfred it would be me that talked with him, but I asked one of the late-arriving officers to grab an official statement from him instead. I couldn't be here any longer.

Spending a few hours away from the latest of this city's fatalities had done me no good. The leads in Denise's case were scarce. Her family and friends were grieving, her husband had been cooperative with the investigation (and why not? He had no reason not to be; he had a solid alibi), and there was no DNA left at the crime scene except what was from the victim herself. I wasn't getting much information back from the feelers I put out on the street, and when I *did* get something, it was either only opinionated banter from those who knew nothing about the case, or it was twisted fucks trying to claim responsibility for something they hadn't done. I didn't like being at a loss. Too many of these cases went unsolved each year; I didn't want this to be one of them.

I couldn't help but think how Ben would feel if it had been his mother that was found dead, dumped like garbage, lacerations cut into her with no explanation as to why. He'd be devastated. We'd both be devastated. Karen and I had gone our separate ways, but nobody's wife or mother deserved to end up as Denise had. I wanted to catch the sick bastard that had done that to her so badly, I had the foul taste of it in my mouth.

My thoughts were getting me so worked up that, when my phone rang, which usually only delivered unwelcome news, I embraced the interruption. It was Lenny. He was down at the morgue, and he wanted me to get there as soon as I could. I hoped he had found something more with Denise's body; something that would lead me in a more positive direction. In fact, I was so expecting that my luck had changed on the case that when I arrived and walked through the doors, I couldn't help but announce what I believed Lenny had discovered.

"Tell me the good news, Lenny," I began. "Did you manage to scrape some of the killer's DNA from Denise's fingernails? Come on, give me something."

Lenny was standing at a counter against the side wall, jotting notes into a binder when I made my loud entrance. He didn't budge from his position, even with the amount of noise I had made with my verbal speculation. Instead, he continued writing for a few seconds longer before turning and presenting me with the bad news.

"Nothing more on Denise yet," he said. "At least, not what you're thinking. I called you here because of what I've found with Eva."

"Just once," I responded, "I'd like things to go my way for a change. Okay, I'll bite. What did you find with Eva? Are we dealing with a homicide?"

"We are." He replied.

Without realizing it, I shook my head and exhaled heavily in frustration. It was becoming an automatic response. "Shit.

Frank's going to blow a gasket when he learns I now have two cases to sort out."

"Well," Lenny continued, "that's why I called you in. I wanted *you* to hear it before I relayed my findings to Lieutenant Garrett." He walked over to the latest corpse in his growing collection of bodies that had yet to be fully processed; Eva was number four, taking up space within the gray slab confines of his gloomy playground. I guess I wasn't the only one who was overworked.

"I think you may still have only *one* case," he continued as he partially lifted the white sheet covering Eva's naked body, exposing the dead woman's left side. He then reached under her back with both hands and carefully rolled her onto her right side so that I could get a look at what would surely give any sane man nightmares.

"Fuck, Lenny," I stated excitedly, but not in a good way, "is that what I think it is?"

"Sorry to say, it's *exactly* what you think it is. *That*, my friend, is the letter E cut into our victim's back. Nothing on this one's head, though."

As it turned out, my earlier disturbing thoughts were leading me in the right direction, after all.

"So, what does that tell us; we have some whack job going around carving letters into people's skin? Frickin' great! Just what I needed to hear, Lenny."

"Well, get ready, Jim," he warned, "because you haven't heard it all yet." He pulled a ziplocked evidence bag and a pair of latex gloves from his lab jacket pocket and handed them to me. Inside the bag was a severely wrinkled piece of paper that looked as though it had been crumpled into a ball at one point and then unsuccessfully ironed out.

"What's this?" I inquired.

"I found it clenched in her fist once I was finally able to pry her hand open," he answered. "You're gonna want to read it; it's addressed to you."

I felt the hair on my arms tug at my skin when he said that. I wasn't sure how to react, but I suddenly had an awful feeling in my gut that I wasn't going to like what I was about to read. I slipped the gloves over most of my hands (enough to keep from contaminating the evidence), opened the bag, and pulled out the paper. It had been neatly folded twice (or at least as neatly as a crumpled piece of paper *could* be folded) to make it fit inside the evidence bag. There were no markings on the outside of the folded paper, only the many crease lines that splintered in all directions across its surface. I handed Lenny the empty bag, unraveled the letter that had now piqued my curiosity, and began to read the handwritten note.

Mr. detektive man. May I call you Jim? Or do you prefer James? I hope this LETTER finds you. You disapointe me. The wispers sed you were smart, but you coodn't figure me out, so I asked "E" to help. Will it do the trick? Or will I find you lacking? You still have much to lerne. I'm on the prowl, and I have no plans of stoping. Five little soljers marched to their death. If you can't catch me, twenty-one guns will fire their final salute. Until we meet again. Ω

I finished reading, and I could feel my heart pounding through my chest. Lenny was looking at me a little funny. I'm sure I was flush, though my brain was on fire. As much as I wished Frank had called Richie in on this one, I saw now it would have made no difference. It would have ended up in my lap anyway. I didn't ask for this case; I didn't *want* this case. Yet, here I was, being called out. Fuck! As much as I didn't like it, I guess it was *my* case now.

Chapter 4

CONNECTIONS

This wasn't how the case was supposed to be. I was supposed to find Denise's killer, who we would have learned was just a strung-out junkie looking for his next fix. I was ready for the whole story. He tried to rob her, get whatever cash he could, but she didn't have any, or she wouldn't give in to his demands. He got a little physical; she fought back. He killed her and cut her for the trouble she caused him. End of story. It all seemed reasonable to me. Only, this story had a twist I never saw coming.

My thoughts immediately jumped back to my meeting with Papa Rio. Truthfully, his words had never left me, but I thought I could brush them aside like they were the rantings of a madman trying desperately to instill fear in his followers. Now, after the latest development, I knew that wasn't the case. Papa Rio told me there would be more death coming my way.

He could have been slinging bullshit, but he was still correct in his prediction; more death came calling. I didn't even contemplate it would revolve around the same killer.

"The press is going to have a field day with this," I said, shaking the hand-written note in my hand. "You know that, right? So, we have some deranged killer on the loose; is that what you're telling me? Some goddamn wannabe serial killer?"

Lenny raised an eyebrow and shrugged his shoulders. "Looks to be the case," he answered. "At least for these two ladies, anyhow." He swung his finger from side to side, pointing at both Denise and Eva.

My eyes followed back and forth between the two as if I were staring at a penlight during an eye exam. "And why the hell is this twisted son of a bitch specifically calling me out?" I questioned, more to myself than Lenny. A familiar Jamaican accent suddenly clamored in my thoughts, *'Death be followin' you, mon.'* Ok, great. That was all I needed, Papa Rio's disturbing words feeding into my already troubled mind.

"I'm afraid you're on your own with that one," Lenny replied. "But I found it an interesting read."

"You're telling *me*," I responded. "And look at this shit. Jesus Christ, I feel like an elementary school student could have written something better than this. Are they even teaching people how to spell these days?"

"You think it might be someone who doesn't speak English very well?" Lenny chimed.

"I'm not ruling anything out at this point, but if the guy is as uneducated as he appears in that letter, maybe he'll make a mistake, and I can nail him before he kills anyone else. Right now, I gotta break the news to Frank; he's going to frickin' love this," I said sarcastically, shaking my head while imagining Frank's reaction.

I handed Lenny the note, pulled my phone from my pocket, and stepped away from the body to clear my thoughts while I prepared to deliver the news. Once again, my eyes shifted from Eva to Denise and back again. Two murdered women, presumably at the hands of the same killer. From my new perspective outside the periphery of the cold bodies, the two women looked as though their deaths were unrelated. If it hadn't been for the letters carved into their flesh..,

My thoughts were suddenly interrupted as Frank picked up the line.

"Lieutenant, it's Jim. I'm down at the morgue with Lenny. Yeah, he called me down here, said he had something. I hope you're sitting down; you're not going to like this. I think we've got ourselves a serial killer. Or at least a repeat offender who thinks he's one."

I had to pull the phone away from my ear for the next few seconds while Frank shouted a slew of expletives that nearly deafened me, even with the phone several inches away. When I heard the rumbling die down, I brought the phone back to my ear and continued.

"I'm going to be here for a little while longer. Lenny's going over the details with me." I shifted my attention to Lenny who was too busy scanning over the killer's hand-written note to notice I had just acknowledged him. "I've got something for the folks in the lab. It's a piece of paper that was in the victim's hand." I didn't feel the need to go into great detail about what the piece of paper was, just yet. "Maybe they can pull some prints or DNA off this thing. Yeah. Don't worry, Frank; I'm handling it. Yeah, yeah, sorry. *Lieutenant.* Yeah, I will. I'll keep you posted." The call abruptly ended, and I pictured it was because Frank, in his usual angered state, slammed the phone down on the receiver. I couldn't blame him. I was feeling that same anger.

I tucked the phone back into my pocket and went to retrieve the killer's note from Lenny. As I approached, he offered his evaluation.

"Notice how he wrote the word 'letter' in all caps?" he stated. "Is that like a joke to him? You know, because of the letters he cut into the victims."

"Not a joke, Lenny," I replied. "A game. He's toying with us, and this little note is his first step toward letting us know he's the cat, and we're the mice. Let me see the note again." I grabbed the paper from his fingers, giving him little choice. It was addressed to me, after all. I should be able to read it when I want.

I studied the words more critically the second time, looking for clues or hidden messages the killer might have dropped. If I was right, and it *was* a game to the killer, then he *wanted* us to play.

"I'm getting a bad feeling about this, Lenny," I continued, keeping my focus on the paper. "It's obvious to me the killer has done his homework; he's probably heard about some of my past cases and is trying to challenge me. The sick son of a bitch needs motivation and excitement. Killing innocent people isn't enough. He needs to know he's better than those hunting him, even while he hunts others." I felt my grip tighten on the paper, and my jaw clenched between each sentence I spoke. "Whoever this sadistic bastard is doesn't view his victims as people. They're only tools in this twisted game he's playing, to be used as he pleases, to string us along. See how the worthless piece of shit wrote that he 'asked E to help'? Eva was holding this note, and even though her name was known to the killer, he labeled her 'E.' It's why she was chosen. E for Eva, just like D for Denise."

"So the killer is playing a game with letters?" Lenny questioned. "First D, now E. Is he trying to spell something?

Like 'dead'? Or 'death'? Or 'December'? It could be anything."

"No," I replied. "I have a feeling it's much worse than that."

"Worse than someone out there killing people?" Lenny questioned.

"Yeah," I replied. "Worse than that. The killer wrote he was disappointed I couldn't figure him out. This note wasn't the first clue the killer had left for us. We just didn't find the first one soon enough: the D cut into Denise's head above her ear. It was too subtle, which is why the larger one was later cut into her leg. It was meant as a flashing neon sign that read, *'haven't you figured it out yet?'* He's saying he's smarter than us, and he's challenging us.., challenging *me*, to catch him. And, what's more disturbing, I don't think this is the start of his game. I think we've joined a little late."

"How do you mean?" Lenny asked.

I shook my head and exhaled deeply, hoping I was wrong but knowing deep in my gut I was right. "It says here," I replied, pointing to the note, " *'Five little soldiers marched to their death.' Five* soldiers, Lenny. We're looking at two of them right now. I think there are three other victims unaccounted for. That would make these two women numbers four and five. If I'm right, I'm beginning to understand why the killer was disappointed. He wanted the attention to come sooner, but we missed his first three victims."

"Five victims?" Lenny blurted excitedly. "So then, something-something-something-D-E. Maybe 'burden'? Or 'border'? Or 'garden'? I don't know what this guy is trying to spell. It could *still* be anything."

"That's just it," I chimed in. "The killer's not trying to spell *anything*."

"How do you know that?" Lenny questioned.

"Because if I'm right, and these *are* victims four and five.., two of the *'five soldiers'* mentioned in that note, then I think *'twenty-one guns will fire their final salute'* means that there will be twenty-one more. Twenty-six victims in all. That's not a random number; it's the number of letters in the alphabet. Victim four was D - the fourth letter of the alphabet. Victim five was E - the fifth letter. I think somewhere out there is our missing A, B, and C."

"You're kidding me," Lenny gasped, a look of concern on his face. "And what about that?" He pointed to the symbol at the end of the note. "Is that supposed to be some kind of signature, his calling card, or something?"

"He's keeping with his theme," I answered. "It's a letter in the *Greek* alphabet. The last letter, actually: Omega."

"Kind of similar to what the Zodiac Killer used back in the seventies?" Lenny questioned.

"Something like that, Lenny; only this one bodes something far darker. Omega, meaning the end. I can only imagine he is referring to his victims meeting *their* end. Or is there a bigger end?"

"This is all blowing my mind," Lenny said. "This is big. Real big. I've never worked on a case involving a serial killer."

"Yeah, well, that makes two of us. I'm going to need you to keep working your magic on these ladies. Find me something, Lenny. There's got to be a connection. Meanwhile, I'm going to deliver this note to the lab. Maybe they can get something off of it."

I held out my gloved palm, but Lenny stood frozen, glancing at it confusedly.

"The bag, Lenny," I said, rolling my eyes. "For the note."

"Oh right," he said as he quickly handed it to me. I could tell he was a little embarrassed by that. He had been holding it in his hand the entire time; I figured he would have understood what I was motioning for. But, as I mentioned, although Lenny was great at his job, he was lacking in other areas.

I took a long, final look at both women before turning in disgust and making my way to the exit. I knew I was leaving Lenny with a heavy burden, but I had to get out of there to clear my head. I'd like to think my feeling of disgust was directed at the sick scumbag who killed those women, but I was placing it on myself, instead, for not having seen the signs sooner.

"Get me something, Lenny," I snapped over my shoulder without turning. And as the door slowly closed behind me, I heard him reply, "I will."

It was late in the day, and the lab techs had all gone home for the evening, so when I stopped in at the precinct, it was only to grab an evidence envelope and drop off the killer's note (I hadn't thought to grab one from Lenny while I was with him). When I walked in, I could see Frank was still in his office doing paperwork, so I tried to keep a low profile. I would eventually have to fill him in on the details, but I wasn't sure I could put up with his overreactive bullshit at that moment.

Quickly grabbing an envelope from my desk drawer, I slid the plastic bag with the evidence into it and proceeded to slink away undetected until I heard a young voice call out.

"Hey, Jimmy. Hold up, man."

It was Mick, returning from a coffee and pastry run for the other newer officers who, like him, were pulling night duty. A few officers requested to keep the shift, even though they had been approved to switch. I'll never understand it, but to each, their own. Anyway, Mick's noisy entrance ensured I wasn't getting away without meeting with Frank, as the Lieutenant immediately glanced up from his paperwork and shot me a glaring look. He pointed at me, then, with two fingers, waved me into his office. I begrudgingly nodded as Mick approached.

"I didn't expect to see you here, Jimmy," Mick said, still holding the coffee tray and bag of treats.

"Yeah, well, now everyone knows I'm here. Thanks, kid."

"Sorry, Jimmy. You still working on that dumpster girl case?"

"Something like that," I replied. "Listen, can you do me a favor, Mick?"

"Sure. Anything, Jimmy."

I leaned over the nearest desk, grabbed a sharpie, and scribbled on the front of the evidence envelope, "Vera, Process immediately for DNA and prints. –JH–"

"Run this down to the Dragon's Lair, would ya," I said, placing the envelope on the tray and wedging it between two coffee cups. The "Dragon's Lair" was what we called the lab because of how Vera ran the show down there. She'd been known to breathe fire up people's asses on more than one occasion. It was her specialty. It was *her* cave, and *she* was the dragon. "When you put it in the locker, make sure Vera's name is facing up. I want her to see it. She owes me."

"You got it, Jimmy," was his reply, nodding eagerly.

"Thanks, kid. Now I have to go and ruffle a few of the Lieutenant's feathers."

"Sorry about that, Jimmy," Mick stated apologetically.

"Yeah. Just get that to the lab."

I stepped away from the young officer before he delayed me any longer. Frank had always been an impatient man; making him wait never went over well. So, when I stepped into his office, and he calmly requested I close the door and take a seat, I expected it to be the only quiet moment before the eruption began. Instead, he clasped his hands on the desk in front of him and gave me an almost sympathetic look.

"Look," he delivered, "I'm not good at this shit, but I wanted to apologize for coming down on you so hard lately."

I sat motionless, almost uncomfortably, unsure of how to react. An apology was not at all what I had expected.

"My blood pressure has been through the roof," he continued. "My doctor's been telling me I need to work a little harder at not getting so riled up about things; my wife's got me on a special diet. It's all driving me nuts."

"Hey, I get it, Lieutenant," I responded. "No apology needed." It seemed like the thing to say, even though I felt like he had a lot more to apologize for than only his rotten attitude of late. "This job has a way of getting to us all."

"You got that right," he replied. "So tell me what you've uncovered about this case? Were you serious about there being a fucking serial killer out there?"

I gripped the wooden armrests of the chair, feeling my arms tense up at the thought of relaying the details of what I'd learned.

"I think it's a distinct possibility," I answered while nodding. "The latest victim, Eva… she had a letter carved into her back, just like the first girl we found. This one was an E."

"Shit! E for Eva, I imagine?"

"That's the theory I have right now, anyway."

"That's just great. What the hell am I supposed to release to the press?" Frank responded. "They've already been beating down my door about the first victim. I can't cause a panic about something that may or may not be, but I can't keep this contained for much longer. I need answers, and I need facts."

"I understand, Lieutenant," I replied. "The fact is, I haven't dealt with anything like this before."

"Didn't your old partner Charlie ever teach you about what he went through back in the eighties with the Midnight Mangler case?"

"He mentioned it a few times," I answered, "but he didn't like talking about it."

"Well, I suggest you start researching his old case files. Maybe there's something in there that can help."

"Yeah, I'll do that."

"Now, what about this paper you found in the girl's hand?" the Lieutenant probed. "What's going on with that?"

I had hoped he'd forgotten about it.

"I had Mick drop it off at the lab. We'll see what Vera comes up with."

"Mick?" Frank questioned. "That rookie meathead? He'll probably lose it on the way downstairs."

"Hey, take it easy, Lieutenant," I said heatedly. "Mick's a good kid."

Then, for a moment, there was an awkward silence that somehow felt much worse than any yelling Frank could have drilled into me. I had to speak up.

"Can I go now?" I asked, nodding my head toward the door.

Frank unclasped his hands and pointed at me, "Whoever it is, we gotta get this clown off the streets. I need you all in on this; you hear me?"

I nodded in agreement.

"Good," he continued. "Now get out of here. And make sure none of this leaks to the press. It'll be a goddamn circus."

I took no time to spring from my chair and exit his office. It never had an accommodating feel. My original plan was to drop off the evidence to the lab and then head home, but now it seemed I'd be taking a trip to the basement for some take-home research assignment. Just what I was looking for, some light and joyful reading material.

The archives at the station dated back to the thirties. For anything earlier than that, one had to go to City Hall to search *their* archives. When I first started on the job, the basement was a mess, filled with boxes piled anywhere and everywhere with no particular organization to them at all. I'd always been amazed when someone found what it was they were looking for down there. Of course, it always took them hours to search in that pit. But, a few years back, the city paid for a complete overhaul of the station, including efforts to clean up the criminal case archives. They brought in an independent company to organize and catalog all the files by year and date. They did a great job, don't get me wrong, but the city could have spent a little extra money on beefing up our servers and had everything scanned in electronically instead. But I shouldn't complain; I liked the feel of actual folders and papers in my hands instead of that virtual shit on the screen.

I strolled over to the eighties aisle and started scanning through the dates on the boxes. As I mentioned, Charlie didn't like talking about that old case of his, but he hinted about it enough for me to know when it took place. The killer he was after, the Midnight Mangler, kidnapped and tortured four women between Thanksgiving and Christmas of 1986, eventually killing each of them and dumping their bodies right in front of the station to flaunt his audacity. Charlie was the one who took the serial killer down, but that case affected him in ways most people would never understand. I never pushed the subject.

Just then, I felt my phone vibrate. I pulled it out of my pocket and saw I had two text messages. Both were from Lenny, though the first was from fifteen minutes earlier. I hadn't felt it go off when I was in Frank's office. The first message read:

Got the first victim's tox screen back. Her numbers were through the roof. She had so many drugs in her system, I'm pretty sure they caused her death before the killer even cut her.

Then, as a follow-up, Lenny must have felt he needed to clarify things for me:

And by the "first victim," I mean possibly number 4. D. Denise.

Lenny was a good guy, strange as all hell, but all I could do was shake my head at his texts and tuck my phone away. I had more pressing matters at the moment.

After finding the dust-covered box in question, I signed it out, lugged it upstairs, and left as quickly as I could. I didn't want to take the chance of being called into the Lieutenant's office again.

Doing research was always the worst part of the job, especially when researching a case that was almost forty years old. Charlie, himself, had only been on the job for three years when the Mangler case spilled onto his lap. Looking through his notes, *his* guy was a sick fucker too. Although, being a sick individual was a prerequisite for the job if you intended to be a serial killer. But the Mangler, he took the cake.

Like most serial killers, the Midnight Mangler had a particular M.O. Each of his victims was female, between the ages of eighteen and twenty-five, had blonde hair, and worked the late shift at their respective jobs. They each lived less than a block from where they worked, making it an easy walk. Unfortunately, it also made them easy targets.

The killer took each woman, tied them up in his basement, and began cutting pieces off of them until there was little left to cut. After about a week of the torture, if they hadn't already bled out, he'd kill them by cutting their throats. Then, he'd toss the body, and whatever parts he had cut from it, out of his car right in front of the station. He'd then begin his search for the next girl. It was a twisted pattern. I've read enough about these serial fucks to know that patterns meant everything to them. Only, from what I could tell, the killer I was after already seemed different.

I had two victims that had surfaced so far, and nothing that fit any particular pattern except for a letter carved into their skin. They were ten years apart in age. One was blonde, the other brunette. They didn't live anywhere near each other. The only pattern there seemed to be was that there *was* no pattern other than them both being female. Even their deaths had no similarity at all. One was drugged, and the other electrocuted. It's like the killer..,

Wait!

I couldn't believe I didn't see it sooner. The psychopath had been taunting me with the whole alphabet thing, and still, I missed it. I needed to get Lenny on the phone. I had a hunch the killer was feeding us more clues than we suspected.

When I pulled out my phone, I saw I had a missed call from Ben. He'd left a voice message, but it would have to wait until after I got Lenny on the line. It was getting late, and I wanted to catch him before he went to bed. I knew from experience he was an early riser, but I had no idea of the man's sleeping habits.

After a few rings, I began to think I would be stuck leaving him a message, which would have been awful for my current frame of mind. I felt like I finally had something, and waiting until morning would have blown my mojo. Luckily, on the fourth ring, he picked up.

"You'd better not be in bed," I said unapologetically. "I think I've got something on the case." I could hear the excitement in his voice when he asked me what it was. "I'll tell you when you meet me back at the morgue," I replied. "Yes, I mean now. And don't give me any shit. This doesn't even make up for all the times you've woken me up at four in the morning. I don't need your excuses, Lenny. I need you to meet me in half an hour. No, you heard me right; half an hour. All right. Good. I'll see you then."

It felt good to disturb someone else's night for a change. I was getting tired of it always being mine. I grabbed my keys and rushed out the door, leaving all the paperwork I had been going through scattered on the kitchen table.

I arrived at the morgue a few minutes before Lenny, which allowed me to gather my thoughts. I hoped I wasn't wrong about my hunch. It wasn't that I would have felt bad about dragging him down here at such a late hour; I just hated being wrong.

After Lenny arrived and shuffled his way to the front door, fumbling with his keys and grumbling the entire time, I reminded him there was an important reason we were there.

"You can hate me now, Lenny," I began, "but you'll be glad I got you down here once I tell you." I only believed that because of how energized he always seemed to be whenever the subject revolved around the recently deceased.

"Yeah? I'd better be," he responded. "I've already spent way too many hours here today."

"What are you talking about?" I questioned after he unlocked the door and practically shoved me inside. "I thought you loved this place."

"Not at night," Lenny replied. "I have my limits."

He turned on the lights and led me down the stairs to the "dungeon." That was what I called it anyway, the place where Lenny conducted all the autopsies. The large, brightly lit room looked the same as when I had left it earlier that day. The two women were lying on the two tables closest to the entryway, while the other two tables against the far wall still had their male occupants.

"So, what was so important that we had to be here tonight?" Lenny asked.

"D," I replied, pointing at the first table. "For Denise." Then I pointed at the second table, "E for Eva."

"We've already established that, Jim."

"Right," I continued. "At first, I couldn't see anything more in the pattern than that, but then, I realized the true pattern was that the killer was following the alphabet not only with who he killed, but *how* he killed. Denise was drugged. There's the D. And Eva, she was electrocuted. There's the E. The killer is using the first letter of his victims' names to determine how he is going to kill them."

"Or he's determined how he wants to kill," Lenny responded, "and then chooses a victim whose name fits. Okay, I get it. But you could have sent me that in a text. Why are we here?"

"I told you we were missing victims A, B, and C," I answered. "I believe two of them are right there." I pointed to the male corpses across the room. "I need you to look for a letter above the ear. It would be subtle, just like the one you found on Denise."

"Holy shit!" Lenny stated, suddenly rejuvenated by my theory. "Neither of them came in as a homicide. I had no reason to look for anything suspicious, especially not a letter carved into their head. You don't actually think..?"

I shot him a confident glance. "What's his name?" I asked, pointing to the burn victim.

"His name is Bru… Oh, fuck me." Lenny quickly grabbed a pair of latex gloves and hurried to the first table. "It's Bruce," he finished as he began to brush aside the man's singed hair with his fingers. "Shit, shit. I think there is something here. It's faint. Tell me what you see."

I leaned in and focused while Lenny continued to spread the man's hair as best he could. "Right there, Lenny," I said, requesting that he hold his fingers still. I took my phone out and snapped a picture, then zoomed in on the image. "I don't know about you, but I'd say that's a B cut into Bruce's head."

Lenny glanced at the second table. "And now I know what I'm going to find on Cameron over there."

"He's already got the right name for it, doesn't he?" I added as Lenny scrambled to the table occupied by the teenager's corpse and began his exploration. It only took a few seconds for Lenny to respond with a disheartening nod.

"It's there," he said. "There's a C."

I shook my head in disgust. "Bruce was burned. Cameron was killed by carbon monoxide poisoning. Our killer's certainly been busy. Now we just need to find A."

Suddenly, Lenny's eyes widened as he turned his head toward the side wall, where, behind three small stainless steel doors lay three built-in refrigerated chambers. His eyes were fixed on the center door.

"I think I know where A is," he muttered. "Amber in the middle there," he nodded in the direction of the wall. "I've been storing her for three weeks now. She died from asphyxiation."

Chapter 5

Five little soldiers marched to their death. That was the killer's message. And five victims is what we'd discovered so far. There was now no doubt we were dealing with a serial killer. The deranged individual wasn't killing only women; a man and a teenage boy were earlier victims. When I wasn't smart enough to notice he was out there, trying for some reason to get my attention, he escalated from cutting a small letter in his victim's scalps to something more noticeable elsewhere on their bodies. If he wanted my attention so desperately, why'd he wait until his fifth victim to leave me his calling card? It didn't matter; he had my attention now.

I looked at Amber's cold body and wondered why someone would do these things. She was a good-looking girl, twenty years old, shapely, with long blonde hair. She had her whole life ahead of her, and this bastard came along and cut it short.

I didn't blame Lenny for not catching it sooner; her death was from asphyxiation due to a severe asthma attack. Another fucking A-word. Her parents found her dead in her apartment when they stopped in to check on her because she wasn't returning their calls. She was on the living room floor, an inhaler under the coffee table only a few feet from her. Amber's medical history confirmed she was asthmatic, having had several attacks in the past few years, often triggered by anxiety. There was no reason to believe the young woman's death was from anything other than an existing medical condition. The medical report substantiated the cause of death; her airway was swollen and constricted, indicative of a person having an asthma attack. Nobody could have suspected Amber's death to be a homicide. Only now we knew differently because, like the others, the killer had cut the letter A into the side of her head. It was barely noticeable, but it was there, just above her ear.

"It started with this one," I said, breaking the uneasy silence that had fallen between us after learning the truth. "Amber's the key. She set the killer on his path. I need to know why. What was his motivation?" I looked around the room at the sick bastard's handiwork. Five bodies, all innocent people who had met their demise at the hands of that sadistic fuck. He had to be stopped. And whether it was his intent or not, he had only motivated me to want to catch him that much more.

"I need you to check these three over again, Lenny," I said. "Knowing what we've just learned, maybe there's something else they'd missed."

"I'll get on it," he answered while nodding. "But it won't be tonight."

"What the hell, Lenny?" I questioned, irritated at his response.

"Jim, it's almost eleven o'clock. I'm exhausted. If I don't get some sleep, I'll miss something for sure."

I looked at my watch and confirmed; he had a point. I had been so wrapped up in our findings that I had lost track of the time.

"All right, Lenny. Let's call it a night. But I want you on this first thing in the morning."

"I will be," he replied. "How does this mess with your schedule tomorrow?"

"It doesn't," I answered. "I had no plans except looking for more clues about our little freak. Only now, I have to break the unfortunate news to these victims' family members. At least that will give me more people to question and a better chance of learning something."

Lenny nodded as he removed his gloves and tossed them into the trash. I couldn't help but think I was forcing my obsessive need to catch the killer upon him. He didn't work for me, yet I continued to order him around. He enjoyed working with the dead, so he continued to accept. Maybe it was a mutual understanding between colleagues. Still, even if I couldn't respect the man for being the timid mouse that he was, I at least respected his work ethic and all that he did to learn the truth behind people's deaths. Even though important evidence had been missed about these three victims, he'd now do everything he could to make things right. Over the past few years, he'd helped our department more times than I could count. The least I could do was forgive him for this one mishap and his need for sleep, especially since he let me drag him down here so late. And without his help, we wouldn't have been able to prove my theory.

Lenny locked up, and we parted ways. I knew he'd get busy finding out all he could about the bodies in the morning. As for me, I had planned to sort through more of Charlie's old files on the Midnight Mangler. But Lenny was right about what he had said earlier; it was late, and I was exhausted too. If I continued searching for things in my current state, I'd miss pertinent details.

I'd made up my mind on the ride home, convincing myself that sleep was the better option with which to end my night, but when I arrived, the lights were on, suggesting Ben had made his way back to the house instead of staying out with friends until an ungodly hour, which I found to be typical for kids his age. He was a good kid, something for which I didn't give him enough credit. It was only then that it hit me that I hadn't checked the message he had left me earlier.

Staying in the car, I pulled out my phone and listened to the short voicemail:

"Dad, it's me. David's car broke down; we could really use your help. Give me a call as soon as you get this message, okay?"

Shit. I always managed to let the kid down. Well, I'm glad to see he made it home even without my help, but it didn't excuse me for not getting back to him. It was just one more thing on a long list of disappointments for which I needed to apologize.

I got out of the car and walked to the front door, hoping Ben would already be in bed. It wouldn't be the first time he'd left the lights on. When I walked in, it didn't come as much of a surprise to see he was still awake, but I was shocked to see what he was doing.

It was my fault. I had left in such a hurry to meet Lenny at the morgue earlier that I had never cleaned up the paperwork I had been going through. It was all laid out on the table, the gory details of the Mangler's kills, and Ben was sifting through it as if *he* were the detective on the case. He didn't attempt to hide the fact he was looking through police evidence, which I figured was better since it meant he didn't have to lie to me about it.

"Hey, you shouldn't be looking through that stuff," I said calmly, knowing full well it was I who was to blame for exposing it to him. "It's an old police case I was researching."

Still holding a document in his hands, which I could see was a photo of one of the Mangler's victims, he turned his attention to me, a confused look on his face.

"This is the case of that serial killer Uncle Charlie helped catch back in the eighties," Ben said. "Why are you researching that?"

"Whoa, whoa. First off, how did you know about that?" I asked, walking over to him.

"Um, hello, the internet," he replied, looking at me as if I hadn't known of such a thing.

It was true that someone could learn about the Midnight Mangler and the detectives who were involved in the case by simply reading about it online, but there were details about those old murders that had never been released to the press. I didn't need Ben reading about all that awfulness.

"Oh my God," Ben asked, sitting up in his chair. "Is that what your current case is about? Is there a serial killer?"

He seemed a bit too excited. "Hey, stop that," I said as I swiped the photo from his hand. "You know I can't talk about my case, and you know you're not supposed to be looking through these files. Now, come on, pack it up." I motioned for him to get up from his chair so I could be the one who did the *actual* packing up. He stood as I asked him, but he remained fixed at the table, staring at me through bellicose eyes.

"I'm not a kid anymore, Dad. I can handle this stuff."

"For one thing, Ben," I said as I gathered the scattered documents into a neat pile, "you might not be a kid anymore, but you'll always be *my* kid. And as such, you know there are things in my professional life that can't be discussed with other people, not even family."

"Can't you share *something* with me?" Ben pleaded. "Just the smallest thing? I want to know about what you do."

Shaking my head, I picked up the pile of papers and tapped the edges against the table to straighten them out, then threw them into the accordion folder that had housed them. I tilted my head and looked at my son, whose eyes begged for his father's attention more than for the police detective who stood before him. And at that moment, his father spilled out.

"There's someone out there who's killed five people that we know of so far. He's dangerous, so you need to be careful. That's all I can say right now. And you can't let anyone know until we alert the media. You got that?"

He nodded his head and gave an approving look. "Thanks, Dad. And what's the second thing?"

"What do you mean?" I asked, shoving the large file folder under my armpit.

"Well, you started by saying 'for one thing,' which would indicate you had more than one thing."

"Oh yeah," I nodded. The kid was showing his deductive skills. Well, his old man is a detective, after all. "About earlier tonight, I'm sorry I didn't get a chance to return your call. But it looks like everything worked out. And since you took it upon yourself to go through my files, I'd say we're even." I smiled and rubbed his head, of which I knew he wasn't a fan.

"It's okay, Dad," he replied as he shrugged away. "After I didn't hear from you for forty minutes, I figured you must be busy on your case. I called Mom."

"Oh, so your mom came all this way and picked you up?"

"No," Ben replied. "She was working a double shift, so she had Phil come and get us."

That was something I didn't want to hear, but I had to get over myself. I couldn't have it both ways. I should be thankful Karen's new boyfriend was willing to go to bat for the kid when I was unable. If nothing else, it showed he cared for her. But it still felt like a punch to the gut. I wouldn't let it show, though.

"That was nice of your mother's boyfriend," I stated as positively as I could. "I'll have to remember to have your mother thank him for me." Ben wasn't buying it as he rolled his eyes and nodded. "Why don't you go on to bed? It's late." I nudged him. "And you'd better not have nightmares from your late-night reading choices," I joked.

"Yeah, All right," he acceded. "And thanks again, Dad, for sharing about your case. I won't say anything."

I patted him on the shoulder, "Sure, kid." Then he turned and retired to his bedroom. I wasn't far behind. The case just took a significant leap forward, and I had a lot to do come morning, starting with meeting Amber's parents. As if it wasn't bad enough that they'd lost their daughter, I now had to tell them she'd been murdered. I was sure that would be the low point of my day; I could only hope it would get better from there. I'd find out soon enough; it was already past midnight. I had a feeling morning was going to come way too quickly.

Sometimes it was a curse being right. The morning *did* come too quickly. Coffee wasn't working its magic fast enough. It was strong as hell and blacker than night, but it did nothing to clear away the haze in my head. I had a rough night of sleep, thinking about how to break the news to Amber's parents. The last they knew, she had died of natural causes. Well, as natural as a severe asthma attack could be. I'm still not sure how the killer did it. Murder by asthma. I couldn't imagine there'd been too many reports written about that in the past.

I should have filled Frank in on what I was doing this morning, but he would have held me back until he could get the state police involved. I didn't want them to hinder my investigation. If Amber *was* the killer's first victim, then I didn't want to waste any time. I needed to learn what I could about who she was or why the demented psycho chose her as the catalyst for his twisted game. I would catch the Lieutenant up after meeting with the girl's parents. And as he chewed me out, I'd keep reminding him of the good job I'd done and about everything I'd learned about this case in such a short time. Yeah, that'd go over well.

The moment of dread was upon me. It wasn't my first time delivering such news, but it felt different somehow. These poor people were already mourning the loss of their daughter; now I was about to kick them while they were down.

I strolled up the walkway to the front door, readying myself in case one of them became overcome with rage. It was a rare occurrence, but I'd seen it once before. Years ago, Charlie had been attacked by a distraught father when the man learned his son had been shot in a gang-related incident. I had to tear the overly-aggressive man away and arrest him for his uncontrolled actions, but he was let off the hook because of the extenuating circumstances. Having a teenage son myself, I understood how one could easily lose control as he had. I suspected Amber's parents would be more reasonable.

I didn't get the chance to knock, as the door opened when I reached the top step.

"Oh, hello," The woman said, surprised at my presence outside her door. Her husband bumped against her from behind since she had suddenly halted their obvious departure. "May I help you?"

"Mr. and Mrs. Rhaines?" I asked. "Amber's parents?"

The man immediately stepped in front of the woman defensively, brushing her back with his arm.

"Who are you, and what's this about?" he questioned.

"I'm sorry, Mr. Rhaines," I replied. "I'm Detective Jim Haddick with the Southbridge Police Department. If you have a few moments, I'd like to speak to you folks about..," I hesitated, gleaning the look in the mother's eyes as she peered over her husband's shoulder. "It's about your daughter's death."

I noticed Mrs. Rhaines' hand grip her husband's arm as the words left my lips. He acknowledged by turning his head slightly in her direction before focusing back on me.

"I'm sorry, detective," the man replied, "we'd like to help you, but my wife and I have been through quite a lot these past few weeks. Not to mention, we're on our way over to our daughter's apartment to clear out some of her things. That goddamn landlord of hers only cares about getting the place rented again as quickly as possible."

I was glad to hear the daughter's apartment had been untouched.

"I understand," I offered, "but what I have to discuss is important. I promise I won't take much of your time."

"Mitch," Mrs. Rhaines jumped in, her soft voice barely audible, "it's about our little girl; let's hear what he has to say."

Mr. Rhaines shook his head and sighed heavily before giving in to his wife's request, stepping aside to open his home to me.

"Come in, Detective," he said, backing away from the door, "before I change my mind."

I nodded, "Thank you, sir. I appreciate it," and stepped inside their quaint home. No sooner had I closed the door behind me than Mr. Rhaines verbally lashed out.

"What is this about my daughter's death? And why did they send a detective here to talk to us? What's going on?"

He was obviously newly agitated and distraught.

"Nobody sent me; I'm here on my own. We've recently discovered something regarding your daughter's cause of death."

"I don't understand what that means," Mr. Rhaines said. "Amber died from an asthma attack."

"Yes," I replied, "that *has* been confirmed. But we believe the attack was somehow induced by someone else."

"What are you saying?" Mrs. Rhaines questioned. "What does that mean?"

"I'm sorry to have to tell you this, Mrs. Rhaines, Mr. Rhaines, but your daughter's death has become part of an ongoing murder investigation."

"What? Murder?" Mr. Rhaines questioned as his wife covered her mouth in shock and stumbled back, falling onto the couch while tears began to well up in her eyes. "She had an asthma attack. How is that..?"

"I understand your confusion," I continued. "Unfortunately, I can't elaborate other than to say that we are looking further into the matter. I'm afraid I'm going to have to ask you to hold off disturbing anything in Amber's apartment until we can get forensics there to look things over."

"But we've already packed up some of her belongings," the father said.

Fuck! Of course, they did. And why wouldn't they have? Their daughter has been dead for three weeks. There was no suspicion of foul play. They had a right to her property. So much for the apartment being undisturbed.

"Do you have any of those personal belongings here?" I asked. "Anything you may have taken from the apartment?"

"Well..," he turned to his wife, who had already begun to sob, "we have a few boxes of her things in her old bedroom. We haven't gone through any of it yet."

"May I?" I requested.

"If you think my little girl's death was deliberate, and going through her things may help you find answers, then by all means. It's this way." He pointed to his right down the hall.

While Mrs. Rhaines stayed behind, rocking herself back and forth on the couch, perhaps in a state of shock, Mr. Rhaines led me down the hall to a small bedroom on the left. The room lay as empty as a vacant dorm room during the summer months. Other than three taped cardboard boxes situated in the center of the floor, it felt as though nobody had ever occupied the space.

"Is that all of it?" I asked.

"That's all we have," he responded. "There were a few items we tossed into the dumpster behind the apartment, but nothing of any significance."

I hated hearing that. In such a case as this, who knew what was significant or not?

"When was that, Mr. Rhaines?"

"It was last week sometime. Tuesday, I believe."

That was unfortunate. The waste management company would have emptied the dumpster by now. There were still the remaining items in Amber's apartment to be examined, but for now, these boxes were all I had.

"Do you mind if I..?"

"Please," Mr. Rhaines quickly interjected as he grabbed the top flap on one of the boxes and peeled away the tape. "As

I've said, we haven't gone through any of this yet. We were grabbing things and throwing them into boxes, not paying attention to what they were. I think we were too numb from it all."

"I completely understand," I said as I squatted by the first opened box. There were some magazines on top: Elle, Marie Claire, Mademoiselle, Women's Health, nothing out of the ordinary for a twenty-year-old. Below them, there was a health-club membership I.D. attached to a lanyard, two used movie tickets to the latest Tom Cruise movie, a pair of sandals, sunglasses, some hair ties, a rolled-up scarf, and a half-eaten pack of Wint O Green Lifesavers. Digging deeper into the box, I came across a handful of pictures, some loose, some framed. I sifted through the loose ones first, admiring the beautiful landscapes she had taken while her father stood over me, delivering commentary about each of his daughter's adventures.

"Did your daughter travel a lot?"

"Any chance she could," he replied, "since she was seventeen. It was difficult to keep her in one place for too long."

"Some of these pictures are amazing," I expressed, rounding out the last of them.

"Yes, Amber had an eye for that sort of thing."

I nodded as I set the loose pictures aside and started on the framed pictures. There wasn't anything unusual about the first few pictures: a graduation photo of Amber with her parents, a picture of her showing off a third-place medal after a 5K road race, and one of her kissing an older woman on the cheek, which I could have guessed was her grandmother, even if Mr. Rhaines hadn't immediately blurted out that fact. But when I reached the fourth picture, it gave me pause. It was a close-up photo of Amber and another person from the shoulders up. The other person was unrecognizable due to someone having scratched out their face. Was it Amber who did it or someone else? I held it up and turned my attention toward Amber's father.

"Have you seen this picture before? Do you recognize the other person in this photograph? Was your daughter involved with someone?"

"No," he replied, shaking his head. "And I don't think I've seen that picture before. Perhaps my wife knows about it." He turned his head to the door and called out, "Dear, can you come in here for a moment?"

While we waited for Mrs. Rhaines' arrival, I flipped through the remaining frames, none of which gave off any questionable vibes, and there was nothing more in that first box except for some well-used textbooks. Mrs. Rhaines slogged into the doorway, her cheeks still red and damp from the tears she tried her best to wipe away.

"What is it?" she asked, her words devoid of all sense of purpose that I was sure had, at one time, exuded happiness and joy.

Mr. Rhaines snatched the picture from me and handed it to his wife.

"Do you know what this is about; who this other person is?"

Mrs. Rhaines looked at it curiously, "I don't know who this is." She ran her finger down the glass over the faceless person. "Was this with Amber's things? Who would do that?"

I stood and grabbed the top of the framed picture, gently so as not to upset the woman, but just enough to let her know I required it back. She complied and released it to me.

"It could mean nothing at all," I responded. "Perhaps someone your daughter was upset with, and she overreacted one night? Still, I'd like to take this if I may, along with these other two boxes. I promise I'll get them back to you."

"You don't think that person had anything to do with my daughter's death, do you?" Mrs. Rhaines asked, her distraught voice coming through loud and clear.

"I wouldn't want to speculate, ma'am," I replied. "But if it's not too much trouble, I would like to get a list of your daughter's friends, people she might have hung out with, coworkers, and such. I'm sure one of them would be able to clear this up."

"Of course," Mr. Rhaines replied. "We didn't know her coworkers that well, but we'll get you as much as we can."

"Thank you." Just then, my phone started vibrating a hole in my pocket. "Excuse me," I said, tucking the frame under my left arm. I pulled my cell from my pocket just as the vibrating stopped. It was a missed call from Frank, but I also saw I had a missed text message from Lenny from ten minutes earlier.

```
I'm sorry, Jim. I couldn't help it. Lieutenant
Garrett was asking me too many questions. He'll
probably call you next.
```

Shit! I guess I now knew what Frank wanted. I was hoping to hold him off until I got back to the station, but he wouldn't be happy if I kept him waiting any longer. I'd have to call him back.

"I have to get going, folks. Something urgent has come up. I'll just grab these boxes and be out of your hair."

"I'll help you with that," Mr. Rhaines said as he bent over and picked up the nearest unopened box.

"Thank you, Mr. Rhaines." Before picking up the second box, I extended my hand to Mrs. Rhaines, to which she obliged. "I'm very sorry for your loss," I expressed, as images of my own son flashed in my head to remind me what she must've been feeling. What they *both* must've been feeling. "I'll be in touch."

I released her hand and watched it drop to her side like she was carrying a cement block. Then, I turned and placed the framed picture on top of the second box, freeing up my other hand for ease of lifting.

As Mr. Rhaines and I made our way to the front door, with Mrs. Rhaines leading the way to open it for us, I reminded them of their obligation in all of this.

"So, if you could gather up some of those names - people your daughter knew - it would be very helpful. I'll send an officer back to retrieve them."

Mrs. Rhaines nodded as I walked past her. "Yes."

Mr. Rhaines and I loaded the boxes into my car, then I gave him my card and shook his hand.

"If you think of anything else," I stated, "even the smallest thing, please don't hesitate to call me."

He didn't release my hand right away, instead gripping it tighter.

"If someone killed my little girl, Detective, you need to find that person; you need to find them and stop them from doing this to anyone else's daughter."

I nodded, and he released his grip. "I'll do everything I can," I assured him. "In the meantime, this is an ongoing investigation; I would appreciate your and your wife's cooperation. No more going to your daughter's apartment until we clear you to do so."

"I understand," he replied.

"Take care, Mr. Rhaines." I gave him a final nod before getting into my vehicle and driving off, shaking my head at the thought of the entire situation. You got used to it after a while, but the minutes immediately following those unpleasant instances lingered on your mind until something just as awful came along to distract you from them. In this case, the distraction came quickly. I had to call Frank back, and I knew it would not be a pleasurable conversation.

I scrolled through the contacts displayed on my dash until Frank came up, only he wasn't listed as Frank; I had him programmed in as "S.O.B." instead. I thought it would make me feel better when I had programmed it that way, but it only served as a bitter reminder of the past. One of these days, I'd have to change it back, but for now, "S.O.B." would receive my return call.

"Hey, Fr…Lieutenant; it's Jim."

"What the hell is going on, Jim?" he started, his raised voice echoing through the car's speakers. "I gotta hear from Mort that this case is bigger than we thought?"

"Yeah," I replied. "Lenny mentioned to me that he filled you in. I was actually heading to the station now to update you."

"Goddammit, Jim. I'm getting hounded by the Captain every day about this fucking case, and you're keeping things from me?"

"No," I responded, finding myself arguing with my radio. "I wasn't keeping anything from you. I had a lead that I couldn't sit on. Jesus, Frank; you wanted me on this case; now you're going to pull this shit?"

"What am I supposed to think?" he questioned. "You don't tell me what's going on."

"I told you; I had a lead."

"Well, you'd better get your ass in here. I have a meeting with Redfern this afternoon, and if I don't have something to report, he's going to rip me a new asshole. Which means I'll be ripping you a new one right after. Got it?"

"Yes, got it. I'm on my way now, and I've got some things with me. I'll fill you in when I get there."

"You sure as hell had better."

"Lieutenant. Frank. It's not good."

"Get in here, Jim."

The line went dead after that.

We've had our differences, Frank and I, especially after what he'd done, but he wanted the same thing we all did. He wanted the criminal element off the street, and he wanted justice for the victims of the heinous crimes those criminals committed. For that, anyway, he had my respect. Otherwise, I would have transferred to another precinct long ago.

He could be a bit much at times, but his irritation wasn't completely without warrant. I should have contacted him last night after I discovered the killer's pattern. At the very least, I should have phoned him first thing this morning. But if I had, he would have insisted I go in to catch him up on all the details first. That would have caused me to miss Amber's parents, and the Rhaines would have gone and disturbed more evidence at the girl's apartment. It worked out better my way. I hoped I could convince Frank of that.

Pulling into the station, I saw Richie having a smoke in his vehicle. It wasn't allowed on the property, but most guys snuck a drag here and there to relieve their nerves. The job could get to you sometimes, so, for the most part, brass turned their cheek to it. You couldn't expect a person in our line of work to shy away from their vises just because there was a policy against it. It wasn't a reasonable expectation. And, since Richie was out here, maybe it would work in my favor. I didn't want to lug both of these boxes on my own.

I purposely parked in the row behind his, in a space diagonally from his driver's side, so I was easily noticeable from where he sat. I got out, walked around to my passenger side, and grabbed the first box from the front seat. I knew Richie had seen me through his side mirror, as evidenced by him rolling up his window as I approached, leaving just enough of an opening for his cigarette smoke to escape. I could appreciate someone not wanting to be disturbed on their break, but I wasn't going to let him off that easy.

I saw him shaking his head as I stepped up to his window. He was doing his best to look the opposite way, pretending he hadn't noticed me standing there. With his window slightly cracked, I could have just called him out, but I decided on a more subtle approach since I'd be asking for his assistance. Extending my knuckle from under the box, I lightly tapped his window a few times. He turned and looked at me with an expression conveying disappointment about his unanswered wish that I continue to walk past his car without stopping. Some things weren't meant to be. He rolled his window down, allowing a plume of nicotine-infused smoke to fly free from its captivity, dousing me with the reminder of why I had quit years earlier.

"Hey, Jim. What's going on?" I could hear his annoyance for having been disturbed; he wasn't doing much to disguise it.

"I've got a second box in my backseat," I said, nodding sideways. "Would you mind giving me a hand with it?"

He leaned his head out the window to look at my car as if to calculate the distance. Like it would somehow play a part in his decision. He must have deemed it manageable since he rolled his window back up and opened his door, grumbling under his breath as he did so.

"Yeah, I can give you a hand," he said with a noticeable sigh, dropping what was left of his cigarette to the pavement and stomping it with his shoe.

"Thanks, Richie," I acknowledged as he brushed past me without another word.

Like me, Richie was in his mid-forties, though he moved like he was nearing sixty. The years had not been kind to him, perhaps from an over-indulgence of smokes and alcohol. Since his second divorce, he'd stopped caring as much about his health, instead, choosing to let himself slowly wither away as a forgotten, middle-aged, old man. His waistline was thinning almost as much as his quickly, graying hair, which he rarely bothered brushing anymore since he was showing more scalp than he was mane. I watched as his hitched stride leaned more toward being a hobble than a march and imagined he'd be walking with the assistance of a cane in only a few years. It strengthened my theory that if the city didn't bring you down, divorce, depression, or alcohol would. Maybe a combination of the four. I lived in this city, and I'd already gone through a divorce. It occurred to me that I was hanging by a thread. I was one traumatic incident away from becoming Richie. I hoped this case wasn't that one shove over the edge.

Richie had gathered the box from the backseat and slowly joined me by his car. Before we headed inside to drop them off at their resting place beside my desk, where crumpled pieces of paper and stacked coffee cups had taken up residence, he stopped my advancement by jumping ahead of me and stared me down as if we were about to brawl.

"How did you get this case?" Richie questioned, almost as if looking for an excuse to start that said brawl. "The Lieutenant still favors you over the rest of us, huh?"

"Honestly, Richie," I began, treading lightly to keep from provoking him, "I think I'm the last guy he favors. I told him I didn't want this case, so he went and stuck it with me anyway. That frickin' guy is always looking for ways to stick it to me." (*Or stick it somewhere else*, I thought).

"This thing's too big for you, Jim. You gotta know you're in over your head."

I glanced at him curiously. Though his words rang true, I probably *was* in over my head; I wondered how *he* knew.

"Richie, what do you even know about the case I'm working on?"

"I know it's not an isolated homicide. You've got yourself a twisted fucker who's killing people. That's all I need to know."

"Okay," I responded, slightly annoyed, "but *how* did you know?"

"I straight-up confronted the Lieutenant," he answered. "I overheard him on the phone with you earlier, and it sounded like something big. I marched right in on him and asked what was going on. Why all the hush about a homicide? He told me it wasn't just one; it was multiple. I asked him why he didn't assign someone else to the other case; he told me there *was* no other case. What the fuck's going on, Jim? Do you got yourself a spree-killing nut job?"

I guess the cat was out of the bag. If Richie knew, everyone knew (or they soon would). I wish Frank would have kept it to himself until after I met with him. Now I had to smooth things over with Richie, who probably felt he was the more qualified to handle the case. He wasn't; not in his current state. The thing was, even if I wanted to give it to him, there was little chance of that happening, especially not after Frank learned about the note personally addressed to yours truly.

"It might be something like that," I returned, trying to appease his curiosity without giving any definitive answer. "I'm still trying to work out the details. That's why I've got these boxes; I'm hoping something will pan out and lead me in the right direction."

"So, you don't know shit yet," Richie retorted, a smug look on his face as if he hoped for my failure.

"Not a lot, no," I replied. "I imagine that's why Frank wanted to see me. He probably wants to ream me out for slacking on this case."

It was easy telling someone things they already believed, even if it wasn't true. And Richie, he wanted to believe. He wanted so badly to believe I was a failure - that I couldn't get the job done - if only so that it would make him feel better about his life swirling down the toilet. I wasn't against leading him down that road if it kept him off my back. I could play the naïve detective if I had to.

"I really appreciate your help, Richie," I continued, nudging him with the box I held, hinting at my urge to move inside. "Maybe I could bounce a few ideas off you later today. I mean, it might help me out with this thing; it's overwhelming."

I was laying it on thick, and from the arrogant look on his face, he was eating it up.

"Yeah? Well, you know, Jim," he replied, "I'd like to help, but I'm kinda swamped with my own cases right now. Freaking things just keep coming in; you know what I mean?"

"Oh, I do," I answered, slinking around him since he hadn't picked up on my subtle hint. "Still, thanks for helping with these." It finally sank in as I walked away from him, talking over my shoulder. He quietly followed.

After dropping the boxes at my desk, and me grumbling about having to meet with the Lieutenant, Richie smirked as he glanced toward Frank's office.

"Good luck with that," he said. "Better you than me."

Then, he trodded off toward the restroom, leaving the rest of his questions either forgotten or unasked, which, unknown to him, had been my design.

I looked toward Frank's office, his door closed and blinds barely open. I wasn't looking forward to going in there. After talking with him on the phone, it didn't seem like Frank had gotten a whole lot of information from Lenny, only that the case had suddenly become bigger. Good boy, Lenny.

Frank had only scratched the surface. And now, as I made my way to his office, he was about to learn just *how* big this case had become. Help us all.

Chapter 6

B

"**G**oddammit, Jim!" Frank raged, slamming his fist on his desk after hearing the news. "You should have come to me with this," he expressed again for the third time. "Five deaths? I can't keep this quiet. Redfern's going to have my ass."

I guess he didn't like what I had to say. That's fair; I didn't care much for saying it.

"Frank, I..."

"Shut your mouth, Jim! I swear to Christ. And that's Goddamn 'Lieutenant' to you!" He pointed a stern finger at me, which reminded me of my rebellious high school years when I spent many days in the principal's office, receiving the same unforgiving gesture. I didn't like it then, and I sure didn't appreciate it now. "What the hell were you thinking?" he continued. "And don't give me some bullshit story about having to check out a lead. I could have sent a couple of officers in your place."

I sat up in my chair, ready for things to turn ugly but decided to keep cool. Enough was going on with this case that I didn't need to add to it, especially since we both knew Frank was right.

"With all due respect, Lieutenant, another officer wouldn't have known what to look for. Hell, I'm still trying to figure it out myself. What I *do* know is that we've got five bodies down at the morgue, each with the same calling card. Lenny and I determined which was the first victim, and I decided to pay a visit to the girl's family. Her death was made to look like an accident, and they deserved to know the truth. And since we don't know who we're dealing with here, Lieutenant, the killer could be anyone, even someone in that house. I had questions that couldn't wait. Plus, until late last night, this was all just a hunch. I needed proof before I was willing to sound any alarms."

"And did you find anything out?" Frank asked, his tone still elevated but milder than his previous rant.

"It's hard to say," I replied. "We only just found out about the other three victims. We don't have a lot to go on yet. I don't think her parents had anything to do with it, but I grabbed a few boxes of the victim's items to have forensics go through. You're going to have to get the lab folks to her apartment, as well as to the other two victims' residences. And quickly. We may have already missed our opportunity to find something."

"And you're sure these deaths are all connected?" he asked. "It's the same person who killed them?"

"It's the same person," I answered, nodding my head. "He's made sure we knew they were all his handiwork. And not just because of the letters he carved into them. He..," I hesitated, well aware of what Frank's reaction would be, but I couldn't keep it from him any longer. "He left a note with his last victim. Eva."

"Jesus Christ, Jim. How long have you known this?"

"Since yesterday afternoon," I replied. "Lenny found it crumpled in the woman's fist once he finally managed to pry her hand open."

"Hold on," the Lieutenant interrupted, putting his hand up to stop me, his eyes narrowing, just then realizing what that meant. "This is the piece of paper you told me about on the phone? The one I asked you about when you were in my office yesterday afternoon after you left the morgue? You mean to tell me you had a note from this psychopath killer and didn't tell me about it?"

I remained silent, shifting my eyes downward, a clear indication of my guilt.

"What the fuck, Jim?" His response was understandable. "Where's the note now?"

"It's in the lab being analyzed for DNA. Contrary to how this has all played out so far, I *am* responsible when it comes to some things, you know."

"Not responsible enough, I'm learning," was Frank's retort. "We've got a sadistic killer on the street, and you're keeping information from me; information that's vital to this case. I can't let this go, Jim. I can't have my men running around this city with their own agendas. I hate to do it, but you've left me no choice. I'm going to have to take you off this case. I want you to fill Richie in on all the details; he's taking this one. He might not be quite the detective you are, but at least he communicates his findings."

I looked at Frank from across the desk, straight-faced and readily prepared to let him know why that wasn't going to happen.

"You're not taking me off this case, Frank." Yeah, calling him by his name was a little jab to let him know how serious I was. "And you're sure as shit not giving it to Richie."

Frank's nostrils flared, and the veins in his neck and forehead began to protrude. I'd say I'd upset him.

"Give me one good reason why I should keep you on this case?" he seethed, his teeth clenched tightly together.

"Because the note I told you about; it was addressed to me. That twisted son of a bitch has made this personal. He's toying with me, Frank, and he's made it clear he wants me on this case. If you take me off of it now, there's no telling what this demented freak might do."

Silence won out as Frank stared me down, his face turning bright red with anger.

"You son of a bitch," he said under his breath. Then he pointed his finger at me a second time, eliciting the same internal response as the first time. "Enough of this shit. I'm not holding onto this, you hear me? I'm filling the Captain in. He has to be made aware there's a goddamn serial killer on the loose. You'll get your wish, Jim. You can remain on this case, but, so help me, if Redfern comes down hard on you, I'm not coming to your defense. You got that?"

I nodded, "Got it."

"He's going to bring the state police in on this; you know that, right? He doesn't have a choice. The FBI will be here soon enough too. Just wait and see what kind of circus show this is when that happens."

"I know that," I answered, "which is why I had to do things the way I did. They're going to fuck things up."

"*You've* already fucked things up," Frank replied. "You'd just better hope you can get more from these other victims before the Captain shifts the whole case over to his friends at the barracks."

"Does that mean I can go?"

"It means you've got a head start," he replied. "I want you on the second victim. I'll call Vera's group and send them over to what's her name's apartment. The first victim."

"Her name's Amber, Lieutenant."

"Whatever. I imagine you've got a day at best; you'd better make the most of it. This place is going to become a madhouse real quick."

"And what about Cameron?" I asked. "He's the third victim."

"Get me the information, and I'll get a couple of men over there to break the news to the family. I'll have Vera send a couple of hers over there, too. Jesus, this thing's already a mess."

"Yeah, well, until yesterday, we couldn't have known."

"And do you think the Chief is going to give a rat's ass about that excuse? Or the Mayor, for that matter? Damn it, Jim, you should have come to me," he shook his head in frustration, "but, what's done, is done. You *will* be submitting a full report by tomorrow morning. I'm not fucking around anymore. I don't care if you have to stay up all night to do it. Understand?"

I nodded. Words would have only made things worse.

"Good. Now get the hell out of my office."

I immediately jumped from the chair and stormed out of the office as quickly as possible. All things considered, that could have gone a lot worse. I was still on the case, and I still had a little time before Redfern was alerted, and he called in the stateys to muck up the water. But now that it was out there, at least most of it, I could get back to doing what I did best.

I was hoping to check out Amber's apartment, but I wasn't about to push Frank's limits any more than I already had. I'd settle for checking in with Bruce's wife. Maybe I'd get lucky and find out she was the killer. Case closed. Wishful thinking.

I stopped at my desk and grabbed the framed picture from the top box of Amber's belongings. I didn't want it left in the open where it could mysteriously grow legs and walk away. We were all police officers, but sad to say, not all trustworthy. And since the picture of the scratched-out figure seemed like the only item so far that could possibly have something to do with this case, I'd rather it was kept safe with me.

On the way to victim number two's house, I thought I would give Lenny a call to see how he was faring with the three latest bodies discovered to be the killer's handiwork. I imagined he would have been up since the crack of dawn, going over every inch of them with a fine-toothed comb. If there was anything to be found, he would have found it. And after his phone rang for what seemed like forever, he finally answered.

"Hello?"

"Lenny, it's Jim. How's it coming with the newest three?"

"They're actually the earlier three, Jim," he responded as if we hadn't already determined that the night before. "And I've got nothing."

"What do you mean, 'nothing'? There has to be something. This guy can't be that good."

"He's probably not," Lenny returned. "There might have been something had the bodies been inspected for foul play from the start, but they've already been processed and handled by the funeral home. Any evidence we might have found has already been washed away."

"So we've got squat," I said, a hint of agitation in my voice.

"It would seem so," he answered. "I'm still going over them, but it's not looking promising."

I exhaled heavily, again with the automatic response, sounding my frustration. "All right, Lenny; you keep at it. Oh, and hey, you've still got all the addresses of the victims, right?"

"Yeah," he replied, "it's all here. Why; what's up?"

"I'm almost at Bruce's house now to ruin his wife's day. Can you send Cameron's address to the Lieutenant? He's going to send someone from forensics over to the kid's house."

"Yeah, sure thing. I'll send it over as soon as we're off the phone."

"Thanks, Lenny. And you let me know if anything more turns up with those bodies."

"I will, Jim. Good luck."

Yeah, 'good luck,' I thought as I ended the call. I needed it, too. I had five bodies, no leads, no witnesses, no suspects, no motive, and a killer who couldn't spell and who seemed to have some personal grudge against me. Maybe it *would* be better if the state police got involved. I could wash my hands of it; let *them* catch the sick bastard. Why did it have to be *my* mess? "Because, asshole," I reminded myself aloud while pulling up to Bruce's address, "this is still your city, no matter how shitty it is." I just hoped the Chief and the Mayor had big enough balls to tell the stateys we were working together and that I would remain the lead on the case. Maybe our solidarity would keep the Feds from bullying us out when they came.

I got out of the car and walked across the unkempt yard to the front door. Either Bruce was the regular mower of the lawn, or his wife hadn't yet stopped grieving long enough to do the yard grooming. I'd forgive her for such a transgression.

As I knocked on the door, I noticed a small handcrafted sign hung to the right of it engraved with the greeting, "The Lazerows." It was a good thing, too, as it occurred to me that, before that moment, I hadn't learned of the victim's last name.

I had been too preoccupied with other things. I still didn't know the wife's first name, which would have been quite embarrassing had the sign not been present to at least allow me to greet the woman as "Mrs. Lazerow." I clearly had too much on my mind. I wouldn't make that same mistake the next time. Hell, I'd hoped to catch this son of a bitch before there *was* a next time.

After a minute of unanswered silence, I knocked a second time, then heard footsteps tromping across the floor along with a few muffled obscenities before the door flung open.

"Yeah?"

The middle-aged woman who answered was as unkempt as the yard. She was wearing dark blue pajama pants that had one leg tucked into her sock halfway up her calf while the other floated freely at her bare ankle. The food-stained, white tee shirt she wore was riddled with holes that looked as though a mouse had scavenged nesting material from it. Her shoulder-length, graying hair twisted in all directions in knotted clumps, clearly having been untouched for days. The smell of menthol wafted from the cigarette drooping from her partially-open lips while her squinting eyes tried to adjust to the daylight.

"Hello, ma'am; are you Mrs. Lazerow? Bruce Lazerow's wife?"

"I was once," she replied in a hoarse voice. "Who the hell are you?"

"My name is Detective Jim Haddick," I stated while flashing my badge. "I'm here regarding your husband's death."

"My idiot husband got himself dead a couple of weeks ago," she replied. "Burned up. I'm surprised it didn't happen sooner. I told him I didn't like him playing with that torch of his. Lucky he didn't burn the whole house down."

I thought it was a strange response from someone who recently lost their spouse in what appeared to be a tragic accident. Everyone grieves in their own way, but this somehow seemed different, cold, and uncaring. It was going to be rude of me, but I was going to say it anyway.

"Excuse me for saying, ma'am, but you don't seem too hurt over your husband's death."

"Hurt? Why should I be? We haven't been married in years. Not really, anyway. Only on paper. Love left this household long ago. Probably shortly after the third time I caught him cheating on me. The lousy slob had it coming. I'm happy to be rid of him."

That was an unexpected development. In less than two minutes, if this woman turned out to be the killer, she just offered up a motive for at least her husband's murder. But no way did she look organized enough to pull something like that off.

"What's this all to *you*, anyway?" she questioned in her rough, raspy voice as she removed the cigarette from her mouth, the burnt ash from the tip falling to the floor.

"Well, ma'am," I began, "I'm investigating a case, and we have reason to believe your husband's death wasn't an accident. If you wouldn't mind, I'd like to ask you a few questions. May I come in?"

She brought the cigarette back to her lips and took a long drag, staring at me through suspicious eyes before blowing the smoke back out in my direction. Then, with the cigarette clenched between her first two digits, she pointed sternly at me.

"You'd better be who you say you are," she said. "I don't need no fucking weirdo rapist coming in here."

She opened the door wider to allow me entrance.

"Don't mind the mess," she continued, "the maid hasn't been here yet."

Her sarcastic tone wasn't lost on me. Neither was her house, which had trash littered about the floor. It seemed the yard wasn't the only thing that needed upkeep. It always amazed me how people could live like this, brushing aside their garbage and filth instead of picking it up and removing it. But I wasn't here to judge her lifestyle.

"Thank you for inviting me in," I said, to which she replied, *"as long as you're not a pervert vampire either."* I smiled and shook my head as words escaped me just then.

"I'd ask you to sit," Mrs. Lazerow said, "but I'm afraid I've misplaced the sofa."

It was true; the furniture was buried under piles of laundry that had yet to be folded. What little surface area wasn't covered in bunched clothing was, instead, covered in piles of newspapers and magazines.

"It's quite all right, ma'am," I assured her. It was just as well; there was no telling what I might pick up if I sat down.

"So, what do you mean Bruce's death wasn't an accident?" she questioned. "I came home from the grocery store and found him on the floor, his damn body pinned under that metal rack I'd asked him to fix for the umpteenth time. His goddamn torch was still flaming after it had burned through his stomach. I thought heat was supposed to cauterize wounds, but his insides spilled out of him and made a mess of the floor. I scrubbed it for days and still couldn't get the stain out."

The way she was rambling, this woman clearly had no emotional attachment to her late husband. I interrupted before she could continue more of her gruesome discovery.

"Yes, well, we believe we may have found a link between your husband's death and another homicide we've been investigating."

"I didn't realize there were other people as stupid as my husband who'd gone and burned themselves up." She responded.

I smirked uncomfortably and nodded, not quite sure how to respond. I decided to keep with the questioning instead.

"So you say your husband cheated on you?"

"All the time," she quickly answered as if she knew the question was coming.

"Do you know any of the women he was seeing?"

"I don't know any of them," she replied. "I didn't *want* to know any of them. I did follow him once, though. It was early on when I first had my suspicions about his improprieties. He thought he was being so slick and secretive, telling me he was heading to the bowling alley with his bowling buddies. He always underestimated women, but he shouldn't have underestimated me. I mean, he actually thought I'd believed him. You've seen his carcass by now, I imagine. Can you picture that fat fuck bowling?"

She didn't wait for me to respond before she continued.

"I couldn't either, which is why I followed him. That son of a bitch met some blonde floozy out in front of a hotel - the cheapest one in the city, I might add. That was *so* him. Cheap bastard."

I tried my best to take notes but found myself unable to figure out what it was I should be writing.

"And this behavior continued?" I asked.

"Oh yeah," she answered, taking another drag from her worn-down cigarette. "Fourteen years of it."

Did you happen to know or see who his latest affair was before his death?"

"Nah. Probably some cheap bimbo. They *all* were if you asked me. He probably paid them. I can't imagine a woman wanting to fuck him for free."

"Right," I responded, nodding my head in agreement, not fully aware of why I had just responded in such a way. "I hate to ask you this, but may I get a look at where you found your husband's body?"

"You're not one of those sickos who get their jollies off this stuff, are you, Mr. Haddick?"

"No, ma'am. I promise; I'm only looking for something that might help my investigation."

"All right, then. I suppose you don't look too *un*-trustworthy. I'll take you to the top of the stairs, but I'm not going down there. I stopped doing that days ago. The smell of burnt flesh still lingers, making me sick. Not the smell, mind you, but the thought of me inhaling some of that good-for-nothing bastard's DNA into my own."

Mrs. Lazerow was such a charming woman. I began to question whether Bruce was having tawdry affairs because of how cynical she was or if she became this cynical because of his affairs. Either way, it didn't matter. A man had been murdered, and I had a job to do.

As stated, she led me to the basement stairs but refused to go down with me. She had asked if I was the crazy one before she invited me into her home. In hindsight, I should have asked her the same before I descended alone into the basement. I wasn't so sure of the woman's mental stability. I had to convince myself there was no need to worry.

One thing was for sure, she wasn't wrong about the smell. *I* was now the one currently inhaling Bruce's burnt DNA. The stain she referred to was very prevalent on the concrete floor, a misshapen oval where most of his blood had pooled, but with tentacle-shaped strands extending away from the oval where some of his entrails had slid after falling from his mid-section. The metal shelving unit leaned awkwardly against the back wall, no doubt untouched since hastily thrown aside by the paramedics when they were extracting Bruce's body from beneath it. The cause of the victim's death, the large acetylene tank and torch, were situated against a hefty-looking workbench just in front of where the blood stain remained. On that same workbench, covered in welding dust, were scraps of metal fragments and half-welded trinkets. I scanned the area for any signs of foul play other than the shelving unit having toppled. There wasn't much to see. But as I turned to make my leave, a glimmer of light reflected off a piece of copper on the workbench, gaining my attention. It was only partially exposed, buried under an old rag, but it showed me enough to pique my interest. Even from several feet away, I could see that the flat piece of metal had a distinct shape. As I moved in closer, I recognized it as something that, in this case, had become synonymous with death: the letter B.

With slight trepidation, I slowly peeled away the rag to find out what else might be hiding. As I did, my skin crawled as a chill swept across me. The piece of copper wasn't just the letter B, but instead, three letters welded together, forming a partial word. There was finally a connection for which I had been hopelessly searching.

Using the rag that had, moments before, been covering the copper, I gathered the piece of evidence, careful not to disturb any possible prints, though I doubted there would be any. Sweeping my eyes across the bench one more time but finding nothing else that stood out, I walked back up the stairs to speak with Mrs. Lazerow.

Just as I reached the top of the stairs, her shrill voice pierced into me like dozens of tiny needles.

"You find something you liked?" she asked, nodding to the item I held, a newly-lit menthol between her lips. "You can take all of it if you want; it's all junk I have to get rid of, anyway."

"Yes," I replied. "I'd like to take this piece if I can." I showed her the item and watched closely for her reaction. There was none.

"As I said," she continued while shrugging her shoulders, "it's all junk to me."

"Thank you very much, Mrs. Lazerow. Oh, one more question before I get out of your hair, and I hate to ask this, but is there anyone who can corroborate that you were at the grocery store the day your husband died?"

Suddenly, she erupted into a fit of laughter, combined with a bout of uncontrollable coughing as she tried to speak.

"Haha, you think, haha, I killed my (*cough, cough*) husband? (*cough, cough*) Oh, sweetie, haha, (*cough*) I would have (*cough*) haha, killed him years (*cough, cough*) ago if I had the stomach for it."

"I understand," I replied. "It's just a formality. But just the same..,"

Her laughter subsided, and she stared at me with those uncaring eyes.

"You're the detective, Mr. Haddick. I'm sure you could scrounge up a video from the store or get a copy of my credit card purchases. That'll tell you all you need to know."

I smirked annoyingly at her comment.

"Oh, come now, detective," she added. "What's with the dour expression? Don't tell me you're just like my husband; always underestimating women."

And just like that, I had heard enough.

"Thank you for your time, ma'am," I nodded. "I'll keep you posted should I find anything more about your husband's death." Then I walked past her in the direction of the front door, plowing through a plume of mentholated-infused smoke.

As I opened the front door to walk out, I heard her raspy voice call out.

"If you *do* find something, you can keep it to yourself. I could give two shits. Fucker got what he deserved."

I closed the door behind me, shaking my head in disbelief. Somehow, leaving there, I felt dirtier than the actual house had been. The whole thing was an awful experience. But as I got into my car and placed the piece of evidence on my front seat, the soiled rag opened to expose the letters, reminding me that not *all* of it was awful. I now had something connecting two of the victims. A subtle smirk came to my lips. I found myself reading the letters aloud.

"A-M-B."

It looked like Bruce might have had something going on with Amber, and he was making her a little gift. Poor bastard never got the chance to complete it, though. Was she his latest and last affair? In my mind, a romantic relationship didn't seem to fit, but I couldn't rule it out. Everyone had their reasons for things. Whatever it was, the killer wanted them both dead. But what about the others? How did they fit into all of this? I needed to get over to Cameron's house.

Chapter 7

I hated the idea of having to call the Lieutenant with every piece of information or evidence I'd found, but it's the price I now paid for having gone against procedure. I'd made my bed. Not to mention I'd be up all night writing a report to appease the man.

I pressed S.O.B. on my contacts list, hoping he wouldn't answer. Luck wasn't with me.

"Lieutenant Frank Garrett."

Just hearing his voice riled me. "Lieutenant, it's Jim. I just left the second victim's house."

"And how did that go? Did you come up with anything?"

"I think I found something that may connect two of the victims. I have it with me. I'm on my way to victim number three's house now. Maybe I can dig up something there also."

"Peretti and Newsome are already there. They've informed the family. Two lab techs are there, as well. They don't know what the hell they're looking for."

"That makes three of us," I responded. "I'll know if I see it, though."

"And *I'd* better know if you see it, too; got it?" he responded.

"Hey, I called you this time, didn't I?" I was thinking of the time I'd get to drag him out of bed in the middle of the night. I couldn't wait.

"God damn right you did. And you'd better keep with it."

I shook my head and rolled my eyes, which would have gotten me reprimanded if he could have seen me.

"And what about the Captain?" I asked.

"I told him what was going on," Frank replied. "He's not happy; thank you very much. I had to calm him down before he had a coronary. I was able to keep him at bay, telling him we were currently working on a few leads and that I'd have a full report on his desk tomorrow morning. You owe me that, Jim. That's the best I could do. He's got an itchy trigger finger, but he's holding off notifying the state police until he gets your full report."

"He'll have it," I answered. "I'll get it done."

"You'd better, or it's both of our asses. Don't fuck this up."

"Can I get back to my *real* police work now?"

"Watch yourself, asshole."

"Love you too, L.T." I hung up, assuming the conversation was over. I would have hung up even if it wasn't. There comes a point when nothing more productive can come from it without adding fuel to the already existing fire. I knew some of my comments provoked his negative attitude toward me, like poking an angry bull. I didn't care. I kept at it. That son of a bitch started it. Things could never go back to the way they were. Especially not after what he had done. He had to know that.

My thoughts were getting off track, but the sudden incoming call pulled the reins to steer me back in. The highlighted "Mort" on my dash let me know it was Lenny.

"Yeah, Lenny, whatcha got for me?"

"I've got a puncture wound; that's what I've got."

"A puncture wound?" I inquired. "Like from a needle?"

"Yeah, from a needle."

"On who? where?"

"On the kid. Cameron. I found the injection sight on his neck."

"I'm on my way over to the kid's house now. Any idea of what might have been injected?"

"No way of telling at this moment," Lenny replied. "Or maybe not at all. It probably would have been something fast-acting; a high dose of Ketamine, or maybe Propofol. That's what I would've used. You know, if the goal was to render the kid unconscious."

"Or if you were a twisted killer on the loose?" I added.

"Yeah, that too," he responded.

"Hey, what's the kid's last name?" I asked, not expecting another fortuitously hung sign to tip me off.

"It's, ah, hold on a sec..,"

While I waited for Lenny's return, my phone started beeping at me, informing me I had another call. Jesus, suddenly everybody wanted me. I glanced at the screen and saw it was Ben.

"Okay, Jim, I'm back," Lenny informed me just before I switched the line over to my son. "It's Bogadinski."

"Thanks. I'm going to have to let you go, though, Lenny; my kid is calling. Nice work finding the injection sight. See if you can find the same on any of the others. We'll talk later."

"Oka..."

I felt bad hanging up the way I did, but I didn't want to miss my kid's call again. He'd start thinking I was ignoring him on purpose. I'd never do that, but if I had stayed on the other line, Lenny would have rambled on until I had missed it.

"Hi, Ben; what's up?"

"Are you going to be home late tonight?" he asked.

"I'm working a case right now, Ben. I don't know when I'll be back home. I've got a couple of leads that need following up. Why, what's going on?"

"I thought maybe we could hang out and watch a movie later. Like we used to do when..."

He stumbled on his words, but I knew what he was going to say. I thought I'd take the pressure off and finish the sentence for him.

"When we were all a family?" I asked.

"I know it can't be like that, Dad," he answered. "But just you and I would be cool, wouldn't it?"

"Yeah, listen, Ben. It does sound cool. But I've got a lot going on right now. We just got a break in this case; my superiors are riding my ass; I've got a report I need to get done tonight. I don't think I'm getting home until late. Sorry, bud."

I could hear his disappointment in the overwhelming silence that overtook my car speakers. I was never good at this part. I didn't know what to say to make him understand. It was easier to retreat into what I *did* know.

"I've got to get going, Ben," I said, hating myself for it. "I'm pulling up to one of those leads now. Maybe we can catch a movie another night?"

"Yeah, okay, Dad," he said softly. "No problem. Do your thing."

Then he hung up.

It wasn't hard to detect sarcasm and resentment in his voice. He'd always worn his emotions on his sleeve. I couldn't blame him. He had a mother who cared more about her personal life than his and a father who spent more time at his job than he did with his family. I'd harbor resentment, too. But at the moment, I didn't have time for that. I'd make it up to him.

I pulled up alongside the grass by the mailbox. The garage door was wide open, and the lab techs within were dusting Cameron's car for prints. The kid's parents were holding each other in a tight embrace at the foot of the garage entryway, the mom looking as though she would collapse if not for the father holding her steady, while the two officers, Peretti and Newsome, did all they could to keep them calm. The parents had most assuredly demanded an explanation. The officers couldn't have asked or answered many questions about a case they knew nothing about, so I was walking into this cold.

As I approached, the father turned and looked at me with sullen eyes, his wife's tears drenching the breast of his shirt as her cheek clung to his chest. I didn't extend my hand to introduce myself, thinking it best to let his arms continue to comfort his wife. The two officers nodded and backed away, allowing me to step in to relieve them.

"Mr. and Mrs. Bogenski, I'm Detective Haddick."

"It's Bogadinski, Detective," the husband corrected me.

"My apologies, sir. I'm sorry for this unwelcome intrusion. I'm sure the officers informed you why this was a necessary imposition."

"They told us our son didn't kill himself. They said someone murdered him."

"Oh, they did?" I shot the officers a nasty glare before turning back to the parents. "It's an ongoing investigation, sir, but yes, we have reason to suspect there might have been some foul play involved in your son's death."

Mrs. Bogadinski began to sob louder at my words, making my heart sink further into my stomach.

"But how?" Mr. Bogadinski started. "Why? We found him alone in his car. What foul play? What have you found out about Cameron's death?"

"Perhaps we should discuss this inside," I offered. "Let the forensics team continue out here."

"We don't *want* to go inside, detective," the husband loudly expressed, his emotions heated. "We want to know what's going on. Who would have done that to my son?"

"I understand your anger, sir. I have a son of my own, just about the same age as Cameron. Trust me when I tell you, we're doing all we can to find the person who did this."

I tried to persuade them to relocate inside, gesturing toward the front door, away from the eyes and ears of any curious neighbors, but they weren't agreeable to my intimation.

"What is it they're looking for?" he nodded in the direction of the lab techs. "What are they expecting to find?"

"Anything that might lead us to who did this to your son," I replied. "Maybe the killer left behind some prints, some hair; something."

"It doesn't make any sense," Mrs. Bogadinski said, peeling herself from her husband's arms. "Why would somebody want to hurt our son? And why in such a way?"

"I can't get into the details of it," I replied, "but we're dealing with a twisted individual. This person may have committed other acts."

"What do you mean?" Mr. Bogadinski questioned. "Like, he's killed others?"

"Again, I can't go into any details," I reiterated.

"The hell you can't," Mr. Bogadinski snapped, almost shoving his wife aside to stand eye-to-eye with me. "This is my son we're talking about," he raged.

Peretti and Newsome took a step forward, but I waved them back. Even the lab guys paused their inspections to be ready for any sudden violence that might've erupted.

"For almost two weeks now, we thought our son took his own life. *Two weeks*, Detective. And now, we find out that he might have been killed by someone else; someone who has possibly killed before?"

"I didn't say that, Mr. Bogadinski."

"You didn't have to," he responded. "I saw it on your face the moment I asked the question."

"Please, calm down, sir; we're just trying to do our jobs."

"Calm down?" he questioned angrily. "You expect me to calm down? Might I remind you, Detective, if you *had* been doing your jobs, you would have caught the son of a bitch before he killed my boy."

He wasn't right about that, but he wasn't entirely wrong, either. With the number of homicides this city recorded each month, we needed to do a better job of cracking down on the criminal element. But not all deaths are suspicious, as was the case with this one, and not all criminals are as devious as the fucker we're dealing with now.

"At the very least," Mr. Bogadinski continued, "I demand to know why you think Cameron was murdered. His car was still running when we found him. The fumes were so bad we could hardly catch our breath when trying to get him out of there. We were told he died from carbon monoxide poisoning. How could someone have killed him in that way?"

I glanced back at the lab techs, who responded by shrugging their shoulders and shaking their heads. Their silence spoke volumes. They hadn't found anything with the vehicle that screamed foul play. Shit. I was hoping to have something more to share with the parents than a letter and a puncture wound. And I *couldn't* share the letter.

"Did your son take any medications?" I asked. "Was he perhaps diabetic?"

"No," Mrs. Bogadinski chimed in through her drying tears. "Why do you ask?"

"We found some evidence on Cameron's body that we believe connects him to another homicide victim."

"What kind of evidence?" Mr. Bogadinski asked.

I couldn't tell him about the letter carved into his son's temple, but here went nothing.

"We found a puncture wound on your son's neck," I began. "The type of wound delivered from a needle. It's only a theory at this point, but I believe someone might have injected your son with something – a sedative perhaps, to knock him out. That would have given the killer enough time to set up this elaborate scenario to make your son's death look like a suicide."

"But why?" Mr. Bogadinski questioned. "If someone wanted to kill someone else, surely there're faster and easier ways to do it than by carbon monoxide poisoning. None of this makes any sense."

"There are other theories we're looking into as well," I assured the parents, though we didn't have nearly enough. "I promise you, folks, we're going to keep digging until we get to the bottom of this. I won't rest until we have a suspect in custody. That's why we're here, trying to do all we can."

"Detective," Mrs. Bogadinski softly spoke, "this doesn't have anything to do with the letter, does it? The one cut into Cameron's head?"

I felt my arms go numb as the words echoed in my brain. What the hell just happened? How could Cameron's mother know about the letter? For a moment, I knew what a deer felt like in a car's headlights. What the fuck was going on here?

Chapter 8

DROPPINGS

Sometimes clues in a case drop into your lap unexpectedly, and sometimes they smack you in the face like a brick. As bricks go, that one was pretty solid.

"Excuse me, ma'am, would you..," I fumbled for my words, "what did you just say?"

"We thought he was getting involved with some bad people," she explained. "Like maybe he was doing it for some gang initiation."

"Doing what?" I asked.

Cameron's father jumped in, "We caught him cutting that damn letter into the side of his head," he announced. "He was using one of our kitchen knives, leaning into the bathroom mirror, trying to carve his initials or some shit."

"You mean he did that to himself?" I questioned, somewhat skeptical and wondering if the parents had gotten nervous and were trying to misdirect me or cover up something more sinister, like possibly their involvement.

"He assured us it wasn't what we were thinking," Mrs. Bogadinski said. "It wasn't a gang thing."

"He told us it was one of those online challenge things that's all over the internet these days," Mr. Bogadinski added. "Those goddamn things have kids dumping ice water on themselves or eating laundry detergent or who knows what else, for Christ's sake. All we know is that he said he wouldn't do it again. Then, we came home to find him in his car the way we did. Those fucking social media sites need to be shut down."

"Wayne!" Mrs. Bogadinski gasped.

"Tell me I'm wrong," he responded, turning his attention to his wife for a moment before turning back to me. "We thought that's what it was all about, another imbecilic online challenge to see how long he could inhale fumes or something."

It all sounded plausible. Not all those online challenges were as harmless as trying to walk up stacked milk crates. There've been plenty of kids who've died from some of the moronic challenges posed online. I could see how the parents would favor that excuse over their child being the victim of a homicide. If it hadn't been for the other victims and the note left to me by the killer, I might have drawn the same conclusion. But if they're telling the truth, and Cameron *was* cutting the C into his own head, what about the other victims? Were they all part of some idiotic online challenge? I found it hard to believe such a thing by the victims we had encountered. Was the killer masterminding a challenge, then killing the participants? I needed more answers, but all I was getting were more questions.

"How long ago did you catch your son cutting himself?" I asked.

"It had to be about a month ago." Mrs. Bogadinski answered. "Maybe a little more."

A month ago? That's before even the first victim, or at least the first we knew about, was killed. This kid was carving a letter into his head before the killings began. Assuming the other victims *didn't* cut themselves as Cameron had, was the killer copying what Cameron had done? If so, that would mean the killer knew Cameron and what he had done to himself.

"Do you know if your son knew anyone who disliked him? Someone with whom he might have made enemies?"

The parents turned to each other, shaking their heads and shrugging their shoulders as if looking for the other's acknowledgment that perhaps they didn't know their son as well as they should have.

"No," Cameron's father replied, "we don't think there was anyone like that. I mean, everybody who knew Cameron loved him. And he was friendly to everyone."

"Perhaps there was..."

"Sir!"

My words were interrupted by one of the lab techs.

"We may have found something."

We all turned at once to see one of the lab techs sticking halfway out of the vehicle's back door, head-first, his arm extended and his gloved hand holding what appeared to be a business card. I immediately marched over to check it.

"What is it?" I asked. "Whatta ya got?"

"It may be nothing, but it was tucked under the backseat cushion and looked out of place. It's a card from something called '*The Letter Group.*' No name or number, but there's text on the back that reads, '*Let your letter shine as brightly as you do.*'"

"The Letter Group?" I turned to the parents. "Do you know what that is? Have you heard of it before?"

"No," said the mother, shaking her head. "Wayne, have you..?"

"No, I haven't heard of that. What do you think it is?"

"I don't know," I replied, "but since it's the only odd thing they've found in your son's car," (and, I thought, the only item that bears a possible connection to the killer) "I'd like to take it as evidence if you wouldn't mind."

"Of course," Mrs. Bogadinski agreed. "If you think it will help."

"That's my hope, ma'am," I replied before turning to the lab tech whose arm was outstretched. "Bag it up, boys. And if there's nothing else, why don't we leave these folks to their evening? I'm sure we've rattled them enough."

It *wasn't* enough. I knew it; the lab techs knew it. Hell, even the uniforms knew it. Sometimes you had to take wins when you saw them and then get out of Dodge before they turned to dust in the blink of an eye. I wasn't finished with the Bogadinskis, but I now had something to look into that could possibly move this case forward. It wasn't lost on me that this "Letter Group" business card happened to show up during a homicide investigation, where the killer's victims all had letters cut into them. Clever. It wasn't a stretch to think it could be related to this case. It had to be. Now I wanted to find out what that little slogan on the back of the card meant. *Let your letter shine as brightly as you do.* Did that make any sense?

I had research to get to - to find out what I could about this group - and I still had a report to file before Frank hung me out to dry by my balls. He'd love that; I wouldn't give him the satisfaction. No, for now, it was time to leave here.

"Mr. and Mrs. Bogadinski," I began, "I'd like to thank you for your cooperation, and I'm very sorry you had to learn about the unfortunate news surrounding your son's death. I hope you can understand the reasoning behind this unexpected intrusion. Please know that we will do everything in our power to find out who did this horrible thing." I presented my hand to Mr. Bogadinski, unsure if he'd be willing to oblige. He was. "You have my word," I added as he gripped my palm tightly within his.

"You'd better," was his response. Not at all unexpected, but I noticed his wife cringed as he said it, perhaps thinking he had overstepped a boundary. Under ordinary circumstances, she would have been right, but this case was anything *but* ordinary. If I were in his shoes, and it had been *my* son, I might not have been as reserved as he was.

Our hands released, and I signaled Peretti, Newsome, and the lab boys to pack it in. As they did, I reached into my shirt pocket and pulled out my card.

"If you think of anything else, folks," I handed it to Mr. Bogadinski, "don't hesitate to call me."

"We will, Detective," Mrs. Bogadinski responded, nodding her head and squeezing her husband's arm. Mr. Bogadinski nodded while keeping his eyes fixed on the card I had handed him. Then, I gave a final nod and walked out of their garage, following behind the uniformed officers who had just gotten to their patrol car.

"Thanks, boys," I waved in acknowledgment as they sat in their car like good little officers, waiting at the ready in case we required any further assistance. Halfway down the driveway, I stopped and waited for the techs, who were lagging with their toolboxes of goodies. They had the one piece of evidence I wanted, and I wasn't letting them leave until I got a good look at it.

"Let me see the card," I stated, pulling out my phone while one of the techs raised a clear sealed bag, showing me its contents. I snapped a couple of pictures before sending the techs off with a clear directive; "Check it and let me know what you find, would you?" As if they didn't know their job.

I didn't mean to be that way; it was just in my nature. I felt I couldn't afford any mishaps in this case. This guy, whoever he was, has been running rampant for too long already. Frank was gunning for me, and I was sure Redfern would be eager to do the same. The state police would soon be involved, and as much as they claimed they were here to help - and I have no doubt they believed that - they'd only get in my way and slow my progress. So, if I could put some urgency into those lab boys getting me something off that card, I'd do it again without a second thought.

I took a final glance up the driveway at the grieving parents and wondered how I would be handling things had it been *my* kid. But I couldn't think that way. It *wasn't* my kid. And as long as I was around, it'd *never* be my kid. Sad thing was, there wasn't a parent alive who hadn't thought the very same thing, including those two. They did seem a bit relieved it wasn't a suicide, perhaps thinking their son taking his own life reflected poorly on their parenting, but they were grieving just the same. And whatever we did as parents to convince ourselves in our little fantasy world that we could get through this life unscathed, it didn't matter; shit still happened. Sometimes, it was a steaming pile, like what I felt on my shoulders right now, and we each had to struggle to dig ourselves out. The problem was, even if you dug yourself free, the smell remained no matter how much you cleaned yourself up. I would know; I'd been living with the stench for eighteen years. But I had to do everything I could to ensure the public's safety. What else did I have; this was my home, and I'd be damned if I would desert her when she needed me - when *this community* - needed me most. I owed them that much.

I made my way to my car and watched the lab van drive past me, followed by Peretti and Newsome in the cruiser. As I pulled away, my thoughts strayed in multiple directions. Did the kid really cut himself as the parents said? Was it all just some ridiculous online challenge? Would they have had reason to lie? And what of the card found in the kid's car? I pulled up the picture of it on my phone and read the back text again. '*Let your letter shine as brightly as you do.*' What the hell was that even supposed to mean? The only thing it meant to me was that it was no coincidence it was in Cameron's car. What I didn't know was if it was something Cameron previously had in his possession, perhaps something he misplaced or tossed in his backseat, or if it was something purposely left by the killer - a message for us to find. Either way, I was now getting more curious to learn if Vera and her crew had found anything at Amber's place.

I scrolled through the contacts on my dash until Vera's name popped up and then hit dial. I should've been calling Frank, but fuck him; I'd be back at the precinct in a few minutes. I could catch him up then. I was more interested in what Vera had for me.

"This is Vera," she answered gruffly.

"Sounding lovely as ever, my girl," I responded.

"Same to you, Jim, you feminine fuck," was her retort. Vera always had a mouth on her. I think she might have been a truck driver in another life. "Did you get the little present I left for you?" she asked.

"Present? No," I replied. "What present?"

"I put it on your desk," she answered. "Call it a gift. You're welcome."

"I'm not at the station; I'm heading back there now."

"So, if you're not calling about that, then what is it?"

"We found something at the third victim's house," I relayed. "A business card from some 'Letter Group.' Did you find anything like that? Or maybe something linking your vic with any of the others?"

"Jim, I don't even know who the other victims are. Frank had a real stick up his ass and told me to get my group out here to look for anything that seemed suspicious. Fucking twit, that guy. I don't mind telling you; this is a shit show. And *you*, you fucker, got me running analysis on some piece of paper turned in by a kindergartener or some shit. Came up with diddly squat on that, by the way; fuck you very much."

"And how would I have known that, Vera," I asked, "unless I sent it to get checked by the best forensics woman I know?"

"Blow me, Jim. That flattery shit doesn't work on me."

She really was a great gal once you got to know her.

"Anyway," she continued, "your creepy little friend Mort told me what you were dealing with. Holy fuck!" she exclaimed. "Five bodies? That's impressive. You managed to snag the Holy Grail of homicide cases. Good for you."

Vera had a sick sense of humor to go along with her wit.

"You talked with Mort?" I asked. "I mean, Lenny?" It was tough getting away from calling him by his nickname when my colleagues slung it around so prevalently.

"Hey, I have to get my information from somewhere," she replied. "Your lips are tighter than your ass cheeks, for Christ's sake. It sounds like you got yourself a real whack-a-doo, Jim."

"Yeah, yeah," I responded. "Anyway, the other victims' names are Bruce, Cameron, Denise, and Eva. Anything like that?"

"Maybe," she replied. "One of the boys *did* find a list of names inside a scratch pad on the dead girl's dresser. Hold on."

I could hear her muffled voice as she pulled the phone from her ear. *"Hey, Danny, you still got that pad with the list of names?"* A few seconds later, her voice erupted loud and clear through the speakers again. "I got six names, Jim. There're no chicks on the list, though. And no last names either. But yeah, there's a Bruce and a Cameron on it. The other names are Steve, Matt, Jay, and Ralph. Jesus, someone named their kid Ralph? What is this, Happy Days? Poor son of a bitch."

Did I mention she was a great gal once you got to know her?

"Well, that's two names on the list," I stated. "I'm going to assume they're our victims. Is there anything else on there that might explain what the list is about?"

"If there were, don't you think I would have led with that, you dumb fuck? Pain in my ass."

"Sorry, Vera," I apologized, but only to keep her sedated, "I know you know what you're doing."

"Damn straight, I do."

"Listen, I'm pulling into the station now; keep me abreast of anything you find, will ya?"

"Abreast, huh?" she responded. "Why does it always come down to tits with you guys?"

"Funny, Vera. Hey, thanks for the information. Make sure I get that pad of names."

"Of course."

"Gotta go," I said as I pulled into my parking spot.

"See ya, shit-for-brains," was her response. Then the line went dead.

That Vera, she's going to make a lovely wife someday. I can't wait to see the poor schlep that marries her. He won't know what hit him.

I stepped from my car, trying to focus my thoughts. Frank was going to be expecting a status report from me. What the hell did I have? I had a dead kid with a carved letter on his head, like the other victims, only he supposedly did that to himself a month earlier. It would have made him the perfect suspect, practicing for his later kills, if he hadn't wound up dead the way he had. And why was Amber compiling a list of names, two of which ended up deceased? Maybe they're *all* dead, for all I know? And then Bruce, I find he was making some homemade piece of shitty art with Amber's name on it. How did they all know each other? And what about Denise and Eva? How are they connected to the other three? I've got a picture with a scratched-out face, a business card of a company I've never heard of, and a goddamn maniac on the loose playing some twisted alphabet game. As far as I was concerned, I had nothing.

I walked into the station with the items I'd gathered and saw Richie staring me down from his corner desk, a smug look on his face as if he knew I was in over my head. I ignored that I even noticed him and continued to my desk to drop off the framed picture and partially-fabricated metal name. On my desk, as Vera had mentioned it would be, was a case file at least five inches thick, a worn rubber band stretched to its max, holding it together. In classic Vera style, there was a post-it note affixed to the top of it with a message: *"I thought you'd be interested, limp dick. Call us even."*

I didn't know if what I'd find inside the folder would be enough to make us even, not after that whole Internal Affairs incident from the year before, but I was willing to let it slide if she provided me with anything valuable.

I placed the picture on the box containing Amber's items, and the piece of metal on the floor, leaning it against the side of my desk, and just as I started to lift the corner of the folder to peek inside, Frank's voice clamored out.

"Haddick!" he shouted, looming in his doorway. "My office. Now."

Vera's present would have to wait. I made my way to Frank's office, glancing in Richie's direction once again to see a smirk on his face. Why did he have to be such an ass? Did he think this was all a joke? He should be wanting to help catch this killer instead of treating it like it was some goddamn competition. It didn't matter; I couldn't let his misguided resentment get to me.

I stepped into Frank's office, and he motioned for me to close the door. I prepared myself for the verbal spanking I was about to receive. I pulled up a chair to sit while my ass was still intact when he stopped me.

"Don't bother," he said. "You won't be in here long enough to get comfortable."

Relief similar to a quick bandaid rip washed over me.

"What's going on, L.T.?"

He looked at me glumly, almost apologetically. "I wanted you to hear it from me first," he replied. "Redfern went and contacted the state police."

And just like that, the relief I felt so briefly was gone just as quickly.

"What the fuck, Frank! You said I had until tomorrow to pass in my report."

"And you still do, but the Captain was getting too much heat from the Chief. He wasn't taking any chances that there could be some blowback on him. You know these assholes are only interested in advancing their careers. They don't want any bad publicity hanging over them."

"Redfern doesn't even know what's going on," I said.

"He knows enough," Frank responded. "He knows there're multiple homicides, and he knows we're looking like a bunch of inept kids out of our league."

"That's bullshit, Frank, and you know it."

"Of course, I know it. This shit just sprang up on us from out of nowhere. But I did warn you; you knew it was coming."

"So what does this mean for me?" I asked, feeling like a ton of lead weight.

"It means you better have that report done by 8 a.m. We've got Redfern and the State Police Captain coming in for a full briefing on this thing."

"That's not what I meant," I countered. "What's this do for my investigation?"

It's still yours," Frank replied. "You know how this works; they're not getting involved to take the case away from you. Who knows, maybe they'll even do some good. We could use their support."

"Fuck that!" I stated heatedly.

"Hey!" he yelled, slamming his fist on his desk. "I'll have none of that. What's done is done. Whether you like it or not, we're all in this together. We need to get this psycho off the streets, and if the state police can help with that, then goddammit, you *will* get on board."

It was a little surprising to me, but Frank seemed like he actually cared just then. He had *me* believing it, anyway. And, as much as I hated to admit it, he was right. The stateys had more resources they could draw upon than we did. I was aiming my frustration in the wrong direction. It was only because we all knew what the next step would be, and that was what we were all dreading.

"All right," I submitted. "I'm on board; I'm on board."

"Good; now, what's the latest?" he asked.

"Not a lot," I answered. "Except, it looks like the first three victims were somehow connected. Maybe."

"What about the other two?"

"I don't know yet. I'm still trying to sort out the details."

"All right," Frank replied, nodding agreeably. "I know you're doing your best. Just make sure this is all in your report. I don't need those fuckers thinking this department isn't on top of things."

"Is there anything else?" I asked, eager to get out of there.

"That's all I've got," Frank responded. "I just wanted you to know where things stood."

"I appreciate it, Frank."

"Good. Now get out of here and get back to work." He nodded his head toward the door, signaling me to leave. And as I began my exit, he howled out one last jibe.

"And Jim," he paused for a moment, only for effect as to get his point across, "it's Lieutenant."

I nodded and closed the door behind me.

That didn't make my day any brighter. I knew it wasn't Frank's fault. Redfern cared more about covering his ass than he did about actual police work. Now I had to worry more about catching the state police up to speed than I did detective work. The joke was on them; *I* wasn't even up to speed on this case yet. I couldn't let it bother me. I still had work to do, and I still had some investigating to get done.

Getting to my desk, the fat file folder that sat in front of my keyboard was a reminder that others in the department still knew what good old-fashioned police work was all about. Most were willing to help however they could; others wandered from the path. Yes, I was looking at Richie, sitting in the corner with his shit-eating grin. What had happened to him? When did he stop caring?

I had to stop thinking about things I couldn't control. I wasn't the babysitter of this department. That was Frank's title: Lieutenant Babysitter. Right now, I had to get my head back in the game.

I was curious as to what Vera had left me. She said she talked with Lenny to get information. God knows the things he told her. You'd think those two would get along better than they did, being in a similar line of work. But Lenny's eccentricities were a bit much for most people to handle.

I sat down and pulled the worn rubber band from the folder, expecting it to break based on its apparent age and the noticeable cracks along its surface. Surprisingly, it didn't, and my fingers were thankful for it. Flipping open the front cover exposed a handful of old newspaper clippings and articles about the Manson Family murders from 1969. What the hell was this, I thought, shaking my head while reading headlines of Helter Skelter in bold print. I slid a few of the clippings aside and came upon other articles about the Zodiac Killer from the same period. Rummaging deeper into the file, scattered clippings detailing Ted Bundy's and John Wayne Gacy's killing sprees took center stage. Then the Boston Strangler and the BTK killer. It was clear, the folder contained a collection of articles about different serial killers throughout the ages. Jeffrey Dahmer, Son of Sam, Richard Ramirez, Ed Kemper, and many others – all killers showcased between the manila folder's covers. Southbridge's very own Midnight Mangler made the cut, as did Aileen Wuornos and the Hillside Strangler. There were even photocopied reports and sketches of H.H. Holmes and Jack the Ripper, both murderers of the late 1800s.

Where did Vera get this, and what was she trying to tell me? I already knew we were dealing with a serial killer, but the one I was after didn't fit the bill of any of these other sadistic bastards. But as I continued perusing through the pile of dated papers, I came upon a small stack paperclipped together, a second fluorescent post-it stuck to the top article and placed purposely to gain my attention, the words, *"Check this out,"* scribbled on it, and a hand-drawn arrow pointing up to the headline. It took my eyes only a second to focus on the bold print but several more to catch my breath after reading it.

"*Alphabet Murders stump police.*"

The newspaper clipping, taken from the Rochester Tribune, was dated November 30th, 1973. Another article, cut from the Rochester Times-Union, dated November 27th of the same year, had a headline that read, "*Another Alphabet Killing.*" A third article from earlier in the year, April 4th, declared, "*A Second Double-Initial Child Found Murdered.*"

Article after article within this small grouping of newspaper clippings, the story was the same. Between November 1971 and November 1973, three child slayings were attributed to a serial killer some reporters dubbed "The Alphabet Killer" as early as the second victim. All three female victims were pre-adolescents, and all three had first and last names starting with the same initial.

I was a bit confused as to what I was supposed to learn from the stories other than the victims having been coincidentally chosen by the letters of their names. Although awful in their own right, none of those past murders resembled anything like what my killer was doing. Sure, the murders seemed to be related to letters, but that was about where the similarities ended. I would need Vera to explain what this was all about.

Shuffling the papers back into the folder and sliding the file off to the side of my desk, I pulled out my phone and sent Vera a brief text.

I found the kid-killer articles. What am I looking at here? Not sure what to take from them.

While I waited for a response, I pulled up the pictures I took of the card found in Cameron's car and stared at the words. "The Letter Group" stood out in bold white lettering on a plain background of dark blue. On the rear, with its colors reversed, "Let your letter shine as brightly as you do" taunted me like an empty bottle of vodka to an alcoholic.

I slid my keyboard closer and searched for "The Letter Group" on the internet, hoping to find an easy connection, but all that came up were sites about grammatical word groups and pronunciations in the literal sense. Searching for the rear quote offered nothing but more frustrating results. If it was a business, it didn't have a website. If it was a *secret* business, well, it was at least successful in that category. But in this city, in this district, even a business that wanted to remain secret wouldn't be able to fly under Papa Rio's radar. Perhaps another visit to the Ruby Room was in order. Just then, my phone buzzed. It was Vera's response.

There was another killer who murdered based on the alphabet, fucktard. Only yours is already more prolific. I've practically handfed you the killer's moniker for when the press comes calling. What do you think about The Alphabet Killer 2.0?

The text left me at odds. I couldn't believe Vera was buying into the publicity aspect of the killings. I felt the need to reply.

That's what this is about; giving the killer a name? Jesus, Vera, I thought you had something useful for me. Where did all this stuff come from, anyway?

Once again, while I waited, I thought I'd start going through the box of items I took from Amber's parent's house. I placed the picture with the scratched-out face on my desk and opened up the flaps of the top box. One at a time, I removed the contents, reviewing them for anything that looked like it could be something of interest. I wasn't finding anything that caught my attention. I moved the top box aside and opened the second box, expecting more of the same. I only pulled two items from it when my phone buzzed again.

```
It's my own personal stash. I love all that serial
killer shit. That stuff would give me a hard-on if
I had a penis.
```

I just smirked and shook my head. There was nothing I could say to that. Vera would have to settle for my simple quip.

```
TMI. Lol. ☺
```

I never knew that woman was so into psychopathic killers. All kinds of other shit, maybe; but who was I to judge? We all had our vices. Mine was work, and it was time to get back to it.

Before I could put my phone down, it started vibrating in my hand. It was Ben.

"Hey, what's up, kid?" I asked while sifting through the second box.

"I just wanted to let you know I'm going out with David tonight. We're going to catch a movie."

"You didn't have to call me for that," I answered. "I trust you."

"I was just letting you know you didn't have to worry about me disturbing you while writing your report."

That line felt worse than any knife stabbing into me. I suppose I had it coming. I hadn't been paying much attention to Ben since he'd been at my place. I couldn't help it, but maybe I could let *him* help.

"Speaking of this case," I said, still removing articles from Amber's box, "maybe you could help me with something."

"Really?" Ben responded with excitement. "What do you need?"

"I'm busy going through some evidence," I replied, "and I really gotta get started on that report. Have you ever heard of some internet challenge where people are being asked to cut themselves?"

"Cut themselves?" he questioned. "How do you mean?"

"I mean cutting a letter into their skin. Have you heard of anything like that?"

"No. That's fucki.., I mean, that's weird."

"Nice catch. Do you think you could do a little online research for me? You're good with that stuff."

"Sure!" Ben said. "An internet cutting challenge. Got it. Anything else?"

I heard Ben say something, but it didn't register as my attention was diverted after having removed a few more items from the box, revealing something that immediately connected Amber and Cameron. It was the same "Letter Group" business card, being used as a bookmark and sandwiched partially between the pages of a periodical.

"I'm gonna have to let you go, Ben." Before he could respond, I had already hit the "end call" button.

I pulled the card from the magazine and leaned back in my chair.

"The Letter Group," I said softly to myself, flipping it over in my fingers to reveal the unusual message on the backside. Amber and Cameron both had the card, and I wanted to know why and what it was. Unfortunately, it wouldn't be tonight. I had to get started on that damn report; there was no getting around it. But I hoped Papa Rio was ready because, like it or not, he was going to be seeing my pretty face again.

Chapter 9

THE WICKED WAYS

I heard the door open, and I rolled over in bed, glancing at the glowing blurry numbers lit on my nightstand clock. I could barely make out that it was 2:15 in the morning. When I heard the heavy steps, I thought it best to learn who it was before I reached for my gun.

"Ben, is that you?" I called out.

"Yeah, Dad; it's me." His voice sounded muffled through the closed door. "Sorry if I woke you."

"It's past two in the morning," I said. "What are you doing out so late?"

"David couldn't get out of what he was doing earlier," he returned, "so we went to a later movie. Then we hung out for a bit downtown and watched the drunks leaving the bars."

"Did you have a good time?" I asked. "You weren't doing anything stupid, were you? Besides waking me and hanging around bars, I mean."

He opened my bedroom door; the hallway light behind him caused my eyes to squint while they tried to adjust to the invading luminescence.

"Nah, nothing stupid," he answered. "Did you finish your report?"

"I did," I responded, glancing at the clock to do some quick calculating in my head. "Just a few hours ago, actually."

"That's good. And I tried finding stuff online about that internet challenge thing you asked me about earlier. I couldn't find anything. Are you sure it's a real thing?"

"I'm starting to doubt it," I replied. "I wasn't convinced from the start."

"What was it about, anyway?" Ben asked.

"Nothing," I replied. "Don't worry about it. Get some sleep, will you? And I'm not mad that you're home late; just next time, text me so I don't shoot you by mistake." I said it with a smirk so he knew I was joking. With everything else going on in his life, I didn't need him worrying about *that* too.

"All right, Dad. Sorry again for waking you. Good night."

"Good night, kid," was my response just as he closed the door. I didn't know if he had heard me or not, but I would fall back to sleep thinking that he had.

The morning seemed to come crashing in earlier than usual. The coffee wasn't dripping fast enough. I was beginning to wonder if I had even slept at all. If I did, it wasn't a sound one, that was for sure. After being woken up in the middle of the night, my mind was restless with thoughts of the killer's twisted game and what his motives could be. How did he choose his victims? I knew at least three were somehow connected. I was hoping to find out more once I met with Papa Rio again to discuss this "Letter Group." He had to know something about it. But first, I had to meet with Frank, Redfern, and the State Police Captain so I could give them everything they needed to hinder my progress on this case. It was sad I thought that way, but I'd been through enough murder investigations to know how it worked. It never seemed to go *more* smoothly once they got involved. It would mean a lot more red tape.

While I waited for the rest of my cup to fill, I checked on Ben, who, at the moment, hadn't seemed to be letting my morning ruckus bother his sleep. I'm glad at least one of us could enjoy the comfort of their bed. He was out quite late; he'd probably be in bed for a few more hours. Although, admittedly, part of me wanted to wake him.

Going back into the kitchen, I finished making my coffee and grabbed my jacket, which hung over the back of the chair. I went into the living room to retrieve my laptop and report, which were both sitting on the coffee table, when I noticed a few of the pages were sticking out of the folder. It didn't take superior detective skills to know that Ben had been going through my report. Damn it! I still wasn't used to the kid staying here, and I certainly wasn't used to having to keep my things from being out in the open. I couldn't blame him; I was just as curious at his age when my dad would bring home case files. And I knew Ben was interested in what I did and only wanted to help where he could, but there was some serious shit in my report. Not to mention the kind of trouble I could get into if anything got out before we released it. He knew better than to say anything, but I'd need to have that talk with him tonight when I got home.

I gathered the folder under my arm, took a sip of my coffee, and headed out. On my way to the station, I thought I'd call Lenny to see if he'd found any suspicious puncture wounds on the other victims.

"Hey, Lenny, it's me. I didn't hear from you last night about those other bodies. Did you find any puncture wounds on any of the others?"

"Yeah, sorry, Jim," he replied. "I didn't get to it."

"What do you mean you didn't get to it?" I asked, my voice raised higher than it probably should have been.

"It was my sister," he replied. "She got taken away in an ambulance."

"Jesus! I'm sorry, Lenny. Is she okay?"

"It was heroin; she tried to OD again. I had to get over to watch her kids until my mother could get there."

"Shit, Lenny, I didn't know."

"It's okay," he answered. "I don't advertise it. Anyway, I'm getting back to the morgue this morning. I'll have an answer for you in a few hours."

"That's fine," I responded. "I'm meeting with the big boys in just a little bit to go over what we've got so far."

"The Chief's going in?" he asked.

"No. But I've got to deal with Redfern and his buddy at the state police. I'm sure Redfern will ham it up for the Chief and make it sound like he's got the whole thing under control."

"Well, you knew it was only a matter of time before the state police were called in on this. I'm surprised it'd taken this long."

"If I had my way," I stated, "it would've taken even longer. Listen, I've got to run. I'm pulling into the station now. Sorry to hear about your sister."

"Thanks."

"Yeah. Talk to you later."

After hanging up, I thought more about what he had told me about his sister. I could almost understand why Lenny was the way he was. I imagined his work was more of an escape for him, something to keep his mind distracted from his personal life. But it also made me realize I didn't know much about the man. What other personal shit was he dealing with?

I couldn't get caught up in whatever Lenny was coping with; I had my own issues to sort out. I shouldn't be here right now. I should be at the Ruby Room questioning Papa Rio about the Letter Group. That was exactly how the state police's involvement was already fucking things up. Yeah, they had the resources, but they expected police work to get done by sitting in meetings all the time discussing what next steps to take. If I had to report to my supervisor every half hour, I'd still have a list of unsolved crimes on my desk.

As soon as I walked through the door, I could feel the thick air as everyone was uncharacteristically stiff. That meant the State Police Captain was already present, and they were trying to impress him. I've seen it a thousand times. I'm sure Frank got on his soapbox and told everyone he wanted them to look sharp and be on their best behavior. Captain Redfern probably regurgitated it soon after. They weren't going to let our boys look bad in front of the state police. That would reflect negatively on them, and they couldn't have that.

I didn't make it ten steps to my desk before Mick jumped at the chance to intercept me and fill me in on their whereabouts.

"Jimmy, you got some visitors here for you."

"Yeah, Mick, I know," I responded, trying to swerve around him.

"They're in the briefing room," he told me. "I can tell it's something big. Is this still the same homicide case you're on? The chick with no face? Why didn't you tell me it was big enough to bring in the other guys?"

"They're all big, Mick," I stated, somewhat annoyed. "We're talking about someone's life here. She was somebody's wife, mother, daughter; she could have been *your* wife for Christ's sake."

"Geez, Jimmy," Mick replied. "Sorry, I didn't mean it like that."

I looked at his remorseful expression and realized I had perhaps been a bit hard on him. I slapped the side of his arm to break his sudden dour mood.

"I know, kid," I stated. "I didn't mean to come down on you like that. This meeting has got me on edge. You know me; I'm not much of a people person."

"It's all right, Jimmy. I get it. You got a lot going on."

"Yeah," I assured him, "that's all it is."

"Well, let me know if you need anything, huh? And oh," he continued, "Gina wants to have you over for dinner sometime. She thinks you've been avoiding her."

"I'm not avoiding her," I answered. "Just her cooking. And don't you dare tell her I said that."

"Yeah, it's not the best," he answered. "I don't understand it. The *cat* won't even go near what Gina cooks. Fuck; just thinking about it, now I'm depressed." He grimaced and shook his head. "Anyway, I've got to get going. Good luck in there." He motioned toward the briefing room before turning and walking toward the exit.

"Thanks," I murmured, knowing he was no longer paying attention to me. It was just as well, I had to get on with it. Things wouldn't play out well if I kept my superiors waiting much longer. I held the report firmly in hand and headed for the briefing room. Of course, they had the blinds drawn, not wanting others to pry on what could be a very high-profile case. At least, not until they were ready to release it to the press, which, by my estimation, would be later that afternoon now that the state police were getting involved.

I could hear them talking as I approached (the walls weren't as sound-proof as they would have liked). I didn't bother knocking before I entered; this was *my* show, after all. Still, I can't say I wasn't somewhat shocked when I walked in. Frank was at the front of the room, leaning on the podium as if he was delivering dailies to a packed house. Chief Copelli, whom I hadn't known was going to be in attendance, was by Frank's side, jawing with Captain Bessell from the State Barracks. In front of the stand, Captain Redfern stood with his arms crossed, nodding attentively, while listening to a story presented to him by a fifth person I was unaware would be invited to the meeting. It was Richie, and my blood began to boil at first sight.

"Ah, Jim," Captain Redfern turned his attention in my direction, "glad you could make it. Detective Saunders was just filling me in on how you had reached out to him for some much-needed help on this case."

I quickly turned my stare to Richie, who had a shit-eating grin on his face.

"Oh, he did, did he?" I spoke with obvious irritation in my voice.

"Yeah, you know," Richie jumped in before I could set the record straight, "how you asked if you could bounce some ideas off me? We all get it, Jim; it's a big case. Sometimes we need a little help. Personally, and I was just telling Captain Redfern this, I think it's respectable that you recognized your limitations and reached out to me. Not everyone would do that."

I felt my jaw and fist clench in unison. I was about to lose it when Frank loudly spoke up, perhaps noticing my controlled rage.

"Gentlemen, shall we get to it?" He expressed.

Richie immediately took a seat like a good puppy, displaying his willingness to be a team player. I continued to stare him down, hoping he'd look up to see my utter disgust at his obvious stab to convince the Captain of my incompetence. My fiery focus was undeterred until Frank loudly called my name.

"Jim," he clamored, "you know Captain Bessel of the State Police Department."

"I do," I stated, gathering my anger while striding forward to greet him, my hand extended. "I had the opportunity to work with you and your officers on the Aaron Moody case a few years back. Good to see you again, Captain."

"Right, right. The Moody case," he uttered, shaking my hand. "Shame we ended up finding that boy in that awful condition."

"Yes, it was terrible," I added, releasing the Captain's hand and swinging it toward the Chief. "Chief Copelli, I didn't expect to see you this morning."

"*I* asked him to come," Captain Redfern blurted. "I thought we'd need everyone brought up to speed on this one. You've got a full report?" he asked.

"As full as it can be," I replied, handing it over to him. "There are a few more leads I've got to look into once we're through here, but that's all of it, in a nutshell."

My words might as well have fallen on deaf ears once I handed over the folder. They looked like a pack of wild dogs slobbering over prey as the others gathered around Captain Redfern to peer over his shoulder at the paperwork. Even Richie got up from his seat to stand behind the pack so he could feel he was a part of something. I glanced at Frank and nodded toward Richie, my face still stern. He peered back and shook his head at me as if to say, "not now." All right, maybe not now, but I *would* have words with him when this little shindig was over.

As expected, the questions began to fly, starting with Captain Bessell.

"You currently have five confirmed deaths attributed to the same killer?" he began. "Why are we just hearing about this now?"

"We only learned of the connection between the victims two days ago. The person we thought was the killer's first victim was discovered five days ago. As it turned out, there were three other murders before that. We didn't make the connection because two of them were meant to look like accidents, and the third, a suicide."

"Why would the killer go through the trouble of making three of the murders appear as something other than," Captain Redfern questioned, "and then not cover himself with the other two? Are you sure the cases are even related?"

Before I could respond, Chief Copelli jumped in.

"Yes, Detective Haddick, I'm interested in hearing your theory on that, myself."

"It's no theory, sirs," I responded. "We *are* dealing with only one killer. We're still trying to determine the killer's motives and figure out why his latest two victims' deaths weren't disguised as accidental. There are a lot of moving parts here."

"Which is why he was asking for a little help," Richie loudly interrupted from the rear, causing the others to turn and recognize his presence. "Isn't that right, Jim?"

I sneered at his comment but kept my cool. "It's true, I did ask Detective Saunders if I could bounce some ideas off him if needed, but he seemed disinterested at the time, reminding me of his own heavy workload. Because of that, I chose not to involve him."

"It's lightened up now, though," Richie added.

"Oh, I bet it has," I stated.

"Can we get back to it, gentlemen?" Frank jumped in, recognizing the tension.

"Anyway," I continued, "as I was saying, we're still trying to piece things together."

"I don't understand," Captain Bessell spoke up. "You're making it sound like we've got ourselves a serial killer running around this city, yet your report indicates all of the victims were killed in different ways. That hardly sounds like the work of a serial killer. They usually have a pattern, and they stick to it."

"It's all in the report, Captain," I pointed at the folder that sat open in Redfern's hands, "but if you need me to explain it to you, the killer *does* have a pattern; it's just not something you would typically pick up on."

"Which is..?" the Chief questioned.

"If you look at the victims' names: Amber, Bruce, Cameron, Denise, Eva, he's choosing his victims sequentially in alphabetical order."

"That could be a coincidence, Detective," the Chief stated.

"I'd agree with you, sir, if it wasn't for how each of them was killed. Amber – asphyxiation. Bruce – burned. Cameron – carbon monoxide. Denise – drugs. Eva – electrocution. This guy's following the alphabet. Five letters so far."

"Fuck!" Richie's voice rang out.

Frank gave him a dirty look.

"Sorry," he apologized.

"If what you say is true," Captain Redfern jumped in, "how can you be certain we're only dealing with five bodies? How do you know there aren't others?"

I looked at Frank for his support, and he nodded his approval for me to continue.

"The killer left a note with his last victim, Eva. It was addressed to me, and it basically declared he had already taken five lives and that he was going to continue until he made his way through the entire alphabet. Our killer is five letters deep, gentlemen, and he's just getting warmed up."

"Why was it addressed to you, Detective?" Captain Bessell asked.

"I wish I knew, Captain. I think he's messing with me."

"Where is this note now?" Redfern asked.

"I had it sent to the lab to be analyzed," I replied. "No luck."

"So, that's it then," Redfern stated. "We've got a homicidal maniac on the loose."

"I don't like that we're just learning about this now, Detective," Captain Bessell stated. "We're already behind the eight ball on this. People are in danger, and they don't even know there's a killer out there. We need to get ahead of this. What kind of ship are you running here, Captain Redfern?"

"Hey, hey," Chief Copelli barked, "I'll speak with my officers, Captain. In the meantime, what are you suggesting?"

"We need to get the word out there. We need to speak to the press. If the killer is going in order, and his last victim was E, then we can assume he'll be looking for an F name next. We have to at least alert the public to this."

"I agree," the Chief said. "Captain Redfern, I want you to set up a press conference for this afternoon. Gather what you can from Detective Haddick's report and fill the hounds in about this psycho. And you know damn well they're going to be looking for a catchy name for this guy. I want you to come up with something before *they* do. If left in their hands, they'll be calling this the Sesame Street Murders or some bullshit."

"Chief," I interjected, raising my hand in front of my chest to gain his attention.

"What is it, Detective?"

"I think I may already have a name for our guy."

"Well, what is it?" he inquired.

I couldn't believe I was even considering this. That damn Vera, bless her soul; she got in my head.

"The Alphabet Killer."

No sooner did the words leave my lips than Officer Newsome burst through the door.

"Sorry, sirs. Lieutenant Garrett..."

"Not now, officer. Can't you see we're in a meeting?"

"Yes, sir," he answered. "But this is urgent, sir."

"Oh, for Christ's sake; what is it?"

"Mr. Manfredi from the diner just called. He found one of his waitresses dead in the freezer."

"What?" Frank expressed. "You're kidding?"

"No, sir. He thinks someone killed her."

Being the detective I was and also being suspicious of just about everything, I had to play my part.

"Not to sound insensitive," I began, "but people have accidentally locked themselves in freezers before. Why would Mr. Manfredi think she was killed?"

"He said the freezer didn't lock," Newsome replied. "And also, there was blood."

"Officer Newsome, did Mr. Manfredi happen to tell you the waitress's name?"

"I believe he said it was Francine," the officer replied. "He found her body frozen."

I glanced over at the other officers; they all had stunned looks on their faces as if they couldn't believe what they had just heard. There were seven of us in the room at that moment, and yet, you could have heard a pin drop. Welcome to the game, gentlemen. Glad you could join me.

Chapter 10

needed this shit like I needed a hole in the head. I expected Frank and the two Captains would accompany me to the crime scene, but I hadn't expected they would suggest Richie tag along. *"Maybe he can provide some insight,"* they said. *"Wouldn't hurt to have a fresh set of eyes on the case."* They could all blow me. Richie was only there because he couldn't stand that I had been named head detective, not only on this case but in our department, as well. He'd always held a grudge about that. The first chance he saw to wiggle his way into the good graces of Captain Redfern, he almost tripped over himself rushing to the front of the line. Frank tried to keep him back at the station, reminding Richie that he had his own report on the Slattery case due by morning, but the two Captains insisted. Heaven forbid they'd have to massage his poor, underappreciated ego. I couldn't stand the guy anymore. Now I

129

was stuck having to babysit his sorry ass. Just what I always hoped for when combing through a crime scene.

Manfredi's Diner was a local eatery from where most of the guys at the station ordered their takeout. It was decent food at a favorable price, but murder victims didn't usually come with the check. And although the diner's slogan was "a meal to die for," a phrase more fitting now than ever before, it looked like someone took it a bit too literally.

Half of the men at the station probably knew Mr. Manfredi's waitresses better than they knew their own wives. The ladies were good listeners if you needed an ear to chew on, quick to fill up your coffee if you were running low, and most importantly, not too hard on the eyes. Francine worked the late shift at the diner, a second job in what seemed like an overwhelming task to try to pay off her student loans. Had she graduated from college, something nobody in her family had done previously, it would have been easier, but she dropped out after only a year and one semester, choosing to attend Cosmetology School instead So, during the day, after she finished her classes, she worked as a manicurist at the Sunshine Salon over in the plaza on Highland Ave. She dreamed of owning her own nail salon someday, promising to give all the officers' wives discounts if it ever became a reality. Just another dream crushed under the heel of this city.

The brown-haired waitress was found dead in the back corner of the walk-in freezer, her body propped up into a seated position, her legs extended in front of her. Her head was tilted back and to her right side, resting against the wall, her frozen eyes locked on her bare arm just below her sleeve. If there had been any doubt this woman's death was linked to our killer, it was immediately dispelled by the familiar marking carved into her forearm.

"What the hell is that, Detective?" Captain Redfern inquired, pointing to the open wound where the blood had crystalized over the flaps of skin. "Is it what I think it is?"

"I don't know, Captain," I replied sarcastically, still upset about the whole situation with Richie. "If you think it's a painted-on butterfly, then no, it's not what you think."

"Watch yourself, Haddick," the Captain replied. "You're walking on thin ice."

Everything went silent for a few seconds. All of us, including the Captain himself, realized his coincidental choice of words. Then the world resumed.

"It's the letter 'F,'" I answered. "Our guy is at it again."

"Son of a bitch," Redfern blurted. "So this is number six, then? Goddammit! Lieutenant Garrett, I want your men out on the street, scouring for this psycho. I don't care if they have to work double shifts around the clock; I want this asshole caught. And Jesus Christ, where is forensics?"

While Redfern continued his ranting, puffing his chest in front of Captain Bessell, I squatted beside the body, examining Francine's frozen corpse, her pale-blue skin almost translucent against the backdrop of her white and yellow striped uniform, the intricate lines of her veins on full display like a spider's web. The carved F on her right forearm had streaks of dried blood running vertically down the inner part of her arm, where it had dripped from her skin before freezing in little droplets on the floor. In her right hand, held loosely between her fingers, a black pen with the words "Manfredi's Diner" printed on it. I glanced over at her left side, her arm resting beside her, forearm faced up. Held in that hand, to go along with the pen in her right, a guest check pad, no doubt meant to look like she was taking an order. Upon closer inspection, I noticed there was scribbling on the top page. I couldn't quite make it out, the paper partially hidden by Francine's icy fingers.

"Hey," I interrupted the meeting of the minds behind me. "Anyone got a tissue or handkerchief?" I could have waited for forensics to arrive; they'd have gloves, tweezers, and other such tools, but my way was more fun, especially seeing the men's faces after I shut their conversation down. They each patted their pockets, scrambling to find something when all they had to do was step out of the freezer and grab a napkin from the counter. It didn't take a detective to realize that. A moment later, however, Richie stepped forward and handed me a lace doily that he pulled from his jacket pocket. I felt myself shoot him a bemused look as I took it from him, but I wasn't going to ask. I didn't want to know. Or, maybe I did.

Scrunching the doily between my fingers, I grasped the pad's edges and carefully wiggled it free of Francine's cold grip. I stared at the page and could feel my blood pressure rise.

"What is it, Detective?" Captain Bessell inquired just as Vera and her forensics crew showed up to take over where I had left off.

"Ah, shit," Vera announced. "Not quite the frozen treat I was expecting."

I looked at her and shook my head in disapproval. It wasn't the time or place for such commentary.

"What?" she questioned as I walked past her. "It was just a joke." Then she turned to Richie, "What's up his ass?"

Just as I walked past Captain Bessell, Captain Redfern belted out, "Where are you going, Detective?" It didn't stop me from walking past him too. Frank was next in line, and of the three of them, I respected him the most (that thought left a bad taste in my mouth), but if I didn't still have the waitress's pad, he would have received the same treatment.

He looked me in the eye and could see I was distraught.

"What is it, Jim?" he asked quietly. "What's on the pad?"

"I gotta go and do what I was supposed to do before this mess happened," I said, pressing the pad into Frank's chest as I walked out of the freezer.

"Hey!" he yelled. "You can't just walk out of here. We've got a body."

"You've got Richie," I replied over my shoulder as I continued for the front door. "I'm sure he's got things under control." Then I walked out.

Richie hobbled to Frank to reassure him, "I can handle this, Lieu. What's on the pad?"

The Lieutenant turned the pad over to read the scribbling as the two Captains stepped forward in curiosity.

Detektive Jim. You shood have known the LETTERS woodn't stop. Not until I'm dun. Pleeze tell me you've learned of "The Group" by now. All these clues, and still I am free to play the game. Have I put too much faithe in you? I had faithe in F once, too, but she let me down. So I had to put her on ice. Six lay silent. Twenty more still roar. Maybe G will fare better. Until the next time. Ω

"Shit," Frank stated under his breath. "Where are you going, Jim?"

* * *

I shouldn't have left the way I had. Frank probably thought I was serious when I said Richie had it under control. Richie couldn't tell the difference between his head and his ass. He was smart enough to know who's ass to stick his head up, though.

Vera and her crew would take care to look things over well enough. Where the fuck was Lenny, though? I'd have thought he would have been all over the crime scene. I pulled out my phone and sent a quick text.

Dead body. Manfredi's. Where r u?

I shouldn't let it concern me. With Frank, Redfern, and the state police now involved, things were going to happen. But they weren't happening fast enough, and now Francine was dead. Fuck!

Why was I letting this scumbag get to me? And why was he making it personal? What made me so special? It didn't matter anyway. For whatever reason, I was his muse, and he would continue to call me out. His little notes were only part of his jabs, meant to knock me down. The joke was on him. When you'd been knocked down before by someone you cared about and still managed to pick yourself up and carry on, there was nothing anybody else could do to drop you that low again.

Just then, my phone buzzed.

Just got here. Lt. Garrett said you stormed off like a bat out of Hell. He showed me the note. Are you going where I think you're going?

Yes, I texted back. *Keep it to yourself. I'll be in touch.*

No prob. I know how to play dumb.

That little interruption managed to cool me down. At least enough to contemplate the killer's message. Did he slip up? He said he "*had faith in F once, too.*" He knew her personally and not the same way her customers knew her. He wasn't picking his victims at random. He knew them all, and I had a feeling it had something to do with "*The Group*" he mentioned. He was obviously referring to the Letter Group, and that was exactly why I was paying Papa Rio another visit.

I still didn't understand why the killer had chosen me. Was it someone I had previously put away? Who did I piss off so badly that would make them go to such lengths? It didn't make sense. And as I arrived at my destination, I hoped I would get some answers.

The Ruby Room had a decent-sized parking lot adjacent to the building. I didn't bother with it, choosing to park right out front of the main entrance in a restricted parking zone. What were they going to do, call the cops on me?

The moment I stepped from the car, I could see the bouncer take notice and put his hand up to try and stop me while pointing at my car.

"You can't park there, sir," he warned, extending his arm to the side to impede my advancement.

It was funny how, at that moment, all I could think about was how he called me "sir." Either this guy was brand new, or Papa Rio hadn't yet enrolled this one in douchebaggery 101. I almost hated being that guy who could give two shits. Almost.

"Do you see my car there, asshole?" I questioned while flashing my badge. "Then I guess I *can* park there. Now get out of my way; I'm seeing the man one way or another. I'd rather it be with you still standing." I could take this guy, couldn't I? Probably not, but if I stared at him long and hard enough, he'd start to believe it. He glanced at my car, then back at me.

"Whatever, man," he said, dropping his arm to his side. "This is just a part-time gig, anyway."

I strode past the large man, feeling confident in my new-found talent of gazing intently into another's eyes. I couldn't leave it at that.

"And if there's even so much as a scratch on it when I get back," I cautioned, "I'll have your ass."

I didn't watch to see his reaction as I walked through the door, but I was confident there was a finger involved.

There wasn't much of a crowd inside, which meant all the hired help's eyes were on me as I made my way to the narrow hallway leading to the back stairwell. There was a single goon sitting on a stool at the opening of the gray passage. He began to stand as I approached, but a quick flash of my badge as I opened my jacket, along with a full display of my sidearm, and he sat his fat ass back down in a hurry.

"Don't get up," I stated as I walked by. "I'll see myself to your boss's palatial estate." That time, I took the opportunity to glance back. It was as I suspected. What was with these guys and their fingers, anyway?

Taking the stairs two at a time, I quickly got to the top, where it appeared I caught the lumberjack guarding Papa's door by surprise since he immediately straightened himself and swiftly reached into his jacket.

I placed my hand on my service weapon while raising my other hand and waving my index finger as a warning, shaking my head in objection as I continued forward.

"Be smart, guy," I advised. "It doesn't have to go down like this."

The brute shot me a confused look as he pulled his hand from the flap of his jacket. My muscles tensed and jerked, and I felt my heart striking the inside of my rib cage until I noticed the radio he held was not an immediate threat. Taking a deep breath and relaxing my hand, I shook my head at the grunt again.

"Maybe next time you could just announce what you're doing."

The big man glared at me as he brought the radio to his lips. His smug look never changed.

"Sir, that asshole is back. What would you like me to do?"

"He's a guest, mon," Papa's voice squawked out as the door buzzed open. "Let him t'rough."

Papa Rio's watchdog stepped aside to allow me entrance.

"That's *Detective* Asshole to you," I said, staring the large man down as I passed. His tough-man stance wavered just a bit. The intense glaring thing I had suddenly adopted was working out for me. I'd keep that in mind.

"Officer Haddick," Papa Rio greeted in his thick Jamaican accent, "welcome back. What brings you to my humble abode dis time? Have you run out of corrupt politicians willing to donate to the policeman's ball?"

"Quit the goddamn charade, Alvin," I said, knowing it would elicit an irritated response.

Papa Rio stood from his chair and slammed his lion's head cane on the polished cherry desk.

"The name's Papa Rio, mon," he yelled. "Disrespect me again, Detective, and your boy will be mourning over your dead carcass."

"You know I have a son, huh?"

"It is my job to know about everybody in dis city," he replied. "Especially dose who could pose a t'reat to me and my business."

Everyone knew his "business" was dirty, but he was good at keeping that dirt off his hands.

"Then tell me who this fucking lunatic is going around killing people on my str... on *your* streets."

The room went silent for a moment. I knew it was best to let Alvin believe he was all-powerful. I hoped he had the information I wanted, and I felt feeding his enlarged ego was the best approach to pulling it from him.

Papa Rio licked his lips before curling them into each other and turning his eyes downward onto his desk.

"He eludes me," he stated, sounding almost flustered. "He is a ghost, only to be seen when he is ready to be seen."

"So much for knowing everybody in this city," I jabbed. I could tell it annoyed him as he quickly got to the point.

"Why are you here, Detective?" Papa Rio snidely asked, looking back up at me, his patience wearing thin.

I pulled the mysterious business card from my pants pocket, marched up to Papa's desk, and slammed it down next to his cane.

"I want to know about this group," I demanded. "And don't give me any of your shit about not knowing what it is. I know damn well something like that wouldn't operate without the great and wise Papa Rio knowing about it."

He wasn't pleased with my attitude. His unflinching gaze made me realize my stare had a long way to go to reach his level of badassery.

His eyes shifted to the card, then back to me, his lip curled in disgust.

"I knew of dis group, yes, mon. But they have not met in many weeks. Not since their leader got busted on drug trafficking charges. He's currently serving his sentence in BrentRidge, mon."

"Could someone else have continued in his place?" I asked. "Another group, maybe?"

"As you said, Detective, a group like dat wouldn't operate wit'out me knowing 'bout it."

"All right," I continued. "The guy who got busted; what's his name?"

"Carmine Lemon."

"I know of Carmine," I said. "I didn't know that lowlife was into whatever this 'Letter Group' shit was. What exactly was it, anyway?"

"I cannot tell you dat, Detective, only dat they used to meet in secret a couple of times a mont'."

"Not too secret for you to know about it, though?"

"No secret is too secret for me, Detective. I just don't concern myself wit' t'ings dat are of no consequence to me."

"Yeah, well this 'no consequence' of yours is leaving a trail of dead bodies in my city."

"I understand, but I have given you everyt'ing I know. The rest is up to you and your boys wit' the flashy badges. Now if you don't mind, Detective, I have a club to run."

He picked up his cane and pointed it toward the door. "I trust you can see yourself out?"

I gritted my teeth and held my tongue. He had been as cooperative as I could have expected and provided me with some information I didn't previously have. I'd comply with his wishes; I might need him again someday. I picked up the card from his desk and quietly walked away as the familiar buzzing sound droned, and the door clicked open.

I squeezed by the large oaf standing guard, thinking I should say something snarky but decided against it. With my luck, that's when he'd pull out a piece and shoot me in the back. Then what? This case would be left in Richie's hands. Hell no. I'll stay breathing, thank you. But as I exited the building and walked past the lone bouncer looking after my car, I couldn't resist.

"Your boss wants to see you," I said, signaling my thumb over my shoulder.

"Fuck!" he responded. "I knew you was gonna say something."

I let him off the hook as I got to my car door. "Nah, you're good; I was just fucking with you. Thanks for taking such good care of my vehicle."

"Asshole," was his reply as I slid into my seat. *I* thought it was funny, anyway. Too bad my next stop wasn't going to be.

I wondered how the others were doing at the crime scene but couldn't bring myself to call Frank to check in. I had more important things to check on now that I had another lead. Papa Rio filled some of the gaps about The Letter Group but not enough. If I wanted more, I'd have to go to the source, and that meant calling in a favor.

I got on the horn and dialed an old friend of mine. He'd found himself working as a Private Investigator over on the east side after he'd lost his job on the force. It was a good move for him, and he'd chosen the right clientele. The overpaid white-collar snobs of that neighborhood were the only ones that could afford his services. And those folks had lots of dirty laundry for him to air out. I just hoped he would pick up.

And then, right on cue, he did.

"Marty, you old stiff, this is Jim Haddick."

"Jimbo, how the heck are you? You still working for next-to-nothing pay at that thankless job of yours?"

"Yeah," I replied, "it's a living."

"Not much of one," he jabbed. "Hey, how's MacGovern been these days?"

"He retired six years ago," I replied. "Frank Garrett is my lieutenant now."

"Frank? That sorry son of a bitch? I feel for you, man."

"Yeah, me too."

"I'm telling you, buddy," Marty continued, "I'll create an opening for you if you want to get in on this sweet deal. It's easy money, and these people have deep pockets."

"Maybe I'll take you up on that offer someday. But listen; the reason I'm calling is I need a favor."

"Sure," he complied, "what do you need?"

"Is your brother-in-law still the Warden over at BrentRidge Correctional Facility?"

"Yeah, almost ten years now."

"I need to talk to an inmate," I said. "Do you think you could pull some strings and get me on the visitor's list?"

"When does this need to happen?" he asked.

"I'm on my way there now," I answered.

"Shit, Jim"

"I know," I responded. "I wouldn't be asking if it wasn't important."

"Who's the inmate?" he asked.

"A two-bit hustler and sometimes drug trafficker named Carmine Lemon. He's got information about a case I'm working on, and it can't wait. I've got to get in to see him."

"Let me see what I can do, Jim. If you don't hear from me, it means my brother-in-law was in a giving mood."

"Thanks, Marty. I appreciate it."

"No problem," he replied, "it's the least I can do."

"Well, maybe not the *least*," I fired back.

"Let me get on that before it gets too late," he said. "Give Karen and Ben my best, will you?"

"I'll do that," I replied.

"Good hearing from you, Jim."

"Yeah, same," I responded, hitting the "end call" button.

I guess Marty hadn't heard about Karen and me splitting. I didn't feel the need to tell him, either. I also didn't feel bad about putting him on the spot as I had. That was only *one* of the favors he owed me. There was still a handful more left unclaimed, and he knew it. If he wanted to clear his debt, he'd convince his brother-in-law to let Carmine out of his box to meet with me. And then I'd hopefully get some answers. Inmates didn't usually share a lot with police officers. I wondered how much leverage the warden would offer me if I wanted to get a little physical with the creep. Wishful thinking; I could never be so lucky. But one way or another, Carmine was going to give me something.

Chapter 11

MEDIA FRENZY

The waiting was killing me. I was thankful the Warden allowed my visit, but did he have to take his sweet time getting the prisoner ready? The plain, white cinderblock walls at the visitor check-in area weren't doing it for me. Not to mention, the officer at the window kept glaring at me suspiciously. Did I really look that shady to keep his distrusting attention? I already showed him my badge and gave up my weapon; did he want a blood sample too?

While I waited, I took the time to send a few texts, looking for updates. Lenny was the first to respond.

I wish I could tell you I had something, but Captain "high-on-his-horse" Bessell kept me from examining the body. He said he only needed me to declare and report on Francine's estimated time of death. The smug ass told me I'd have more time

with her once her body was delivered to the
morgue. I'm still waiting for it, by the way.

And there it was; the state's slow take-over of this case. Already Captain Bessell was calling the shots, and Captain Redfern was just standing back, letting it happen without putting up much of a stink. He always *was* a candy-ass.

Then, my phone exploded again as Vera's response came through.

I can't believe you left me there with that dumb
schmuck Richie. He spent the entire time harassing
Manfredi as if the old man had something to do
with it. What a putz. Everyone knows a serial
killer wants to remain low-key. It's always
someone people least expect. Look at Ted Bundy.
Nobody had a clue about him. Anyway, our girl
didn't put up a fight. There was no sign of a
struggle. My guess is she knew the killer. There
were some smudged prints on the pen. I'm guessing
they were Francine's. I haven't gotten the pad
from Frank yet, but I doubt we'll find much on it.
The guy we're dealing with is too smart for that.
I guess that clears Richie from being a suspect.
Lol.

It was disturbing how much Vera seemed to be getting a kick out of this. Since learning of her infatuation with serial killers, I wasn't sure if I could look at her the same again. Still, she knew her stuff; and having someone on the case who had studied up on these types of killers was probably a good thing. Hell, she probably knew more about the killer than...

"Detective Haddick," the voice rang out from behind the opening steel door, waking me from my wandering thoughts.

"Warden Bishop," I greeted, standing from the uncomfortable bench left for those visitors who were unlucky enough to have to wait for entry – which was all of them. "Thank you for accommodating my request on such short notice."

"I'm happy to help, Detective. Martin told me you were working on an important case, though I was surprised to hear you wanted to speak with Carmine Lemon about it. I would have expected someone from Vice rather than Homicide."

"I understand," I replied. "It's a tricky case. I'm hoping Carmine might be able to provide some information about a suspect in a murder investigation."

"Well then," the Warden stated, "by all means, we shouldn't keep the man waiting. You'll have to leave your phone with the officer." He waved his hand toward the window, the officer still eyeballing me skeptically.

"Of course," I agreed.

The window officer presented a small plastic container for me to drop my phone into. As I was about to, it rang. Looking at the screen, I saw that it was Ben. Horrible timing. The officer behind the window gave me an annoyed look as I debated answering the call.

"Something you need to take, Detective?" the Warden asked.

"Oh, ah, no," I answered, hitting the button and sending the call to voicemail. "Nothing important; it can wait."

"Shall we then?" he asked, nodding his head toward the door.

I placed my phone in the container, smiling half-heartedly at the officer collecting it. "Let's get this over with," I replied.

The Warden escorted me through the door, continuing the conversation about Carmine.

"He's quite a character, that Carmine."

"Is he?" I questioned. "I only knew him as a low-life dirtbag."

"Oh, no," the Warden expressed in disagreement. "Mr. Lemon has shown quite an improvement during his short stay. He's become somewhat of a spiritual guide, you might say. Many of the inmates look up to him."

"Is that right? Sounds to me like he's building himself a little cult following."

The Warden raised his eyebrow at me, "I wouldn't call it a cult."

"Sorry, Warden," I said. "It probably wasn't the right choice of words, although, before he'd ended up here, he had coordinated another group that *could* have been considered a cult. It makes me wonder if he's up to his same antics."

"Well, I assure you, Detective," the Warden continued, "Carmine Lemon has been a model inmate. I'm sure you'll see that for yourself. The visitation hall is just ahead; you'll have the room to yourself, but there will be two officers present if you need anything."

"You won't be staying?" I asked.

"I've got a prison to run, Detective. I'm sure you can handle things from here."

I nodded.

We stepped into the small visitation hall, my interviewee facing away from us, sitting at a round table in the center of the room. He was viewing a muted, flat-screen television hung in the corner above a second doorway that led out into a darkened corridor. Carmine knew we were there but refused to peel his eyes away from the screen to acknowledge our presence. As the Warden had stated, there were two officers present, each posted by one of the doors at opposite sides of the room.

"You'll have half an hour, Detective," the Warden said. "I assume that will be enough time to gather the information you seek."

"More than enough," I responded. "Thank you." I hoped that was true, anyhow.

"Glen," the Warden spoke to the officer standing closest to us at the entryway, "see to it that Detective Haddick here finds his way to the exit when he's through with the prisoner."

"Yes, Warden," the officer acknowledged.

"Well then, Detective Haddick, I wish you continued luck in your investigation." The Warden offered his hand, which I accepted with a firm handshake. Then, he walked away, leaving me alone to question Carmine.

I turned to the officer standing beside me, "you've got my back if things go sour, right?" He looked at me and smirked as if I was joking. I wasn't. Not really.

I wasn't worried about Carmine doing anything stupid (he'd done enough of that already), but I was used to interrogating people at the station; this was a different playing field.

Carmine was taller than average but scrawny. He wasn't very appealing to the eyes, either. He kept his short, dark hair slicked back with whatever greasy product was available. He had a pock-marked face that was partially disguised by a horseshoe mustache that made him look like he'd just walked off the set of a porno. That a man with Carmine's looks could convince anyone to listen to what he had to say was a wonder to me. Papa Rio seemed to think he was an influential guy, and the Warden all but confirmed it. What's the saying; you can't judge a book by its cover. Maybe not, but you could certainly dislike the story within.

I walked toward the center table, maneuvering my way around a few untucked chairs along the way, their tubular metal frames and hardwood seats looking as though they'd come straight from a 1970s grade-school cafeteria. I pulled up the seat across from Carmine, his eyes still fixed over my left shoulder on the television behind me. I didn't say anything right away, instead waiting to see if my sitting in silence was enough to draw his attention away from the screen. It wasn't.

"Carmine, I'm Detective Haddick with the Southbridge Police Department. If you wouldn't mind, I'd like to ask you a few questions."

"It's a free country, man," he spoke, his eyes never swaying from over my shoulder. "Well, free for you, not for me."

"Mr. Lemon, this..."

"Hey, hey, hey," he interrupted, his eyes finally shifting to meet mine, "Enough with the names, man. We're all judged by our names. From Judas to Hitler to Mother Teresa. We need to shift the paradigm of how people think. You may address me as C."

"C?" I questioned.

"That's my letter, man," he replied. "With a letter, there is no misconception. I take on a new form but remain the same. I'm just me. I am C."

The man obviously had a few screws loose. Did he believe all that horseshit? He spoke of not being judged, but that was all I wanted to do now.

"Okay.., C. I'd like to ask you a few questions about the group you established." I pulled the business card from my pocket and placed it on the table before him. "Can you tell me about The Letter Group?"

He glanced down at the card, a subtle smirk penetrating his unpleasant features.

"We all have the desire to fit in, Detective. Those who give themselves to the way of the letter, to abandon the name they *were*, and to be accepted as they *are*, choose to shine above the named ones."

"What the hell is that supposed to mean?" I asked, somewhat surprised he was willing to open up so easily.

"It means we all possess a light within ourselves; a light we tuck away for fear others will steal it from us. But by becoming a letter, man, we unshackle our fears and turn them into strength. We *become* the letter that is us, and because of it, we can let our letter shine as brightly as we do."

I wasn't getting it, and he could tell, as I picked up from his irritated tone and shifting body language.

"Yeah, yeah," I said, brushing off his ridiculous comments, "I've seen the slogan. What I need to know is, who are the members? Who was in this little group of yours?"

"The lost," he answered. "The weak; the downtrodden. Those who were missing something in their lives, man. Through me, they found a connection to others who were like them. Where once they felt they didn't belong, The Letter Group offered community, love, hope, and most importantly, acceptance."

"That's great, and all," I interjected before his nonsense ramblings wasted more of my time, "but what I meant was, I need to know the names of your members. You must have had a list of attendees or something. How many members were there?"

"We numbered in the hundreds," he snapped. "And haven't you been listening at all, Detective? There were no names in the group. Everyone went by their letter to maintain anonymity. Some even chose to brand themselves with their new identity, symbolizing their yearning to discard their old life, and embrace their new one."

"Are you kidding me right now?" I seethed, sitting up in my chair, incredibly annoyed by his nonsensical banter. "Is that something you encouraged, having people mutilate themselves for the sake of feeling accepted into your goddamn group?

Well, let me tell you something, *Carmine;* I believe someone in your group has taken your sermon gibberish a bit too seriously. Someone out there is killing people and leaving a little calling card with each victim. Only, this calling card is a goddamn letter cut into the flesh. And you sit here and tell me you don't know the names of any of the members of your group. How convenient for you."

"The Alphabet Killer," Carmine mumbled.

"What?" I questioned, shocked at his response. "What did you just say?"

Without another word, he pointed to the television behind me. I twisted in my seat, then almost fell out of it from what I saw. A recorded press conference had taken place, with Captain Bessell of the state police, front and center, at the podium microphone. Behind him, Frank and Captain Redfern stood statuesque, showing their support. A news ticker along the bottom of the screen scrolled a repetitive message, "Recent murders in Southbridge attributed to a serial killer dubbed 'The Alphabet Killer' by State Police Captain Bessell."

"Hey," I announced, pointing to the second officer standing just below the television. "Any way you can turn up the sound on that thing?"

The officer glanced up at the television, then reached around to the front and pressed the volume button a few times.

"...assured your local law enforcement and the state police are working together to get this killer off the streets. The public's safety is our number one priority. The Mayor is already putting a plan in place to enlist the aid of surrounding law enforcement agencies to help increase the police presence on the street. Until such time, we advise people to be cautious when going out alone. Especially at night. Thank you."

The news then switched back to the studio.

"A disturbing message earlier today by Police Captain Bessell, as authorities have so far uncovered six victims by a purported serial killer. Once again, we take you back out to the Southbridge Police Department, where news correspondent Harmony Veloy reports. Harmony?"

"Thank you, Nick. I'm standing outside the Southbridge Police Department, where just over an hour ago, State Police Captain George Bessell gave a press conference, alerting the public that there was an investigation underway into a possible serial killer on the loose in the city. Although he didn't go into details about any of the victims, Captain Bessell did announce that the police have christened the suspected predator, 'The Alphabet Killer.'

"Now, Channel 46 news has learned the latest victim attributed to The Alphabet Killer was a waitress who worked at the local landmark eatery, Manfredi's Diner. Francine Douglas, 38, was found frozen to death inside the establishment's walk-in freezer. No other details are available. Police have since cleared the owner of the diner, Mr. Vincenzo Manfredi, as a possible suspect. Mr. Manfredi was noticeably shaken and refused to comment at this time. As always, we'll keep you posted as developments arise.

"This has been Harmony Veloy with 46 News. Back to you, Nick."

"Thank you, Harmony. Are you getting a general sense of the public's reaction to this latest development?"

"Well, Nick, the people I've spoken with so far have shown great concern over this terrifying news. You can almost feel a sense of dread in the air. There are already whispers that this killer might be worse than another serial killer this city was

frighteningly familiar with back in the eighties: the Midnight Mangler."

"Thanks, Harmony. Awful news for the city of Southbridge. In other news..,"

I'd heard enough. It was out there now. We didn't know enough about this guy yet, and now Captain Bessell's decision to alert the public was going to bring people crawling out of the woodwork, confessing to crimes they hadn't committed. We'd have to dedicate resources to weeding them out, no matter how ridiculous their claims, even though I already knew none of them would be our guy.

"You can turn that shit off now," I barked to the officer. He complied. Then, I turned back to Carmine, who had a huge smile on his face.

"Something funny, asshole?" I questioned.

"Funny? No," was his response. "You said the killer was cutting letters into the victims. This is a wonderful thing, man! The word of the letter is getting out there. Don't you see? Someone has learned to free themselves of their troubled life. They're teaching the way of forgiveness and acceptance. They're embracing their letter to the fullest."

This guy was off his rocker. He couldn't see that what the killer was doing was a terrible thing. He thought it a means to propagate his misguided message. I wasn't going to get a name from this nut job, but if the killer was a member of Carmine's group, maybe he could provide me with a letter.

I couldn't believe I was going to ask this, but it was the only way he'd listen. "Tell me, C; was there any letter in your group that you feel might be acting out in this way? Was anyone pushed out of the group for not believing? Any letter that wanted to help spread your word as much as you?"

He smiled at me with a sinister grin. "They *all* wanted to spread my word, Detective. They were all my good letters."

"Yeah," I said. "And you're a fucking piece of work, *Carmine*. Officer," I announced, standing from the table, "take me away from this demented shithead."

I felt like I had wasted my time. As much as I hated the thought, if I wanted anything useful from this slimy bastard, I'd probably have to come back and indulge his misguided bullshit fantasies. But in my current mood, I couldn't pander to his obscene idiocy.

I was quickly escorted out the way I came, stopping only to gather my weapon and phone. I saw I had four missed calls: three from Frank and one from my ex-wife. Fantastic. Just what I needed. The day was going swimmingly so far; why not keep the train rolling?

Chapter 12

ON THE TRAIL OF A KILLER

I used to get an excited feeling in my stomach when a big break in a case would fall into my lap. I thought that's what I was onto when I learned of The Letter Group and its righteous champion. What a disappointment that was. Carmine Lemon was a crackpot who didn't know any of the members. Instead, he encouraged all who joined to embrace shortening their names to just their first initial. I couldn't believe people actually bought into his delusional fantasy. But they did. The weak-minded would buy into anything. The Kool-Aid of Jim Jones and the followers of NXIVM and Charles Manson were proof of that. Not to mention the twisted members of the FLDS or the extremist suicide bombers willing to take their lives, along with innocent people, in the name of Allah. People really were just sheep, and because of that, what did I have to show for it?

I had two theories, and neither one got me any further in my investigation. Assuming all the victims were connected in some way, and that connection being that they were all part of the now defunct Letter Group, then I could reasonably assume the killer was either a member of the same group, or he was targeting them for some reason. Either way, I had no name and no member roster to pull from. I couldn't pin down a suspect, and I couldn't warn anyone who could be in potential danger of being the psychopath's next victim. The only thing I knew with any amount of certainty was that the next victim on the killer's list would be someone whose name began with the letter G. Great! That narrowed it down to probably a few thousand people in this city. The best I could hope for was that the lab folks were able to pull some usable DNA from Francine or the note the killer left behind. Maybe that's why Frank was so desperately trying to reach me. I figured I had cooled down enough to return his call. If not, screw him. He was lucky I'd kept my cool this long dealing with him. I dialed the S.O.B.

"Jim, where the fuck are you?" Frank bellowed when he answered his phone.

"I'm on my way back to the station now," I answered. "What's going on? Did you get anything from Francine?"

"Why the fuck should I tell you, asshole?" Frank barked. "You walked away from a crime scene right in front of my boss and the State Police Captain, making our entire department look bad. When you pull your goddamn stunts like that, I'm the one left dealing with this shit. Redfern already threatened to pull you from the case. It took all I had to convince him to keep you on. You'd better tell me wherever the fuck it was you took off to was worthwhile."

"I went and visited our friend, Papa Rio, to see if he had any information about that wacky support group. I have a hunch all of the victims belonged to it. I suspect that's how they are being targeted."

"And what did you find out," he asked.

"I found out the group was run by that greasy dirtbag Carmine Lemon, but they haven't met in weeks."

"So let's pick up Carmine and see if he's got anything to say," Frank suggested.

"The man's in prison, Lieutenant. But I took a trip to BrentRidge to question him. I'm coming from there now; that's why I couldn't answer your calls."

"What the fuck, Jim," he responded. "Don't you think I should know about this shit before you run off like that? Christ!" The line went silent for a moment. Then Frank's voice erupted again, "Well, what did he have to say? Did he give you any names?"

"That's just it;" I replied, "the people in the group didn't go by names. They were all letters."

"Letters? What the hell does that mean?"

"It means Carmine didn't know squat about who attended the meetings. They were all Bs, or Ts, or Qs for Christ's sake. And now our guy is picking them off one at a time. I'm telling you, Frank, the deeper I get into this case, the more dead ends I keep hitting."

"Yeah, well you're going to like what I have to say even less. Captain Bessel called it into Washington. The FBI is sending over some agents from their field office."

"What the Fuck, Lieu?" I raged.

"You knew it was coming, Jim. It was only a matter of time."

"Of course I did; just not yet. That should have been Redfern's call. So much for working together; Bessell's got

Redfern kissing his ass. Next thing you know, he'll be calling in the goddamn National Guard."

"All right, that's enough, Jim. We're all under a lot of pressure here. The FBI was getting involved, no matter what. If it wasn't today, then tomorrow. And right now, the way things are going, we can use all the help we can get."

"It doesn't mean I have to like it," I griped.

"Then don't like it, but you're going to work with it. Now get back here so Redfern doesn't lose confidence that his decision to keep you on was the right call."

"Aye, aye, Lieutenant," I responded snidely. "I'll be there shortly."

"And when you get here, go see Vera; she said she's got something for you."

"Did her team find something at Manfredi's?" I asked.

"I don't know. She wouldn't tell me, and I wasn't asking. You know how that woman gets. She would have likely chewed my head off just for questioning her."

It was comforting to know that being an IA nightmare like Vera was all it took to keep Frank off your back.

"All right," I said, "I've got another call to make. I'll see you soon."

I hung up without waiting for his response. He'd get over it. There were more important conversations to be had. I hoped Vera had something for me. For now, I wanted to check in with Lenny while I could, to see if Francine's body was able to tell him anything more than what we all saw.

"Lenny, it's Jim. I assume you've already started on Francine."

"Yeah," he replied. "And you're lucky I like you, Jim. You caught me at a bad time. I was in the middle of weighing her organs. I'm going to need a fresh pair of gloves now."

"You didn't need to go into that kind of detail," I said. "Ending with 'I like you' would have sufficed. But tell me what you've got so far."

"The first part you already know. Francine froze to death, or more accurately, her organs shut down due to her sustained exposure to the extremely low temperature. But what you didn't know is how the killer managed to keep her in the freezer long enough for that to happen."

"I assumed he injected her with a sedative the same way he did Cameron."

"You would have thought that," Lenny explained, "but no. And here's the part you're going to be glad you left when you did. When it was finally time to remove the body, they had to scrape the back of her head from the wall. Blood and partial brain matter had frozen to it like a tongue to a flagpole. She was struck from behind by something blunt and heavy, cracking her skull open. I found traces of iron oxide - that's rust – at the opening of the wound, so we know the object was metal."

"I thought you said she froze to death." I reminded him.

"Oh, she did," Lenny replied. "The blow didn't kill her, but it did render her incapable of moving. She wasn't paralyzed, mind you; at least, not in the traditional sense. But the trauma inflicted would have been severe enough to cause acute Cerebellar ataxia. With the damage I saw, it's a sure bet she lost motor function in her extremities, which is why there were no signs of a struggle. And, in all likelihood, she remained conscious even after being struck. She sat there, freezing to death, the door to her salvation right in front of her, and she couldn't budge from her position."

"Fuck, Lenny," I expressed. I only hoped Francine couldn't process what was going on. I didn't want to think about the terror she must have been experiencing.

"That's not all," Lenny added. "The killer cut the F into Francine's arm while she was still alive. She stared into that sick-o's eyes while he carved her, and she felt every bit of it but could do nothing to stop him."

"Jesus," I gasped. "Do I need to hear this? You got anything more for me? Preferably something a little less graphic?"

"As a matter of fact," he continued. "That wasn't the only F on Francine."

"The bastard cut her twice?" I questioned.

"Oh, no. Sorry, I didn't mean to suggest that. She had a tattoo on the back of her left shoulder. It was the letter F with the words 'shine bright' below it."

"Let your letter shine as brightly as you do," I mumbled, shaking my head.

"What was that?" Lenny inquired.

"Nothing," I answered. "That confirms Francine was a member of the same group as the others." It also confirmed, at least in my eyes, these people were into that shit enough to permanently mark themselves. Calvin didn't carve a letter into his head because of some internet challenge; he was proudly branding himself a card-carrying member of that secret society of freaks. But whatever motivations they had for joining The Letter Group, they didn't deserve to die for them. "Fucking cults," I let slip.

"So that's it then?" I continued. "The killer hit Francine with something, knocking her immobile, propped her up against the freezer wall, cut her, then waited for her to freeze to death."

"Don't forget he also wrote you a note," Lenny added. "But yeah, that's pretty much it."

"Yeah, I didn't need the reminder, Lenny. Listen, thanks for the update. If anything else comes up, let me know."

"You got it, Jim."

We hung up, but I couldn't keep my thoughts from lingering on the conversation. Francine was always such a pleasant woman. To think about what that maniac did to her tears me up. Those waitresses are like family to Manfredi. He must be devastated. But what of Francine? Why was she a member of that group? Carmine said the members were all lost, people looking for acceptance. Was she looking for that? I guess you couldn't always tell from appearances who was hurting inside. What was so terrible in her life that she needed to join Carmine's merry band of misfits? What was so bad in *any* of their lives? Maybe it was a copout. We all had our problems, but we didn't all seek support from misguided fanatics to solve them. And now, because of it, someone had sentenced them to death.

I couldn't keep thinking about that as I pulled into the station. The two non-discreet, large black SUVs parked in a row gathered my attention. Shit, it had begun.

Collecting myself and taking a deep breath, I got out of my car and walked into the rear entrance. You would have thought I set off an alarm the way everyone turned in my direction the moment I set foot in the building. They couldn't have made it more obvious how I had been a topic of discussion. Maybe the boys in black were interested in what I had to say.

They were all huddled in the briefing room: Frank, Captain Redfern, Captain Bessell, Chief Copelli, and four suits. If I hadn't already guessed what they were talking about, Mick was about to spill the beans as he came rushing over to me before I could make it to my desk.

"Hey, Jimmy," Mick greeted me, his head turned toward the small gathering as if keeping watch to ensure they didn't see him. As if he was doing something wrong just by approaching me, and he didn't want them to notice. "The Feds are here, man."

"I can see that, Mick," I said.

"Yeah, well, it's about your case."

"I know that too. It was bound to happen."

"Why didn't you tell me you were on a serial killer case?"

I looked over Mick's shoulder, spying Richie at his desk, Mick's eyes shifting between me and the briefing room.

"You mean Richie hadn't already told you?" I questioned.

"What's Richie got to do with any of this?" Mick asked. "Is he involved too?"

I was taken aback by his response. Richie wasn't one to hold back information if a gloating opportunity arose. Why was he suddenly so quiet about this particular case?

"He only just got involved this morning, kid. Captain Redfern felt we needed more resources. That's why the Feds are here too."

"They gave a press conference to the news stations earlier," Mick said. "Captain Bessell called the perp 'The Alphabet Killer.' It's like something straight out of Sesame Street or something."

My thoughts immediately turned back to Chief Copelli's earlier concern about the press coming up with the killer's moniker. Hearing Mick just now, I guess it was a valid point.

"Listen up, people," Captain Redfern's voice erupted from the briefing room doorway while he rapped on the metal casing. "We need everybody in the briefing room in two minutes. Bring your notepads." Then he disappeared back into the room.

"Sounds like everyone's getting involved now, kid," I said, brushing Mick aside to gain passage to my desk. "We're not the ones in charge anymore."

Like a good officer, Mick dashed to his desk to grab a pad and pen. And like an ass-kissing officer, Richie was already walking to the room like he was ready to rush in for Black Friday deals. The sight of it turned my stomach. I didn't bother with the notepad; I already knew the information they'd be regurgitating.

I decided to wait for Mick to gather his things. It always took him a while to find where he last placed his essentials, and I didn't want him to be the last one walking in alone. We had all been in those situations before, and they could be very uncomfortable. Mick was a little slower in the head than most of the other officers. He didn't need to be the focus of ridicule more than he already was.

Once Mick had himself together, I slinked around my desk to walk with him.

"Hey, Jim, where's your pad?" he asked.

I smirked at him as we entered the briefing room and whispered, "I hope you're a good notetaker, Mick." His stutter-step and widened eyes let me know he thought I was serious. I liked the kid, but I wasn't letting him off the hook by telling him I wasn't.

As we took our seats, I noticed Redfern give me a disapproving glance. It stood to reason; it had been *my* case, and I was the last to enter. He probably felt I was irresponsible or perhaps disrespectful. Irresponsible, never. Disrespectful.., eh. But also, it was my case. I should've been up with them instead of on the outside looking in.

"As most of you are aware by now," Captain Redfern started, "and for those of you who are not, Southbridge has a killer roaming our streets. Over the past week alone, there have been three homicides attributed to this maniac. This department has since confirmed that, over the last several weeks, there have been at least three other murders identified as belonging to the same killer. Six homicides, ladies and gentlemen. We're dealing with a serial killer."

I noticed a female agent standing off to the side, wincing at that comment.

"Because of the nature of these murders," Redfern continued, "and how the killer is marking each of the victims by cutting a letter somewhere on their body, we've given him the name 'The Alphabet Killer.'

"What we know so far: the individual is killing people in alphabetical order, choosing his victims by the first letter of their name. He's also killed each of them differently, their causes of death beginning with the same letter as their name. We believe the killer is male and that he may have had some connection to each of his victims. There's not a lot to go on at this time. The maniac has vowed to continue killing until he finishes the alphabet. We won't let that happen. Chief?"

"Thank you, Captain," Chief Copelli responded, stepping up to the podium. "Many of you weren't around when this city was in a stranglehold from another serial killer: the Midnight Mangler. More than thirty-five years ago, the Southbridge Police Department, with its capable detectives and officers, worked diligently to bring that killer to justice. We'll do the same with this one. But times have changed, and as our technology has advanced, so too have the criminals preying upon the innocent.

"Working together with Captain Bessell and the state police, we've taken the necessary steps to expand our resources by calling in the FBI to aid us in this investigation. They will be working with Captain Bessell and Captain Redfern, helping to set up a special task force dedicated to finding and apprehending this heinous killer. To provide you with more information about what you can expect to happen over the next couple of days, I'd like to introduce Special Agent Marion Hayes."

Chief Copelli stepped back from the microphone, taking his place in line with the Lieutenant and the two Captains. The nicely-dressed Agent Hayes, wearing a fitted, cliché black blazer over a white, buttoned-down shirt, and black slacks, stepped forward, her blonde hair pulled tightly into a bun at the back of her head.

"Good afternoon," she spoke. "As Chief Copelli had stated, I am Special Agent Marion Hayes from the Bureau's Pierre field office." She motioned to her left. "The gentlemen to my left are Agents Brynn and Pease." She then swung her arm in the opposite direction. "And to my right is Special Agent Cordell.

"I want to be clear that, although the FBI will be taking point on this investigation, we fully intend to work with the Southbridge Police Department in conjunction with the state police to track down the aptly-named 'Alphabet Killer.' I would also like to add that, contrary to what Captain Redfern and Chief Copelli had earlier stated, this is not a serial killer we are after, but rather, what the FBI refers to as a spree killer.

"You'll all be given a dossier, detailing everything we know about the killer's M.O. and his victims. I don't think I have to point out to any of you the sensitive nature of this in-formation. It shall remain confidential until such time we deem it pertinent to release any portion to the press.

"That being said, we're dealing with an unpredictable killer who has thus far eluded capture."

I raised my hand, thinking I couldn't remain silent any longer. All eyes turned in my direction. I stood out like a five-foot basketball player on an NBA all-star team. Special Agent Hayes glared at me as if she wasn't used to being interrupted. She'd learn; I was good at it.

"Yes?" she asked, nodding her head at me.

"I'd say the killer *was* predictable. We know he's planning for his next victim to be someone whose name begins with the letter G. That could be an edge we can use to our advantage."

"Yes, thank you for that," she responded. "And you are..?"

"Detective Jim Haddick," I announced. "I'm the reason you have the information you do on this lunatic. This was my case."

"Well, Detective Haddick," she said smiling, hiding her real emotion, something at which *she* was no doubt good, "we don't throw the word 'lunatic' around so frivolously until we're able to gather enough facts about the killer and his motives. I'd appreciate it if you refrained as well. I mentioned the killer was unpredictable because we have yet to understand his thinking. We don't know when he'll strike next or what method he'll try and use to kill his next victim. He has proven himself to be very clever, planning out each of his kills, yet if it weren't for the letters or the notes he'd left, we would have never known the murders were connected. As for this being your case, I'm very sorry, Detective. But there's no need to worry; it's in good hands now."

She shut me down with that last comment. She also got my juices flowing. She was a feisty one. I liked it, but I also hated it. My blood was boiling, and I'm sure my face was showing my anger. I would have gotten up to leave, but I knew that would only have made things worse for me.

"Now then," she continued, "Captain Redfern already mentioned this department believes that the killer was somehow connected to each of his victims, though we have yet to establish what that connection is, or if there is any at all."

Yup, my hand went up again.

"Detective Haddick," she acknowledged, "are there more words of wisdom you'd care to share with us?"

"The Letter Group," I stated. "That's their connection."

Special Agent Hayes glanced at her sidekick to her right, shaking her head, while he pulled out his sophisticated spy phone and began typing frantically.

"And what exactly is that, Detective Haddick?" she asked.

"It's a support group to which all of the victims, and I believe, our killer, belonged. If you put your efforts into tracking down the members of that group, you'll not only narrow down the list of possible victims, but your killer could potentially be among them."

Hayes turned to Special Agent Cordell, looking for confirmation. He shook his head and shrugged his shoulders.

"We've read your report," she countered. "And we have nothing in our database that supports your claim about this 'Letter Group' even existing, Detective Haddick."

"You need it spelled out in your damn database to support a claim that something exists?" I fired back. "I just found out more information this morning. Had you bothered to brief me before this meeting or had included me in your little secretive gathering, I would have given you the details."

Haddick!" Redfern shouted. "That's enough."

"You're right, Captain," I announced, standing from my seat. "It *is* enough."

"Sit down, Detective," Frank urged from beside Redfern, his hands motioning for me to calm down.

"I've sat through enough of this bullshit, Lieutenant," I snapped as I walked to the door, stopping only to make one last comment. "Let me ask you something, Special Agent Hayes; how does the Bureau solve any case if the information isn't in that database of yours?" Then I walked out. I'd catch hell for it, but it felt too good not to.

I had more important things to do than sit through a meeting, going over details from a report that *I* provided about a killer that *I* discovered. I knew this was going to happen. I warned Frank this investigation would go to shit. And here we were; welcome to Shitsville.

There was nothing to do about it now. The Feds would work the case the way they wanted, but it wouldn't stop me from collecting information on the side. Vera said she needed to talk with me. I might as well start with what she had to say.

I took the stairs down to the Dragon's Lair, leaving behind my frustrations. I could see Vera analyzing the killer's latest note, comparing it to the first one, but she hadn't noticed me standing just beyond the lab's little glass cage. I knocked on the reinforced window to gain her attention. She glanced up, pointed toward the door on my left, and sauntered over to unlock it for me.

"You're looking happy, chuckles," Vera said sarcastically, opening the door, my annoyance from the briefing room not yet wiped clean from my face. "Is it that bad up there?"

"It's *that* bad," I replied.

"I believe it," she responded. "Don't even get me started on the shit those outsiders are pulling, Jim. Can you believe that fucking twat Bessell took credit for naming this guy The Alphabet Killer? That was *my* idea. Only, he didn't even use the '2.0,' which would have been more accurate. You know this is going to confuse the historians all to hell."

I didn't dare tell her it was me who refrained from using the numeral suffix when I suggested the name.

"I think they'll manage to keep the two cases separate," I assured her. "Anyway, what is it you wanted to talk with me about? Tell me you've got something on the killer."

"I thought I had a partial print of our killer," she communicated with much agitation, "but it turned out to be a thumbprint belonging to your creepy little friend, Mort. That twerp gets too excited around dead bodies. Anyway, it turns out he couldn't resist taking a peek at the note the killer had written."

"Yeah," I acknowledged, "he mentioned Frank had shown it to him."

"He could have put on gloves first," Vera expressed. "The dumb asshole. He got me all tingly inside for nothing."

"That must have been a strange experience for you," I joked.

"Don't you worry about me, ass wipe," she returned. "I get plenty of locomotives wanting to park in my caboose."

I cringed. "That was a bit more than I needed to know."

"Pantywaist," she added.

"Listen, I'd love to continue the banter," I said, "but if you don't have anything more, I'd just assume head back upstairs to accept the ass-chewing I'm going to get for walking out on the FBI's little party."

"Oh, I've got more," Vera said, walking back to her desk. "I've been comparing the two notes the killer left. They're very similar in that they both look like they've been written by a first-grader. You might've thought this guy was either uneducated or a foreigner. Maybe both. But I think he's smarter than he's letting on. And it's all in one word."

"What do you mean?" I asked.

"Take a look," she said, sliding the two notes to the side of her desk so I could read them. "Here's the first note," she pointed. "See how he spelled the word, 'lerne'? Now take a gander at note number two."

"'Learn.' He spelled it correctly," I said.

"Exactly! That 'a' in there trips up uneducated people all the time. And foreigners? Forget about it. They can't spell English words for shit. This guy's not stupid. He knows how to spell, but he's trying to lead you to believe otherwise."

"I wondered if that was the case," I responded. "Thanks, Vera."

"Don't mention it. Unless it's to my boss at review time. Then shower me with love, baby. Vera needs a new pair of shoes."

"I'll keep that in mind," I answered, smirking. "You got anything else for me?"

"Isn't that enough, you greedy fuck? Christ, I've probably given you more than anyone else has."

"Almost," I replied.

"Mort doesn't count," she responded. "That bug is up at all hours looking for clues. I'm only a nine to five kinda lady."

"Lady, yeah," I returned, heading back toward the glass door. "Thanks again, Vera."

Just before the door closed behind me, I heard Vera's voice chime, "Munch, munch, sweet cheeks." An obvious acknowledgment of my earlier comment about going upstairs to get my ass chewed out. Once I was up there, it didn't take long, and it was worse than I expected.

The briefing room was cleared out, and everyone was back at their desks. The Feds had departed, along with Chief Copelli and Captain Bessell. Frank and Captain Redfern were in the Lietenant's office having a heated discussion from the look of it. I thought I had gotten off easy until Redfern spotted me.

"Haddick!" he yelled, causing everyone to look up from their newly-distributed reading material. "Get your ass in here."

All I could think of was, "let the ass-chewing begin," with the occasional "munch, munch," and Vera's face flashing before me. It was an amusing thought until I stepped into Frank's office, where any sign of amusement had packed up and left over a year earlier. I thought I'd be the bigger officer by beginning my apology.

"I know things got a little heated earlier..."

"Shut the fuck up, Detective," Redfern jumped in. "I've heard just about all I can take from you. We've dealt with your bullshit long enough. You're lucky you lasted on this case as long as you had, and you can thank Lieutenant Garrett for that. He's the one that vouched for you. Then you go and pull that shit you did in there," he pointed to the briefing room. "In front of *my* superior and the goddamn FBI. Enough is enough."

"So that's it, then?" I questioned. "You're taking me off the case?" I turned to see the regret in Frank's eyes. "Frank, you know I..."

"Sorry, Jim," Frank interrupted. "Not just the case. I'm going to need your badge and your sidearm."

I felt my heart sink into my stomach. "I'm being suspended? Are you fucking kidding me?"

"Think of it as a forced paid vacation, Detective," Frank stated, trying to relieve the soreness my ass was feeling. "Two weeks. Take the time off; think about how you want this case to go. It's the FBI's show now; that's not going to change. But you can still contribute. You can still help catch this psychopath if he's still out there when you come back. You'll just have to learn to play by a different set of rules."

"This is unbelievable," I said, shaking my head and staring at Frank. "Eighteen years, Frank. Eighteen years I've served this department and never once have I been suspended. Suddenly, the FBI comes swooping in on my case, and you're suspending me?"

"Don't turn this around on me, Jim. I warned you this would happen. This case is getting to you."

"All right, enough of this," Captain Redfern interjected. "Hand over your badge and firearm, Detective. Don't drag this out longer than it needs to be. You're lucky I'm not recommending you see the house shrink before returning."

I gave the Captain a nasty look. "You want my badge?" I said, unclipping it from my belt and tossing it onto Frank's desk. "My gun?" I unholstered it and slammed it down. "It's yours." Then I turned to storm out. But of course, I was me, so I couldn't just walk away without at least one final remark.

"Tell Miss Agent Fancypants, 'good luck.' She doesn't realize what she's gotten herself into. None of you do."

That felt better. That was the mic drop moment. I walked away thinking I had maybe struck a nerve in them that would linger long after I was gone. In reality, it was me that felt it more than they would. They'd go on working the case without me. I'd never been away from police work since I joined the force. And now I had two weeks with nothing to do. This was going to be the longest two weeks of my life.

Chapter 13

SLUM CITY

I began to think bad luck held a dark cloud over my head wherever I went. My ex-wife hated me. My kid was on the fast track to doing the same. The boys at the station thought I'd lost it. And I was stuck at home, receiving daily updates about the case from the nightly news and stewing over the decisions made by the Mayor and the FBI.

It hadn't always been like that. I used to be a respected member of the force, able to remain calm in the most daunting of circumstances. My objectives were clear, and I always maintained my composure in high-stress situations, even if those situations involved idiotic decisions made by my superiors. It wasn't ideal, but I could get past it. Lately, though, something had changed within me, and I didn't like the dark path it was leading me down.

I wish I could say it was the case that had put me on edge and that everything would go back to normal once the killer was caught, but that would be too easy. Although the case wasn't doing me any favors, I knew the real cause for my miserable disposition could be narrowed down to a single incident about a year and a half earlier, a pinpoint in time, from which I'd never quite fully recovered. And maybe I never would. But none of that had anything to do with the past two weeks. No, that I could attribute to the self-loathing despondency I felt because of my time away from work.

It started the day I got that bullshit suspension. As one could imagine, I wasn't in the best of moods. I had never been taken off a case before, let alone asked to turn in my badge and gun. Over the years, I'd seen other officers suffer the same indignity, some even taking pleasure in the time off, but I swore it would never happen to me. Yet there I was, driving home after having just had the bad news delivered, my thoughts still raging, and the slightest thing able to set me off. It was almost as if the universe knew, and it said, "let's fuck with that guy." That was when my phone rang.

I saw that it was my ex. In hindsight, knowing my frame of mind at that moment, I never should have answered it. But I also knew she had already called once before, and although I had good reason for missing it the first time, dismissing it a second time would bring the full fury of her wrath upon me, fire and brimstone included. But also, she seemed like a good target for my hostility. So I thought, bring it on. I always said we learned more from our mistakes than our successes. As mistakes go, answering the call was a big one.

"Karen," I started, "I don't know if this is the best time right now." I did try to warn her.

"It's never a good time, is it, Jim?" she answered, her voice like nails on a chalkboard. "Didn't you see I called earlier?"

"Yes, I did," I replied. "I was busy."

"Why didn't you call me back?" she snapped.

"Why didn't you leave a message?" I snapped back.

"Do you always have to be that way?" she asked. "Why do I always have to be the responsible one? You saw I called; you should have called me back."

"You? The responsible one?" I poked, like poking a raging bull. "Our son is staying with me right now, Karen, because you're too busy going out all the time with your new boyfriend, Phil. You weren't paying any attention to him."

"That's a bunch of bullshit, Jim, and you know it," she responded. "Don't try to turn this around on me. Ben is staying with you because he wants attention from his father. He never got any when he was younger, so now he's trying to make up for the lost time. *You* never took the initiative."

Words always cut deepest when they were true. That comment was no exception. I knew where the fault lay; I didn't need to be reminded of it every time she called.

"Do we really need to do this?" I questioned angrily. "I'm dealing with a whole lot of shit right now."

"I know," she replied. "I saw it on the news. You've got some crazy killer running around the city. That's why I'm calling. I don't think being in the city is the safest place for Ben right now. I think he should come back home with me. At least until you catch the guy."

"Are you kidding me right now? I'm a cop, Karen. There's no safer place *for* him to be? You always do this to me. You want me to spend more time with him, then, the first chance I get, you already want to take him away."

"It's not like that, Jim," she countered. "I'm thinking of *you*, too. I know you've got your hands full with this case. You can't keep watch over Ben all the time. If he goes out, you'll always be wondering where he is, worrying if he's safe. He'll be a distraction, and you won't be able to focus on what you need to do, which is getting that lunatic off the street."

"First of all, our son is not a distraction. Second of all, as shitty luck would have it, I just got suspended for two weeks, so I've got plenty of time to spend with Ben. And third, we don't throw the word lunatic around so frivolously until we're able to gather enough facts about the killer and his motives." Ok, that last one was an unnecessary jab, meant only as something to irritate her. It worked for Special Agent Hayes; I figured it would work for me too.

"What?" she questioned emphatically. "You've been suspended? What did you do? They can't suspend you when there's a killer on the loose."

"Well, they did," I answered. "If you'd like to take it up with those in charge, I can put you in touch with my boss, Frank; I'm fairly certain you know *him* well enough."

The line went silent for a moment before she started back in. "I'm sorry that happened to you, Jim. I'm sure they'll be just as lost without you as you'll be without them. More so, even. You're a good cop. You always have been. They won't be able to catch this guy without you."

"Thanks for trying to cheer me up, but I hope they *do* catch him. I'm tired of thinking about it all the time. This case needs to be put to rest, and the killer locked in a cage so our lives can all return to normal."

"I still don't think Ben should be there," Karen said.

"If the kid wants to stay, Karen, he's staying."

"I'm just concerned for his safety, Jim. Don't you get concerned at all?"

"Of course I do. And if I thought Ben was in any danger, I wouldn't hesitate to drop him off to you. Listen, the kid wants to stay here for a while; let him stay. I'm home for the next two weeks. There's nothing to worry about; he's going to be fine."

"And, if after two weeks they haven't caught the killer, and you go back to work?" she questioned. "What then?"

"Then, we'll re-evaluate things at that time. Christ, Karen, I can only do so much."

"I was only asking, Jim. You don't have to be an asshole about it."

"Well, I *am* an asshole," I replied. "Or did you forget all the times you made sure I knew it while we were married?"

"You know what?" she said. "I'm done. I'm sorry I even called."

"That makes two of us," I remarked.

"Well, here's another one for you," she replied. "Go to hell, ASSHOLE!" she yelled. Then she hung up.

As I said, nails on a chalkboard. I shouldn't have answered the call. Not that it would have gone any differently had I been in a better mood. We always brought out the best in each other.

If that had been the worst thing that happened during my two-week suspension, I would have considered it a win. But that dark cloud overhead hadn't finished raining on me yet, and I could hear the thunder rolling in. It was only a matter of time before the lightning struck.

Ben didn't come home that first night, which made me seriously consider Karen's words about how concerned I could get. After he didn't answer my first few texts or my phone call, I began to wonder if she might have picked him up without telling me. I couldn't ask her, though, as that would have given her ammunition had I been mistaken. He eventually responded, letting me know he and David had gone to the movies, which is why he didn't receive my messages until after they left the theater. They were going to grab a bite to eat, and then hang out at David's new apartment.

Karen's voice rang in my head, so I told Ben not to go out after getting to David's place unless it was to come back home. She must have really gotten to me. Anyway, he told me they were going to binge-watch some fantasy show that was the latest craze and that he probably wouldn't make it home. I imagined it felt good to have his freedom, but also, perhaps he was preparing himself for dorm life for when he would be attending college in the fall. I knew it weighed heavily on his mind. It would be his first time away from home for an extended period.

When he returned home the next day and asked why I wasn't at work, I broke the news to him about my suspension. He was very upset about it (almost as much as I was), but I quickly learned how much more upset he could get when I asked him how his night at David's went.

"So, how'd it go last night with you two?" I asked. "What show are you guys watching?"

"It was fine," he answered. "We're watching 'Kingdom's Rise: Worlds Torn Asunder.'"

"The name sounds interesting," I said.

"It is. It takes place in medieval times. There are seven territories splintered across the land, each ruled by these horrible kings. Then, a mysterious kingdom suddenly appears in this area known as the forbidden wasteland, and each of the kings from the seven territories sends their armies to lay siege to it to learn of its secrets. It's got some cool battle scenes, lots of blood."

"Well, maybe we could watch it tonight," I offered. "We can start it where you left off. You can fill me in on what I missed."

"Oh, but I already told David I'd go over again tonight to continue watching it. It's kinda our thing."

"You weren't going to check with me first?" I asked. "What if I had made plans for us to do something tonight?"

He looked at me awkwardly. "You *never* make plans for us, Dad. Besides, you're usually too busy with your work cases."

"Well, I'm not busy now. I told you I don't have work for the next two weeks."

"I didn't know that when I made plans with David."

"So tell David you'll go over to his place tomorrow night. Why don't you stay home tonight and hang out with your old man? We can order pizza, talk about your upcoming plans for college, and watch some of that kingdom show; it'll be fun. What do you say?"

"I say, 'where is this coming from?' You never wanted to do these things before. But now that you suddenly have free time on your hands, you expect me to rearrange my plans to cater to your needs?"

"That's not what I was saying, Ben."

"Then what *were* you saying?" he questioned. "Because it sure sounded like that to me. And why do you suddenly care, anyway? Oh, right, because it's convenient for you."

"Maybe it's that I think you're spending a little too much time with your friend and not enough time at home."

"What's that supposed to mean?"

"It means you're always out with David," I snapped. "It's always, 'David this' and 'David that.' If I didn't know any better, I'd think the two of you were dating."

The words slipped out before I even realized where my head was going. The angry look on Ben's face told the whole story. If he decided to take a swing at me at that moment, I wouldn't blame him and probably wouldn't try to stop him. I deserved it. I thought it best to try and calm the raging waters before they became even rougher.

"Ben, I.., I mean there's nothing wrong with being gay." I couldn't believe I was saying these things and how unprepared I was to have such a conversation. "*Are* you gay, son?"

"Dad, what the hell!" he shouted. "No, I'm not gay! And neither is David. Not that I owe you an explanation, but his girlfriend broke up with him a few weeks ago, and he's been having a rough time with it. That's why we've been hanging out; I've been trying to keep his mind occupied. God, I can't believe you'd even say that."

He stormed past me on the way to his bedroom, slamming his door so I understood how upset he was. If that didn't do it, the silent treatment for the rest of the night sure did. At least until Ben removed himself from the bedroom later that night with a backpack slung over his shoulder.

"Hey, where are you going?" I questioned, not with harshness but with curiosity.

"I told you, I'm going to David's," he replied.

"You haven't had dinner yet; let me cook you something."

"Don't worry about it; we'll get takeout."

"Well, if you're going to go, let me drive you."

"Dad, don't bother," he said, continuing his stride toward the door. "I'd rather walk."

"Now, wait a minute," I said, grabbing him by the arm, my fatherly instincts kicking in. "You can't be walking alone across town. You've seen the news; you know the case I'm working.., I *was* working. It's not safe for you out there. Not at night. Let me drive you."

"Let go of me, Dad," he yelled, yanking his arm free from my grip. "This city's always been dangerous; you never cared before. Because there's some killer out there that you haven't been able to catch, *now* you're worried about me? Don't get so overly protective just because you aren't working. I can take care of myself. I've been doing it for years."

"Ben, hold on..,"

I couldn't get the words out fast enough before he was already out the door. He was thoughtful enough not to slam that one, though I was sure he struggled with himself not to. I had this awful feeling building up inside, and I couldn't tell if it was frustration or anxiety. I knew Ben could take care of himself, but there was no telling what that maniac on the street was capable of.

I think, deep down, I knew there was nothing to worry about. If the killer's words rang true, his next target would be someone whose name began with the letter G. Ben wouldn't even be a blip on his radar. It still didn't sit well with me. How could I trust a killer? I couldn't. But I trusted Ben. I knew if I sent him a text telling him to let me know when he made it to David's apartment, he'd at least be responsible enough to do that. And he was, but the entire forty minutes spent pacing back and forth in the living room, waiting for it to come through, was more difficult than I would have imagined. I'm going to need distractions.

The week didn't get much better as it dragged on. The tension between Ben and me remained. Every day, I tried to make up for my careless choice of words, and every day, he'd ignore my apology. I didn't think I had ever been his favorite person, but I was beginning to feel like I was now his *least* favorite. He was going to have to talk to me, though. Argument or not, I wouldn't tolerate the disrespect much longer.

Ben spent most of that first week over at David's apartment, which meant I had only the news to keep me company. I should have turned it off after the reports of the Mayor's decision to enforce a city-wide curfew, but I was a glutton for punishment. And it *was* punishment, too, listening to the press conferences held by Special Agent Hayes and the State Police Captain as they promised a heightened police presence on the street in their continuing efforts to track down the killer. Watching Richie standing beside Captain Bessell, hamming it up in front of the cameras as if the situation was well under control, was burning me up. He acted as though it wasn't a big deal that a killer was out there. And *that* was the guy they would rather have in charge of the investigation? The thought of it was giving me an ulcer. I was on edge, frustrated, and disgusted about the whole thing. I had to let it go. And I tried, too, until the start of the second week.

I had made a concerted effort not to turn on the news since it only succeeded in riling me. Evidently, if it wasn't going to be the news that did it, something else had to take its place.

Just as I sat down to enjoy an episode of Law & Order (yes, I could still enjoy police dramas), the phone rang. I instinctively pressed the "answer" button before it registered in my head that it was my ex calling.

"Hello."

"That's you they're talking about on the news, isn't it?" she asked, jumping right in. "Why didn't you tell me?"

"I don't know what you're talking about, Karen."

"Turn it on, the news," she demanded. "You'll see what I'm talking about; they just read a note from the killer."

"What?" I hollered, flipping to the station. I sat at the edge of my seat, ready to spring forward at the television.

"They just read a note," she repeated.

"Sh, sh, let me listen."

"…received anonymously. The note had been found with the killer's latest victim, Francine Douglas, and was purportedly left by the Alphabet Killer himself, perhaps to taunt police investigators. One particular officer had been called out in the killer's note, referred to only as 'Detective Jim.' We reached out to the Southbridge Police Department for more information, but they refused to comment on the validity of the note or about who the specific officer was that the killer had called out.

"When we return, Meteorologist Donna Vasquez breaks down your five-day forecast…"

"That *is* you, isn't it?" Karen reiterated.

I was speechless for a moment, replaying in my head what I had just heard. I hadn't realized my silence until Karen snapped at me once again.

"Jim? Is it you in that note?" she questioned, and quite loudly at that.

"Yeah, it's me," I answered.

"Did you know about that? Did you see the note?"

"Yes, I knew," I replied, my voice elevated, but less at my wife than the situation. She wouldn't see it that way.

"So the killer is calling you out specifically," she started, "and you didn't think to tell me? You son of a bitch. If the killer knows you, he probably knows you have a son."

"I couldn't say anything," I snapped very coldly. "You know that. As for the killer knowing I have a son.., will you relax about that?"

"No, I will not relax about that. I don't want Ben staying with you anymore. Put him on the phone; I want to talk with him."

"Well, you can't," I responded, "he's not here."

"Where is he? You're supposed to be watching out for him."

"He's been staying with David for the past few days."

"What the fuck, Jim. There's a killer out there and you let him stay at a friend's house? You were supposed to be spending time with him. What happened to the whole, *'he'll be safe with me,'* bullshit?"

"He's eighteen years old, Karen," I said heatedly. "Christ, I can't keep him locked up. He can go when and where he wants. Or don't you trust our son enough to know he'll be smart about being careful?"

"I trust our son," she yelled. "It's that maniac on the street who's killing people I don't trust."

"Well, if he's going to kill again, it's not going to be Ben."

"How can you say that?" she questioned. "You don't know that fucker."

She was right, but I had to ease her mind before she had a stroke. There was already enough weighing me down; I didn't need her ending up in a hospital on my conscience as well.

"He's named the Alphabet Killer for a reason. This guy has a pattern. There's a purpose behind his choice of victims. He won't stray from that. If he kills again, I'm sure it will be someone whose name begins with a G."

"That doesn't make me feel any better," she said. "I'd still feel more comfortable if Ben were home with me."

"You'll have to take that up with him," I replied. "I'm not exactly his favorite person right now."

"Why not? What did you do this time?"

I hated that she automatically assumed it was me who did something wrong. It *was*, of course, but why did I always have to be her first choice? Although, if the roles were reversed, and Ben wasn't speaking with *her*, I'd probably have the same reaction, placing the blame on my ex before I even considered it to be Ben's fault.

"I said something I shouldn't have, and he got bent out of shape." I wasn't going to get into details.

"You? Say something you shouldn't have?" she questioned sarcastically. "Huh, I wonder how that could be?"

"Yeah, you don't need to keep pounding into me how much of an asshole I am. It wasn't *all* my fault. Ben had some stake in it too." Way to go, Jim, for shifting some blame onto your son like that. I really *was* an asshole father. "Anyway, I can't stay on the phone with you, Karen. I have to check in with Frank to see how the fuck the news got ahold of that note. You can go ahead and give Ben a call if you want. If he decides he wants to go back with you, I won't stop him."

"So kind of you to permit me to call my own son," she said as if looking for reasons to continue the argument.

"Karen, enough already. You know what I meant. Just give Ben a call and let me know what he decides. I have to go."

I hung up, not waiting for her to start anything more with me. It was like she enjoyed our spats or something. Maybe Phil wasn't spicy enough for her, and her constant fighting with me was the only thing that gave her satisfaction. I could do without it, though. I'd had enough of it during our marriage; I didn't need it now that we were divorced.

My thoughts went back to the newscast. Someone had leaked the killer's note to the press, and I wanted to know who. Not that it was the worst thing, the public knowing what he wrote. Maybe hearing the words directly from the killer himself would encourage all the Georges, Gingers, and Garys of this city to be more cautious. Even so, someone had to be held accountable for supplying that information to the news station.

I stared at the glass face of my phone, wondering why I was even considering calling Frank. He hadn't done me any favors; why should I concern myself with it? Because I was a cop, dammit. It was in my blood. They could try to force me out, but it would always be a part of me. I knew it; my family *learned* it. It was my worst enemy. There was never any question; I was going to make the call.

My thumb slid across the phone's surface to initiate the action, but a sudden incoming call beat me to it. As coincidence would have it, it was Frank.

"Yeah?" I answered as if I had no interest in what he had to say. He didn't need to know I was just about to call him. It worked out better this way. I didn't want to come across as needy.

"Jim, we got a problem," Frank stated.

"No shit," I replied. "You let somebody leak information to the news. I bet your FBI pals are having a fit."

"It's not that," he said. "But when I find out who gave that note to the press, heads are going to roll. And I swear to God, if it was someone in my unit, their ass is mine. But no, I called for another reason. There's been another homicide. The same M.O. It's our guy."

"What the fuck are you telling me for?" I questioned. "I'm still on suspension, remember? Besides, Richie's your guy. And you have the FBI calling the shots, and I know damn well they don't want me involved."

"*They* made the decision. They asked me to call you."

"Don't fuck with me, Frank."

"I'm not, Jim. They want you back on the case. Starting immediately."

"How the hell did that happen?" I asked. "And who do I have to thank for making that call?"

"You can thank the Alphabet Killer when you catch the son of a bitch," Frank said. "It was *his* doing."

"What the hell are you talking about?" I questioned.

"Just get your ass to the parking garage over on Shuster. The killer left you something."

Chapter 14

G

The crowd was a little bigger this time, like flies swarming around a fresh turd. It was understandable, given the circumstances. It was early evening, a public location, and the sound would have drawn people's curiosity. The uniforms were doing a decent job of crowd control, keeping the onlookers back behind the police tape. A channel 46 news van was parked along the curb in front of the adjacent building, its reporter and cameraman standing just beyond the crowd, recording their unapprised version of events. And in the thick of it, standing over a sprawled body on the garage's concrete floor, Special Agent Hayes and her three cronies, along with Frank and Richie from my department, two state police officers, and Lenny, who was squatting over the blood-soaked corpse. I felt like the odd man out, having arrived late to the party.

"So, what do we have here?" I questioned, walking up behind one of the suits. Frank saw me and began walking over from where he stood on the opposite side of the victim.

"Male, African-American, middle-aged," the first agent offered with no emotion. "Single gunshot wound to the back of the head," the second agent added.

"I can see that," I said. "And based on the brain matter sprayed on the floor, it was close range."

"Mort says the killer couldn't have been more than two feet behind the victim," Frank jumped in, pulling me away from the FBI and state police.

"Frank… *Lieutenant*, what's going on?" I said in a hushed voice.

Quietly, he replied, "I don't have to tell you you're not on Hayes' favorite persons' list. Do us all a favor and play nice, huh."

"I'm not here to make trouble, Lieutenant," I replied. "*You* called *me*, remember? Whatever bad blood is between Ms. FBI and me can be placed on the back burner. This is about the case, nothing else. I'm here to do my job."

"All right, Jim," he replied. "Just don't lose your head as you did at the briefing."

"Is that an appropriate choice of words, Lieutenant, given the victim's condition?" Unsurprisingly, he gave me a dirty look, so I changed the subject. "What's up with Lenny checking out the body? I thought they didn't want him doing that until it was at the morgue?"

"That was Captain Bessell's thing," Frank responded. "He had a stick up his ass. Besides, Mort just got here before you arrived. The Bureau boys, and lady, held him back for a little while to let Vera finish her part, but then they set him loose."

"Isn't Lenny's apartment right around the corner?" I asked. "He must have heard the gunshot. What took him so long to get here?"

"What can I tell you?" he shrugged his shoulders. "I'm not his fucking keeper. We called him when we got here; he didn't answer. When he arrived, he told us he was in the shower."

"Huh," I nodded. "Okay, you said Vera was here?" I questioned.

"Yeah, she's a couple of rows in," he pointed over his shoulder, "checking out the victim's car." He tapped me on the arm and motioned toward the agents, who were signaling for our return.

When we joined the others, Special Agent Hayes turned and greeted me.

"Welcome, Detective Haddick; glad you could make it."

I was unsure if it was sincere, but as Frank said, I'd better play nice.

"Special Agent Hayes," I said, nodding my head. "Have you found anything yet?"

"The murder weapon was only a few feet away from the victim; a Glock 19, 9mm rounds. It's registered to a Mr. Gaston Warber, who has since been confirmed to be the unfortunate victim you see before you."

"Wait, he was shot with his own gun?" I questioned.

"From what we've been able to piece together," Agent Hayes continued, "we believe the weapon was stolen from Mr. Warber's vehicle; his driver's side window had been smashed in. Ms. Snell and her people are currently examining the vehicle for evidence."

"If that's true," I stated, "the killer had to have known his intended victim kept a gun in his car. And he had to know which car it was. That confirms it for me; our killer knows his victims."

"Or, he watches them for a while before striking," offered Special Agent Cordell.

"That's unlikely," Lenny's voice rang out as he stood from the body. "I mean.., if you want to hear what I think. Sorry, I wasn't eavesdropping; I just overheard."

"Sure, Mr..?" she paused, unsure of his name.

"Shurek," he announced. "Leonard Shurek."

My eyes widened in shock. Lenny had always been a timid individual. Standing up as he had and injecting himself into the conversation wasn't like him. Maybe this was something new he was trying, but I had to question "*Leonard.*" Since when did he go by Leonard? He must be trying to impress.

"Ok, Mr. Shurek," Hayes said, accepting his request, "why don't you tell us your theory?"

"Well, it's been just over a month since the killer's first victim. I mean, we're talking four weeks. Gaston here is number seven. If our killer had to stake out each of his victims, to learn their habits and locations, how much time would that take? That's just over four days between each killing. Plus, I'm sure there's a lot of planning involved before taking someone's life the way this guy has been doing it. When would he find time to eat and sleep? I think Jim's.., I mean, Detective Haddick is right. This Alphabet Killer already knows them all and already has it planned out. Then it's just a matter of when."

"That's very insightful, Mr. Shurek," Hayes said. "Very interesting."

She didn't realize how interesting it was. I had known Lenny for years, but besides conveying all the gory details of how a person died, he'd never shown an interest in stepping into the spotlight and conveying his theories about criminal analysis. Dead bodies were his thing, not vocalization. It's like I'd stepped into Bizarro World.

"I believe the killer knew where and when his victim was going to be today," Lenny surprisingly continued, "because he already knew him and his routine. He smashed the guy's window, took his gun, and waited for him to return. There are plenty of cars for him to hide behind. Then, when Gaston was returning to his car, the Alphabet Killer ran up behind him and shot him. He's smart too. Smart enough to wear gloves. No fingerprints that way. You may have also noticed there are no cameras around and not a lot of foot traffic. This was an ideal place to catch Gaston alone, and The Alphabet Killer knew it. This location was planned for a reason. It was calculated."

"I find it unusual, Mr. Shurek," Hayes spoke, "that you keep referring to the killer as 'The Alphabet Killer,' while the rest of your colleagues simply say 'killer.'"

"Well, that's his name isn't it?" Lenny said. "That's what Captain Bessel came up with. What's the point of naming the guy if we're not going to use it?"

"Yes, I suppose you're right," Special Agent Hayes agreed before glancing curiously to her right at Special Agent Cordell. "Now then," she continued, turning back toward Lenny, "what can you tell us about the body?"

"The obvious shot to the head," Lenny started, squatting back down. "It was square to the back; the victim didn't react to the Alphab.., um, the *killer* sneaking up behind him. He never knew the guy was there. The killer wouldn't have had much time. The city invested in the ShotSpotter detection system last year, so the police would have been notified of this location. Not to mention the sound would have brought unwanted attention to him. With the victim lying face down as he was, the killer lifted the back of Gaston's shirt and cut a G into his lower back. He was rushed. The letter wasn't cut as clean as the ones in his previous victims."

"Is that all?" I asked.

"That's it," he replied. "This one is pretty cut and dried; excuse the pun."

I turned away from the body for a moment and glanced toward the gathered crowd at the entrance, all of them gawking and trying to catch a glimpse of the horrific sight, their phones held high as they proudly snapped pictures of the scene. What was wrong with people?

"Do we know if there were any witnesses?" I asked Special Agent Hayes, keeping my eyes peeled on the crowd.

"My agents and a couple of the other officers already questioned those that were here when we arrived. Nobody saw anything."

"Right," I said, "they never do. Nothing except Mr. Warber's body here in its unsavory condition. I bet those first few people who arrived will have nightmares for the next few days. Serves them right for running *toward* the sound of a gunshot."

I turned back to the body; Lenny was still looking over the letter carved into the victim's back as if he were inspecting a piece of art, while Richie stood over him like an understudy, watching his every move.

"Listen," I began, speaking with Special Agent Hayes, "I know we got off on the wrong foot, but I'm not even supposed to be here. You have Detective Saunders there. Why did you request my reinstatement in this case? Lieutenant Garrett said the killer left me something, and I don't think he was referring to the body. What's going on?"

Hayes turned to me and replied, "To be clear, Detective Haddick, I didn't enjoy making that decision. I've read your file. You're brash and arrogant, and you fly off the cuff. You like to do things your own way, skirting procedures and never looking back at the repercussions of your imprudent decisions. Your decision-making is irresponsible, to say the least. This is a very delicate case, and we can't afford something going wrong. If I felt I had a choice, you'd still be serving out your suspension."

I guess she laid it all out there for me. So much for playing nice. It was fine. I had thick skin. I was more interested in why she felt she had no choice, which I assumed was forthcoming when she reached into her blazer pocket and pulled out a small, plastic, ziplocked bag containing a familiar-looking piece of paper. The killer left another note.

She handed me the bag, which visibly displayed the message without having to be removed.

G-Men, G-Men, all around. I see you on the street with the other officers, canvasing for me. Now I've given you MY version of a G-Man. But where has my favorit detektive been? Where are you, James? I see the other officer on the news, but he is not you. Our game isn't over. If you refoose to play, I will take twice as many. Your choice. Shall it be one H or two? Nineteen more is a lot for sure, but thirty-eight would sure be grate. Decide quikly. I'm on the hunt. Cheers. Ω

"Looks like you've got yourself a fan, Detective," Hayes stated. "He wants you back in his twisted little game, threatening to kill even more people if you're not on the case. If I didn't pull you back in, and this letter ever leaked to the press like the last one, it would be a PR nightmare. Which reminds me, you wouldn't happen to know how the news station got ahold of the last note, would you?"

"If you're trying to accuse me of something, Agent Hayes, you don't have to be so subtle; you can just come right out and say it."

"Not accusing, Detective," she said, "just asking a question. And it's *Special* Agent Hayes."

And she said *I* was the arrogant one.

"I don't know how the note ended up in the hands of the news," I replied. "But I noticed it landed there after you folks showed up."

"Now who's making a subtle accusation?" she questioned.

"Not an accusation," I replied, "just an observation."

She smirked. And although it wasn't in a good way, it was the first sign I had seen from her that made me realize maybe she *wasn't* a robot.

"Tell me," she began, "why do you think he's singling you out?"

"How the hell should I know," I retorted. "You think maybe it could be my irresistible charm?" I couldn't be sure, but I thought I heard a soft chuckle when she exhaled. Two human moments in less than a minute? Perhaps I've judged Agent Hayes too hastily.

Just then, from across the garage, a voice boomed out. "We've got something!"

Vera's shrill yell was a godsend; the timing couldn't have been better. The conversation with Hayes wasn't to my liking.

"Although, it's not a heck of a lot," Vera added, walking past the bloody body, a black trash bag in her hand. "We found a steel pipe under the car, most likely the implement used to smash the window. No prints on it, though. Fucker!"

"Vera!" Frank quickly interjected, his way of letting her know to watch her language in front of the Feds.

"Sorry, Lieu; I say what I mean. Anyway, there are traces of blood at one end of it. I don't think it's from our guy, but I'd be willing to bet it's got Francine's DNA all over it. You saw the back of her head; I bet this is what the killer used to brain her."

"Was that necessary?" Frank questioned, giving her a stern look.

"If he wanted to knock her out, it was," she responded.

"That's not what I meant, and you know it," Frank said, his tone growing harsher.

I thought it might be a good time for me to jump in.

"Vera, perhaps you can continue explaining your findings."

"That's pretty much all I've got until I get this back to the lab to analyze the blood sample. I mean, pretty simple smash and grab. Nothing else from our guy left behind."

"Thank you, Ms. Snell," Agent Hayes said. "I'd appreciate a copy of your results."

"Of course," Vera replied, her face showing annoyance. "This isn't my first rodeo." Then she turned to one of her lab techs while holding up the plastic bag, "Yo, Zach, take this back to the lab and get started on it, would you? The FBI wants results."

Good ol' Vera, never afraid to stick it to someone. In her own way, of course.

"Lieutenant Garrett," Agent Hayes spoke up, "may I have a word with you, please?"

Frank gave a sideways glare to Vera and shook his head in frustration. He must've thought he was getting scolded. I was just thankful it wasn't me for a change.

The two of them went off to the side to have their chat. I stayed glued to Vera, staring at Richie while Lenny gave him a lesson in medical examination.

"Look at him," I said, nodding my head forward. "Can you believe that guy?"

"I know," Vera remarked. "The little twerp. He gives me the creeps. I swear he gets his jollies off of playing with dead people."

"What?" I responded. "I was talking about Richie."

"Oh, yeah, he's a creepy dude too. But you'd better get used to him; I hear you're going to be working together as partners on this thing."

"Fuck that," I said. "*Let* the killer claim twice as many victims if that's the case."

"I'm being serious," Vera affirmed. "Frank and the FBI chick were discussing it before you got here. I'm sure that's what they're talking about right now. I don't think Special Agent blondie over there trusts either one of you to work this investigation alone."

"Well, I hate to break it to you, Vera, but that's the *only* way I work."

"You'll have to take it up with Frank then," she said. "But I hope you're right; even a girl my size can't handle two dicks at once."

Vera smiled and nudged my arm, "Get it? Dicks. Because you're both detectives."

"I got it, Vera," I nodded.

"I'm just trying to lighten the mood here," she added. "Listen, I'm going to head back; there's nothing else for me to do here. I'll tell Danny to hang out in case forensics is needed." She began to walk away, talking over her shoulder, "Let Frank and your girlfriend know I'll be working really hard on that report."

I shook my head and smirked. What else could I do? Girlfriend. Yeah right.

Without Vera or Frank around me, I felt like an odd duck, swimming alone on a secluded pond. I wasn't about to chat it up with Special Agent Cordell or the other two Feds, who were engrossed in a conversation of their own. The state police officers had nothing to offer me in which I cared to listen. And Danny, the lab tech, stood by himself, farther away from everyone, waiting for Frank and Special Agent Hayes to finish their discussion so he could be released. As much as I disliked the idea, it appeared Lenny and Richie were my best option.

I strolled over beside Richie, listening to Lenny explain the difference between a penetrating and a perforating wound. It wasn't my subject of choice. I preferred something less nauseating. Even so, I waited until a break in Lenny's descriptive storytelling before I interjected. I'm a hell of a guy.

"I don't see the transport wagon, Lenny," I said, glancing to my left and right. "How are you getting the body back to the morgue?"

"I contacted Barry," Lenny replied. "He should be here any moment."

"Barry's back?" I questioned. "I haven't seen him since he went out for his surgery."

"He just came back last week. He was supposed to be out until the end of the month, but I asked him if he could come back early. With all these bodies the killer keeps sending my way, I can't keep up by myself."

"Do you even have enough room for this guy?" I asked.

"I do now," he answered, "I released Amber and Cameron's bodies a few days ago. The funeral home came and got them."

"So that's it, then?" I asked. "What we have is what we got?"

"That's it," he responded. "I'd gotten everything we're going to get from those two. The other two ladies, Denise and Eva, will be leaving in the next day or two as well."

"What about Bruce?" I asked.

Richie snickered under his breath.

"Something funny?" I questioned, staring hard at Richie.

He glanced at Lenny as if deciding whether he should answer the question. Lenny piped in.

"I can't get the guy's wife to sign the release. What's up with her?"

"She was a real treat to visit, too," I replied sarcastically.

"I can only hold onto him for another week before things start going really bad," Lenny continued. "The funeral home isn't going to like having to do all the extra paperwork to release him on her behalf."

"They're going to have to, aren't they?"

"Seems like it."

"Lenny," I inquired, "with all these bodies going away, why did you need Barry to come back early?"

"You think this is all I've got going on, Jim?" he snorted. "There are other crimes in this city that result in deaths. Dirtbags don't take timeouts to give us a break. Plus, my sister's having all kinds of problems right now. My mother keeps pulling me away from my work at the worst times. What can I do; she's my mother. I needed Barry back right now."

As if on cue, the crowd parted, letting us know Barry had arrived with the morgue's van.

"Hey, Lenny," Richie spoke, staring at Barry through the windshield, "I always wanted to ask you this - is Barry the Assistant Medical Examiner or Assistant *to* the Medical Examiner?"

"He's my assistant," Lenny answered. "Why?"

Richie looked at him with a furrowed brow, "Nevermind, it was a joke."

"Oh. Well, it was terrible."

I just shook my head and turned in time to see Frank and Hayes returning from their pow-wow.

"What's the word, Special Agent Hayes?" I inquired, trying to keep things light and copacetic between us.

"I think it's time to clean up here. I need everyone gathered at the station tomorrow morning for another briefing. Mr. Shurek, you'll see that things are taken care of with the body?"

"Yes, ma'am. I mean, Ms. I mean Special Agent Hayes."

There's the Lenny I knew, nervous and tongue-tied around authority, especially when it was a woman.

"Lieutenant Garrett," Hayes continued, "I assume you'll have your men stationed here a while longer to keep the crowd at bay."

"They'll remain here until everyone has cleared out," Frank answered. "How do you want to handle the press?"

"Special Agent Cordell and I will take care of that," she replied. "Detective Haddick," she held out her hand, "I'm sorry it had to be under such circumstances, but welcome back to the fold. I look forward to working with you."

It was completely unintentional on my part, but I reached forward cautiously to shake her hand as if I was about to be bitten by a snake. I think she noticed my hesitation and smiled.

"Thank you," I replied, knowing her actions were all about politics.

Then, she nodded to her agent buddies and proceeded to head toward the garage entrance. I waited a minute for them to get out of earshot before I confronted Frank.

"Lieutenant, I didn't like the sound of that. What are we in for tomorrow?"

"Probably that shit show you've been expecting from the start. You'll hear it tomorrow. In the meantime, get some rest. It's going to be a bumpy ride, and I'm going to need you guys firing on all cylinders."

He turned his head and saw the lab tech, Danny, standing alone and stiff, waiting for direction. "What the hell are you looking at? You're dismissed."

Danny nodded nervously and slithered his way out of sight.

"So now what?" I asked.

"Now go the fuck home. You too, Richie. Tomorrow's going to be a busy day." Then he walked away toward his car.

I wanted to think things were going to get better, but the only thought that ran through my mind at that moment was: welcome back to Hell.

Chapter 15

MOTIVATIONS

Why is it that whenever you need to get some good sleep, you toss and turn all night, thinking about how you need to get some good sleep? By four in the morning, I'd had enough pretending that I was going to drift off. It wasn't happening. My brain wouldn't allow relaxation. I felt like this investigation was going nowhere, and we were all puppets, dangling from an invisible hand. The problem was, it wasn't the FBI manipulating the strings; it was the sadistic maniac who had this city gripped in fear. Parents would no longer let their kids walk the streets, women were afraid to go out alone, and the Mayor imposed a 10:00 curfew. Then, the Feds were called in to help solve the case. So far, they were no real help.

Sure, the FBI could provide resources and databases to which we wouldn't generally have access, but that was only helpful if we could find some trace of the killer's DNA. So far, we had squat. If we had a fingerprint, a name, a description, or even just a stray pubic hair that had fallen from his pant leg, maybe we'd be onto something. Instead, except for Vera and Agent Hayes, we'd all been left standing with our dicks in our hands. Well, maybe Vera too. It wouldn't surprise me if she were hiding something in her pants. That's still undetermined.

I still didn't know why this guy had taken such a personal interest in me. Was this some personal vendetta? Was he trying to fuck with me until I went batshit crazy? Because right now, the way I was feeling, he was succeeding in his efforts.

On top of *that* growing mound of horse dung, the FBI was crawling up our asses like this was *their* investigation, and neither the Chief nor Captain Redfern had the balls to step in and shut it down. Seeing Frank's face last night after his brief discussion with the female version of Jack Bauer, it was clear to me that Special Agent Hayes was calling the shots. And although Kiefer Sutherland did a bang-up job portraying the tough-as-nails agent in the series "24," I think even he would have had a hard time with Hayes. Her good looks aside, she rubbed me the wrong way. I'm sure Frank knew that and was tickled pink about the entire situation. The bastard. Still, there was something about Hayes that I couldn't get off my mind. Her tough exterior commanded respect, and she wasn't afraid to give shit back to anyone who gave her shit. I suppose that was something.

There was no sense dwelling on the subject. Better to focus on catching the murderous son of a bitch who was toying with me. He'd obviously been keeping tabs on me; he knew I wasn't out there looking for him. Was the note he'd left his attempt at drawing me back? Should I be thankful? Not when he'd threatened to kill twice as many people had my superiors decided not to call me. It was funny how one could love a job when *wanting* to do it but hate it when obligated. And the Feds seemed more concerned with the public's reaction should the note get out than they were with saving people and stopping the asshole responsible. That's the only reason Hayes and her band of uptight misfits requested my return. If the horror continued, they couldn't be looked harshly upon, even though they'd done nothing to prevent the killer's blatant disregard for human life. Okay, maybe I was being too critical. They *are* here to help, and they want to catch this guy as much as we do, but Fuck; enough with the meetings and ass-chewings, and let's get down to some actual police work. The whole thing just bothered me.

Seven people dead, and we were no closer to finding this guy than when we first learned of his existence. I felt much more confident when I thought Denise's homicide was an isolated incident. Now, I began to wonder if we would ever catch the freak.

At least one thing I could feel relieved about was that Ben was no longer staying with me. At first, I thought it would be better if he were at my place where I could watch him and protect him, but with the killer stalking me, possibly even knowing where I lived, it was best if Ben kept his distance for a little while. I knew his mother had reservations about that. I'm sure she'd rather him back with her, but apparently, she's upset him as much as I did, and he had no intention of going back any time soon. As long as David was willing to put up with him being a temporary roommate, I was okay with it.

I was thankful the morning was passing quickly; I felt anxious about getting to the station. There was only so much time I could spend with my own thoughts before I became restless and impatient. Special Agent Hayes called an early morning briefing, requesting all available officers to attend. And although we didn't report to her or the FBI, Frank made it abundantly clear in his late-night text that the Chief expected full cooperation from his officers, or there would be severe consequences. I could probably skip out on it without facing another suspension since it was my necessary involvement in the case that forced my reinstatement. After all, the killer made it quite clear what he would do should I be stripped of my duties. But I wouldn't play that card. Because although some people in this city probably didn't deserve saving, they also didn't need me risking their lives by disobeying a direct order. Or an indirect one, as it were.

When I arrived at the station, I was on edge and raring to go. A group of younger officers had huddled around Richie's desk like he was a celebrity, questioning him about what he thought the morning's meeting was. He had no answer, of course, but he had no qualms pretending he did, telling them he wasn't allowed to divulge information. I chuckled, but maybe a little too loudly.

"Don't worry, Jimmy," a voice erupted from behind me, "I know he's full of it."

Mick always favored me over Richie. And why wouldn't he? I was his older brother's best friend growing up. When we were kids, Mick was a needy pipsqueak who always wanted our attention, which we never gave. Being nine years younger than us, he never understood why we didn't want him hanging around when we were with our friends. It was only after his brother Henry killed himself that I felt a responsibility to Mick. I took him under my wing as a surrogate big brother. I think he'd always looked up to me since then.

"He plays it off like he knows his shit," I responded. "Those rooks just eat it up, don't they?"

"Only because they don't know whose case this really is," Mick answered, lightly poking my chest with his index finger.

"You talk as if you think it's still mine," I said. "Well, kid, let me tell you; it ain't. Not sure it ever was."

"What are you talking about, Jimmy? Of course, it is. You're the smartest guy in here. If there's anyone who can figure out who the killer is, it's you. I have faith in you."

"That makes one of us," I replied.

Then, Frank's booming voice interrupted our conversation.

"Haddick! In my office," he demanded.

"That was quick," I said quietly to Mick. "It hasn't been five minutes, and I'm already on Frank's shit list." I tapped him on the shoulder, "I'll see you in the briefing, Mick."

Mick nodded as I shuffled by him en route to having my fate delivered upon me. Who knew being sent to the Principal's office week after week in high school would prepare me for what was to come in my adult life daily? Oh, how I'd come full circle.

I entered Frank's office prepared for the worst, expecting they'd changed their minds about my suspension. He was propped up against the front of his desk, partially sitting on the edge with his legs extended forward, one crossed over the other in a somewhat relaxed posture. His arms were at his sides, his palms pressed firmly against the top surface, supporting more of his weight than the desk was.

"Lieutenant, I..."

"Shut up, Jim," he interrupted. "There's been a lot of tension between us lately; I've noticed it. With all the shit that's been going on, the Feds being here, we can't afford to let others see us like this. So, I'm stepping up. We need all our resources on this, and I'm not too big to admit that I'm glad you're back on the investigation. Nobody works a case like you, even if those assholes in their fancy suits don't see it. So, before you go in there today, I need you fully dressed."

He reached behind his back with both hands, then swung them forward to present me with my badge and gun.

"You'll be needing these," he said, smiling. "Welcome back."

I was stunned. Was this a moment we were having? I suddenly felt like an ass for harboring the negative feelings I still couldn't suppress. I didn't know what to say or how to react. It was like I was supposed to be nice but couldn't quite bring myself to get there. Still, I nodded and smiled as if everything was forgiven, even replying "thank you" before grabbing both of my previously confiscated items from his hands.

"Now get the fuck out of my office, would ya," Frank added. "We've got a briefing to attend. And try not to piss anyone off this time."

"Right," I replied, exiting his office with him following behind.

In the Briefing Room, everyone was already seated, waiting quietly for whatever announcement was to come. All the top brass were present again, including both Captain Redfern and Captain Bessell, Chief Copelli, and the four FBI Agents assigned to the case. I took my seat beside Mick, who was playing a word game on his phone, while Frank strolled over to stand beside Special Agent Cordell. Captain Bessell was having a whispered conversation with Special Agent Hayes until Chief Copelli placed his hand on Bessell's shoulder and nodded to Hayes. Hayes nodded her reply and took to the podium.

"Thank you all for coming," she started, straight-faced while scanning her audience. "Thank you, Chief Copelli, for organizing this on such short notice." She nodded in his direction once again. "Captain Redfern, Captain Bessell, for your continued support," she acknowledged. "As you are all well aware," she turned, looking back at the rest of us, "there is a killer at large in this city who has thus far eluded all three of our agencies' efforts to locate and capture him. He has so far killed seven people that we are aware of and has threatened to kill more, taunting us with cryptic notes, challenging us to catch him while he hints at his next victim. We have had no witnesses to any of the crimes step forward, we've been unable to obtain any trace of the killer's DNA from any of the crime scenes, and we currently have no..," she paused, glancing at Captain Redfern, "...*firm* suspects. We're dealing with a ghost, people.

"We believe the killer to be male, most likely Caucasian, age undetermined at this time. We don't have a lot to go on. What we *do* know, is that he is organized, calculated, and very patient. Because of that, and because of yesterday's most recent homicide, the Mayor contacted our three agencies to discuss our ongoing efforts. With that, in conjunction with the already-established curfew, the Mayor has decided to approve the Bureau's recommendation for a city-wide sweep.

"What does this mean for most of you?" she continued. "Starting tomorrow, the Southbridge Police Department, partnering with the state police and the FBI, will be going door to door, conducting interviews of its citizens. Your objective is to look for suspicious activity: strange behavior, unusual body language, or anything else that seems a little out of the ordinary. If there is anyone you find to be acting dubious or apprehensive, we ask that you encourage them to come in for questioning. We need people talking.

"Not all of you will be taking to the streets. Some of you will continue your normal police duties, which will also consist of sharing responsibility for monitoring a tip hotline that we will be setting up. Now, we've worked closely with your Lieutenant and Captain to partner each of you with someone. You will all be handed assignments after this meeting, along with instructions on how to carry out your interviews. I suggest you take this seriously and read through the packet before tomorrow. For those of you who will be involved in the sweep, we will convene here in the morning before heading out to our locations. We need everyone on board with this. Is that clear?"

A low rumble emanated from the attendees. It was easy to tell many of us weren't pleased with taking direction from someone outside the department.

"Special Agent Hayes asked if it was clear," Chief Copelli shouted, causing those slumped in their chairs to sit upright at attention and respond affirmatively.

"Yes, sir."

"Yes, Chief."

"Yes, it's clear, Chief."

"That's better," he responded. "Remember, this is a directive coming from the Mayor's office. Whatever your feelings are about this, you can dismiss them here and now. We all have a job to do, and we all want the same thing. Lieutenant Garrett will hand you your packet on the way out."

With that comment, Frank grabbed the stack of binders on the table beside him and walked to the door.

"As Special Agent Hayes mentioned," the Chief continued, "you'd better study them well. We need you all ready for this by tomorrow." Then, after a long pause as he scanned the room, "Dismissed!"

It amazed me how even the disinterested officers rushed to grab their packets. Were they in that much of a hurry to be disappointed? Was I?

I snatched the binder from Frank's hand as I exited, making a beeline to my desk. I ruffled through the first few pages of objectives to get to the pairings, which I was sure most of the others were doing, as well. Out of curiosity, I slid my finger down the column, reading each line to learn who everyone's partner was. I wondered who the lucky bastards were that got stuck catering to the whims of the FBI brats. Newsome got Agent Brynn. Iverson was paired with Agent Pease. Poor Mick ended up with Special Agent Cordell. That wouldn't be easy; I felt for the kid. But not as much as I did for Peretti; he got stuck with Special Agent Hayes. I'm sure he was going to have a great time with her all day. Though admittedly, being paired with an attractive woman wasn't the worst thing. I imagined watching her hips swing as she walked would be too much of a distraction for me to concentrate. I guess it was a good thing I wasn't partnering with her. Why did that thought almost feel like a disappointment? Whatever; back to the list. Only a few names further down, I saw who my partner was.

"What the fuck," I mumbled to myself, seeing red. I glanced up from the page and saw Frank sitting at his desk. He was too busy writing to look out and notice how livid I was, but I imagined he was laughing on the inside about the whole thing. I slammed the book down on my desk and stormed into Frank's office, closing the door behind me and ready to trade blows.

"What the hell is that all about," I exploded, "partnering me with Richie?"

"Calm down, Jim," Frank said. "Everyone had to get assigned to someone."

"Why him?" I raged. "You know I can't work with him. I *won't* work with him. Give me Mick, or Newsome, or even StMartin, for Christ's sake."

"Goddammit, Jim," Frank shouted, standing from his desk and pointing his finger at me. "You heard the Chief; we've got a job to do. The situation we're dealing with is bigger than your bruised ego. Deal with it."

"This is bullshit!" I replied. "You need me on this case; why am I being punished? It was your idea to stick Richie with me, wasn't it? Just another way to stick it to me."

"What the fuck are you talking about?"

"You know goddamn well what I'm talking about, Frank," I shouted, looking straight into his eyes.

"If you've got something to say to me, Jim, just say it."

I stared heatedly at the man, my hands clenched, ready to jump over the desk at him for what he had done to me. He stood just as firm, his face red with anger, ready to face whatever I could dish out.

"Why'd you do it, Frank?" I questioned. "We were friends. Why Karen?"

"Jesus Christ, Jim; is that what this is all about?"

"You're damn right it is," I replied.

Frank shook his head, dropping his chin to his chest in a moment of guilt. I knew he felt it, but I'd never once seen it.

"It just happened, Jim," Frank began. "It was a one-time thing. And it was over before it even began."

"Over for *you*, maybe," I responded. "You could walk away; you *had* your fun. But I had to live with the knowledge of what you two did behind my back. Our marriage was never the same after that. You drove a wedge between us."

"That's bullshit, and you know it, Jim," Frank responded. "Your marriage was shaky long before the Christmas party, and you were the one holding the wedge. You were so drunk that night you probably don't remember how it all went down. Karen was fully prepared to go home with you once you complained about not feeling well. *You* were the one that pushed her to stay, asking if I could take her home."

"I meant *our* home, Frank," I jumped in. "Not yours."

"It wasn't like that, asshole," he countered. "You were never around. And even when you were, you weren't. You were, and still are, a mess. Look at you; you're your own worst enemy. Well, let me tell you, Karen needed something more, and you weren't there to give it to her."

"So you decided you'd give it to her instead, huh?" I said through clenched teeth.

"Is that what you think, you son of a bitch?" Frank replied. "Let me tell you the unedited details. While we were still at the party, I held that woman in my arms for forty minutes while she sobbed uncontrollably, telling me how much she loved you and how you never returned that love. She needed someone to console her that night. It should have been you, not me. But I can't change that. Neither of us planned for what happened, and if I could take it back, I would. Believe me. And I'm sure she feels the same."

"None of that matters now," I answered as I felt my fists unclench.

"I'm sorry, Jim," Frank said. "It happened, it was an accident, and it's in the past. But I'm not the one to blame here."

I knew he was right. Deep down, I had always known. The job always came first. My family was something I took for granted. I always thought they would be there, no matter what. First, I pushed Karen away. More recently, I pushed Ben away. Though, with the Alphabet Killer on the loose, that may have been a good thing for now. When this was over, I would make sure not to take Ben for granted any longer. He needed me to be present in his life. He needed a decent father, and I wanted to be that for him. I *would* be that for him. I just hoped he would let me.

"Listen," Frank added, interrupting my thoughts. "This whole mess we're in, we need to figure this out. We still have to work together. There's a sadistic killer out there, and you seem to be the guy's focus. I need you clearheaded. If you need to go a few more rounds, I'm right here, let's have it. Otherwise.., are you good?"

I stared in silence for a moment, letting his words sink in. I had already admitted to myself my blame was misplaced. I had no more reasons to be angry.

"I'm good," I nodded.

"Yeah? You're good?" he questioned a second time.

"Yeah," I replied. "I'm good."

Then he did this funny thing where he swung his finger back and forth between us.

"How about us? Are *we* good?"

I stood silent, wondering how anything could ever be good between us again, but then realized, perhaps, there was never anything *wrong* between us; only a fool who couldn't accept his own mistakes.

"Yeah, Frank," I replied. "We're good."

"Good," he stated. "And just so you know, it wasn't my decision to put you and Richie together. That was Hayes' call. Captain Redfern approved it."

"Hayes," I said, shaking my head. "I should have known. Sorry, Lieutenant."

I turned to leave, but Frank called me back.

"Hey," he expressed, his hand extended as a gesture of good faith. I reached forward to reciprocate, but when I grasped his hand, he gave it a slight yank and looked me in the eye, "I told you before, call me Frank." Then he smirked and released my hand.

I smiled and nodded before turning for the final time and walking out of his office. I didn't know if the broken fence between us could ever be fully mended, but I thought we had both taken strides in the right direction. Now I needed to learn how to take those same strides with others.

Chapter 16

WHILE WE SLEEP

I'd like to say it's been a while since I had a frozen dinner, but as a divorced cop living alone, my lifestyle wasn't always the most glamorous. At least when Ben was staying here, I put in a little effort when it came time for dinner. I didn't enjoy cooking for only one person. Without the added parental responsibility, my efforts were best focused on other things, such as reviewing the next day's plans for sweeping the city.

I wasn't the biggest fan of the Mayor's decision, but I understood his reasoning. If we could catch the killer off guard and instill a little fear in him, perhaps he'd act suspiciously and give himself away. Had that been the Mayor's sole motivation, I might have respected the decision more, but it was an election year, and he needed all the votes he could get after last year's municipal budget debacle. This stunt was nothing more than a campaign to grab voters' attention, to let them know he was serious about catching the killer and ridding the streets of crime. If it worked, though, I wouldn't complain; but I still wasn't going to vote for him.

As I sat eating my freezer-burned, imitation steak patty and rehydrated mashed potatoes at the living room coffee table, I perused through a few pages of the detailed packet. Richie and I had been assigned about six blocks, Franklin Street down to Seventeenth in the lower west district, right in the heart of Papa Rio's territory. That was a good draw; it would give us an excuse to drop in on my little friend Alvin once again. He put me onto Carmine Lemon; maybe he'd have something else for me.

I didn't get many pages into the binder when the knock on my door grabbed my attention. My first thought was that Ben had decided to come back but had forgotten or misplaced his key. It wouldn't have been the first time the boy had shown such irresponsibility. Just the same, as I opened the door, thinking how good it would be to have him back, even if for only one night, my joy immediately departed when I saw it was Special Agent Hayes standing outside my door instead.

"Agent Hayes.., sorry, *Special* Agent Hayes, what are you doing here?" I realized, just after the words left my mouth, it wasn't the nicest of greetings.

"Detective Haddick," she began, "I apologize for dropping by unexpectedly like this. May I come in?"

Why did I suddenly feel nervous? I *didn't* want her to come in, but I kinda did, which is why my involuntary reaction of swinging the door open and stepping to the side to allow her entry overrode my better judgment. A visit from someone of the opposite sex wasn't a frequent occurrence. I'd decided it was a momentary lapse.

As she brushed by me, a subtle hint of her perfume invaded my senses, sending my thoughts swirling to an earlier time when Karen would douse herself in the liquid. It was the same scent, her favorite, Light Blue by Dolce&Gabbana; I'd recognized it immediately. Oddly, I'd just now realized how much I missed it. I felt a slight smirk tear at my lips, and I shook my head in response as I closed the door.

"So, Special Agent Hayes, what brings you out this way?" I questioned, walking swiftly past her purposely on the way to the living room so I could catch another whiff of the floral-scented fragrance. "I was just reviewing the details of our assignment for tomorrow."

"I'm glad you're taking it seriously, Detective," she said, following me into the next room.

Hayes' unexpected arrival caused me to forget I had also been eating dinner when her knock interrupted me. Upon entering the room, a feeling of embarrassment grabbed me when I noticed the microwaved dish was still sitting on the table, the flavorless gravy within already forming a congealed layer of film over the half-eaten cardboard meat. I quickly dashed to the table, scooped up the dish, and fled to the kitchen, leaving her alone in the living room for a moment. I quickly returned after feeding my dinner to the trash, hoping my mug wasn't as red as it felt, and noticed that Hayes had an amused look on her face.

"Yeah," I said, scratching the back of my neck. "I was just grabbing a quick bite of something before bed."

"It's quite all right, Detective," she answered, smiling. "I've had my share of similar nights. But I'm somewhat partial to the turkey dinner."

"Right," I nodded uncomfortably. "Well, Special Agent Hayes, I'm afraid you have me at a loss. What's this about; was there a break in the case?"

"Oh, no, nothing like that," she responded. "And please, can we dispense with the formalities? We're not at work right now. Call me Marion."

"Okay," I replied awkwardly. The way she said it caught me by surprise. I swear I felt my heart rate increase. "I suppose this is where I tell you to call me Jim."

She smiled and looked down, looking unnerved herself, before speaking.

"I think we got off on the wrong foot. I wanted to apologize for any misunderstanding there might have been between us. I realize this had been your case before my men and I were assigned. I wanted to speak with you before the initial briefing, but there wasn't time. I intended to speak with you afterward, but when you stormed out, I figured it wouldn't have been a good idea at that moment. I realize I could have handled things better. But once I regained my senses, I remembered why I was excited to have the opportunity to work with this department. So, I wanted you to know the Bureau is not taking anything away from you. If you believed my behavior was unprofessional in any way, I assure you, it's because the boys in Washington are bringing a lot of heat down on us. And I think we're all a little distraught over the lack of evidence in this case. That's not a reflection of your investigation. On the contrary, you have an impeccable record. It does help establish, however, the kind of able mind with which we're dealing. As you know, our perp isn't just randomly picking targets. He's very methodical in his approach, and he knows how to clean up after himself. That's not something your run-of-the-mill criminal is adept at doing."

"Tell me about it," I said. "Pardon my French, but it's like the demented fuck knows what we look for in a crime scene. That makes him even more dangerous."

"I agree," she responded. "I'm glad we can see eye to eye on some things."

"Some things, sure," I replied. "But one thing we don't see eye to eye on, however, is why you partnered me with that kiss-ass, son of a bitch, Richie."

"Yes, I spoke with Lieutenant Garrett about that. He informed me you weren't pleased with my decision. I'm sorry, Jim. That wasn't my original intention. But I also don't have time to pay attention to schoolyard riffs."

"Well then, what *was* your intention?" I asked. "To see how good my babysitting skills were?"

"Actually," she replied, "if you *must* know, I was planning to have the two of *us* work together. The problem was, I needed everyone on their game, and I realized our working together would have been too much of a distraction."

She was right about that. Even now, I had a hard time focusing. But I wasn't about to let her know.

"What are you talking about?" I questioned. "I might not agree with some of the decision-making on this case, but I've never let that get in the way of good detective work. I wouldn't let whatever tension there was between us distract me from doing my job."

"I appreciate that, Jim," she stated, dropping her gaze to the floor again. "I, um..," she hesitated, nervously picking at her fingernail, "I wasn't worried about *you* getting distracted."

She tilted her head up slightly, lifting her eyes to mine, an embarrassed smile on her face.

"Oh," I muttered, feeling a nervous tingle run down my spine. "But I.., I mean, we're..,"

"I completely understand, Jim.., Detective Haddick. I probably shouldn't have come, but I wanted you to at least be aware of why I made the decision. I guess I was hoping to dispel some of the negativity you've felt toward me so you could better focus on your duties tomorrow."

Focus on my duties? I thought. How the hell would I be able to do that now? An attractive woman who I thought was out to get me had just admitted to having feelings for me. At least, I think that's what just happened here. Did that happen? Or am I making it up?

"Well, Detective," she continued, "we have ourselves a busy day tomorrow. I'll let you get back to your review of the assignment. Again, I apologize for stopping in unexpectedly, and I'll see you bright and early tomorrow morning."

She nodded and turned to make her way for the door as the lingering smell of her perfume wafted across my nose. The smell got me every time. It was like I couldn't control the thoughts running through my mind. Damn it!

"Agent Hayes," I called to her before correcting myself. "Marion."

She paused at the door and turned, "Yes, Detective?"

"It's just that I haven't, you know..," I froze for a moment, staring at her tender features, wondering what sort of nonsense had spewed from my lips. I was sure it wasn't supposed to happen like that. I was supposed to have control of my emotions. I was.., "Fuck it!" I announced, as I quickly marched over to her, forcing her back against the door as I pressed my hungry lips to hers. She had every opportunity to push me away, but I tasted the want in her returned kiss. I wasn't about to let her walk out the door, and she no longer had the desire to leave. We both had needs we wanted to fill. She was going to stay a while longer.

Damn it; she should have pushed me away.

* * *

The sound of her pant fabric sliding against her smooth skin awakened me. The hint of her shadowed silhouette as the blooming rays of the sun crept in through the slight gaps in the window shade, showering her with their light as she dressed, was an indication that night had faded into morning. I lay silent for a moment, not wishing to disturb her while I admired every curve of her body. She fidgeted with the last few buttons on her blouse, turning her eyes to me and noticing I was staring back.

"Sorry, I didn't mean to wake you," she said in a hushed tone.

"You didn't," I replied. "I'm a light sleeper. What time is it?"

"It's just after five o'clock," she replied. "Don't get up; you've still got a couple of hours before you have to be at the station."

"It doesn't seem right that *you* have to be up this early," I responded sympathetically while selfishly wanting her to come back to bed.

She smiled, "Yeah well, had we been at *my* place, I'd be the one creepily watching you get dressed right now, and I'd practically be kicking you out so I could get another hour of sleep."

"Is that so?" I questioned playfully.

She looked at me tenderly, the early light reflecting off her cheek, "No," she said softly. "I'd probably trick you into coming back to bed."

"It wouldn't be much of a trick," I said. "But what's this about 'creepily'?"

"What would *you* call it," she asked. "staring at me in the dark while pretending to be asleep?"

"When you put it like that..," I answered, rolling my eyes. "At least let me make you a coffee before you leave." I pulled the covers aside and sat up, swinging my legs to the side of the bed.

"No, please," she stated. "I've never enjoyed the taste of coffee."

I should have guessed that; I'd never once seen her with a cup of Joe in her hand. It was just as well; I didn't make the best coffee. And I didn't have anything else to offer her unless she wanted a freezer-burned toaster strudel.

"That's fortunate," I replied. "You've just saved yourself from the worst coffee you've ever had." She smiled, which was the reaction I'd hoped to elicit. "Hey, listen," I continued, "can I ask you something?"

"You can ask."

"At the briefing yesterday, what did you mean when you said you didn't have any firm suspects? That would imply you had at least *a* suspect. Care to share?"

She squinted and gave me an awkward smirk. I wasn't sure how to take that, but the words that followed made it clear.

"Sorry, Jim," she began. "I know we're all working together on this, but that's information I can't divulge at this time. It may be nothing. If anything comes of it, I'll let you know."

"It sounds like you don't trust me," I said.

She stepped between my bent legs, leaned in, and kissed me. "I trusted you last night," she said softly after peeling her lips from mine, our foreheads resting against each other. She flashed her beautiful smile again, making my tense shoulders drop. Then, without warning, she shoved me back. "But that was when I was Marion," she said as she reached for her shoes on the ground, a devilish twinkle in her eye. "This morning, I need to be Special Agent Hayes. And that woman doesn't trust anyone, not even the man she slept with."

"Yet," she added.

All I could do was smile.

"But I've got to run," she continued, slipping on her second shoe. "Really, don't get up. Thanks for last night, Jim. I'll see you in a little bit."

I sat up from her abrupt shove, my head shaking in disbelief while listening for the sound of the front door as it closed behind her. I couldn't keep from smiling like I was that acne-covered teenage kid with a crush all over again. What the hell was wrong with me? I just slept with the lead FBI agent on this case. And although it was fun, I should learn to keep my penis in my pants. I'd be in a world of shit if this ever got out. But wait, what was I worried about; I didn't initiate anything. She came over to my house unannounced. And I'm certain she came on to me first. Right, like any of that mattered. IA would have my balls in a sling if they learned of this. It would make even Vera's issues seem tame in comparison. Oh, for fuck's sake, what have I gotten myself into?

Chapter 17

CLEAN SWEEP

I felt their eyes upon me the moment I walked through the door, their suspicious gazes reading my every move as if they knew what I'd been up to the night before. They didn't, of course, and I realized it was all in my head. But it felt real enough to keep me on edge.

"Look who decided to grace us with his presence," Frank announced, throwing his arms into the air, a shit-eating grin on his face.

I glanced up at the clock while people snickered, then responded in kind by throwing two fingers, one on each hand, into the air to match Frank's overreaction.

"Don't you think that's a little harsh, Frank?" I questioned jokingly. "I'm only two minutes late."

"Hey, two minutes later than the rest of us is still late. Now, take a seat like everyone else. Captain Redfern and Captain Bessell will be joining us shortly."

I surveyed the room, noticing everyone had already paired up with their partners for the day. Richie had an empty seat next to his, which he tapped on to get my attention. Suddenly, I was the cool kid in class, and he wanted to sit next to me as if he thought he could somehow absorb my coolness through fucking osmosis. I'd sit next to him out of professional courtesy, but we weren't suddenly going to become friends. And he was going to be sorely disappointed; no amount of cool could rub off on that guy.

I took my seat, and Richie immediately leaned in to grab my ear.

"Glad you could join us, buddy," he whispered. "Not that it matters; our friends from the Bureau haven't arrived yet."

"And why is that?" I asked.

"Something about Special Agent Hayes running late or some shit," he replied. "I wouldn't be surprised if she was up all night banging her partner, Cordell."

I faked a smile at his comment, but only because he'd never know how close he was to the truth. He said he wouldn't be surprised about Cordell. I wonder how surprised he would be to learn who she *did* bang last night. I let it slide and told him the Feds were always late; it was like a power trip.

Just then, the doors to the briefing room burst open, and the two Captains walked in, followed by the four agents. Hayes purposely tried to avoid looking in my direction, but I caught her sneaking a glance as she scanned the audience, pausing for a second to make eye contact. Her face showed no emotion that would give away her secret. She was good, whereas I was struggling to tame the butterflies in my stomach. As she said, Marion was gone; this was Special Agent Hayes standing before us. I could only hope she wouldn't get too carried away with her change in character and try to reenact how our last briefing went.

"Thank you all for coming," Hayes began after taking the podium. "I trust you've all read the packets you were handed yesterday. You should all know your assignments. I don't think I have to tell anyone here how important it is this mission goes off without a hitch. Stick to your schedules, people. We're all out there working this together, and we're pouring a lot of resources into this city-wide sweep. We're expecting results, so keep your questioning thorough and on point. We obviously want to keep the element of surprise; there will be absolutely no talking to any reporters.

"I will tell you this; it's not unusual for an endeavor of this magnitude to take up to two weeks or more, but your superiors, as well as those of us from the Bureau, are fully confident that with your efforts, we'll have our man in custody sooner than that. Even so, you all know this is a dangerous individual we are after. Keep your wits about you and stay safe out there."

She subtly shifted her eyes to me as she spoke those last words. I caught the hint.

"That is all I have," she concluded.

She stepped away from the microphone, making way for Captain Redfern to step up and say a few words.

"You've all got your orders," he began. "Now, let's get out there and catch this son of a bitch." He ended it with a head nod toward the door, short and sweet, signaling for us to exit.

Like a mass exodus, and with much enthusiasm, everyone rose and piled for the door, looking to be the one to catch themselves a bad guy. I wasn't as enthusiastic as the rest of the group. Maybe it was my experience. The killer had been a few steps ahead of us from the start. He'd shown that he was capable of avoiding detection. He was smart and focused. So if

I didn't seem as eager to go hunting for this maniac, it wasn't because I didn't want to catch him; it was because I wasn't sure how ready I was to learn who the deranged individual we were dealing with was. Someone like that could mess with your head. He'd already been fucking with mine, and look what it'd done for my cheerful disposition.

Walking out of the briefing room door, Richie grabbed my arm. "Jim, hold up," he requested. "I've got to make a quick phone call. Let me stop at my desk for a minute."

That was fine with me; the longer Richie stayed away, the better. I could find something at my desk to keep my attention until he was through.

While I ruffled through some paperwork, my pocket began to buzz. I pulled out my phone to see a welcoming surprise; Ben was calling. I tried to talk with him every day, even if only for a few minutes, but the previous day slipped away from me, especially with the unexpected late-night distraction. He must have noticed and was checking in on me, something I, as the responsible parent, should have done.

"Ben, what's up, bud? No, I'm fine. Yeah, sorry about that; I didn't get the chance to call yesterday."

As I suspected, he was worried about his old man.

"No excuses; it was my fault. It was a busy day, and we were all gearing up for today's big event. No, nothing like that. I wish it *were* a party. Wait, I take that back. No, I don't. Not with these clowns, anyway. No, we've got a major thing starting today. We're going door to door on a sweep of the city, questioning residents and hoping to get lucky with this investigation. So, if a police officer comes knocking on David's apartment door, don't panic; nothing's happened to me. He's just going to ask you a few questions."

Just then, I noticed Marion making her way toward my desk. Peretti had split off from her to use the restroom. Was it too much to assume she was going to tell me how much of a great time she had last night and that she couldn't wait to do it again? Probably, but I could hope. I did feel jittery, though.

She stood in front of me as I raised my index finger to let her know I would only be a moment.

"Hey, Ben. It was good to hear from you, but I'm going to have to cut this short. The FBI needs to speak with me." I smiled and gave Marion a wink. "No, I'm not in any trouble. Thanks for caring, though. Talk to you later, son. Bye."

"That was your son.., Benjamin, is it?" Hayes inquired.

"Yeah. Yeah, it was," I answered. "He was checking in on me since he didn't hear from me yesterday."

"Ah, very thoughtful of him," she responded.

"He's a good kid," I said. "Listen, Marion, about last night; I wanted to tell you..,"

"That's why I've come over here, Detective Haddick," she interjected. "It was a mistake that I went to your house last night. We're both professionals, and we're working together. Getting involved now could seriously jeopardize this case. The timing is wrong, and we both need to stay focused."

"Are you saying you didn't have a good time?" I asked.

"Of course I did," she replied. "That's not the point. It should never have happened, and I apologize if I made you believe something different. Neither of us needs that kind of distraction."

I shook my head with an embittered smirk. "You know something, Marion; I'd rather you had just come over here to wish me good luck."

She wrinkled her nose up at me and nodded. "Very well, Detective Haddick. Good luck. And by the way, it's Special Agent Hayes."

Why did everyone feel the need to make sure I understood what their titles were before parting ways? Did they all attend the same "bug up your ass" class? I watched her walk away, which was bittersweet. I wanted her to stay, but she sure looked good from behind. The timing couldn't have been better; Richie had finished his call and was on his way over.

"What did the agent lady want?" Richie asked, peering over at her as she reconnected with Peretti.

"Nothing," I replied. "Just wanted to wish us luck out there today."

"Did you tell her we didn't need it?" he commented. "With the two of us working together, this case is as good as solved."

I looked at him with his cocky smirk and wondered how he could think like that after all he'd learned about the killer. Did he think we were all sitting on our thumbs, waiting for his unparalleled detective skills to come along and help us through this? Freaking moron. I had to work with him, but I didn't have to listen to his garbage.

"Let's go, Richie," I said while walking away from him so he wouldn't see the irritation on my face. "We've got a lot of ground to cover."

"Yeah, okay," he responded, hobbling forward, trying to keep up with me. "I'm coming."

I didn't slow down to wait. If Richie couldn't keep up, that was on him. Maybe I could use that as an excuse to ditch him somewhere along the way. Not likely. He'd cry too much to Frank or Captain Redfern. I felt like I was in a no-win situation here. The day had already started with a bang; it might as well keep going in that direction.

The problem I had with this exercise in futility was that, for the most part, the residents we were dealing with were either the retired elderly or the stay-at-home moms, neither of which were considered possible suspects. And neither demographic would be out and about at the time the murders had taken place. We had a better shot at picking up on suspicious behavior when we stopped in at the local businesses along our route, but even then, it was usually only a supervisor or manager who would meet with us.

Searching into the early afternoon had so far gotten us nowhere. Richie had been on my nerves for three-quarters of that time, repeating phrases he'd remembered from syndicated episodes of Columbo and Starsky and Hutch like this was some television drama. For me, it was more of a horror movie playing in my head; the kind where the bad guy won. I couldn't let that happen. I was going to stop this guy; if it was the last thing I did.

After hitting up the last two apartment buildings, which only resulted in Richie getting scratched by a feisty cat (I told him not to pet it, but it *did* make me smile), we landed at my anticipated destination, The Ruby Room. I was kind enough to park in the side lot this time, but only because I wanted to torture Richie by forcing him to walk farther. We had already taken ten flights of stairs between the previous two tenements; I was sure he could handle a few more yards. At the very least, I could hope by the next day that his bad hip and wrecked knees would be enough to keep him bedridden so I could be on my own.

I heard some grumbling as he stepped from my vehicle, pausing for a moment to rub his knees as I continued toward the front of the building. As I said, I wouldn't wait for him. I rounded the corner and saw the same heavy-set bouncer standing watch at the door from when I was last here. It was good to know Papa Rio was doing his part to maintain the employment rate in this city.

The big lug recognized me immediately and shook his head before gesturing with his hands and questioning my presence.

"Nah, Man," he said, "not again. What you doin' here now?"

"Relax pal," I responded. "I parked in the lot this time. Can't you see I'm playing the good cop today?"

Just then, Richie staggered his way around the corner.

"He's the bad cop," I said, shooting my thumb over my shoulder and winking. "You're not going to want to let that guy in, if you know what I mean" I nodded my head sideways, requesting he step aside, which he did. For me, anyway. He then squared himself back to the front, arms crossed about his chest like a statue to hinder Richie's progress. As I continued for the door, I heard Richie say, "Out of the way, shithead." I turned and yelled, "I'd be careful, Richie; he's big."

"Jim, tell this lumbering oaf he's interfering with an investigation, and we'll haul his ass in if we have to."

I didn't bother to turn that second time, instead yelling as the door closed behind me, "What's that? I can't hear you, Richie," and continued into the lobby.

I knew it was mean, but with almost the entire force out on their assignments, Richie knew he didn't have any backup unless there was an actual crime or some other emergency. He wasn't getting in here because he was all bark and no bite. And in his condition, even his bark wasn't too threatening.

Now that I was able to lose Richie, I could concentrate on what I wanted to ask Papa Rio. I'm sure he already knew I was coming; he had feelers out everywhere, feeding him information. I was hoping some of that information would contain clues to who our Alphabet Killer was. I was going to find out soon enough.

Having been to the nightclub three times in as many weeks, Papa's men had already become accustomed to seeing me, making no effort to stop me or stand in my way. That also meant Papa had given them orders to allow me to pass. I swear the man could smell me coming.

When I got upstairs to the long hallway leading to Papa's office suite, I noticed immediately that his usual doorman was absent, replaced with a much smaller version of a man. If push came to shove, this guy was someone I could handle, so my feeling of being intimidated lowered tremendously.

"Where's the oak tree I usually see planted here?" I asked.

"His wife went into labor this morning," the hired muscle answered. "Don't worry; Mr. Rio has already given explicit instructions to let you in."

Without turning his attention from me, the smaller watchdog unfolded his arms and swung his right hand to his side, where he proceeded to knock four times on the door behind him. A short buzzing sound followed, and he stepped to the side to allow me entrance.

When I walked through the door, Papa wasn't in his usual location behind his desk, but instead, standing to the left of me, staring at a large painting hung above his built-in fireplace. His back was to me, but I could see he was holding his lion-headed cane in his crossed arms, his head tilted to one side like he was examining the extravagant piece of art.

"I've had dis painting for five years, mon," he announced, unmoving from his stance. "I don't t'ink I've ever liked it."

"So why do you keep it?" I asked. "Are you fond of the sight of cavalrymen on horseback?"

"Some t'ings you keep around because you recognize their worth," he answered as he turned to face me. "It's why I keep you around, Detective."

"Now see," I responded, smirking and shaking my finger at him a few times, "that's just what I was thinking about you, Papa."

He stared at me unamused, his nostrils flaring and his eyes spitting daggers. Then, in a heartbeat, he raised his chin slightly and flashed a huge smile as if he was in on some joke I was unaware of being played on me.

"Come, Detective Haddick," he waved his arm to the leather sofa, "have a seat."

"You know I'm not much for sitting on the job," I stated. "I came seeking more information."

"You t'ink I don't know dis, mon?" he responded. "You flood my streets out there, looking for your letter killer, and when you have not'ing else, you come to Papa. But what of you and the FBI lady?"

I stiffened up. It was one night; how could he have learned about us?

"Why do you two have not'ing about the killer yet?" he questioned.

Right, of course, that was what he meant. I quietly exhaled a sigh of nervous relief.

"This guy is always one step ahead of us," I answered. "It's like he knows what we do and what we're going to do. He knows how to cover his tracks."

"And you t'ink I know how to *un*cover dem?"

"I don't know what to think anymore," I replied. "I'm grasping at straws here. You should know I don't enjoy being here, coming to you for help like this."

Just then, I couldn't help but grab for my pant leg as Papa Rio watched my movements intently. My phone was doing a dance in my pocket. Richie must have given up arguing with the human blockade at the front door and wanted me to come to his rescue. Fat chance of that happening. I reached into my pocket and hit the ignore button to send it to voicemail. I'd listen to his ranting later and laugh about it.

"I appreciate that you pointed me in the direction of that slimy rat Carmine, but the Feds don't seem to think as highly of your suggestion as I did. He's not our killer; that much we know. And they don't think he's credible enough or smart enough to be working with someone on the outside. I know there's some connection to his group; I just don't think he's involved. What else can you tell me?"

"I can tell you not everyt'ing will be as clean anymore," he replied. "Like the painting, your worth to me is quickly fading. Perhaps I put too much faith in you, Detective, t'inking you could catch the man. T'ings have changed, and now t'ings are going to get messy."

"What do you mean by that?" I asked. "What's changed?"

Papa stared at me with a look of death in his eyes. Whatever was going on, he wasn't taking kindly to it.

"Your killer made a mistake," he said through clenched teeth. "His last victim.., Gaston was my cousin."

That explained the exasperation in his voice.

"Now he has incurred Papa's rage," he continued, "and I promise you, Detective, I will not be held back by the same law dat handcuffs you."

"Now, hold on a second, Papa," I said, putting my hands up to de-escalate his growing anger. "I understand where you're coming from; I do. But this is a police matter; let us handle it. I can't have you getting involved and interfering in our investigation." I placed as much fury in my stare right back at him. He knew I meant business, and I wasn't about to back down. Papa Rio and his men getting involved would only make matters worse.

"I will give you t'ree days," he said. "If you do not have the killer in custody by then, havoc will rain down upon this city as you have never seen."

"I swear, Alvin, if you do anything stupid..," As much as I wanted to continue the discussion, my vibrating pocket once again drew my thoughts away. This time I pulled it out to chide Richie for his constant disturbances, but when I looked at the screen, I saw that it was Mick calling. I hit the speaker button.

"What is it, Mick?" I answered, annoyed. "I'm kinda in the middle of something here."

"You're not gonna believe this, Jimmy," he responded. "Agent Cordell doesn't know I've been trying to call you, but I thought you should hear this. We just finished raiding a house. I think he and the FBI lady had this planned from the start."

"Had what planned?" I asked, staring at Papa Rio's expression while speaking into the phone.

"I think we did it, Jimmy," Mick said. "I think we got our guy. Fuck! You gotta get down to the station."

"You're kidding me." I expressed. "Why the hell are you sounding like that's a bad thing? We've got the son of a bitch." I nodded positively toward Papa Rio, relieved his rage wouldn't destroy this city.

"Because of whose house we raided," Mick replied. "It's Mort, Jimmy. Fucking Lenny. We're bringing him in now."

My stomach flipped. "I gotta go, Mick," I said, stunned at what I had just heard. "Thanks for the call." I hung up, unsure if Mick even responded.

I stared at the silent phone for a minute, trying to make sense of things. What the fuck just happened. I looked back at Papa and could feel the blood rushing from my face as I tried to form coherent words.

"I.., I think I gotta.., I gotta leave now."

Not the smoothest I've ever been, but Papa's nod let me know he understood.

I turned and rushed out of there as quickly as I could, accidentally bumping Papa's small door crony as I hurried by him. I didn't apologize, and I didn't look back. I had other things on my mind. He'd get over it. I took the stairs two at a time. I couldn't get out of the joint fast enough. I couldn't wrap my head around it. I felt like I had been betrayed. I wanted to throw up, and my legs felt like rubber.

Walking out the front door, the large bouncer was still standing guard as if he was defending a fortress. Richie had given up on gaining access and had taken to leaning up against a signpost by the curb's edge. I tapped the lumbering oaf on his bicep on my way past.

"Thanks," I said. "I'll owe you one."

Richie shook his head in disgust as he pushed himself from his leaning position.

"Asshole. I can't believe you just left me out here."

"Shut up and get to the car," I said, walking quickly by him. "We've got to get to the station."

"Why? What the hell is going on?"

"They think they caught the Alphabet Killer. They're taking him into custody."

"Holy shit!" Richie exclaimed. "That's great news. Why do you sound miserable?"

"Because it's Lenny," I said. "It's been fucking Lenny all this time."

Chapter 18

CUSTODY

Richie wouldn't shut up the entire ride back.

"I knew it!" he said. "I knew there was something about that guy. I never liked him from the moment he started the job. I'm telling you, I've got a nose for these things."

"We don't know anything, Richie," I responded. "They just brought him in for questioning."

"Oh, he's our guy, all right. I've suspected it for some time now. He's a creepy little man who gets off on death."

"It's part of his job," I reminded Richie.

"I get that," he replied. "I'm not an idiot."

I wanted so badly to remark, but I showed some restraint.

"Of course, he works with dead people," Richie continued. "But he enjoys it way too much. I mean, did you ever see the way he stares at the bodies sometimes? It's not normal, even for someone in his profession. There's something not right with that goddamn freak."

"So, that's your investigative theory?" I questioned. "Because he enjoys his job and stares at dead bodies, that makes him our guy?"

"It's not just that," Richie replied. "He gives off eerie serial killer vibes. Don't tell me you haven't felt them. Plus, you see the way he dresses, all nerdy-like. It's fucking weird, is what it is."

I looked over at Richie in perturbed annoyance.

"Are you even listening to yourself?" I asked. "That's what you've got; the way Lenny dresses? And you wonder why you didn't make head detective. Frickin' moron."

"Oh yeah?" he responded, showing his irritation. "They brought him in for *some* reason, smart ass. You got anything better?"

Suddenly, my thoughts shifted back in flashes to the different crime scenes. There were some strange things I couldn't quite wrap my head around. They didn't mean much at the time, but knowing what I know now, they should have triggered my instincts.

"See? You've got nothing," Richie said.

"I've got stuff, shithead."

"Let's hear it, then."

"For starters," I began, feeding into Richie's nonsense, "he lives right around the corner from where the last victim was killed, and he had conveniently showered before arriving. Perhaps he was washing off blood spatter or gunpowder residue."

I didn't know why I was suddenly so willing to condemn Lenny before I even knew what evidence the Feds had.

"And there's been other things, too," I continued. "Like how Lenny's thumbprint has been the only print found on a piece of evidence so far."

"What the fuck?" Richie reacted. "I didn't know that."

"Yeah. Vera found it on one of the killer's notes. She left it out of her official report after questioning him about it."

"And you didn't think to question him yourself?" Richie asked.

I was more frustrated with myself than I was with Richie's comment. I wouldn't let him know that, though.

"Hey, shut the fuck up," I replied. "You know we've all handled evidence without gloves at one point or another. Lenny's constantly working with the bodies, and it was *one* stray print."

"What else you got on the little fucker?"

"It's just stupid shit," I replied. "He'd make these comments like, '*that's what I would have used if I was the killer.*' Christ; it was almost like he was giving me the answer."

I shook my head and slammed my palm into the steering wheel. How couldn't I have seen it sooner? I know how; Lenny's one of us. He's always helped us solve the murders. We never suspect one of our own to be involved. But shit, it was all right there in front of me. I still didn't know why I was telling Richie all this. It must be the shock. I didn't want to believe it was true, but...

"He knew everything we knew," I continued. "That's how he was able to stay ahead of us. And he knew what we'd be looking for, so he knew how to cover it up. That son of a bitch was playing me for a fool this entire time. I should have seen it from the first note. "*May I call you Jim? Or do you prefer James?*" Lenny had just laid into me the day before for calling him Mort instead of by his name. It's all been a game to him."

"Damn right, Jim," Richie agreed. "Now you're getting it. We've got that slimy twerp dead to rights."

I pulled into the station, heated from my wandering thoughts. The Feds' black SUVs were both there, as was Captain Bessel's cruiser and Captain Redfern's car. I wasted no time exiting my vehicle, leaving Richie to fend for himself.

This started out as *my* investigation. If the killer turned out to be Lenny, I sure as shit was going to be there to nail his ass to the wall. Either way, he had a lot of explaining to do. But first, I needed to know what they had on him.

I barged through the doors, uncaring about making a scene. Agents Hayes and Cordell were gathered in a tight circle with Captains Bessel and Redfern. The other two agents were just outside the periphery, listening intently. Mick and officer Peretti were standing together off to the side of the room as if having been shunned. I guess they were only important enough to be paired with the Feds out in the field but not enough to be part of their secretive discussions. Typical. But I wasn't one to let that stop me from butting in where they didn't want me. Hayes said the Bureau wasn't taking anything away from me. As far as I was concerned, that meant it was still my case.

As I approached the group, Agent Hayes broke away, putting her hands up to my chest to stop me.

"Hold on, Detective," she stated, remaining professional amongst her peers. "I know you must be upset, but this isn't the time. Come with me; we need to talk."

She grabbed my upper arm and dragged me to the opposite side of the room from where Mick and Peretti were standing. Once we were alone, she dropped the formalities and began talking in a whispered tone.

"What are you doing here, Jim?" she asked. "You're supposed to be out interviewing people."

"Why? You've already got your man."

"Who told you that?"

"Never mind that," I said. "Why didn't you notify me?"

"We were about to," she answered. "There's a lot going on here that you don't know about."

"But *you* knew all along, didn't you?" I said heatedly. "You and Cordell there had this planned from the start."

"Not from the start," she replied. "But yes, we've had our suspicions for a while."

"So, tell me what the fuck is going on!" I inadvertently shouted.

The other agents and the two captains turned in our direction, to which Hayes threw her palm up toward them, assuring them she had things under control.

"First, I need you to calm down and listen," she said, piercing me with her cold stare. "Agent Cordell informed us that Mr. Shurek was acting nervously as soon as he answered the door. Even so, when my agent asked if they could go inside to ask some questions, the suspect allowed him and your officer to enter. That was a fortunate mistake."

"A little *too* fortunate, it would seem," I remarked. "Our guy has been able to avoid detection this long; do you think the killer would be careless enough to let anyone into his place if he had something to hide?"

"We found items belonging to some of the victims, Jim. He didn't even attempt to hide them, probably thinking we'd never get close to him. They were sitting in plain view on his television stand."

"How do you know they belonged to the victims?" I asked.

"Mick noticed the waitress' nametag almost immediately," she offered. "After that, it wasn't difficult to notice what else he had in his possession: a small ankle bracelet with a dangling heart that has the name Eva inscribed on the back, an envelope addressed to Gaston Warber, a wallet-size photo of Denise, with her kids."

"Fuck!" I exclaimed.

"It was all there in the open," she added. "And that's not all. We also found a few syringes, probably used to subdue his victims, and a picture of the killer's second note on his phone, the one that mysteriously found its way into the hands of the news."

"You got a warrant for that already?" I questioned.

"We didn't need one; he offered it up."

"Why the hell would he do that? He must know how that would make him look?"

"That's what we're hoping you can find out."

"What do you mean?" I asked.

"He said he's willing to cooperate but that he'll only speak with you."

"What about a lawyer?"

"He's waived his rights, said he doesn't want one. He only wants you. Why do you suppose that is?"

"I have no frickin' idea; maybe because I've always been friendly with him."

She stood silently for a moment, exhaling from her nose and staring intently at me as if she were expecting some grand revelation. It wasn't coming.

"Well, anyway," she said, "that's why we were about to contact you; we want you to talk with him. Maybe you can get a confession out of him."

"Where is he now?" I asked.

"We have him in room two. And Jim..," she paused, looking deeply into my eyes. "When this is all through, maybe we can.., talk about things?"

I knew exactly the kind of talk she wanted to have. And I was a sucker for it. I kept my mouth shut and nodded agreeably. She smiled and redirected her head toward the gathered group.

"Let's tell the others."

We walked over to explain my acceptance. Richie, who had made his way in soon after Hayes pulled me to the side, was leaning against his desk, shaking his head as if realizing he was no longer part of the club. I wasn't about to break the news to him, but he was never part of it, to begin with.

"Detective Haddick has agreed to sit with Mr. Shurek," Agent Hayes stated to the group.

Captain Bessell spoke up, "You do realize what we're asking here, Detective? We understand Lenny has worked with this department for years, helping to solve homicide cases. Are you sure you can handle this, treating him like a suspect instead of a colleague?"

"Are you through, Captain?" I questioned, feeling more confident in my role. "I know what it is you're all after, and since I'm the only person Lenny is willing to talk to, I suggest you get out of my way and let me do my fucking job."

I couldn't be sure, but I thought I saw a slight smile on Agent Hayes' face. The same couldn't be said for the State Police Captain, whose eyes narrowed in frustration. I didn't care what he thought or how he felt. I *had* a boss, and it wasn't him. Plus, I was still annoyed I wasn't part of the team that knocked on Lenny's door. Or, at least, given a heads-up about the FBI's suspicion.

The group broke apart, readying themselves to send me into the interrogation room. As soon as I was free, Mick quickly marched over to catch me before it all took place.

"Jimmy," he began, "what do you think? Can it be true? Is Lenny the Alphabet Killer? I mean, it's Lenny. He's one of the good guys, right?"

"I don't know, kid," I answered. "You were there with Cordell; you tell me. Did he really have all that stuff in his apartment?"

"From the victims, yeah," he replied. "But I'm not buying it. Plus, he said it wasn't how it looked. Something doesn't feel right."

"Well, I appreciate that, Mick. I do. But sometimes, if it walks and quacks like a duck..," I shrugged my shoulders and gave a half-hearted smirk. "Listen, I should get going before they think I've changed my mind. Don't worry, Mick; if there's any chance Lenny didn't do it, I'll make sure he's cut loose."

"All right, Jimmy. I know you've got this."

I tapped Mick on the arm and smiled to assure him it would be okay. Mick had a big heart and didn't like to see bad things happen to those he knew. He was somewhat of a naïve simpleton, always hopeful, who only wanted to believe the best in people. He was one of the lucky ones who hadn't yet let this rotting city tear him down. For that, I gave him a lot of credit.

As I turned away from him, I saw Special Agent Hayes waving me forward into the hallway leading to the interrogation rooms. I guess they were in a rush to get things going. I only hoped I was on my game. I had never questioned one of our own. At least, not about something as serious as this. And although Lenny didn't work for the Southbridge PD, he'd worked enough cases with us that made it feel like he was part of the family. This whole mess wouldn't be easy. On the other hand, if he *was* our killer, I wouldn't be against getting stuck alone in a room with him for a short time. He'd quickly learn how even family members could sometimes be motivated to commit horrible acts against one another.

I stopped at the interrogation room doorway, glancing in through the window. Lenny sat at the table, unaware of my presence, his head hung downward, tucked into his palms as so many regretful criminals did after being caught. I couldn't begin to understand why he would only talk to me. But whether he was ready or not, Lenny was getting what he wanted. I hoped I was ready.

I stepped through the door, the sound immediately alerting him of my entrance. He peered up at me through his horn-rimmed glasses with a look of relief, his cheeks puffy and red.

"Oh, thank goodness," he expressed. "I wasn't sure if they'd let you see me."

"I'm here," I stated. "Though I'm not sure why, you son of a bitch."

"It wasn't me, Jim," he said. "Look at me; I couldn't do the things the killer has been doing."

"That's not much of a defense. I've seen the worst kinds of things from people that look just like you."

"But you *know* me, Jim," he said. "I'm telling you, I didn't do those things."

I slid my knuckles across the table's smooth surface on my way to the empty seat across from where he sat. He said he'd only talk to *me*, but he knew I wasn't alone. Behind the large plate glass mirror on the wall that reflected our every move, others were watching, listening, salivating over wanting a confession. The audience was in place, but I had him face-to-face.

"Okay, Lenny," I began, "you say you didn't kill anyone. So then, tell me about the victims' belongings found in your apartment."

"It's not what you think," Lenny stated. "I'm not a sadistic killer collecting items from each of his victims. I know they do that sort of thing."

"Then why did you have them? Help me to understand."

"It was the day I called you into the morgue to look at what I'd found with Eva's body. There was so much going on that morning, and my mind was moving a mile a minute. There was the discovery of the letter on her back, the crumpled note in her hand. I hadn't even realized I'd placed her anklet in my pocket until I'd gotten home. I had every intention of returning it the next day, but the longer I stared at it, the more I kept thinking about what she had gone through, what she must have been thinking in her last moments. I told you before how each body had a story to tell, and I know how this all sounds, but it's like she was telling me through that piece of jewelry.

"When I went in the next day, I took the picture from Denise's wallet. I know I shouldn't have done it, but there were several other pictures, so I didn't think anyone would miss one. I'm not crazy or perverted; I'd just never been a part of a case like this before, and there was something about these victims that called to me. Their anguish, their pain.., it struck a chord, you know?

"And then Francine," he continued. "She was a great woman. We all loved her. I just wanted something to remember her by. I figured her name tag was no big deal."

I shook my head in disgust. "I want to believe you, Mort," I jumped in, calling him by his nickname to rile him. "But this all sounds like a bunch of bullshit to me. Even if what you're telling me is true, that's tampering with evidence. Someone in your position knows better than that. Oh, but that's right; I remember now. What was it you texted me? *'I know how to play dumb.'* Is that what you were doing when you wrote those notes - playing dumb so nobody would think twice about it being a smart guy like you?"

"I didn't write those notes," he said through clenched teeth. "And don't call me Mort. You know I don't like that."

"Oh, you don't like that, Mort?" I prodded. "Well, that's too damn bad. You wanted me; now you're going to have to deal with it. As for the notes, you had a picture of one of them on your phone."

"And I offered it up right away," he jumped in. "Once they thought I had something to do with the murders, I knew they would eventually find the picture. I took it after Lieutenant Garrett handed the pad to me."

"And that's when your thumbprint landed on it?" I questioned.

"Yeah," he replied. "There were so many people around, and Captain Bessell was watching me like a hawk. When he grabbed the Lieutenant's attention away for a moment, I knew it might be my only opportunity to get the picture. I wasn't even thinking when I switched the pad to my ungloved hand so I could grab my phone. I snapped the picture and tucked the phone back in my pocket."

"How convenient to have an answer for all the evidence against you. But why, Mort?" I asked. "Why take the risk? What was so important that you needed a picture?"

"I wanted to do something," he said. "I wasn't sure what at the time. Francine's death really hit home for me. It just felt like things weren't happening as quickly as they should. Maybe if they had, she would have still been with us. And then you got suspended, and everything was going to shit. I couldn't think straight. So I sent a copy of the note to the news station, hoping it would either draw our guy out or light a fire under the Feds' asses. And look, it helped get you back in the game."

"The game, huh?" I questioned. "That's what this is to you?"

"That's not what I meant, Jim," he responded, shaking his head. "I just meant you're the best detective I know. You needed to be on this case. I know I shouldn't have done it, but I couldn't *not* do it."

I stared at Lenny from across the table, his body displaying a nervous tension while his eyes were pleading with me to believe him. However unusual, nothing he'd said so far was so extraordinarily unbelievable. People did crazy things during stressful situations. His poor decisions might have been a bit extreme, but totally feasible given the stresses of his line of work. Handling the dead all the time must do funny things to a person's psyche.

"I was told they found syringes," I stated. "It doesn't look good, Mort. You know the killer injected at least one victim with a sedative."

"Those aren't mine," he answered. "I confiscated them from my sister. I hadn't gotten around to disposing of them yet."

"Right," I said. "The convenience of having a heroin addict as a sister, access to all the syringes you need. Such an easy excuse. Reasonable doubt won't be enough to save you, you sick fuck. I wonder if you even *have* a sister."

Lenny's face turned sour at my comments. It was easy enough for us to find out the truth about his sister's condition, but I wanted to see his reaction. It was the look of someone telling the truth.

"I *have* a sister," he stated, his voice raised. "It's not the easiest thing dealing with her. My mother can't handle it and is threatening to take her kids away."

I exhaled heavily, feeling like a piece of shit. Nothing in my gut was telling me Lenny was lying. Everyone looking in was expecting me to get a confession out of him, but all we had to go on was a bunch of circumstantial evidence. Nothing proved he was the Alphabet Killer. I was going to take one more stab at it.

"Did you kill those innocent people, Mort?"

"No," he replied. "I didn't do it."

"Come on, Lenny; it's me," I said more reservedly. "We've worked together for a while now. You wanted to speak with me; I'm right here. Tell me what it is. Are you the Alphabet Killer?"

"I'm not the Alphabet Killer, Jim. I screwed up; I know that. That's why I asked for you. The rest of those people don't know me as you do. They're going to believe what they want. But you *know* me. You know that what I'm saying is the truth."

"That's just it, Lenny," I responded. "I thought I *did* know you. But after all of this, everything I've just learned, I don't know anymore."

I rose from my chair, continuing to stare at Lenny in disapproval. I then turned my glance toward the large mirror and shook my head. I wasn't getting anything more out of questioning our only suspect.

"You should get comfortable," I said, turning back to Lenny. "You're going to be here a while."

I didn't look back as I walked out the door, but I heard his head slump back into his palms. He was feeling the regret. I wondered if it was from his misguided actions and mishandling of evidence. Or if it was from being found out as the killer? Right now, I couldn't be sure. Why the hell couldn't anything be easy?

Chapter 19

ALIBI

"What the hell was that, Haddick?" Captain Bessell loudly questioned as he stepped through the observation room door.

"That was called questioning a suspect." I replied snarkily. "Have you been out of it that long?"

"Watch it, Detective," Captain Redfern interjected.

"Well, what do you want from me, Captain?" I asked. "I went in; I questioned him. I'm sorry he didn't confess. Did it ever occur to you that maybe he's not our guy?"

"Maybe if you had grilled him instead of acting like he was your best goddamn friend," Captain Bessell raged.

"Take it easy now," Captain Redfern said, throwing up his hands between us to keep us separated. "Detective Haddick asked the questions, and he got answers. They may not have been the answers we wanted, but it doesn't mean they weren't true."

"Captain Redfern is right," Agent Hayes' voice rang out. "Detective Haddick knows the suspect as well as any of you."

"Better," I jumped in.

"There you have it," she said, staring down Bessell. "You were in there, Detective," she continued, turning her attention to me. "What are your thoughts?"

"It's tough to say," I replied. "Lenny was acting nervous, but who wouldn't be when faced with the same situation? If you're asking me if I think he killed those people, my gut tells me he didn't do it."

"That's bullshit!" Bessell yelled. "You're losing your touch, Haddick. The guy's nervous because we caught him with his pants down. The victims' belongings, the syringes, the note on his phone.., his goddamn thumbprint on the killer's note. Which, by the way, was news to us."

He turned to Captain Redfern. "I think you should have a talk with your lab personnel about withholding that little piece of evidence, Captain Redfern."

Then it was back to me. "That little weasel is our guy," he continued, pointing down the hallway in the direction of the interrogation room, "of that, I'm certain. And you, Mr. Great Detective," he pointed his finger at me, "couldn't break him."

"First of all," I began, glaring at him sternly, "don't point your finger at me like I'm one of your little whipping boys. Secondly, were you even listening to anything that was said in that room? So, he had items from the last four victims. I'm not saying it looks good, but he explained them. That only makes him guilty of bad judgment and tampering with evidence. But what about the first three victims? If he was the killer, he would have collected items from them too."

"And he may have," Captain Bessell responded. "We're still going through his apartment."

"You know something, Bessell," I began. "You're just looking for someone to pin it on. You could care less who goes down for the crime, isn't that right? As long as you can say you got your man. Well, I hate to break it to you, Captain, but down here in the slums, we need hard evidence to hold someone in custody. Everything we have to this point is circumstantial, at best. Maybe you should go study up on your fucking law books."

Things got heated quickly. I had to walk away. The only remark I recall hearing after that was Agent Hayes' words, "I'll speak with him."

I heard the tapping of her heels on the floor, gaining on me from behind, but I continued forward, looking to put some distance between myself and the State Police Captain's over-inflated ego. Only after I turned the corner into an empty hallway did I pause to wait for Hayes to catch up with me. I was still bitter about the way she brushed me off this morning after coming on to me the night before the way she did. Maybe I'd have it out with *her* too. That son of a bitch Bessell put me in a confrontational mood, and I wasn't looking to restrain myself.

She came around the corner quickly, probably expecting to have to chase me down, then stumbled back after almost colliding with me. I wouldn't have minded; I'd be lying if I said I didn't enjoy her body against mine.

"Detective, I..,"

"Save it if you're going to defend that asshole back there," I said.

"I wasn't," she replied. "Bessell was out of line. You did what you needed to do. Mr. Shurek isn't the killer."

"Just like that?" I questioned.

"Oh, he's not out of the fire yet," she stated. "There's still a lot he has to answer for. Mr. Shurek has done some questionable things, without a doubt. But your gut is telling you he's not our guy, and I trust your judgment. That man's not a killer. We will, of course, be following up with his sister. And Ms. Snell is currently testing the syringes for any sedatives or other substances used to incapacitate. We'll know soon enough of the results. We'll also be doing a full investigation into Mr. Shurek, which will now use up resources we don't have."

"So it's back to square one," I stated.

"That's exactly why we wanted people to remain diligent out there searching. Although we've had our suspicions about the medical examiner for a little while now, I've never been one hundred percent convinced. It was better to keep everyone on their assignments. We could use a few more suspects in this case."

"That's what all this was about, wasn't it?" I questioned. "You had it planned from the start. You just needed a legit excuse to get over to Lenny's place without anyone knowing. You could have confided in me, Marion."

"I'm sorry, Jim," she said. "I couldn't take the chance of someone alerting him in advance and allowing him to hide evidence. Clearly, it was the right call since it was all there in plain sight."

"And you thought I would have warned him?" I questioned. "If there was any merit to your suspicions, if the possibility was there that he was the Alphabet Killer, you should have known I wouldn't have informed him. I want to catch this guy more than anyone."

"I understand," she responded. "But you also need to understand why I couldn't share that information."

"You could have confided in me," I said. "Especially after last night."

She smirked, then dropped her head for a moment. Was it from embarrassment or out of guilt? Either way, I was glad my comment triggered some emotion from her. It meant she pushed Special Agent Hayes aside to make way for Marion.

"Jim," she said softly, looking back into my eyes, "last night was..,"

"You can stop yourself right there," I spoke over her. "I get it. I'm not exactly the kind of guy someone like you would get involved with. Hell, I know I'm not the easiest. Let's call it what it was, shall we? We had a fun time, that was all. Now we can get back to solving this case. Except you'll have to count me out for the rest of the day. I've had enough of this shit; I'm going home. You can tell Redfern I suddenly came down with the twenty-four-hour flu."

I walked away, even as she said, "Jim, wait." I pretended I didn't hear her as I walked through the door leading back into the office area. Richie sat at his desk, shaking his head, still looking upset. I wondered if it was because of what I put him through earlier in the day or if he finally realized how *uni*mportant he was to the powers that be. Either way, I think he'd gotten the hint.

I stopped by my desk and grabbed a notepad and a few files. I was going home, but it didn't mean I was giving up for the day. There was still plenty to review, and I did my best work alone. They had Lenny in custody, but they'd only be able to detain him for so long if they weren't going to officially charge him with anything. I didn't see that happening. They didn't have enough against him to charge him with the murders, and if the D.A. learned what little evidence they had, there's no way she'd be willing to prosecute. She'd need more. Maybe the FBI's investigation into Lenny would expose something, but I doubted it. As much as I wanted to believe we had caught the killer when I first heard they'd brought Lenny in for questioning, he wasn't the killing type. I saw that in his eyes. He respected the dead too much to carve letters into their skin.

As I gathered up the last of the files from my desk, I could feel Richie's eyes burning a hole in my back. He had to know I was leaving, which left little for him to do. He should be grateful; without me around to capture the attention of the brain trust still gathered in the corridor, he could swoop in and act like he was suspicious of Lenny all along. Then I could hear all about it tomorrow.

I didn't bother looking Richie's way when I walked from my desk, heading for the door. Maybe I was being harsh on him. What can I say? I held a bit of a grudge. I didn't like the guy after what he had done (Did I ever like him?). I'd eventually get over it, but for now, it gave me comfort to dislike him publicly.

I walked to my car, stopping first at the passenger side to drop off the pile of folders onto the passenger seat. It was a decent amount; it would keep me busy for the night. As I walked to the driver's side, my phone began buzzing. I pulled it from my pocket and saw it was my ex. Jesus, will the torment ever end? I didn't answer it right away, choosing to start the car first so the Bluetooth would activate.

"Karen, what did I do this time?" I assumed she was calling to bitch me out about something; it was the only time I heard from her.

"Have you talked with Ben?" she asked.

"Yeah, we talked this morning."

"And did he tell you where he was?"

"I assumed he was at David's apartment," I replied.

"Well, he wasn't," she retorted. "He was at the hospital."

"What? What happened? Is he all right?"

"It wasn't him," she replied. "It was David. I guess he cut himself pretty badly. He needed stitches."

"What did he do?" I asked. "How did he cut himself?"

"I don't know; Ben wouldn't tell me. He seemed upset, so I didn't harp on the subject. I didn't know if you had heard anything."

"I didn't, no," I responded. "Why the hell didn't he tell me when we spoke?"

"He probably tried, but you weren't listening, as usual."

And there it was. That's the Karen I knew. It must have been my fault. It was *always* my fault.

"Thanks for the guilt trip, Karen. Will there be anything else you'd like to add? Maybe you'd like to remind me how horrible of a father I am. That's always fun. Or did you only call to put me in my place for not knowing about David?"

"Oh, stop the act," she replied. "You know damn well you've never been the best at listening."

"That's bullshit, Karen, and you know it." I felt myself gripping the steering wheel tighter as I weaved through traffic. She'd probably love it if I got into an accident. "I listen," I continued. "I've *been* listening. Unlike you, I don't throw it back in your face when he says things about you and your new boyfriend. Or don't you know? Have *you* been listening?" Now I was being childish with her. Why did I let her rile me like that?

"Eat shit, Jim," she yelled into the phone. "I just thought you should know where your son has been all day."

Then she hung up, which was fine with me. Her screeching was causing my skin to crawl. It was for the best; it would allow me to call Ben to find out what happened. It sounded serious. Maybe they needed a ride home.

I dialed him up on the phone, but after a single ring, it bounced me to voicemail.

"This isn't Ben; it's Ben's voicemail. Leave a message."

"Ben, it's your father. Give me a call when you get this. I heard there was an accident. I want to make sure you're all right. Call me."

I'm sure he was fine, but I wanted to let him know I was concerned. I hoped he and David weren't doing something stupid. He'd tell me when he called back. For now, I'd think only good thoughts until I had a reason to think otherwise. Unfortunately, I was pulling into my driveway, which guaranteed the good thoughts would disappear sooner than I'd hoped. I had a night of studying ahead of me.

It had been a few hours since I left Ben a second message, asking him to call me. I'd understand his lack of a response if he was still at the hospital. That place never had the best cell service. I had a hard time believing he was still there, though. If David only needed stitches, he would have been out hours ago. I was about to grab my keys to head over to David's place when it occurred to me that I had no idea where the kid lived. Suddenly, my ex's voice rang in my ears, telling me everything that was wrong with me being a father. Shit. How could I have never thought to ask Ben where the place he was staying was? Maybe I was a horrible father after all? I was always too preoccupied with work to be a part of Ben's life. He must have felt that. If I had been around when he needed me, like when David's car broke down, I'd have known where he was staying. Even worse, that meant Karen's boyfriend knew more than I did, and therefore, she did too. And there was no way I was contacting Karen to ask for David's address. I'd never hear the end of it. Even though, in this case, I deserved whatever lashing she would have dished out. I couldn't even tell her it was because I trusted our son. She would have known it was only an excuse. I'm such an idiot.

I was working through stuff in my head when I saw the headlights through the curtains. All I could think was how thankful I was such businesses as Uber existed. Ben was home safe.

I rushed to the door to greet him, my nerves calming with each step. He'd never understand the feeling, but I did, and I was ready to show him. And as I opened the door..,

"Ben, thank G..,"

I stopped myself in midsentence when I realized it wasn't him.

"Sorry, not Ben," Agent Hayes said, shrugging her shoulders while delivering an awkward smile.

Even after realizing my mistake, I stuck my head out the door and peered past my unexpected guest, looking for signs of Ben's arrival as if he had pulled up alongside her. He hadn't.

"Marion, what are you doing here?" I asked.

"I was afraid if I phoned you, you wouldn't agree to my stopping over."

She might have been right, but she was here now. And somehow, seeing her outside of work, she just seemed different. I stepped aside.

"Come on in," I said, nodding my head.

"Thank you," she replied, stepping past me, the scent of Light Blue capturing my senses again. I swear, the woman must spray herself, knowing she's on her way.

I was never good at deciphering hints from women, but I took that to be one. I closed the door, looking at her figure from behind as she stared away into the living room.

"Care to sit down?" I asked, brushing past her in the direction she had been facing.

"Sure," she responded. "That would be great."

I led her into the next room, where she gravitated to the cushioned chair located to the left of the sofa.

"Light reading?" she questioned as she walked by the coffee table, the files in disarray across its surface.

I slid between it and the couch, swiping the folders into a manageable pile on one side of the table.

"Yeah, well, I have a hard time leaving work *at* work. And since I left early, I felt obligated to bring something home."

"I know the feeling, Detective."

"We're not at work now," I replied. "You can call me Jim."

She nodded her response.

"So, what brings you here this time?" I asked. "Did someone get Lenny to confess?"

"No," she replied. "And we won't. Mr. Shurek will be released tomorrow, but we'll be keeping a close watch on his activities from now on."

"Then.., what?"

"Jim, I didn't like the way we left things. When you interrupted me earlier in the hallway, what I was going to say, was that last night was very special to me. I've just never been good at the whole relationship thing. Being a woman in my position, in our line of work.., it's always been tough. Men are easily intimidated. I didn't feel that with you. What you said about us having fun.., it was. Very much so. And what I seem to be rambling on about is, well, I'd like to continue that fun."

My ears perked up with excitement as a nervous chill ran down my spine.

"Marion, I..,"

"Wait," she said, putting up her hand to prevent me from finishing. "I don't want to jeopardize things between us, but I *will not* jeopardize this case. It's much too important. To both of us. So, if you'd be willing to wait until we catch this..," she paused, almost as if she were struggling to find the word. "…Fucker."

She smiled. It was easy to tell that one was for me. Perhaps it was a hint that I needed to tone back my foul mouth. I smiled back.

Just then, Ben walked through the front door, a large duffle bag slung over his shoulder. I quickly jumped to my feet as if I had just been caught doing something I shouldn't have been. Marion did the same.

"Ben!" I expressed with surprise. "Hey. I've been calling you. How'd you get here?"

"I got a ride," he answered.

"I didn't hear a car door," I said.

Ben's eyes shifted to Marion.

"I imagine you didn't," he replied.

Marion smiled and immediately stepped forward, her arm extended to shake Ben's hand.

"Hello, Ben," she greeted him. "I'm a coworker of your father's. He's spoken very highly of you."

"He has?" Ben questioned, grasping her hand.

"He has," she reassured him. "But I'm afraid I must be going." She turned to me and offered her hand in the same fashion, for which I obliged. "Thank you, Detective Haddick," she said. "I appreciate you going over the details of the case with me. And next time you act like an ass, I won't take it so lightly."

"Of course," I replied, nodding. "Let me walk you out."

"No need."

"Well, to the door, then." I placed my hand on her lower back as I walked beside her, guiding her to the door. I hoped she understood it as more than me rushing her out. I opened the door for her, and she slowly walked by, giving me a wink as she stepped out. I smiled and nodded, unable to convey my feelings verbally.

I closed the door and turned to give my full attention to Ben.

"That was the FBI lady, wasn't it?" he asked.

I looked at him in curiosity. "Now what made you think that?"

"Gee, I don't know, Dad," he began. "Could it be the black SUV with the 'U.S. Government' plates?"

"Oh, well, I guess that would do it," I answered.

"So, are you guys seeing each other, then?"

"Whoa, hold on there, buddy. First of all, that's none of your business. And second of all, the answer is 'no,' okay. The 'FBI lady' and I are not seeing each other." I shot him a snarky glance. "But wait, hold on. Before we go any further, Your mother called me and said you were at the hospital. Something about David cutting himself and needing stitches. Do you want to tell me what that was about? What happened?"

"I don't know what happened," he replied. "He came home this morning with a large gash in his arm. He was bleeding all over the place, trying to hold the skin together. I had to rush him to the hospital. I kept asking him how it happened, but he wouldn't tell me. The doctors said he would have bled out if I hadn't gotten him there in time."

"Jesus! Is he still there?"

"He's back home," Ben answered. "Thirty-seven stitches."

"You had me worried, Ben. I left you a couple of messages asking you to call me back. I was about ready to put out an APB on you." I walked closer to hug him. I wanted him to know I was ready to be there for him. He stopped me before I could get my arms up.

"I've been a little preoccupied, Dad," was his response. "When we got back to the apartment, he told me he wanted me out."

"What? Why?" I questioned.

"I don't know," Ben replied. "He told me to take my things and get out. He's been acting strange. I mean, he had been ever since his girlfriend broke up with him, but it's been worse lately. I think he tried to kill himself."

"If that's true, you can't leave him by himself."

"I contacted his mother; she said she was going over."

"Okay, that's good, at least," I said, relieved. "Why didn't you tell me when we spoke this morning?"

"I wanted to, but I knew you had a lot on your plate. I didn't want it to distract you from your case."

"Ben..," I shook my head, feeling angry with myself for making my son feel like his father's job was more important than *he* was. I wouldn't let that happen again.

"Ben, I'm sorry about your friend," I opened my arms and stepped toward him, "but I am so glad to have you back here with me."

Almost instantly, Ben lunged forward into my embrace, squeezing me tightly. I hadn't felt that kind of love from him in years. I could get used to it all over again. All he ever wanted was to be included in my life, to learn about what his old man did. While holding him, I looked down at the pile of folders on the table, noticing I hadn't done the best job straightening them. One of the files sneaking out from the top was the folder Vera had given me with her collection of serial killer articles. It gave me an idea.

"Hey, Ben," I began, peeling myself from his grip. "What say you give me a hand with this case?"

"Wait, really?" he asked, a huge smile on his face.

"I've been looking at these files all day," I said, "and I'm not getting anywhere. Maybe I need a fresh set of eyes."

"Okay," he replied. "What do I do?"

I couldn't let him look through the Alphabet Killer files, but there was no reason he couldn't dig through Vera's folder. There wasn't anything in there that a kid his age didn't already know, especially with the internet. All someone had to do was search online for serial killers.

"Come on," I said. "Sit down." I grabbed Vera's folder from the pile and handed it to him. "That's a folder of past serial killers. I want you to look through it and see if you can find any similarities between any of them and what you know about our guy."

"The Alphabet Killer!" he exclaimed.

"Yes," I said, nodding. "The Alphabet Killer. Just don't tell your Mom I let you look through those," I said, grinning.

I watched as Ben began flipping through the pages, his smile never fading. Why was I so hesitant to have him be a part of my life? I'd always kept him so guarded against it, wanting to keep the darkness of the job from tainting his innocence. I couldn't protect him from it forever, and he was now old enough to see some of that darkness for himself.

"Hey, Dad," Ben looked up to get my attention.

"Yeah, son?"

"There's some pretty cool stuff in here. Where'd you get all of these old newspaper clippings?"

"I actually got them from a friend," I replied.

"Well, whoever it is," he said, "it looks like they've been collecting for a long time. I bet they know more about the killers than even the killers did themselves. I wonder if the Alphabet Killer has something like this. If he does, it's probably how he learned to keep from getting caught. It wouldn't surprise me. Who knows what goes on in their heads? It's really great that you're letting me help you.

Ben's voice faded out. I faked a smile and continued to nod whenever he looked at me, but it wasn't real. He continued talking, but I could no longer concentrate on what he was saying. He just made an observation that I had never picked up on. Either that or I was unwilling to admit the possibility. I shifted my eyes to the folder he had on his lap, and a horrible feeling crept up inside me. A lot of effort was put into collecting all of that material. Was I being paranoid? For what reason would someone need it? Was it really only a hobby? I'd already had to question Lenny about *his* odd behavior. Now another person crept into my mind. My wheels were spinning. I hated what I was thinking.

Chapter 20

Waking up at four in the morning was never a fun thing. I couldn't keep my eyes shut. My thoughts kept wandering, thinking about Ben's words the night before.

I wonder if the Alphabet Killer has something like this. If he does, it's probably how he learned to keep from getting caught.

I hadn't thought of it before then, but perhaps the killer *did* have it all this time. We'd been thinking the killer was a man because of the strength needed to drag a body. It seemed like a valid argument since most murderers turn out to be men. But even Vera had joked on numerous occasions how she was more a man than most of the officers at the station. It wasn't only her mouth; she had the bulk too. And the more I thought things through, the uglier things seemed.

The woman was obsessed with serial killers, having collected articles and clippings over the years. I'd known Vera for a long time, yet she remained secretive about her infatuation until this new killer suddenly surfaced in our backyard. She *did* mention how serial killers liked to remain low-key. She said it was always the ones you least expected. It made sense; the longer they remained undiscovered, the longer they could keep up their killing ways. Vera was also the one who came up with the name "The Alphabet Killer 2.0." Then she became upset when they excluded "2.0" from the title and worried that it would confuse historians because of the previous Alphabet Killer from the seventies. She took it very personally.

I also knew these types of killers were egotistical and self-absorbed, wanting credit for their kills. Vera had no problem leaving out Lenny's thumbprint from her report. Was it because he was "one of us" or because she didn't want someone else credited with Francine's murder? And like Lenny, being in forensics, she'd know how to avoid leaving evidence. She'd know how to remain undetected and could tamper with or eliminate any incriminating evidence against her. The question was, could she have flown under my radar this long? I was going to find out. I hoped I was wrong, but the more I thought about it, the more things stacked-up against her.

I asked Vera to meet me at the station early that morning so we could review a few things still missing from the report. I wanted to get there before having to go out on our assignments. She wasn't happy about it, sending me a few nasty expletives, but she agreed.

Because of my inability to sleep, I arrived at Vera's cave a few minutes early. That was fine with me. The wait allowed me to clear my head. If Vera was a viable suspect, I didn't want to give away my hand too early. While I waited, I peered in through the glass door. It always amazed me how many things the folks down here had their hands on. The job had to be tedious, processing every piece of evidence tossed their way. I was glad it wasn't me stuck down here.

I saw that the handgun used to shoot Gaston had been bagged and tagged, and the pipe used to smash his window lay beside it. On Vera's desk, segregated into individual baggies, I noticed the items confiscated from Lenny's apartment. There were only the four items that we had previously discussed. I guess that meant the state police hadn't found anything else, as I suspected they wouldn't. And now, with my attention drawn elsewhere, the reason why might've been right under our noses.

"Jesus Christ," Vera's voice rang out as she descended the stairs. "Fucking fuck, it's early. You dicks enjoy getting an early start like this? Fuuucckkk! A girl needs her beauty sleep."

As serious as the situation was, I couldn't help but snicker at her boisterous entrance. I had to act as I always had around her; I didn't want her to pick up on anything. And since I hadn't yet shared my thoughts with anyone, I had to be careful.

"Oh sure," she continued, "laugh it up, ass hat. Do you think my good looks and sexy exterior come naturally? I now know why you fuckers call me the Dragon. I saw my face in the mirror this morning and punched the shit out of the glass, thinking a beast was about to eat me. Don't get me wrong, I enjoy getting eaten by a man-beast now and again, but that was some scary shit."

Vera wasn't an especially attractive woman, and she knew it. She wasn't dealt a favorable hand in the looks department and being a bit on the heavier side, her body was what most would consider less than desirable (though she claimed to have suitors constantly beating down her door). What she lacked in sex appeal, she made up for in smarts, though you wouldn't know it, listening to her talk sometimes. Say what you wanted; Vera had a way with words. The killer did, too, though used very differently. Should that mean anything? Vera herself even concluded that the person who wrote the notes was smarter than what they wanted people to think. Vera was an intelligent woman, but the way she presented herself always led others to believe otherwise. She always said she liked it that way; it kept men guessing. It was advantageous to let them think that her mind was as dull as her figure. Perhaps she used that advantage in other ways as well.

"Do you mind telling me what was so important that you had to get my fat ass down here at the butt crack of dawn," she said as she slid by me, swiping her magnetic security card in the reader to open the locked door.

"I wanted to check on a few things," I answered, following her through the doorway. "Having to deal with Richie and the Feds, I feel like I've been out of touch with some of the evidence that's been collected lately."

"No shit, Sherlock," she replied. "I was wondering when you were going to come calling. Perfect timing, too. Although an hour later would have been preferred. Just last night, I got the results of the analysis we ran on the dried blood found on the pipe. I'd rather give my findings to you before handing them over to those government hacks."

"And what's the verdict?" I asked.

"Just as we thought; it's got waitress juice all over it."

"Christ, Vera. A little respect, huh? Some of us were friends with Francine."

"Sorry, Jim. I didn't realize you two were that close."

"We weren't," I replied. "It's just.., I don't know." I ran my fingers across my forehead, hoping to relieve some of the tension I was feeling. "I've been looking over that folder you gave me. You know, your private stash. There's some sick shit in there. I guess it has me a little rattled."

"Yeah, well, don't get too used to it," she responded. "I'll be expecting that back when you're all done."

"Soon," I said. "Hey, how did you get into all that serial killer stuff anyway?"

"Are you kidding me?" She responded. "I work in a crime lab. That shit's in my DNA."

"I suppose that makes sense," I countered. "I'll tell you what, with all the research you've done on those whack-jobs, I'm glad you're on our side. You probably know more about getting away with murder than most of the demented nut jobs you've studied."

"You bet your ass, I do," she replied excitedly as if it were something of which to be proud.

Her candid response assured me she didn't suspect my reasoning for questioning her, but it hadn't left me with a good feeling either. I had more to ask, but my sudden vibrating pocket distracted my thoughts. I pulled my phone from my pocket, thinking Ben must have woken up and wondered where I'd gone off to so early. Instead, it was a text message from Frank.

```
Get your ass into the station. We've got another
body. It looks like our guy struck again last
night.
```

"Shit!" I let out audibly.

"What now?" Vera asked. "Did you forget your tampon this morning?"

"Funny," I replied, giving her a jagged look. Having been discreet about my early arrival, Frank didn't realize I was already in the building. And it appeared Vera hadn't yet been alerted of the disturbing news, though if she had, and if she were the killer, it would come as no surprise to her. Still, she had no idea what I had just been notified of, and I aimed to let that secret remain until I had the chance to learn more. I had a few more minutes to question Vera without raising suspicion.

"It was my ex-wife pestering me again," I answered. "She never gets enough of it. I'll deal with her later." I turned my stare to Vera's desk. "So," I continued, pointing at the items splayed out to steer us back on course, "the pipe was used to strike Francine and to smash Gaston's car window. That's now confirmed. Were you able to get anything else off of it?"

"Just the blood," she confirmed. "Unless you consider some sand granules from the parking garage useful."

"That doesn't help," I said. "What about this other stuff?" I waved my hand back and forth over the bagged items on her desk. "Were you able to get through it all?"

"Don't get your panties all up in a bunch," she replied. "Danny and I were working overtime on all this shit. We didn't get out of here until after nine last night."

Perfect, I thought. That was an important tidbit of information. Although I hadn't asked, Vera offered up what I needed. If there was another homicide last night, I had only to verify the time and her alibi, which shouldn't be too difficult. Pulling my phone from my pocket again, this time with the pretense that I had received a second text, I glanced at the screen with what I hoped was a convincing sneer.

"Oh great," I played it up, acting with a frustration that had been real from the first glimpse of Frank's original message. "Now *Frank* is gunning for me. He wants me upstairs."

"Sounds like an absolute delight," Vera jabbed sarcastically.

"You *would* say that. Keep up your thing down here, Vera. Let me know if you find anything conclusive on the stuff from Lenny's apartment."

"Of course," she replied. "Now get out of here so I can take a nap."

I shot her a disconcerting look.

"I'm kidding, jack-hole," she said before shooing me away.

I trekked upstairs to Frank's surprise as he caught me rounding the corner from the lower floor. Based on his expression, there was no doubt he expected my arrival later in the hour. What could I say; I was an overachiever.

"Jim, you're here," Frank cried excitedly.

"Yeah," I replied. "I was here checking in on a few things."

"Whatever it was, leave it," he said. "I need you downtown. The Reisling Apartments."

"That's the Bowery district," I responded.

"No shit. You got a problem with that?"

"Yeah, I do," I replied. "It means our guy is branching out."

"I thought that too. Our friends at the FBI are already en route. I want you there holding their hands. I'll keep everyone else on their assignments."

"You're not going?" I asked.

"I have things to clean up here because of the predicament Mort put us in. This latest homicide may have given your little friend a reprieve, but he's not out of hot water yet. He still has a lot of explaining to do. That goddamn weirdo. Now get out of here before I change my mind and let Richie tackle this one instead."

"Yes sir, Lieutenant." Huh, how do you like that? I was able to say it without being condescending. We live; we learn.

The Bowery district was a predominantly Asian-American neighborhood, so named because of its similarities to the area in New York City known for its cheap hotels and flophouses. Like other minorities, the Asian Americans settled in amongst themselves, establishing their own self-contained, social-economic community - similar to Chinatown with its shops and eateries. Unlike Chinatown, however, tourists didn't want to visit this poor, decaying section of the city. Not that Southbridge gets many tourists, anyway.

The Reisling Apartments, located in the heart of the district, were low-income housing units for many of the shopkeepers and their families. Most of the units were one and two-bedroom sardine cans - sometimes supporting up to eight occupants. Even on the best of days, it would be uncomfortable for most. The residents there said it was better than where they had come from. I didn't get how anyone could live like that, piled on top of each other like hamsters. Those people learned how to live in squalor like champs. And on the worst of days, such as the one I just stepped into, at least one of them learned to *die* in the same impoverished condition. When I thought about it, maybe that person was the lucky one.

I stepped into the room, unprepared for what the killer had left behind. From the look of the mostly-coagulated pool of crimson on the floor, the blood had stopped dripping from the woman's feet hours before. The victim's lifeless body was stripped down to only her underclothing and was still hanging from the beam where the room's light fixture was once suspended. She had been cut in several places along her legs and stomach. The white fabric of her under linen was stained red from the liquid that had seeped from her wounds. On the woman's left chest, above her blood-soaked bra, was the familiar calling card of the fiend responsible.

Marion and her FBI cohorts were already present, as was Barry, the Assistant M.E. He was scanning the woman's lacerations and making notations in his pad. Agent Brynn was standing on a chair by the dangling woman, dusting for prints on the tightly-wrapped extension cord that had been the killer's weapon of choice for this particular slaying. Agent Pease was several feet away, carefully analyzing the bloody blade that had been used to slash the victim before ultimately landing in its resting place on the kitchen counter.

"It's a little excessive, don't you think?" Special Agent Hayes stated as I approached. "If the hanging was the killer's intent, why cut the victim so severely?"

"Because they could," I responded. "It's a statement. The killer was bragging about having the time to do what they wanted. We've seen this before with victim D."

"'They'?" Hayes questioned. "As in multiple people? Or do you no longer believe our killer to be a man?"

"I don't know *what* our killer is," I answered. "What kind of person does this sort of shit?"

"Someone who craves attention, Detective," Hayes replied. "Someone who lacks moral restraint. We're dealing with a sick individual who doesn't comprehend that what they're doing is wrong."

"'They're'?" I questioned in return.

"I'm following your lead, Detective," she answered. "Your gut feeling about Mr. Shurek not being the killer panned out. Perhaps we should be listening more carefully to what you have to say."

She looked at me with acceptance in her eyes, something I had only previously seen in her non-professional persona. It was a welcoming surprise.

"So, what's the story with this one?" I questioned, turning my attention to Barry, who was standing behind the victim, writing frantically in his leaflet.

"Hu Xi Minh," he began, flipping back in his notes. "She's 29 and lives alone. She helped her aunt run the fish stand on the corner. Her neighbor from across the hall discovered the body like this when she stopped over this morning."

"The neighbor has a key?" I questioned.

"I don't think they lock their doors around here," Barry answered, throwing his shoulders up. "Probably never had much need to."

"Maybe they'll think about it now, huh?" I responded. "Anyone questioning the neighbor?"

"Captain Bessell and one of his officers are taking a statement from her now," Special Agent Cordell offered. "The woman is understandably shaken."

"And are we sure this homicide took place last night?"

"Well, the neighbor lady said she was with the victim until 11:30 yesterday morning," Barry answered. "So that's our first indication. Although I can't give you the exact time of death just yet, based on the body's rigor and the brownish color of the dried blood around the periphery of the main deposition onto the floor, I would speculate it happened maybe ten to twelve hours ago."

"Ten to twelve hours?" I questioned, immediately calculating backward to help put an end to the horrible thoughts I'd been having about Vera. "Wouldn't the blood be completely dried by now if that were the case?" I asked.

"Not with the humidity in this place," Barry replied, wiping away the sweat that had gathered on his forehead as if to validate his point. "Lousy airflow, too. Now, had these been wood floors," he tapped his foot on the linoleum surface, "you'd see a difference. The linoleum helped keep it all pooled, which impacted its drying time. Plus, it was a lot of blood."

"Yeah, about that," I said, staring at the large H carved into the woman's upper chest. "The cuts she sustained along her chest, stomach, and legs hardly seem like the type of wounds that would produce the amount of blood I see on the floor. What am I missing?"

Barry looked at me from the far side of Hu's rigid body. "You've only seen the good side so far, Detective. We've actually been waiting for you to look at this before we took her body down." He gestured with his pen, pointing up at the backside of the body. "The killer has left you another message."

With trepidation, I slowly made my way around the hanging victim to see the view that had captured Barry's attention. If I had a weaker constitution, I would have lost the contents of my stomach.

From the front, Hu Xi Minh was an unfortunate victim of a disturbed individual who slashed at her and gouged her flesh. From behind, she had been a plaything used for pure enjoyment to hone the killer's craft. The backs of her arms from the shoulders down, and her legs, from the bottom of her buttocks to her ankles, had the skin and muscle filleted from her body, revealing the skeletal structure within. Had that been the extent of the mutilation, it would have already been the most disgusting thing I'd seen inflicted upon another human being. But the killer was not so kind to this one. As Barry had stated, a message was left behind, and Hu's back was the killer's canvas.

Chunks of flesh had been torn away where jagged letters were cut into the skin, forming jigsaw sentences pieced together by the flaps of epidermis left behind. The killer had all the time needed to complete a masterpiece of literature.

"My God!" I said, covering my mouth as I stared in horror at the words addressed to me.

Hello again, Detektive. So glad you are back on the hunt. They can't take you away, this has always been our game to play. Hate me or thank me, which will it be? H was a sweet thing. I hung on every word she said. But she went against her own advice, so now, she hangs instead. Why do they always disapointe? Look where it gets them. But you won't disapointe me, will you? You'll do exactly as you've sed. Stop me, James. Stop me before the alphabet's end, or I'll be forced to start all over again. Wouldn't that be fun? But let's not get ahead of ourselves. There are still plenty of others waiting for me. Ω

Trying to catch my breath, I glanced at Barry, "Please tell me she was already dead."

"You want me to lie to make you feel better?" Barry responded.

"Shit."

"Well, I don't think she was conscious if that helps at all."

"It doesn't," I replied. "But how do you know that?"

Before Barry could reply, Agent Hayes jumped in, "No screams."

We both tilted our heads to peer around the body.

"Well, it only stands to reason," she continued. "Any one of her neighbors would have heard her screaming. Her body wasn't discovered until this morning; she didn't scream."

"And the woman wins a door prize," Barry stated, rubbing the thickly-settled, ginger whiskers along his jawline with the back of his hand. "Miss Minh here was heavily sedated. And not from any legal substances, if you know what I mean. Tracks along the inside of her elbow suggest she was a heroin addict. Most likely, she was in a drug-induced coma. If she was awake, she was probably so high she had no idea the extent of what was happening to her. There's also some blood on the sheets in the bedroom. It looks like your killer started carving his love letter to you there. The stains are far enough apart and consistent with someone lying face down. It appears the blood trickled from each side of her back while he cut into her. Then, after the sicko had his fun with that, he strung her up here, balancing her on this chair," he pointed to the chair Agent Brynn currently stood upon, "and began cutting the skin from her. Once he'd finished, he pushed her off. She thrashed about for a minute; that's the blood spatter you see outside the periphery of the pooled blood. Then she expired."

"Jesus," gasped Agent Cordell.

"Sorry," Barry apologized. "I can't sugar-coat it."

"So, where's the woman's flesh?" I asked.

"The killer was tidy," Barry replied. "It's piled nicely on a dinner plate in the kitchen sink. There was no trail of blood, so it was collected on the plate as it was cut from her, then carefully transported to the kitchen. No mess."

Just then, Captain Bessell charged through the door.

"Look at this," he started, "the prodigal son has arrived. You certainly know how to make friends, Haddick. This guy's got a hard-on for you, doesn't he?"

"What's the matter, Captain?" I responded. "Are you jealous I have more friends than you? Or that they can still get it up?"

He shot me an irritated glance. "I've seen the friends you keep," Bessell said. "One wound up being a suspect, as I recall."

"Oh, you mean that suspect you were so confident was the killer?" I questioned. "Even though I told you he wasn't our guy? How did that pan out?" It was an arrogant retort, but I didn't care. He came in with guns blazing; I wasn't about to sit back and take that from the likes of a blowhard like him, even though I had my suspicions about another strange colleague of mine.

"I'm not willing to concede yet," Bessell stated. "Shurek may still be connected to this somehow."

"Gentlemen," Special Agent Hayes interjected, "are you two finished comparing testosterone levels? We get it; you're *both* right. Can we move on to figuring out our next course of action?"

I immediately jumped in. "I think we need to retrace our steps down the path I had originally started."

"So, what are you suggesting?" she asked.

"These victims aren't chosen at random," I replied. "They're all connected somehow, and it has something to do with the Letter Group. I can feel it. And the message cut into her; how did Hu go against her own advice? Whatever it was, the killer knew about it, and she was murdered because of it. We need to get somebody over to BrentRidge to question Carmine Lemon again. The man knows something. We just have to pull it out of him."

"Well, I think the Medical Examiner knows something," Bessel stated loudly to hammer his point home.

Barry put his hands up in front of his chest and backed away from the hanging body, "I told you what I know."

"Not you," Captain Bessell said, shaking his head. "The other one."

"The fact is, Captain," Agent Hayes began, "with this latest homicide taking place while Mr. Shurek was in police custody, he's no longer a prime suspect. Unless you want to waste more time and place him under arrest for mishandling evidence, all so you can question him about a murder we *know* he didn't commit, we'll have to release him soon. No, I agree with Detective Haddick on this one. Perhaps we were a bit hasty in dismissing Mr. Lemon as someone who could provide some insight into this case." She turned to her partner, "Special Agent Cordell, would you mind taking a trip to visit our friend Carmine Lemon? Find out what was so special about the group's members that would lead someone to want to kill them."

"Yes, ma'am," he replied, nodding in agreement and striding for the door.

"As for you, Captain," she continued, "I trust you haven't received anything so significant from the neighbor that would have broken this case wide open?"

"Nothing we didn't already know. The neighbor was with the victim in the morning but didn't see her the rest of the night. She also claims she didn't hear anything either."

"We expected as much," Hayes responded. "What're your thoughts on all of this, Detective Haddick?"

She turned her full attention to me, making a bold statement to Captain Bessell that I wasn't someone to be dismissed. I let the moment sink in while I gazed at the body dangling before us. Then, I offered my thoughts.

"Let's assume the victims are all members of this Letter Group. They mingle, they tell stories, they get things off their chest. Maybe some of them even get together outside of the meetings to have flings or romantic involvements. Who knows? But the killer is there too, among them, has been all along, learning all about these people: their likes, their dislikes, their triumphs, their faults. Then, something upsets this person. And I think I'm finally starting to understand what's going on in this whack job's head.

"You've all asked why the killer seemed so fixated on me. The psycho's already told us; it was there in the first note. Whoever it is believes I've somehow disappointed them, and because of it, I've become a person of interest. The waitress, Francine, did something to let this person down. It was stated as such in the note the killer left in her hand. Whatever it was, it shattered the killer's faith in her. She couldn't be allowed to live, at least in the killer's mind. When the killer learned I was no longer on the case, the disappointment was so great, the sick fuck was ready to kill twice as many people. And in this latest.., message," I pointed up at Hu's bloody back, "it again speaks of disappointment. *'Why do they always disappoint? Look where it gets them.'* It gets them dead."

"Then I'd look out if I were you, Haddick," Captain Bessell spoke up. "You said you've already disappointed this guy. Maybe you're on his list."

"I don't think so," I replied. "This person would rather torture and torment me. Plus, I think the individual is too smart to try and kill me. I'm a cop. My death would bring too much heat."

"Or perhaps the killer believes you can redeem yourself," Agent Hayes interjected. "This person has done their homework. They don't like being disappointed, and if there is one officer who has shown a clear track record for not disappointing the people of this city, it would be you. Our killer *wants* to be caught and wants *you* to be the one to catch him. They want their faith restored. No more disappointments."

"Then they've come to the right place," I stated with conviction. "I *will* catch this son of a bitch. Then we'll see how well they can keep their disappointment in check."

Chapter 21

Why do I put myself in these situations? I should be out looking for some crazed lunatic who finds pleasure in killing people based on whatever letter is next in the alphabet. Instead, I'd found myself pondering the idea that a colleague could be the killer we've been after all along. How desperate am I getting?

First, there was Lenny, whose innocence was justly proven after another homicide took place while he was still in custody. Unless there was more than one killer, he wasn't our guy. I couldn't believe there was a part of me that actually considered he ever could have been. He's a strange little fucker; of that, there's no doubt. But to believe he was a killer is something I don't think I'll feel good about for a while.

And now, I've found myself mulling over the possibility that Vera could somehow be involved. What's wrong with me?

These were good people. I'd worked with them for years, yet this case had me doubting everything and everyone. Deep down, I didn't think Vera was the killer. Still, could I afford to dismiss even the smallest of possibilities? It's no secret the woman had had her share of problems with Internal Affairs. She wasn't exactly what one would consider a model law enforcement officer. That was painfully clear a few years ago when her brother was killed by a mugger, and after the perp had been arrested, she planted evidence on the scumbag to ensure he wasn't getting off on any technicalities. She was eventually found out, and although I did all I could to defend her from the inevitable backlash, IA came down on her brutally hard. But that didn't make her a killer. Neither did having all that weird shit she'd collected about serial killers. She was maybe a bit disturbed, but who wasn't in our line of work with all the shit we had to go through? And yet, here I found myself checking in with IT to dispel any doubts that lingered in this thick skull of mine. I suppose it was better than sitting at a desk or wasting time knocking on doors. Eliminating a suspect was still working the case, no matter how it was achieved

Every time I walked into the IT department, I half expected all of the techies to have their noses buried in their laptops, playing Minecraft, Call of Duty, or whatever the geeks were playing these days. Instead, it was like a ghost town in there.

"Hello," I cried out from the front of the large counter, which impeded all of us non-computer-skilled morons from entering their super secret domain.

"Yeah, just a sec," was returned from somewhere between the racks of servers, outdated hardware, and old tube monitors.

While waiting for the mysterious voice to make an appearance, I found myself amazed at how much old junk the IT Department kept stored on the shelves as if it would all be useful again someday. The place needed an overhaul similar to what the rest of the precinct went through, but the city never bothered to update this floor. The Mayor claimed it wasn't in the budget. What a crock; the budget issues never seemed to prevent him from getting his hefty raise. Either way, I didn't have time to daydream about the needed improvements, as just then, the person belonging to the voice stepped from one of the server aisles.

"Jim, what's going on?" he greeted.

"Hey, Dennis," I responded. "Where the hell is everybody?"

"Don't even get me started on that," Dennis replied. "Tom called out sick. Monica and Sreeham are setting up the new dispatch system. Um, let's see, Theresa's out on maternity leave. You knew she had a little girl, right?"

"Oh, no shit," I said.

"Yeah, three days ago. Both Mom and daughter are doing fine. So, yeah, what you see is what you get."

"That's okay," I said. "I'll take whatever help you can provide."

"Well, what do you need?" he asked. "Don't tell me your computer shit the bed again."

"No, not that kind of help," I replied. "I need to check the overhead camera footage from the lab last night."

"Sure, no problem, Jim. I'll just need the support ticket with your supervisor's signature."

"Dennis," I began, giving a sideways glance, "you know Frank is up to his eyeballs with that Alphabet Killer shit. He's also got the FBI breathing down his neck. He doesn't have time to deal with signing nonsense paperwork."

"Then get Captain Redfern to sign off on it," Dennis added. "You know I can't access the footage for you without proper approval."

"Cut the shit, Dennis," I replied heatedly. "It's me. I need five minutes. We could have been done by now, for Christ's sake."

"I don't know what to tell you, Jim," Dennis persisted. "I could lose my job."

"You're worried about losing your job?" I questioned. "I suppose that *would* be devastating. Almost as devastating as if your wife found out you've been boning Monica for months. How do you think that would go over, Dennis?"

His face turned as white as a sheet. He knew *exactly* how that would play out. I knew it was a low blow, but I needed to see that footage.

"You think I didn't know that?" I questioned. "I'm a goddamn detective, asshole. Now, are you going to show me the footage or not?"

Dennis scowled while he glared at me with pure hatred. I was burning a lot of bridges lately, but it was all for the sake of good. At least, that's what I kept telling myself.

"You're a son of a bitch; you know that?" Dennis stated, logging into the security footage.

"I've been told that once or twice," I answered, looking over his shoulder at the monitor.

"What are you looking for?" Dennis asked. "Make this quick."

"Pull up last night's footage between eight-thirty and nine o'clock."

A few keystrokes later and we were watching a recorded video of Vera and Danny running some tests on a few articles of evidence.

"Well, I'll be," I said, a relieved smile on my face. "And this is what time?" I asked.

"It's right there on the screen, asshole," Dennis snipped. "20:50 hours." He turned and looked at me snidely while I continued staring at the screen. "That's 8:50 if you didn't know."

"Yeah," I nodded, "I got that. Okay then," I said, slapping my palm on the counter. "That was all I needed. Painless. Thanks, Dennis," I said, smirking. "You've been a big help." Then I turned and walked out as if it had been no big deal, paying little attention to the middle finger Dennis was flipping me behind my back. It wasn't the smartest to piss off the IT folks. I've witnessed them hold onto some serious grudges. I was probably going to pay for that.

I felt a huge weight lifted off my shoulders. The video confirmed Vera was in the lab late the previous night. She wasn't the killer. I almost wanted to head down to the Dragon's Lair and apologize to her, but she wouldn't know what it was about. And if I told her, we'd have *two* killers on our hands. Well, the rest of the force would; *I'd* be dead. I thought better of it and decided I'd settle for a clear conscience. That's a win in my book.

I went back to my desk, where the room was incredibly silent. Almost all the other officers were out on the assignments the FBI laid out. Frank remained behind to finish up the paperwork on Lenny's release. I would have liked to have heard the conversation between Chief Copelli and the Mayor on that subject. Word came down that Lenny would face a suspension of all duties and that there would be a full investigation regarding his questionable activities. And what would that mean for all of the past cases with which he'd been involved? Would they be put under a microscope? Once word got out, defense attorneys would come swarming like flies on shit to overturn their guilty clients' cases. What a mess it would be. Great job, Lenny.

In the interim, Barry would be the acting Chief Medical Examiner until things were cleared up. Not to sound insensitive, but that was fine with me. Don't get me wrong; I liked Lenny a lot, but I just needed someone who knew his shit about dead bodies; I didn't care who it was. If that fell upon Barry, so be it.

Special Agent Cordell was taking his sweet-ass time at BrentRidge, questioning Carmine about the Letter Group. I hoped he fared better than me with that head-case.

Marion and the other two agents stayed in the field, scouring the Bowery district for any possible witnesses that might reveal themselves. They wouldn't find any. The residents in that community were tight-lipped when it came to matters of their own kind. If they knew who it was, they'd sooner lynch the bastard themselves than call the police.

As for me, I couldn't be out there. That's why I stayed at the station to think. I always did my best work in that bustling environment. Unfortunately, with the place being so quiet these days, the current environment wasn't what I was used to. But that was all about to change.

My ears perked up the moment I heard Frank slam the receiver down.

"Jesus fucking Christ!" he yelled, standing from his desk. Even from that distance, it came through loud and clear. I glanced at the wall clock, saw that it was just a few minutes before two, and thought, *that seems about right.* I could see through Frank's open door that he immediately got back on the phone. His head hung down, and from what I could see, his face looked distraught. I couldn't hear what he was saying, but he was rubbing his left temple vigorously as if to discourage a migraine from coming on. When the call ended, and he hung up the phone, this time more gently, he stepped from his desk and grabbed his jacket that hung from the coat rack by his door.

"Haddick!" he called out gruffly, exiting his office. "Grab your coat; you're coming with me."

"What's going on?" I questioned excitedly, standing up and grabbing my jacket from the back of my chair.

"We've got another body," he replied. "This one *just* happened. And we've got a witness."

"You're kidding me," I said, eyes wide, rushing to keep up with him as he headed for the door. My question was rhetorical, but Frank felt the need to answer.

"Do I look like I'm kidding?"

As we walked into the parking lot and Frank led me toward his vehicle, I questioned him further.

"Frank, talk to me. Where are we going?"

"Myrtle Drive," he answered. "Others are on their way."

"Myrtle Drive?" I inquired loudly, getting into the passenger seat. "That's two streets from my house. Fuck!"

Without thinking, I immediately pulled out my phone and dialed Ben. It bounced right to voicemail, which gave me an awful feeling in the pit of my stomach.

"Ben, it's Dad. If you're home, stay inside and lock the door. Call me when you get this message. I mean it. Don't go out. Call me."

I pulled the phone from my ear and looked at the screen to verify the number before hanging it up. It was an unthinking response but something I needed to see. My hands were shaking uncontrollably, which is something I had felt only once before: the first time I held Ben as a baby. Frank couldn't help but notice and tried his best to calm my nerves.

"Your kid's gonna be fine, Jim," he assured me, nodding his head as we pulled out onto the street. It was something people rattled off even when things *weren't* so fine. But I appreciated the sentiment. "This fucker isn't going backward in the alphabet," Frank continued. "Yeah, Ben's good. You know parents always go straight to worst case."

It was strange, but there was genuine concern in his voice as if he wasn't so confident the killer would stick to the rules of his own twisted game. I had that same thought.

"If the killer knows me, he knows I have a son. And he was just around the corner from my fucking house. That son of a bitch is playing with me, Frank. He's playing with me, and he's testing my patience. I'm going batshit crazy over here. I'm about ready to go Charles Bronson in Death Wish on this asshole. This witness had better give us something; I swear to Christ."

"Calm down, Jim. We're going to get this guy. I need you to stay focused."

"I *am* focused," I hollered, slamming my fist against the door's armrest. "Just get us to Myrtle Drive; it can't be only a coincidence this guy was around the corner from my house."

Frank was silent the rest of the short trip. He understood the littlest thing could set me off; he wasn't willing to take the chance. Smart decision.

Pulling up to the address provided by dispatch, we saw an elderly woman in front of the house, sitting on the top step. She wasn't alone, as it appeared Mick had arrived moments before. *How was he here already,* I thought. He was standing over her, taking notes, and occasionally placing his hand on the grief-stricken woman's shoulder to console her.

Frank and I stepped from his vehicle and trekked up the front lawn. We didn't think the owner would mind.

"I'll take it from here, officer," Frank jumped in immediately, allowing me to pull Mick to the side for a moment.

"How did you get here so quick, kid?" I asked.

Mick pointed diagonally down the street, "I was around the block interviewing folks when word came over the radio. I got over here as fast as I could."

"Did you check on the body?" I asked.

"I went in, yeah; she was already dead. Sorry, Jim, I couldn't stay there; I'm not built like you, you know?"

"Hey, it's okay, Mick," I said, placing my hand on his shoulder as he had done to the woman. "It took me a while to get used to it, too." You never got used to it; you only became numb to it.

I patted him on the arm and stepped back to Frank's side to listen to the woman's statement.

"…knew Izzy wasn't feeling well," the woman continued her story. "She was always sick with one thing or another, poor dear. I came over to bring her some homemade chicken soup." She pointed to the Tupperware dish beside her. "That's when I saw him right there through the window," she said, pointing over her shoulder. "He was kneeling over Isabelle's body. I didn't know what he was doing, but I knew he was up to no good. I wasn't thinking. I just yelled, 'Hey,' and pounded my fist against the door. I know I startled him. He jumped up and ran to the back door like a streak."

"And you're sure it was a man?" Frank asked.

"Oh, it was a man," she replied, nodding confidently.

"Would you be able to describe him, ma'am?" I asked. "Anything at all? Hair or skin color? His clothing? Was he thin? Was he overweight?"

"He wasn't overweight," she answered. "He looked fit. He *moved* like it, anyway. It was difficult to see with the glare in the window, but he had dark hair. Brown, I think. He was facing away from me; I couldn't see his face. I think he was white, but that could have been my own reflection I was seeing. Poor Izzy; will she be all right?"

Frank and I looked at each other, realizing the woman didn't know. Frank spoke up, "We're going to have her checked out as soon as the ambulance gets here, ma'am."

"I hope it's soon," the woman said. "The soup is getting cold."

Frank looked at me and subtly shook his head. The woman didn't understand the gravity of what she had just witnessed. At her age, it might've been for the best.

"And where do you live, Ms..?"

"Oliver," she jumped in. "Margret Oliver. You can call me Margie. I live next door," she replied, pointing to the tan house on her left. "Been there forty-seven years."

"And did you see Izzy often?" I asked.

"Who?" she questioned, looking puzzled at my inquiry.

"Izzy," I replied. "You said the woman who lived here was Isabelle."

"No, sir," she answered adamantly. "This is Gretchen's house. We've been neighbors since 1980. I don't know any Isabelle."

The woman was confused, perhaps suffering from dementia. We weren't going to get anything more useful out of her, and whatever we did get, we couldn't trust. So much for a witness. Just another dead end to match the trail of dead bodies.

"Thank you for your help, ma'am," Frank said, offering his hand to help her up from her seated position. "Officer Dooley will see that you get back home safely." He nodded to Mick and gestured toward the woman's house. Mick quickly sprinted forward and grabbed the woman's arm to lead her. "Oh, don't forget your bowl," Frank stated, picking it up and holding it out to her.

"Now, how did that get out here?" the woman questioned, aggressively swiping it from Frank's hand as if she thought he was trying to steal it.

I glanced at Frank, shrugged my shoulders, and smirked, "Well, you *do* look a little shady."

"Smartass," was his reply as he pointed to the road to alert me of Barry's arrival, followed by an ambulance.

Barry pulled in front of Frank's vehicle to allow the ambulance to squeeze into the driveway beside Mick's cruiser. We both watched as Barry exited his car, fumbling with a camera and notepad as he struggled to stretch latex gloves over his hands. Shouldering a leather bag, he trodded his way across the lawn, shaking his head.

"Long time no see, gentlemen," he greeted as he snuck by me onto the steps, stopping for a moment to check the progress of the EMTs in the driveway. "By the looks on your faces, I assume they wasted their gas getting here."

"We haven't gone in yet," Frank said. "But, Officer Dooley checked the body when he first arrived. Yet another homicide attributed to our piece-of-shit psychopath."

"Well, let's get this over with, shall we?" Barry stated, opening the front door.

He stepped inside and stopped in the middle of the floor, staring down at the victim's body, the blood still fresh on the area rug beneath her as it soaked into the fibers.

"I feel like we just watched this movie," Barry commented. "At least this one's not as messy as the last one." He reached into his jacket pocket and pulled out extra gloves. "Here, you'll need these," he said, handing them to Frank and me.

Frank put his hands up, "Oh no, I won't be needing those; I'm not touching shit. That's what Jim is here for." He nodded his head in my direction.

I gave him a sideways glare, "Thanks, Lieutenant."

"Your fucking case," he reminded me. "You get the honors."

I grabbed the gloves and began the laborious task of putting them on while Barry stepped forward and squatted beside the woman's right shoulder. She was lying face up with the majority of the blood isolated on the floor to her left, the singular culprit: an ice pick jabbed into the side of her neck.

At that moment, the EMTs arrived at the door, their medical kits slung over their shoulders. Barry looked at them and rudely waved his hand for them to go.

"Sorry guys; we won't be needing you," he said. "This one will be coming home with me."

Barry's demeanor was very different than that of Lenny's, who would have let the paramedics enter and crowd the crime scene simply because he wouldn't have wanted to rock the boat. It was unexpected but something that made me wonder if Barry should have been the one appointed to the position from the start. Whether he wanted it or not, it was his now.

As Barry continued to inspect the body, I felt Frank tap me on the arm. When I turned to him, he pointed to a chair situated by the front window where, upon its fabric, a great deal of blood had sprayed from the victim's neck. He wasn't pointing to the blood but to the purse sitting on the chair. I was about to step forward when Barry snapped at me.

"Hey! Not yet," he stated, reaching into his leather bag and pulling out some white, wrinkled items. "Put these booties on over your shoes and mind where you step."

I grumbled and gave him a dirty look before complying with his wishes. A dead body at a crime scene; this was Barry's show. I had to respect that.

After fitting the plastic booties over my shoes and feeling like an idiot, I stepped over the woman's legs, avoiding the blood stains, and retrieved the small handbag. Quickly rummaging through, I found a wallet with her identification inside. I held it up for Frank to see.

"Isabelle Stockton," I read aloud. "34 years old. That's our gal." I pointed to the victim.

"Yeah, well, your 'gal' died quick," Barry chimed in. "No visible bruises or scratches. There was no struggle. The arterial spray is focused linearly in one direction. The killer used one swift motion to stab the ice pick into her jugular, probably from behind. He didn't pull it out, probably expecting her to live longer if it remained in place. He would have been right. Based on the wound, however, it appears Ms. Stockton may have immediately collapsed while the killer's hand was still on the weapon. Her falling weight in his hands caused the ice pick to tear open a gash in her neck, forcing the immediate release of blood. I'd say she was dead in less than a minute."

"Jesus!" Frank blurted. "And this is our killer? How can we be sure it's the same guy?"

"Come on, Frank," I jumped in. "Isabelle, Ice pick. It's the Alphabet Killer."

"Well, I don't see a fucking letter cut into her, do you?"

"Not visibly, no," I replied. "It could be anywhere."

"Not really," Barry interjected. "The body hasn't been disturbed from how it landed. If we're not seeing anything, it's probably not here."

"Then the neighbor interrupted him before he could finish what he started," I said.

"It's possible," Barry responded. "Here's something interesting, though. The killer cut off her eyelids."

"What the fuck?" Frank grumbled.

"It's like he cut them off so that her eyes would remain open," Barry added.

"Why would he do that?" I asked. "If she was already dead, it's not like she could see anything."

"I don't think it was for her, Detective. I think it was for us." He looked down at Isabelle's open eyes once again, her stare locked skyward, then slowly tilted his head upward toward the ceiling. "Huh, would you look at that?"

Frank and I looked up to where Barry garnered our attention. Above the woman's gaze, attached to the ceiling by a thumbtack, a familiar note with the killer's unquestionable scribblings upon it.

"You satisfied now?" I questioned, sliding a nearby ottoman beside Barry so I could retrieve the note from the ceiling. I no sooner pulled it free from its resting place than Vera appeared in the doorway with three other officers standing behind her.

"Sorry I'm late to the party, guys," she said excitedly. "What fun stuff did I miss?"

"We don't need that right now, Vera," Frank objected. "You three," he continued, pointing at the officers still outside the door, "the suspect is on foot. You're looking for a Caucasian male with dark brown hair and a medium build. We believe he ran out the back door. Get on the radio and start having officers scour the surrounding streets. That includes you three."

The officers quickly scurried off, realizing Frank was in no mood for arguing. I stepped from the ottoman, staring at the paper in my hand. Vera noticed it immediately, which she vocalized in a way only Vera could.

"Shit Fuck! Is that what I think it is?"

I exhaled heavily, slightly nodding. "It is."

"Well, don't leave us in suspense, Dick Tracy. What does it say?"

I looked at the note and began to read the words.

Do you see what "I" sees, Detektive? The eyes are the windows to the soul. It's too bad "I"'s soul turned black long ago. She couldn't see the rong in what she was doing. But my eyes saw it, and now she'll never see again. Are you finally seeing, James? They've all been a disappointment. Poor, dead "I" was just one of many victims on my growing list. Count it with me, Detektive. Nine down, seventeen to go. As the letters inkrese, the number of sinners in this city dekrese. I'm sure that's one thing in which we see eye to eye. Ω

"That's the golden ticket right there, my friend," Vera stated, her eyes wide like a kid at Christmas.

"Will you cut the shit, Vera?" I shouted. "These are people's lives here. Show some fucking decency."

Vera stumbled back a step, caught off guard by my verbal assault. It served her right. I knew she had some distasteful infatuation with serial killers, but Jesus Christ, enough was enough. She needed to tone her excitement down and focus more on finding evidence. Frank caught on to that, too, as was apparent in his next order.

"Vera, I need you to check for prints. Start at the back door. This guy was spooked and ran out quickly. Maybe he left us something."

I jumped in, "We already know how this ends, Frank. We haven't found a single print at any of the crime scenes except for those of the victims."

"And we probably won't find any here," Vera added. "I can tell you right now; the front door is out. There's no sign of forced entry at all. The note made it sound like the two of them might've known each other. If that's the case, she probably let him in. He never even touched the door. I'll check the back, but I'm not expecting promising results." She looked down at the body, giving it a quick glance. "I'll need the ice pick before they haul her out of here." Then she pulled two small plastic bags from the manila envelope she'd been carrying, turned to me with an annoyed look, and slapped them against my chest. "And the note, before it's contaminated."

She wasn't happy I snapped at her earlier. It might have been a mistake on my part. I'd now have to deal with her more serious side, and things could get ugly real quick. I'd do my best not to disturb the apple cart and bag the evidence as she ever-so-subtly hinted.

Vera scuttled past me on her way to the back door while I slipped the killer's note safely into one of the plastic sleeves. Turning to Frank, I handed him the baggie and voiced my concern about being at the victim's house.

"I gotta get out of here, Lieutenant. That psycho is on the loose and I haven't heard back from Ben. I need to get home; I need to find him. This fucker is in my neighborhood. You've got capable people here. Whatever these guys find, I can comb over it later."

Frank gave me a disgruntled look that slowly faded to that of understanding.

"He's my son, Frank," I added.

Frank nodded his head toward the front door, "Get the hell out of here."

Before I could take a step, Barry chimed in, "Before you go, Detective, you might want to take a look at these," his eyes focused on the coffee table beside his left leg.

"What is it?" I asked.

He reached down and snatched a pile of credit cards from its surface and scanned the front of them briefly.

"I think I know why our victim was targeted," he stated, handing the stack of plastic over to me.

"What the hell is this?" I questioned, shuffling through the credit cards. "None of these belong to our victim. We've got Charlotte, Mary, Andrea.., what did the neighbor say her previous neighbor's name was?"

"Margret," Frank answered.

"Yup, she's here too," I said. "There's a whole stack of people here, and none of them is our victim."

"Those are skimmed or stolen cards from the look of it," Frank added. "Son of a bitch."

"So.., Izzy here has been copying or stealing credit cards and maybe even people's identities?" I questioned. "And our guy killed her because of it."

"'*I's soul turned black long ago,*'" Frank said, recalling the killer's words from the note. "That's gotta be what he was talking about."

"I can't deal with this right now, guys," I said, my mind still preoccupied with Ben's whereabouts. I handed the cards back to Barry, along with the second plastic evidence bag. "It's something; I know. But I need to get out of here."

Not waiting for another response, I headed straight for the front door where, as I exited, I bumped into Mick on his return from delivering the neighbor safely to her house.

"Mick, give me a ride, will you?"

"Sure, Jimmy," he replied. "Let me just tell the Lieutenant."

"He's fine with it," I answered. "Let's go."

Mick was an easy one to push around. He always had been. And he took orders from me easier than from others since I was like an older brother to him. I didn't know if that was good or bad, but for now, I needed it to be that way.

As we got into his squad car and began to pull away, The FBI's black SUV arrived. From the passenger window, Special Agent Hayes waved for us to stop, to which Mick complied. As I said, he was easy to push around. Mick rolled down his window.

"Where are you two headed?" she inquired.

Leaning over toward Mick to respond through his window, "I'm looking for my son. The killer's out there somewhere, and I haven't been able to contact Ben. I don't like that this shit is happening so close to my home."

"I understand, Detective," she said. "Do what you gotta do. Good luck."

I nodded, then sat back in my seat. "Let's go, Mick," I said, waving him onward.

Mick didn't say anything as he pulled away. After hearing what I told Hayes, he understood why I was in such a rush. His face showed concern. Even though he and Ben weren't that close, he had expressed to me how he always felt like he was an uncle to Ben. And although I didn't always succeed at showing it, he knew how much Ben meant to me. At that moment, there was nothing else that mattered.

I think Mick knew I was putting him in a horrible situation. If anything happened to Ben, if that sicko son of a bitch laid a finger on my boy, the badge wouldn't hold me back. There would be more blood spilled. Only, it would be that belonging to the Alphabet Killer. And Mick, he'd have one hell of a decision to make: stop me from killing the man who took everything from me, or go against everything he knew was right and look the other way while I took my vengeance. It's a good thing Mick was an easy one to push around. I'd tell him to look away. Or maybe hold the bastard down.

Chapter 22

INTO THE DEEP END

"Ben?" I called out, my heart racing while I sprinted to his bedroom. "Are you here?" There was no response. "Shit!" I exclaimed. "Ben!" I couldn't stop yelling for him even though I knew he wasn't home.

Mick stood in the doorway, unsure of what to do. He then tried to offer calming words.

"He's probably out with a friend, Jimmy. I'm sure there's nothing to worry about."

"You don't know my kid, Mick," I snapped. "He's never had many friends, and the one he *did* have, which he stayed with for a couple of weeks, just kicked him out of his apartment. I have to find him."

Instinctively, I reached for my phone again and dialed Ben's number. And again, it went directly to voicemail. I hung up and frantically began texting.

Ben, where are you? I need you to call me as soon
as you get this. It's important.

"Goddammit, kid!" I yelled in frustration. "Check your cell phone." I felt like I was being a bit paranoid, but I couldn't help it. When a murder takes place so close to your home, and the killer is roaming free, you suddenly become more protective. When you can't find your kid during all of it, it jumps to a whole new level of fear.

"We gotta go looking for him, Mick," I ordered, striding back toward the front door.

"Sure thing, Jimmy," he agreed, stepping aside to let me walk past as he closed the door behind me. We both rushed to the car in silence, having no clear plan. Once we got in, however, and Mick realized I hadn't given any directive, he opened up.

"I mean, where are we going?" he asked. "Where does Ben like to hang out?"

"I don't fucking know," I barked. "He likes going to the movies. Just drive for now."

Mick pulled away, turning left out of the driveway.

"I'll head toward the theater downtown," he said. "Maybe we'll see him along the way. Do you think he would have gone to his friend's apartment?"

"I don't know, Mick. I don't even know where the kid lives. Fuck, I didn't want to have to do this."

I pulled out my phone and clicked on my ex's number, knowing I would catch hell from her. I knew she'd bitch to me about how lousy of a father I was. What was I to do; Ben was an adult. He could do what he wanted. If she had her way, he'd be locked in his room until he was thirty.

"Hello?" her voice sounded through the speaker.

"Karen, has Ben contacted you?"

"No, why? What's going on?"

That was the question I didn't want her to ask. I didn't have time to get into an argument with her.

"I need to know where David lives," I replied. "Can you give me his address?"

"I don't have his address," she answered.

"Phil brought him home before," I said loudly. "How can you not know where he lives?"

"How can *you* not know where he lives, Jim?" she threw back at me heatedly. "Christ, the kid lives in the city, and Ben was staying with him."

That was exactly what I was hoping to avoid. It didn't help that I had Karen on speaker, causing Mick to stare uncomfortably forward, trying to act as if he wasn't listening. He knew our situation enough to know this was old hat. He'd heard us arguing many times, even while Karen and I were still married. Still, I'm sure it was awkward for him to listen to it now.

"Can you please check with Phil then?" I pleaded.

"Why are you asking, Jim?" she questioned. "Tell me what's going on."

"Jesus Christ!" I exploded. "I just need an address, Karen. Can you do that for me?"

"As a matter of fact, I can't," she stated. "Phil's not here right now."

"Then can you..," my words were cut short as an incoming call from Ben flashed across my screen. I felt a relieved tingle run down my spine. "Never mind; Ben's calling now."

"Jim, are you going to explain..."

I hung up on her to switch over to Ben's call. She'd forgive me. Who was I kidding? She wouldn't. But I didn't care; that wasn't my immediate concern.

"Ben!" I said excitedly. "Where are you? I've been trying to reach you." I could feel the tension draining from me as I held back tears that filled my eyes. I did everything I could to keep my voice steady.

"Yeah, I got your text," he responded. "That's why I'm calling. What's up?"

"Are you okay?" I questioned, automatically assuming the worst-case scenario. "I left you a voice message too. Where are you?"

"I'm fine, Dad," he answered. "Why are you acting so weird?"

"Something has happened," I said. "Can you please just tell me where you are?"

"I'm at the Y," he replied.

"The YMCA?"

"Yeah. It's kind of boring at the house, Dad. I had to keep myself busy *somehow*. Sorry, I didn't get your message until I stepped out. They don't have the greatest cell service here."

"It's okay, son," I assured him. "Stay put, would you; I'm coming to pick you up."

Mick took the next left, finally traveling toward a known destination.

"What's going on, Dad?" Ben asked.

"I'll explain later. Just stay there; I'm close by."

"Okay," he said. "I'll wait here."

"I love you, Ben." The words rolled off my tongue effortlessly, making me wonder why I hadn't said them as often as I used to. That was going to change.

"Okaaayy," he replied, sounding confused by the expression of such feelings. "I love you too, Dad."

My thumb lingered over the "end call" button, unable to press it as if there was so much more for me to say. I never got the chance, as Ben did the honors by hanging up on his end.

"See, like I said," Mick spoke, "nothing to worry about."

"Yeah," I nodded, exhaling a sigh of relief. I didn't actually believe that, though. Somewhere out there, a killer was playing a deadly game, and for whatever reason, he wanted me involved. For the first time, it hit me. As long as that freak was on the loose, I couldn't be sure of my son's safety. Maybe sending him back to his mother's house *was* the right thing to do. If only I could convince Ben of that. I had to. Karen was right; I couldn't guarantee his safety.

The YMCA was only a couple of blocks from the house, but it seemed like hours before we rounded the corner onto its street. I could see Ben standing by the entrance, his duffle bag slung over his shoulder. He started shaking his head as he saw us arrive in Mick's cruiser. We pulled up along the front curb, and I immediately stepped out to give him a hug, which caused him to flinch away.

"What's the matter; can't I give my son a hug?" I said with a smirk, realizing his embarrassment in front of Mick.

"Sorry, Dad, I'm just all sweaty."

"I can see that. Did you have a good workout?"

"Yeah," he replied. "First one in a while."

"Come on," I said, reaching for the back door. "Let's get you out of here."

"You're not going to make me ride in the back of this, are you?" he questioned, his hand extended as he gestured toward the open door.

"What's wrong with that?" I asked.

"People are going to see me and think I'm some criminal."

"Stop it," I said. "You used to love riding in the back when you were a kid. Besides, the window's tinted; nobody will see you."

He shook his head but accepted, rolling his eyes and tossing his bag in the back while sliding into the seat.

"Hey, Mick," Ben nodded.

"How ya doing, kid?" Mick replied, looking through the rearview mirror and putting his hand up as a sort of wave.

The moment I sat down, the questions came like rapid fire.

"So, why did you pick me up?" he asked. "You said something's happened. What's going on; is it Mom?"

"No, it's not your Mom," I answered. "But that brings up something I want to talk to you about." I paused for a moment to give Mick direction. "Bring us back to the station, would you, Mick?" He nodded. Then, I continued with Ben. "I think you should go back and stay with her. Just for a little bit."

"What? No Dad. I like it with you. Where's this coming from?"

I looked at Mick for any sign of silent advice. He saw me glancing at him, shifted his eyes in my direction, and shrugged his shoulders. It wasn't much help. I turned my head sideways, staring at Ben peripherally, hoping he wouldn't freak out once I told him the news.

"There's been another murder. It was in our neighborhood."

"What? Holy shit!" Ben exclaimed. "Oops, sorry, Dad. But seriously, somewhere by us? The same killer?"

"Yeah," I replied. "And that's why I think it would be best if you went back to stay with your Mom."

"No way. I'm not doing it. I'm not leaving you alone, Dad."

" Ben, I..,"

"You can't make me," he shouted over me. "Besides, didn't you say this guy was following the alphabet? He's already past B."

"That's not the point," I jumped in. "This guy, this Alphabet Killer, he's toying with me. He's trying to get in my head. If he's in our neighborhood now, he probably knows where I live. If he wanted to get to me, he could go after you. I can't have you around that. I need you safe."

"Well, you don't have a choice, Dad," he argued. "I'm not going back to Mom's house. So unless you want me out on the street, I'm staying."

"Damn it, Ben!" I shouted. "I'm trying to protect you. Why don't you..?" Just then, my buzzing phone kept me from saying something I might have regretted. I pulled it from my pocket and put it to my ear, letting my frustration loose on the caller instead.

"What?" I yelled into the phone.

"*Wow, someone's in a mood,*" Special Agent Hayes returned. "*I take it you're still looking for Ben?*"

"Sorry," I said, rubbing the side of my head with my other hand. "No, we found him; he's safe. What's going on?" I glanced back at Ben, hoping he would understand how dangerous this was for him.

"*I thought you'd want to know,*" she stated, "*Special Agent Cordell just informed us about what he was able to pry out of Mr. Lemon.*"

"Anything interesting?" I asked.

"*I'll let you decide,*" she offered. "*My agent said Carmine wasn't so cooperative at first. He needed some extra coercing. Anyway, he told Cordell that everyone who joined The Letter Group was broken, one way or another. They all had issues, some of them quite serious. Drugs, alcohol, divorce, depression, break-ups, you name it. It was more of a support group than anything else. Cordell continued to pester him about the members. Carmine couldn't supply any names, or genders, for that matter, but he did eventually recall someone in the group who had been very vocal about some of the other members' activities. He said he thought it was D.*"

"That would be Denise," I said. "She was the first victim we discovered. I wonder what she was so vocal about?"

"*I don't have an answer for you, Detective. I'll let you work that part out. Oh, and before I forget,*" she continued, "*one of the officers at the station said the father of one of the victims dropped off a list of names for you. He said you were expecting them.*"

"That must have been Amber's father," I said. "With everything that'd been going on, I completely forgot."

"*Well, the officer put the list on your desk,*" she added.

I glanced back and saw Ben sitting quietly in the back seat. I didn't know what to do, but I knew I couldn't leave him alone. This case was becoming too much for me. Maybe it was too much from the start. I never asked for it; it just landed on my lap. Maybe it was time to raise the white flag.

"You know what?" I began. "Maybe you should give that list to Richie. He's been wanting this case since he first learned of it. In fact..," I glanced at Mick and then at Ben, "I'm done. I just want to go home and spend time with my son, to be with him and protect him."

Mick turned to me with a shocked look as he pulled into the station.

"I'm sorry, Agent Hayes," I continued, "there's no talking me out of it. I don't need this shit. But I need my son, and he needs his father. And right now, that's all I can think about. Deliver that message to Frank, would you?"

"*Jim, you can't just..,*"

"I gotta go, Marion," I said as I ended the call.

I didn't feel good about hanging up on her, but I've realized there are things in my life that are more important to me. I was thankful Ben was all right, but the fear of losing him had opened my eyes. No amount of doing good in this city was going to clean the filth from under my heels. Why continue to try? Why did it have to be *my* burden? It didn't, and it wouldn't be anymore.

I opened up the door and expressed my thanks to Mick before hopping out. He looked dumbfounded, like a puppy watching its master leave for work. I didn't know what to say, so I remained silent, closing the door. I opened the back door to let Ben out, who looked relieved to be exiting the police vehicle, then handed him my car keys.

"Go wait for me in the car," I said. "I have to go in and grab a few things."

Ben nodded, slung his bag over his shoulder, gave Mick a quick wave, then started for my car. I looked in through the open back door. Mick was staring at me through saddened, unbelieving eyes.

"Thanks again, Mick. And do me a favor, huh; catch that sick fucker."

I watched his head nod as I closed the door. He slowly pulled away, staring at me through the rearview as if he thought this was the last time he was seeing me. It wasn't. I promised I'd still go over and eat his wife's horrible cooking. Just when I thought I couldn't feel worse. But with that thought, I felt a smirk penetrate my lips, and I shook my head as I turned to make my way into the station to gather some things.

The station was still quiet. Everyone was either out looking for the killer or at the crime scene. Not me, though. I'd done enough for the people of this putrid city. And what did it ever get me? A destroyed marriage, a broken family, and a child I couldn't protect. Fuck this shit. Let someone else lead the charge for a change. I wasn't the only detective, and I couldn't be the only one holding this city on his shoulders.

I stood at my desk, staring at the paperwork and other items collected throughout the investigation. Someone could easily pick up where I left off. It's not like we had a lot to go on. Frank would understand. The other officers would understand. And the victims' families would.., I paused, my thoughts flashing to Cameron's parents holding each other in their garage while I promised them I would do all I could to catch their son's killer. I promised the same to Amber's parents. I thought about the sheer terror on Alfred's face when he discovered Eva's body behind his store. And what about Mr. Manfredi when he found Francine dead in the freezer? She was like a daughter to him. And Denise had two daughters who now had to grow up without their mother. None of the victims deserved to die the way they had. They counted on us to keep them safe and protected. I had sworn an oath to the people of this community to do just that; it was my job. I made promises. I wanted to help people. I wanted to protect my family. What father didn't? And as I looked at the box of Amber's things, I couldn't help but think I was letting everybody down. If Ben were killed, I would stop at nothing to find the murderous scumbag who did it. Did these other victims and their families deserve any less? I knew the answer before I muttered the word.

"Fuck."

No matter what I said, I still had a job to do; and I was going to do it. I couldn't rest knowing there was a killer out there. I grabbed the partially empty box and started stacking the files from my desk into it. Lastly, once the box was full, I grabbed the framed picture of Amber and the scratched-out figure, a reminder that her death, as well as all the others after her, would not be in vain. People were counting on me to bring justice for their loss. I wouldn't let them down.

I walked out with a renewed sense of purpose. I didn't want to leave Ben alone at the house, but that didn't mean I had to stop doing what was right. If I had to comb through everything I had again, then that's what I'd do. There had to be something I was missing. The killer *wanted* to be caught. It's why he was playing the game. It's why he was leaving me notes. It was all laid out for me; I just had to find it.

I placed the box and the picture in the back seat of my car while Ben patiently waited for me in the front. He didn't say a word, perhaps nervous I was going to drive him back to his mother's house. I wasn't. He was coming home with me. He was an adult; he'd made his decision. Whatever shit he was going through with his mother, I wasn't going to contribute to it.

On the ride back to my place, I wanted to open up to him, but I didn't have the words. He'd seen me place the box of materials in the back, so he knew all my earlier spouting about giving up was bullshit. I hoped that wasn't a disappointment to him.

Just as we pulled onto our street, my phone buzzed again. It wasn't unexpected. Someone was going to be looking for my ass. I pulled out my phone, ready to explain the misunderstanding, but the text message I received was from an unknown number.

```
You had your three days, Detective. I've seen no
results. It is my turn now. I warned you of my
vengeance. This will come to an end.
```

Shit! That was Papa Rio; it had to be. I knew it because of our previous conversation, but unfortunately, no one else knew of it. Then again, why should I care if he takes the fucker out? Because I was a cop, that's why. We couldn't have people running around like goddamn vigilantes, exacting their revenge on others, no matter how justified it might seem. And sadly, I knew I wouldn't be able to prove who the text came from. Papa

Rio was too smart to do something so stupid as to send a text from his own phone. He would have covered his tracks and discarded the phone so that the number couldn't be traced back to him. That's all I needed right now, another loose cannon on the street.

That concern would have to wait as I pulled into my driveway. I turned the car off and looked at Ben.

"You're stuck with me now, kid."

Ben flashed a slight smile. "Thanks, Dad." Then he got out and ran into the house. I gathered up the items from the backseat and slowly followed suit. Ben had already made his way to the bathroom and started a shower. I decided I would sit on the couch, relax my thoughts, and start sifting through the box's contents. If there was something within these documents, I was determined to find it.

Unfortunately, the task was never as easy as it played out in my head, and fifteen minutes later, I was still staring at the same few documents I had pulled from the top of the stack. It was going to be a long night.

As Ben exited the bathroom to get dressed, I thought about once again asking for his help. It would go against police procedure, but a fresh set of eyes couldn't hurt. It had to be better than going crosseyed, staring at the same bits of evidence and the same framed picture of Amber I'd had from the start.

A few minutes later, Ben stepped out of his bedroom, wiping the remaining water from his hair. Before I could speak up, he offered his own thoughts.

"I know why you do it, Dad," he said, standing beside the couch and draping the damp towel over his shoulder. "I know why it's so important to you. You have to look out for those who can't look out for themselves. There are a lot of people with problems out there, and most of them don't have you to save them."

"I don't know *who* I'm saving anymore, son" I responded, "but I appreciate the sentiment."

"I'm serious," he continued. "Think about everyone you've helped over the years. It's too many to count. So, as much as you wanted to give it all up, I'm glad you decided to keep at it. I'm proud of you, Dad."

"Hey," I jumped in. "It's not your job to be proud of *me*, it's my job to be proud of *you*."

"I wish I could give you a reason to be proud of me," he responded. "I'm not like you, Dad. I couldn't even help David after his breakup, and look how that turned out. He tried to kill himself."

"I don't want you talking like that," I said. "You hear me? I've never been more proud of..," I stopped in midsentence, glancing down at the picture on my lap. Suddenly, a feeling in my gut gripped my insides and began twisting. It was that feeling every good detective relied upon when logic and evidence weren't enough.

"What did you just say?" I asked.

Ben looked at me confusedly, "I said David tried to kill himself."

"Before that," I said.

He shrugged his shoulders, uncertain of what I was asking, "I said I couldn't help him with his breakup."

All at once, Agent Hayes' words flooded my head. It was her relayed message from Agent Cordell that stabbed into me. He said all the members of The Letter Group were broken. They all had issues, including those who had been through breakups. Carmine even remembered a particular member being more vocal about the others. He said he believed it was D. I naturally assumed he was referring to Denise since she was a victim of the Alphabet Killer and had a D cut into her. But now, I feared I may have had it all wrong.

With renewed excitement, I quickly skimmed through the papers in the box, searching for the one file I hoped would eliminate doubt. Marion told me Amber's father had dropped off a list of Amber's known acquaintances and that the file was placed on my desk. I piled everything from my desk into the box, so it had to be there.

A moment later, and with my heart racing, I held the folder in my hands. I opened the front cover and began scanning down the list, praying I wouldn't see it. Unfortunately, praying never did squat for me, and in seconds, I was staring at the name under the "coworker" column that caused my heart to get lodged in my throat: David Forrester. I began to question how I hadn't seen it: the scratched-out face, the breakup, the sudden change in his behavior, and now, his name on the list. It was David all along; I could feel it. How was I going to break the news to Ben about his friend? How could I tell him I believed David was The Alphabet Killer?

Chapter 23

WRONG TURN

"**D**ad, you're scaring me," Ben cried. "What's going on? Why are you looking at me like that?"

I wasn't sure *how* I was supposed to look after finding out my son's friend was the sadistic killer I'd been hunting. The color must have left my face when I first read David's name on Amber's list. I didn't know how to tell him. I just wanted this all to be over.

"Ben, I..," I couldn't get the words out as he stared at me through fearful eyes. He was going to learn sooner or later, but I couldn't bring myself to do that to him. Not as his Dad, anyway. That's when the cop in me took over. "You need to tell me where David lives."

"What? Why?" he questioned.

He had a nervous look on his face, shifting his eyes to the paperwork on my lap and then back to me.

310

"What's going on, Dad?" he repeated. "What is that?"

"Ben, I need to know right now where David lives. Tell me where his apartment is."

"No! Not until you tell me what this is about," he responded. "Why are you asking about David?"

"Goddammit, Ben!" I yelled. "I'm not fucking around! Tell me where he lives."

Shaken by my raised voice, Ben uncharacteristically lashed out verbally in defense.

"I'm not telling you." Then, he aggressively swiped the file from my lap and turned away, curiously skimming through the document to see what had prompted my sudden questioning.

I jumped to my feet, causing the framed picture on my lap to drop to the floor, cracking the glass. Normally, that would have caused me to pause, but in my irritated state, I thought nothing of it as I reached for Ben's shoulder. He tugged away before I could get a solid grip, took a few steps to distance himself from me, then turned to face me, his eyes still focused on the sheet in his hands.

"What is this, Dad?" he asked. "Why is David's name on this list?"

Rather than fuel the already heightened hostility we seemed to have found ourselves in, I reached forward and gently clasped the file between my fingers but left it in his hands until he looked up at me. Then I slowly pulled it away, my sympathetic face giving him all the information he needed.

A look of fear renewed in Ben's eyes as he stammered with his words, "Dad, you.., you don't think..,"

"Tell me where he lives, Ben," I said in a calm voice. "I'll go pick him up and bring him down to the station for questioning, that's all. It'll be better if I do it instead of someone else."

"You can't think he's the killer," Ben stated.

"If he's not the killer," I began, "then there's no reason to be concerned. He'll be on his way, and he can go about his business. It's as simple as that. Now come on; give me his address."

"But he's my friend," Ben said sullenly. "He wouldn't kill anybody."

"And maybe he didn't," I responded. "But I don't have time for this right now, Ben. I need to find him. Tell me where he is."

"I-I'll tell you," he said, "but I'm coming with you."

"Absolutely not," I stated, my voice raised once again. "You're staying put."

"No, Dad," Ben argued. "I'm not going to sit here, wondering what's going on. If you want to know where David lives, I'll tell you. But you're taking me with you."

He was a stubborn kid; I'll give him that. Did he get that from me, or was his mother to blame? Either way, I could see it in his face; he wasn't going to back down. The only way he was giving up David's address was if he went along for the ride. I didn't have time for this. I could take other avenues to try and pin down his address, but it would take too long. If my suspicions about David were correct, I needed to get him off the street before he could harm anyone else. I couldn't believe my kid was holding the cards on this one.

I gave him a stern look, exhaling heavily from my nose so that he knew I wasn't happy. I pulled my keys from my pocket and pointed my index finger at him. "You'll do as you're told, and there will be no arguing along the way; you hear me? Grab your jacket." I couldn't believe I was catering to his demand, but at least it would allow me to keep an eye on him; I'd know he was safe from that psycho.

Ben's eyes widened, perhaps surprised I gave in to his plea. I had little choice. If David was the Alphabet Killer, he was a threat to everyone while he remained on the loose. Ben nodded and darted for his room. A moment later, he emerged, slipping his second arm through his jacket sleeve as he quickly strolled by me to the door.

"Let's go, Dad," he said, opening the door and stepping out.

All I could do was shake my head in frustration.

By the time I walked outside, Ben was already in the passenger seat. I knew he was worried about his friend, but I thought maybe he was also a bit excited to go out on a case with his old man. It could have been exciting for me too, but at the moment, I was only concerned with Ben's safety. Every instinct told me I should be leaving him at home. Instead, I was potentially placing him in danger. It didn't sit well with me. I wouldn't be winning any Father of the Year award, that was for sure. Then again, David knew where we lived. Maybe bringing Ben along was less of a danger.

Bolting from the driveway, I asked again, "Are you going to tell me where he lives now or what?"

"You promise you won't stop the car and force me out?" he questioned, looking at me as if he didn't trust me.

"I don't like that you think you can make demands, Ben, but I'm not going to make you get out. I promise you. I only want you to be safe. If I wanted, I could have made a call to Phil to get his address. Now tell me where we're going."

I could feel his stare upon me as if he were gauging how honest I was being with him. He must have determined my sincerity as he straightened himself in his seat, looked forward, and opened up.

"He's at the Vinmore Apartments on South Street."

"Was that so hard?" I questioned, shaking my head in annoyance.

I hit the address book on my dash and dialed Special Agent Hayes. It was probably overkill, calling in the FBI, but if I was right and didn't report in, I'd never hear the end of it. And since I needed to call in backup anyway, it was as good a choice as any. Plus, they could help keep an eye on Ben.

"Special Agent Hayes," her voice played through the speakers.

"This is Haddick," I began. "I've got a line on a suspect. I've got good reason to believe he's our guy. His name is David Forrester. I'm heading to the Vinmore Apartments now to pick him up."

"Okay, we'll meet you there, Detective," she said. "Don't engage the suspect until backup arrives."

"Screw that," I returned. "I've got this. Besides, there's no way I'm giving this fucker a chance to slip away. I told you before, I'm taking this bastard down."

"Be smart about this, Jim," Hayes said. "We don't need you being a loose cannon. If the suspect you're after *is* the Alphabet Killer, there's no telling what he'll do if you show up at his door. We're on our way. Stand down until we get there so we can make sure the property is covered. We don't want him slipping away."

"I'll keep that in mind," I returned before hanging up. I think she understood what that meant. If I had the chance to take the killer down, I wasn't going to hesitate, not when he'd been so elusive. Once I had him in custody, she could play tiddly-winks with him for all I cared. I just wanted him off the street.

"I think you're making a mistake, Dad," Ben stated. "I know David; he can't be the killer."

"Sometimes you only think you know someone, Ben," I responded. "You said yourself he started acting strangely. Then he kicked you out of his apartment. I'd be willing to bet it was becoming too difficult for him to continue his extra-curricular activities with you there. He needed you gone."

"That's crazy!" Ben shouted. "You've known David for years. Has he ever once given you the impression he could do the things you're accusing him of doing? Do you honestly think he could be a killer?"

"Anyone can be a killer," I said. "I've seen it. Sometimes all it takes is a little push to send someone over the edge. With David, it was a breakup he couldn't handle."

"That doesn't make him a killer, Dad," Ben shouted. "God, why won't you listen to me? He's not like that."

"You don't know what you're talking about, Ben," I yelled back. "I've been doing this a long time. I know you don't want to believe your friend could be the maniac who has been terrorizing this city, but it's time you grew up and realized that not everyone is who they appear to be. Not everyone in your world can be as perfect as you want them to be."

"I'm learning that now, Dad," he jabbed, lifting his left leg and placing his foot on the dash while crossing his arms about his chest. He turned his eyes toward his passenger window to avoid my stare. His face showed his disappointment even more than his body language. I knew he could see me in the reflection, glancing his way every few seconds to check on him, but he wanted nothing to do with me. And to think, we were getting along so well, too. But once again, the job got in the way. It was always the job. But for once, it wasn't about me.

Ben remained silent, shaking his head in denial, probably regretful that he told me where David lived. At the moment, it didn't matter. I could be driving to an empty apartment, for all

I knew. David could be out searching for another victim. I hoped that he was home, but if not, I had no problem waiting as long as I needed until he came back. One way or another, this was going to end today.

Ben continued to stare silently out the window, avoiding any eye contact, even as we turned onto David's street and pulled up in front of the apartment building. I parked along the front curb instead of the side lot, wanting to maintain eyesight of the front door. I ducked my head slightly to peer out Ben's window at the building's face to get a good feel for the layout. The building had gone through renovations in the past year to make it look grander, but it still didn't compare to the two larger apartment buildings across the street. In this case, that was a good thing. Fewer floors meant fewer stairs to climb.

Still choosing to ignore me, Ben didn't want to hear anything I had to say, but right now, he had no choice.

"What apartment number is he in?" I asked.

"You're so smart; why don't you figure it out," he said without removing his stare from the side window.

"This isn't a game, Ben," I said, reluctantly raising my voice again. "People have been killed. Do you understand? Do you want that to keep happening? The best way to prove David isn't the killer is to let me take him in and clear his name. Now tell me which unit he's in."

Ben turned his head slightly toward the front windshield, his lower lip quivering as if he wanted to offer up what I requested. His eyes shifted back and forth like he was struggling to make the decision that he knew was right. Eventually, reason won out.

"You promise you're not going to hurt him." He spoke.

"I'm a police officer, Ben. I'm not going to hurt him. I'm going to bring him in for questioning, that's all."

He looked at me through saddened eyes. He and David had been friends since grade school. I could tell it was hard for him to accept the horrible possibility. In the end, he knew what had to happen.

"Apartment 3C," he offered, turning back to stare at the apartment building through his window.

I nodded, knowing he could see me in the glass, then opened my door and got out. I stood motionless, holding the door open, afraid to walk away without saying something to Ben. I leaned into the doorway to speak with him, to try to make him understand why this was necessary.

"You think I do what I do to help people," I began. "Well, you're wrong. I do what I do to protect *you.* You're everything to me, Ben, and I never want to see you hurt. If there's someone out there that can harm you, I want to stop them. That's why the job always seemed to come first. It wasn't because I didn't care about you; it was *because* I cared about you. It was my job to ensure you didn't grow up in a city where you had to be afraid. I wouldn't let that happen. You're my son, and I love you. I'll always love you."

I knew from his awkward shifting motions he understood, even if he refused to respond.

"Stay in the car and lock the door," I continued, still with no response. "I mean it, Ben. Lock the door and do not open it under any circumstances."

I shut the door and walked toward the entrance, glancing back once to see Ben watching me intently. Once at the building's main entrance, I pulled the front door open and disappeared inside.

Upon entering, the smell of urine and wet dog fur, which permeated the dimly lit hallway, assaulted my senses. The outside façade had clearly spewed lies to all who gazed upon the building's exterior. The annoying buzz of an overhead fluorescent light broke the otherwise silent space as I gleaned four apartment doors, two along each side wall, leading to a singular staircase at the end of the hall. I walked forward, noticing Units 1A and 1C on the left, with 1B and what I assumed to be 1D on the right (the last door was missing the faded, brushed nickel adornment). Passing by 1C, I heard a baby start to cry, which was immediately followed by a woman's shrieking voice telling the "little brat" to "shut the fuck up." That was a distraction that would have normally given me pause. It would have taken me all I had to walk away without at least knocking on the door. But not today; I had more pressing matters garnering my attention.

The Vinmore apartments, like many older buildings in the city, hadn't yet been brought up to current handicapped accessible regulations. Having no elevator, I traversed the creaking staircase up to the first landing, where it took a one-hundred-and-eighty-degree turn in the opposite direction up to the second floor. I wondered if, through the seemingly paper-thin walls, the noise from the stairs often alerted the tenants of unwelcome visitors. I hoped the renters were too used to the foot traffic to pay much attention.

The second floor looked like a carbon copy of the first, with apartments 2A through 2D residing along its two walls. It was safe to assume the next floor, as well, would offer no unusual surprises. Outside apartment 2A, an old, beaten tricycle sat riderless, its makeshift seat fashioned from a small throw pillow that had been duct taped to the shaft. Directly across, at apartment 2B, the occupants tried their best to spruce up the joint with what little they had to work. The equivalent of putting makeup on a pig, a colorful doormat sat in front of the door, a small plant stand with a withering plant begging for water beside it, and an out-of-place picture of William Shatner hung from a nail above it. It seemed like an odd compilation of items, but who was I to judge?

Staying my course, I took the next flight of rickety stairs two at a time, thinking fewer stairs meant less noise. It would have made no difference if they belted out a tune, as when I arrived on the third floor, the very subject of my purpose for being in the building was standing in the hallway, locking the door to apartment 3C. David hadn't noticed me at the top of the stairs as he jiggled his keys in the lock, but I immediately noticed *him*. I also couldn't help but notice what he was wearing. He wore the familiar shirt forever burned into my memory, belonging to that of the scratched-out face, confirming he was the boy in the picture with Amber. Not that it mattered anymore.

I should have stayed silent as I took a couple of steps in his direction, but the impatient police officer in me couldn't help but yell out.

"David!"

He turned his head toward me and stiffened up, a look of shock enveloping his face. Without saying a word, he pulled the keys from the lock and quickly ran up the nearby stairs to the fourth floor. I immediately gave chase, instantly regretting the early warning I had given him. He was younger and faster than me, able to scramble up the stairs at an incredible clip, leaving me to continue yelling more, thinking he would suddenly obey my orders.

"David, stop!" I shouted, scaling the stair treads as only an out-of-shape, middle-aged man could. "Son of a bitch," I grumbled to myself, feeling more winded with each step I took. The adrenaline was all that pushed me forward. The good news was that the building had only four floors, so unless that floor had a different layout than the previous three, he had nowhere else to go; the stairs were the only way to the exit. At least, that's what I thought.

When I got to the top floor, the hallway was vacant. David was gone. My first thought was that he either knew someone on this floor who had let him in or he had forced his way into one of the apartments. I hadn't heard him banging on any doors, and I didn't hear any skirmishing or anyone yelling. Then I saw it. The fourth floor was identical to the lower floors, with apartments 4A through 4D along its walls, except for one subtle difference. At the end of the hallway, just past unit 4C on the left, there was a fifth door, and it was slightly ajar.

I approached cautiously, pulling my gun from its holster, unaware of what to expect. I could see that, unlike the other wooden doors in this building, this one was a bulkier steel door with a levered push-bar. Once I was within a few feet of it, I saw the small, red and yellow metallic placard that read, "Roof Access" just above the aluminum bar. You had to love these older buildings. There was no handicap accessibility, but there was an unlocked door leading to the roof, where an unsupervised child could easily wander up and throw himself off. This city certainly was a special place.

I slowly pushed the door open and peeked around its bulky frame into the darkness. Thankfully, enough light from the hallway outside had pierced its veil, allowing me to see a small staircase leading up to a second steel door. As much as I didn't like it, I couldn't back down now.

Gripping my gun tightly, I darted up the five stairs and pressed my back against the steel surface. I could feel my heart pounding through my chest, and I was breathing heavily. A bead of sweat rolled down from my left temple, which I wiped away with the sleeve of my jacket. I closed my eyes and took a deep breath to calm my nerves, then let the air slowly exhale from my lips. When my eyelids reopened, I decided it was time. I reached down and grabbed the knob in one hand while stepping down a stair to allow the door to swing open. I yanked the door open and jumped out onto the roof with my gun extended, practically tripping over some stray 2x4s scattered about the roof.

Catching my bearings, I turned to my right and saw David standing twenty feet away at the front side of the building. A three-foot-high brick ledge spanned the perimeter of the roof; David was leaning his upper body over it, looking down at the street below. I felt a little better knowing toddlers would have to work a bit at throwing themselves off. I was surprised David hadn't run to the fire escape located at the back of the roof.

"David!" I yelled a second time, my gun still pointed. I could see he wasn't armed, but I wasn't taking any chances. "Step away from the ledge, David."

He turned to me and took two steps forward, away from the short wall. He raised his hands in front of his chest and began shaking them.

"Don't shoot me, Mr. Haddick," he pleaded, shaking his head and looking like he was about to break down in tears. "I didn't do anything."

"Then why did you run, David?" I questioned, taking a step forward.

"You scared me," he replied. "I got spooked."

"Bullshit!" I said. "I know about the Letter Group. I know the kind of shit they were feeding you. I know about your breakup with Amber and how devastated you must have felt. But none of that shit gave you the right to do what you did."

"It.., it was an accident," he cried. "I never meant for any of it to happen."

"I'll tell you what," I began. "Why don't you get on your knees, David? Do you hear me? Get on your fucking knees, you son of a bitch, and put your hands on top of your head."

"But I didn't mean it," he said, taking another couple of steps forward as tears began to run down his cheeks.

"Shut the fuck up and get on your knees. Now!"

He slowly lowered himself to his knees, pleading through his blubbering tears. "It was an accident, Mr. Haddick. I swear! It was an accident. I didn't think she was going to die. I only wanted to scare her for what she did to me."

"What the fuck are you talking about?" I asked, slowly edging myself closer to him. "*Who* are you talking about?"

"Amber!" he yelled. "I thought she loved me. She said she wanted us to be together. Then I found out the truth. She had been sleeping around with others in the group. She kept a list of all her 'conquests,' as she called them. I was just another sucker she could add to her list."

"So you killed her because of it?" I shouted.

"I didn't kill her," David argued. "I mean, not intentionally. I was at her place, and I had just learned what she had been doing behind my back. We got into an argument about it when suddenly, she started shaking and gasping for air. She clutched her chest and dropped to her knees. I knew she was having an asthma attack. She started shaking her arm and pointing to her bedroom; she kept her inhaler on the dresser. I ran to get it, but I couldn't stop thinking about what she had done. I was furious and not thinking straight. All I wanted was to teach her a lesson.

"I walked back into the living room with the inhaler in my hand, but when she reached out for it, I didn't give it to her. I wanted her to feel what I was feeling at that moment. Even when she collapsed to the floor, barely able to take a breath, I stood and watched her. I kept thinking, 'I'll wait another ten seconds.' Ten seconds turned into twenty. Then thirty. I wanted her to squirm. But then, the squirming stopped.

"Once I realized she had stopped moving, something in my brain snapped me back, and I felt the blood rush from my face. I immediately knelt beside her and began shaking her and calling her name, but she wasn't waking up. I didn't know what to do. I panicked and started shaking. I thought she had stopped breathing. I thought she was dead and that I had just killed her. And all because I kept her inhaler from her.

"I got up and started freaking out, pacing back and forth, wondering what to do. It was an accident; I didn't want to go to jail. It was stupid; I know. But nobody knew I was there. I thought if I just left, nobody would need to know. She just died from an asthma attack. It happens every day, right? So I dropped the inhaler near her, and I ran out. It's been bothering me every day since then. You have to believe me, Mr. Haddick. I never meant for that to happen. I was just scared."

"Just scared, huh?" I repeated, sickened by what I had just heard. "And what about all the others?" I questioned. "Were their deaths only 'accidents' too, you twisted fuck?"

David shot me a perplexed look as he tried to quell his tears. I was beside myself with anger, but even in my enraged state, I recognized a look of confusion.

"Others?" he questioned.

It was the last word I remembered hearing before the shot rang out. I had seen the flash of light in the distance behind David. It came from the roof of the building across the street. I wasn't sure what had happened until I saw David fall forward onto his stomach. I instinctively jumped to my left and fell against the brick ledge at the side of the building, peering across the street at the darkened rooftop. I couldn't see a thing, and I wasn't behind any protective cover. The other building was a story taller than this one. If bullets started flying, I was a sitting duck. I did all I could to squeeze tighter against the wall to present myself as a thinner target. I heard gurgling noises coming from David, alerting me he was still alive. I pulled out my phone and dialed 911.

"This is Officer Jim Haddick of the Southbridge Police Department. I need immediate medical assistance at the Vinmore Apartment building on South Street. Male, Caucasian, with a gunshot wound. Suspected shooter on the roof of the building across the street from the Vinmore. I'm going to try to get to the victim. Hurry the fuck up; we're on the roof."

I didn't immediately hang up; they always needed more, but I needed to get to David before it was too late. I put my phone in my jacket pocket and crawled on my hands and knees, clinging to the side of the perimeter wall, even though it offered me no protection. I made it to David's adjacent location without being shot but couldn't take the risk of jumping so carelessly into the open. I was no good to anybody if I was dead. I could see the growing blood stain on the back of David's shirt. He needed serious medical attention. I peered over at the other roof again, still unable to see anything, then looked back at David's twitching body.

"Stay with me, David," I shouted, my heart beating a mile a minute. "I'm coming to you."

With my back pressed firmly against the brick ledge, I started breathing like I was back in Lamaze classes with Karen. Several minutes had passed since the initial gunshot. There had been no second one. Coincidentally, as I watched David's breathing become shallower, I found myself thinking the very thing David had told me, *'I'll wait another ten seconds.'* Like *his* story, ten seconds became twenty. Then thirty. An Image of Amber lying on her apartment floor flashed into my head, and I wasn't going to let that happen to David.

Taking a final glance across the street (however useless it was), I darted out from the safety of the short wall to David's side. I first tried to drag him to the side in case the shooter was still a threat, but from my knees, I couldn't gather the strength. I shifted my body so that I was facing the adjacent rooftop. If there was any movement, I wanted to see it. Placing my gun beside me, I rolled David over to see if there was any blood on the front of his shirt. I needed to know if the bullet had passed through. It hadn't. Blood trickled from his lips as he stared into my eyes.

"It… was… an accident," he said through labored breath.

"It's okay, David," I said. "Don't try to talk. Just stay with me; help is on the way."

"This… is… what I… get," David said. "I… deserve… this."

"David, shut up," I said. "You're going to make it. They're almost here."

I looked away from him for a moment, glancing across the street at the opposite roof. *How could this have happened*, I thought. Why would somebody have shot David? And then, a moment of clarity came upon me. The text message swirled in my head.

You had your three days, Detective. I've seen no results. It is my turn now. I warned you of my vengeance. This will come to an end.

Of course! It had to be. Papa Rio must have had one of his goons following me. He knew I'd eventually find the killer, and then he'd take him out. That bastard!

I couldn't think about that now as I felt David shift his body in my hands.

"How… did… you know… about… Amber?" he asked. "Did he… tell you?"

"Did he tell me?" I questioned. "Did *who* tell me?"

Just then, I saw David's eyes widen with fear as he reached up and gripped my sleeve.

"Look… out!"

The warning came late. I don't think I felt the strike before a blurry haze came over me and everything faded to black.

Chapter 24

THE PRICE WE PAY

As I regained consciousness, everything seemed foggy. How long was I out for; a minute? Maybe two? A voice was speaking, but it was muffled, sounding like I had cotton balls stuffed in my ears.

"No, no, no, no, no," the muted voice spoke. "It wasn't supposed to happen like this. How did everything get screwed up? Why can't I do anything right?"

That was when the voice suddenly became recognizable.

"B-Ben?" I questioned, pushing myself to a seated position and rubbing the back of my head where a large lump had formed. "What are you doing up here? I told you to stay in the car. It's not safe." My voice sounded unfamiliar to me, and my lips were dry. My tongue was sticking to the roof of my mouth.

Everything was still a little fuzzy as I tried to recall what had happened. I was talking with David when something struck me, and I blacked out. David! I had to check on David.

I twisted in my seated position and saw David lying still beside me. I could hear Ben pacing behind me, mumbling to himself and sounding distraught. Trying to dispel the wooziness I felt, I nudged David's unmoving body to try and get a reaction from him.

"David!" I yelled, still confused about what was going on. Blood had absorbed into the rear of his shirt and crept up the sides into view. There was quite a large puddle around him; he'd lost a lot of blood. Still fighting the dizziness, I reached forward and placed two fingers on his neck, searching for a pulse. There was none. A chill ran through my body, and I suddenly felt nauseous. My arm fell limply from David's neck onto the roof's rough surface. My head dropped heavily to my chest as I wiped my hand across my forehead to calm my thoughts. David was dead. My head was pounding, not only from the blow but also from a terror I hadn't felt in a long time.

"This is your fault!" Ben screamed out, snapping me out of my stupor. "You killed him. You killed David!"

Still seated, knowing I wasn't capable of standing, I twisted back to face Ben, who was still pacing back and forth. He was shaking his head while tears streamed down his face. Right away, something caught my attention. In his left hand, I noticed he was holding one of the cut pieces of 2x4 that I almost broke my neck on when I first stepped out onto the roof. But what was more disturbing, which sent a shiver down my spine, was that in his right hand, he held my gun.

"Ben, what are you doing?" I questioned calmly. "Why do you have my gun?"

He stopped pacing and turned to me as tears fell from his chin.

"You shut up!" he yelled, uncontrollably waving the gun and pointing it in my direction. "You promised me you wouldn't hurt him. You're supposed to keep your promises. I trusted you, Dad."

"Ben, calm down," I said. "I need you to hand me my gun. Come on, son; this isn't a game. Give me the gun before someone else gets hurt."

"Like you hurt David?" he cried, saliva shooting from his lips. "After you told me you wouldn't?"

I could see Ben was losing it. David was his best friend. And now, he was dead with blood pooling all around. It wasn't something anyone should witness, let alone someone Ben's age. I had to de-escalate the situation before he did something rash.

"I didn't shoot David," I said, maintaining eye contact while shaking my head.

"That's bullshit!" Ben responded through his tears. "I heard the gunshot, Dad. That's what made me run up here."

"No, you're wrong, Ben," I continued. "That was someone else. Someone on the other roof shot David." I extended my arm behind me, pointing across to the other building. "It was someone who decided to take the law into their own hands, someone who wanted to stop the killer. I was trying to save David. Now, come on; give me my gun."

"You're lying!" Ben yelled. "*You* were the one that wanted to stop him. Only, I told you David wasn't the Alphabet Killer. But you never listen to me, and you shot him anyway."

"I told you, I didn't shoot him, Ben. And as much as I know it hurts you to hear this, he *was* the killer. He admitted to me how he killed Amber."

"No, no, no," Ben yelled, dropping the 2x4 and bringing both hands to his ears as if trying to block out what I had just told him. "That's not what happened," he cried, dropping his hands as he began to pace again. "He didn't kill Amber. That was an accident."

Hearing those words, I suddenly felt a knot in my stomach.

"Wait, you knew about Amber?" I questioned.

"Dad, do you even listen to me?" he asked, keeping his eyes downward. "We're best friends; of course, I knew. He called me in a panic, asking for my advice. He wanted me to talk to you about it, to explain what had happened. But I knew you wouldn't see things straight. You've never listened to me. The job was always more important. Putting people in jail was more important. I wasn't going to let that happen to David. I told him not to say anything. I told him I would take care of things and that no one would know. That's why I came back to the city to stay with you. David needed my help."

"Ben, what did you do?" I asked nervously, not sure I wanted to hear.

He stopped his pacing and turned to me angrily.

"Stop interrupting me," he seethed. Then he began pounding his left palm against the side of his head.

"Stop it, Ben!" I shouted. "You're scaring me. Why don't you give me the gun, and we can talk about this like father and son? Come on; what do you say?"

"No," he said, pointing the gun at me again. I instinctively put my hands up in front of my chest. "You're trying to trick me," he added. "You never listen. Not to me. That's why I couldn't tell you. That's why I had to handle it myself."

"Handle what, Ben?" I asked. "Talk to me. I'm listening now; you have my full attention. And would you please be careful with the gun?"

He glanced at his hand that was pointing the weapon at me, tilted his head in confusion, then dropped his arm to his side.

"Why, why, why do I need to explain this?" Ben mumbled through clenched teeth. "It was an accident," he spoke louder. "He didn't mean it. And he didn't deserve to go to jail for it - not after what she did to him. I wasn't going to let that happen. He didn't do anything wrong. But I knew nobody would believe him, especially not you. So I had to be his protector, his friend.

"David was careless. I had to go to Amber's apartment to find the inhaler. Didn't he know the police could pull prints from it? I knew. But then, he didn't have a detective for a father, as I had. I wiped the inhaler clean and placed it back where I found it. Then, as I was leaving, I saw the picture of him and Amber. That would have been a big problem. I would have taken it, but somebody might have noticed it was missing. So, I pulled the photo out and scratched out David's face. Nobody would know they were involved."

"Okay, okay," I said. "That's not a big deal. You were trying to help a friend. We can talk to Frank about this. We can get you some help."

"Help?" he cried. "I don't need help, Dad. *David* needed the help." He pointed the gun at David's lifeless body. "That's why he had joined that stupid Letter Group in the first place. It was so easy for Amber to convince him to join. David used to tell me all about it. What a group of losers. All they did was confess their problems and their vices, promising they'd give up their aberrant behaviors. I felt like he was swimming in a cesspool of filth. I'm sure you would have hated it, Dad. But Amber loved it. That's what started all the problems. She was really into that messed up shit, even carving an A into her head. That's also where she met the others. The bitch. She just wanted to sleep around. Young, old, it didn't matter. She loved the idea of freeing herself. She even convinced those she slept with to cut their own letter into their heads like they were marking themselves for her. She didn't care about David's feelings. But *I* did.

"Then, after Amber's death, he dragged me to the meetings a couple of times so I could see what it was like. Every time he saw someone with a letter cut into their head, he was reminded of what she had done. He couldn't stop talking about it. He couldn't believe Amber could hop from one person to the next like it meant nothing. Then the meetings just stopped, but he was already so hurt, and I couldn't stand to see him in such pain. I knew what I had to do. Amber had already paid the price, but those others had to pay too."

"What are you saying, Ben?" I asked, slowly pushing myself to my feet. "What do you mean they had to pay?"

"Come on, Dad," Ben cried, raising his arms skyward. "You're a cop. You deal with this stuff every day. People are bad, and they need to be taught a lesson."

"No, no, Ben," I said, waving my palms toward him, "it's not like that."

"Shut up!" he yelled. "You don't think I've watched you all these years? I'm not stupid. I've learned from you, Dad. I know how badly immoral people infect this city. I could see it infecting David. I had to make it stop. The Letter Group wanted to have fun with letters? Well, I could have fun with letters too."

All at once, it hit me. My insides twisted, and my arms became numb. I felt like I was going to vomit, and my legs began to wobble beneath me. My thoughts were swirling in my head, and I couldn't fully grasp what I was hearing. But it was all there; it had always been there.

"Ben, Please," I pleaded, shaking my head in denial. "Please, Ben. Say it's not true. You didn't do anything. Tell me you didn't do anything."

"I did what you taught me, Dad," he answered proudly. "I know I'm not as good as you, but you've been doing it longer. You're the best. But I'm helping to clean up the streets."

"No, Ben; no. What have you done?"

"Yes, Dad. I did what I had to do. It's *their* fault. They shouldn't have let Amber play with them like that. Bruce and Cameron had to pay. So, I learned where they lived – being a cop's son pays off sometimes, you know? They both recognized me from the group and had no problem letting me into their homes. Bruce even showed me his workshop. The idiot. He didn't know he was about to die. He's the one that gave me the idea of how to do it, showing off his torch like I was supposed to be impressed. So, he had a little accident.

"And poor Cameron. It was so easy. Everyone thought he killed himself. The hardest part was figuring out a way to knock him out. But duh, Mom's a nurse. After a couple of visits to see her at the hospital, I had what I needed. You know, they don't keep that stuff locked up as tight as you might think. That blew my mind." He placed the barrel of the gun to his head. "Crazy, right?"

"Ben, Ben!" I shouted, taking a step toward him. "Stop it! Put it down! Don't play around like that!"

"Stay back!" Ben yelled, re-directing the gun at me. I did as he ordered and took a step back.

"Why don't you just put the gun down, okay?" I said, patting my hands in the air in a downward motion. "There's no need for any of this; we can just talk."

"Now, you see," he said with an awkward smirk while dangling the gun sideways in his hand, "that's exactly what Denise said when she found out she was about to die." He grinned and let out a slight chuckle.

Ben circled around me, continuing to wave the gun like it was a toy. He stopped at David's feet, looking morose at his lying body as the grin faded from his lips.

"I loved him, Dad," he said softly before stepping away toward the roof's front ledge wall. "Why can't everybody have these feelings? Did you know Denise was going to leave her husband?" he said, turning back to me. "She wasn't happy. There was no love there. But she was ready to leave her daughters, too. That sickened me. How could someone as awful as that be allowed to live?"

"Ben," I said, shaken by what I was hearing, as evidenced by my quivering hands, "Denise had nothing to do with hurting David. She was innocent. How could you have done what you did?"

He looked at me straight-faced, pushing himself away from the front wall. "It's like you said, Dad. 'Anyone can be a killer.' And don't kid yourself; Denise was far from innocent, the way she was ready to abandon her kids like that. None of them were innocent.

"Eva was a prostitute," he continued. "I bet you didn't know that. She confessed it all to the group. She said she was going to give it all up to start a new chapter in her life. Then I saw her on the corner one day, peddling her body to some guy in a fancy car. I guess the money was too good to give up. But really, *she* was the one who had given up on life. I made sure she understood what that meant."

Listening to Ben talk like that was making me sick to my stomach. What was happening? I couldn't believe what I was hearing.

"Ben, whatever this is," I began, "whatever's happened to you, I can get you help. You're sick, Ben. That's all."

"I'm not sick," he bellowed, striding forward. "You know who was sick? Francine. That's right; she was a member of the

Letter Group too. She was an alcoholic. She joined the group, thinking they could help her. She even lied, telling everyone she had quit. But I saw her, Dad. I saw her through the window after hours at Manfredi's, taking swigs from the bottle. Why would she lie? Criminals lie all the time, too. When I knocked on the door, and she saw it was me, she had no worries about opening the door for a cop's kid. Sucks for her. She never saw me holding the pipe; I hid it well."

"Stop, Ben," I cried. "Can't you see what you've done?"

"*I* see," he replied. "Can't *you?* These were not nice people. They all deserved what they got.

"Gaston was a thug, working for Papa Rio. I know how you feel about that guy. I've been listening to it for years.

"Hu was a heroin addict. She said she was going to get clean, but she never did. She wasn't going to straighten her life out. She didn't even try. She probably would have been dead in less than a year anyway.

"And Izzy, she bragged to everybody about how she was getting rich by stealing identities. That's not right, Dad. You wouldn't stand for that, and neither could I."

"But why?" I questioned. "Why do all of this? Why didn't you just come to me so I could take care of it?"

"I tried, Dad," he responded. "But you never listened to me. You were always so wrapped up in your job. So, I decided to *make* you listen.

"After Cameron, when nobody had paid attention to the good I was doing, I had to make you see. I knew you'd be able to connect the deaths if I gave you a little hint. I cut the D into Denise's head, but since nobody had even questioned the letters in the first three, I had to make it stand out. I needed to get your attention. That's all I ever wanted, Dad. Just your attention. So, I cut another D, a *bigger* D, into her leg. That's what got you assigned to the case. But you still hadn't noticed what I'd done for you. How would you be proud of me if you didn't know I was helping you? That's why I let Eva deliver my note to you. I thought it was pretty clever.

"I knew you'd eventually figure it out, but I couldn't make it that easy for you. Plus, what better way to show everybody how good a detective you are than to have you solve the biggest case this city had ever seen? But then they went and suspended you. How dare they? They had no idea you were the only one capable of catching the killer.., well, catching me. Another one of my notes would ensure they brought you back. And they did. You should be thanking me, Dad. Everything was for you."

Ben smiled, and it burned straight to my core. What was wrong with him? I didn't raise him to be like this. Maybe that was the problem; I didn't raise him at all. As he said, I hardly paid attention to him. I was all about the job. There was nothing else. If anything, it was all my fault. I felt sick to my stomach. I created the Alphabet Killer.

Ben waved the gun back and forth between us. "Look at us," he said. "Bonding over police stuff. You know, I thought you were going to figure it out sooner. But then the FBI lady distracted you. That was a shame, but it allowed me to keep working my magic, bringing you more puzzle pieces, cleaning up the streets like you always wanted."

Just then, emerging from the roof's open door, Agents Hayes and Cordell sprung out onto the roof with their guns raised, causing me to turn toward the commotion. Behind them, Frank, Mick, and a couple of other officers jumped out, their weapons raised as well. Startled by their sudden appearance, Ben darted behind me as he fearfully aimed the gun over my shoulder. He was several feet behind me, with David's body situated between us.

"Ben, drop the weapon and get on the ground!" Agent Hayes ordered.

I threw up my hands, trying to control the ensuing madness.

"Whoa, whoa," I shouted. "Hold on, here. Nobody needs to get hurt. This is all just a misunderstanding. Ben was just about to put the gun down. Isn't that right, son?" I said, glancing over my shoulder.

"Tell them to go away, Dad," he cried. "It can't be them. You have to be the one to take me in. This is *your* case."

"Ben, listen to me," Agent Hayes said. "We don't want anything bad to happen to you. Lower the weapon, now."

"Dad?" Ben questioned, bringing his gunned hand up to rub his forehead with the butt of the weapon. "Why are they here? They're not supposed to be here."

His teeth were clenched, and I could tell he was getting frustrated.

"It's okay, Ben," I assured him, turning my head to the side to see him peripherally. "They're not here for you. They're here for David." I turned back and gave a slight nod to Hayes. "I'm the one that's going to take you in. This is *my* case, remember? I'm the only one smart enough to catch the Alphabet Killer."

Ben shook his head in confusion, looking down at David. Then he snapped his hand forward, pointing the gun toward the officers again.

"No!" he yelled. "You're trying to trick me."

Agent Hayes yelled out, "Your father's telling the truth, Ben. The EMTs are right down there in the stairwell." She pointed toward the open door with her right hand while keeping the gun in her left, pointing at Ben.

"You see, son," I said. "People are here to help David."

"David is dead! You killed him! He was my friend."

"That's right," I said. "He was your friend. And you don't want him up here on this roof. Let the officers take him downstairs where he can be more comfortable. Don't you think that would be better?"

"No, no, no, no, no. Something's not right. They weren't smart enough to catch me. I can't trust them. How can I trust them with David?"

"Ben," Frank's voice chimed in. "You know me. You can trust me."

"You can trust me, too," Mick interjected, stepping out from behind Cordell. "Come on kid, put the gun down. We'll take care of David."

Ben began shaking. I could tell he was struggling, unsure of who to trust. I noticed his arm begin to lower. I thought it would be best if I looked him in the eye so he could see it was his father talking and not the cop who ignored him most of his life.

I looked at Marion and the other officers, trying to assure them I had this under control if they could just keep their cool. Slowly, so I didn't frighten Ben even more, I stiffly turned in his direction, my hands still up in front of my chest. He looked at me with saddened eyes.

"Ben, we're all here to help you," I said softly, staring into his eyes. "Me, Frank, Uncle Mick, we all care about you. I think you know that. I wouldn't let anyone hurt you. But you have to give me the gun; you don't need it anymore. You've done a good job of cleaning up this city. Let me handle it from here. I'm the best cop you know, right?" I smiled. "Give me the gun, Ben."

I extended my palm, an offer of good faith, hoping he'd hand the weapon over. He glanced over my shoulder at all of the officers pointing their weapons at him.

"What do I do, what do I do," he mumbled, looking confused. "I don't know what to do."

"You give me the gun," I said calmly. "Then we talk about things – father and son."

Tears began to form again in Ben's eyes. He looked back at me and tried his best to fake a smile.

"I really screwed up, didn't I, Dad?"

"No, Ben," I replied. "*I* screwed up. I should have paid more attention to you. I should have been a better father."

"You were out catching criminals," he said. "You were stopping the bad guys. That's the greatest father ever. And now I realize.., I think I might be the bad guy."

Ben took a step away, a look of regret on his face, and brought the gun to his temple.

"Ben, no!" I yelled. "It doesn't have to be like this. Put the gun down. I don't let the bad guys die, and I'm not letting you die, either. You're my son, and I need you. Please, Ben, give me the gun."

"But the things I've done, Dad. I shouldn't have done them. I must not be a good person."

I could see his arm tensing up.

"You're my son, Ben," I replied. "You *are* a good person. You were trying to help your father. That's what good people do. And you can't help others if you do this. Put the gun down. Let's help you continue to be a good person."

"But I've killed a lot of people, Dad."

His finger began twitching on the trigger as more tears streamed down his face.

"Please, Ben," I pleaded. "I need you, son. Your mother needs you. Give me the gun. Please. Give me the gun."

Ben began to shake his head, wrestling with the decision only he could make. I stood frozen for a moment as I watched his finger tense up on the trigger. In a heartbeat, I thought of all the times I had let him down, and I wasn't going to let him down again. I lunged forward and grabbed at the weapon, pulling his arm down from his head. He didn't release the gun, instead, gripping it tighter, trying to wrestle it free from my grasp. Neither one of us was willing to give in to the other as we pulled at the gun. Eventually, something had to give. And as the gun fired, we both stared at each other, wide-eyed and afraid. And as Ben's face suddenly expressed pain, I looked at him and smiled, and said, "It's okay."

I could feel the blood soaking into my shirt as I dropped to one knee.

Ben immediately dropped the gun. "Dad!" he screamed. "I didn't mean it." He fell to his knees to embrace me. I reached down and pushed the gun away. As soon as it was clear, the agents and officers charged forward, shoving Ben to the ground as he cried in anguish at what had just happened. I fell backward into Marion's arms as the medics ran in from the stairwell.

"There was a shooter on the other roof," I said to Marion, wheezing.

"The officers caught him trying to escape the building," she replied. "Don't worry about that. Let's get you fixed up."

I looked down at my blood-soaked shirt and then back at Marion. "I think it's too late for that. I'm not sure we'll be able to continue our fun after this case," I joked, wincing in pain.

"Shut up, Jim," Marion said to me, a hopeful smile on her face as the EMTs pulled her away. She really was good at faking her emotions.

I could hear Ben screaming as Mick handcuffed him and pulled him to his feet. They walked him by me, a look of fear on his tear-filled face, and I smiled to give him solace. He'd been through enough. Too much. I wanted him to know his Dad still loved him.

Ben was safely in custody. The Alphabet Killer was caught. The people of this city were safe again. I did what I set out to do and to hell with the consequences. It's what I always did; it was my job. I was a cop. I could finally close the case. I had said I would catch the killer if it was the last thing I did. And with that thought, I felt my eyes close.

Chapter 25

THE LAST LETTER

He sat on the edge of his uncomfortable mattress, alone and confused, staring at the concrete floor, wondering how everything in his world had fallen apart. His family didn't understand him. Some on his block admired him as if he was a celebrity, but even they didn't understand him. If Ben had known how it all would have turned out, perhaps he would have rethought his motives. It wasn't supposed to end as it had. And it ended worse than he ever expected it would.

The trial was swift, the punishment severe: eight consecutive life sentences, one for every life he took. It was the recording that sealed his fate. Even in death, it seemed, his father played a part in bringing another criminal to justice. How was he to know his father had dialed 911, then inadvertently placed the phone in his jacket pocket, the line still open for the operator to gather the incriminating

341

confession of all the murders? It was as if he had planned it all along. The FBI agents also received full details of Ben's nefarious crimes as The Alphabet Killer, having been listening from the stairwell for a time before jumping out with guns raised. They heard all they needed to hear. It was an open-and-shut case and everything the jury required to deliver a guilty verdict. It was a fair and just decision; he understood that now. Had he been among them, weighing in on a similar case, he would have concluded the same based on the pieces of evidence provided in the state's prosecution. Whatever else had been brought to light during the trial was used only to vilify him in the public's eyes, and it was everything he deserved.

Eight months had passed since his inevitable conviction; the sentencing came down like a hammer. He would never see the outside world again. He would grow old in the confines of the pale-gray walls of BrentRidge Penitentiary. He would remain an outcast, even among many of the other unsavory characters who shared the same fate as him. And eventually, he would die in that place, a prisoner in more ways than one. And still, it wasn't the worst fate he could have received. *That* ill fortune fell upon his father.

There was nothing the EMTs could do. The moment the firearm discharged, his father's life was forfeit. From point-blank range, the bullet did more than enter and exit his body. Severe damage to the stomach, intestines, diaphragm, spleen, and pancreas ensured the regrettable outcome. Within minutes, blood had filled his chest. Death was inescapable.

Ben had spent many nights reliving that moment of misery. It was never what he intended. He had only wanted to make his father proud, something disappointingly unknown to him as a child. He didn't blame his father for it; he knew being a police officer extracted a heavy toll. Ben might not have liked it, but it was an inconvenience with which he learned to live.

Still, what young boy didn't crave his father's attention? And as Ben grew older, that attention became almost nonexistent. So, what was an impressionable young man expected to do? It had to be something his father would understand, and what his father understood most was criminals. And after all the years of dedication his father spent cleaning up the streets, could his son do no different?

Had the opportunity not presented itself, it might have been another year or two before Ben could have stepped out from his father's shadow and into the light for which he so desperately yearned. By then, his life might have taken a drastic turn, causing him to question his very reason for living. And that could have ended tragically. Just as it *almost* played out on the roof, it would have been easy for him to get ahold of his father's gun at any time and end it all by putting a bullet in his brain. But how would that have made his father proud? And what fun would that have been? No, it was better to do what he had done, to follow in his father's footsteps and take out the filthy garbage before only the cockroaches were left to scurry around. It was the right thing to do. And with that lingering thought, Ben smirked.

As he stared at the floor between his feet, letting his thoughts wander, he hadn't heard the guard approaching his closed cell until the wooden stick slammed against the bars, startling him.

"Haddick," the CO said sternly, pointing his baton threateningly toward Ben and unlocking his cage, "looks like somebody still likes you. You've got visitors."

Ben looked confused, wondering if Officer Devon was playing a joke on him. He had no friends, and his mother had only visited three times since his incarceration, making it abundantly clear on her last visit that she couldn't do it anymore. She couldn't pretend like everything was okay.

Seeing her son locked behind bars and knowing what he had done to be in that awful place made her stomach churn. He was alone.

He pushed himself from his bed and walked to the edge of his cell, his eyes locked on the officer's stick, wondering if it would be used on him. When Ben tried to step out of his now-open cell, the guard quickly pressed his weapon horizontally against the cell door, preventing Ben's advancement.

"What's the magic word, asshole?" the CO asked, a nasty smirk on his face.

Ben looked Officer Devon in the eyes, unblinking, and with a disturbing smile, answered the officer's unwarranted request.

"You should know by now," Ben began, "words and letters are a specialty of mine. Do you really want to challenge me?"

The Correctional Officer sneered at Ben's comment, pulling his head away a few inches to interpret Ben's ominous expression. After a few silent seconds, the guard curled his lip up and responded.

"Shut the fuck up, Haddick!" he said, pulling his wooden club from the doorway and pointing it toward the cell block exit. "Goddamn freaky lunatic mother-fucker," he continued mumbling as the prisoner walked by him. Ben smiled, holding back a slight giggle.

Before exiting the confines of his secluded, concrete hell, Ben's wrists and ankles were handcuffed. Two officers then led him into a series of hallways until they finally arrived at a private room where Ben had previously met several times with his lawyer. This time, however, two other familiar faces sat at the table in the center of the room. Ben half-heartedly smiled and subtly raised his hand to wave as he was escorted forward to greet his unexpected visitors.

"Uncle Mick," he nodded, sliding into a chair at the opposite side of the table. "Richie. What are you two doing here? Hasn't every book already been thrown at me?"

"Shut the fuck up," Richie barked. "You know goddamn well why we're here."

"Hey, take it easy, Richie," Mick jumped in. "He's just a kid."

"He's *not* just a kid," Richie sneered. "He's a fucking psychopath is what he is. You'd do well to keep that in mind, Mick."

"I don't have to keep anything in mind," Mick's calm voice chimed in. "I've known Ben since he was a baby. Ain't that right, kid?" Mick nodded to Ben, expecting no response.

"Fuck it then," Richie snapped. "You deal with this piece-of-shit killer.

Mick shook his head in disgust at Richie's comment, then turned to face Ben.

"Sorry about that, Ben," Mick said. "Richie can be a real asshole."

Richie grumbled under his breath.

"It's okay, Uncle Mick," Ben responded. "I've had plenty of time to think about things. I understand why Richie is upset. But I still don't know why you are here."

Mick glanced at Richie, then back to Ben with a puzzled look on his face.

"Come on, kid," Mick said. "You gotta know why we're here."

Ben squeezed his lips together and slowly shook his head. "I honestly don't know."

Mick squinted his eyes as if trying to determine if Ben was telling the truth. It was a useless attempt as Ben was too clever to give away any hint of a lie. Instead, Mick reached into his jacket pocket and pulled out a folded envelope, its torn and jagged top edge a possible indication of the officers' frustration.

"What is that?" Ben questioned.

Mick stared at the envelope in his hand. "You really don't know?"

"Sorry, but I really don't know," Ben answered.

"Oh for crying out loud," Richie griped, "give him the goddamn envelope"

Mick placed the envelope down on the table and slid it forward. Ben's eyes shifted downward, unsure if he should take the bait. He noticed the words "Southbridge Police Department" written on the front, though he didn't recognize the handwriting. He slowly brought his cuffed hands from his lap and rested them on the table inches from the envelope. He glanced up at the two officers to gather what their intentions were. When he saw they lacked expression at his sudden interest, he snatched the envelope from the table. Opening it up, he leaned back in his chair and pulled out the letter within. He unfolded the paper, and his face suddenly shifted to irritation.

HELLO, OFFICERS. I HOPE THIS LETTER FINDS YOU. AFTER ALL, LETTERS ARE WHAT I'M ALL ABOUT. YOU SHOULD KNOW THE TIME HAS COME AGAIN. I'VE LET YOU PLAY YOUR SILLY GAMES LONG ENOUGH. WE'LL CALL THAT FIRST ROUND PRACTICE. THE REAL SHOW IS ABOUT TO BEGIN. I THINK YOU'LL LIKE WHAT I HAVE PLANNED.

I WATCHED YOUR CAPTIVE'S PROGRESS. I MADE HIM A HOBBY OF MINE. YOU SHOULD BE PLEASED WITH HIS WORK; HE DID A LOT OF GOOD. THE CITY NEEDED CLEANSING. AND ITS SAVIOR – DETECTIVE HADDICK – FALTERED. THERE WAS ONLY ONE CLEAR PATH TO TAKE.

I LIKED HIS LITTLE GAME. THE ALPHABET MAN. AND HOW HE PICKED THE PLAYERS OFF. LETTER BY LETTER. MAKING THEIR CAUSE OF DEATH MATCH

THE LETTER OF THEIR NAME WAS A DEED WORTHY OF THE INHERITED MONIKER.

IT WAS FITTING THAT HIS LAST VICTIM WAS THE MAN WHO FAILED HIM IN LIFE. AT FIRST, I DIDN'T UNDERSTAND THE SIGNIFICANCE OF HIS DEATH, THINKING THE ALPHABET MAN HAD ERRED. AFTER ALL, HE WAS ON J. YET HIS VICTIM'S FINAL BREATH WAS TAKEN FROM HIM BY A BULLET. THE GAME HAD BEEN PLAYED SO WELL, TO THAT POINT. HOW COULD THE ALPHABET HAVE BEEN BROKEN? I TRIED TO RATIONALIZE THE LOGIC. GUN. GUNSHOT. PISTOL. FIREARM. NOTHING SEEMED TO FIT. THEN, IT CAME TO ME. I REALIZED THE SHEER GENIUS IN HIS PLAN. IT WAS CLEVER AND ALMOST INDECIPHERABLE. BUT I DISCOVERED IT. "J." FOR JIM; DEATH BY JUSTICE.

Ben's scowl exhibited his annoyance at what had been written. The person who wrote the letter knew nothing about him. But as he continued to read more, his expression slowly changed.

THIS IS WHY THE ALPHABET MAN'S LEGACY MUST LIVE ON. THERE IS SO MUCH MORE TO DO. THE STREETS ARE LITTERED WITH VERMIN. THEY ARE A DISEASE. SPREADING PESTILENCE. OTHERS DIDN'T PAY ATTENTION TO HIM. BUT I DID. HIS WORK MUST CONTINUE. I WILL BE YOUR NEW MESSENGER. HE STARTED ON THIS PATH, TAKING THE LIVES OF "A" THROUGH "J." IT IS MY TURN TO CONTINUE WHERE HE LEFT OFF. "K" WILL BE MY FIRST VICTIM. THERE ARE SO MANY TO CHOOSE FROM, AND A KNIFE SHOULD DO JUST FINE. HAVE NO FEAR; I'VE ALREADY CHOSEN HER, THAT BITCH OF A WOMAN. I THINK THE ALPHABET MAN WOULD BE PLEASED. THIS IS THE DIRTIEST "K" OF THEM ALL.

BUT ALAS, I DON'T WANT TO GIVE TOO MUCH AWAY. THAT WOULD HARDLY BE ANY FUN. YOU'LL JUST HAVE TO WAIT AND SEE WHAT I HAVE IN STORE. I'VE GOT GREAT PLANS FOR US. SO MANY LETTERS LEFT; SO LITTLE TIME. ENJOY THE CALM WHILE YOU CAN. YOUR WORST NIGHTMARES ARE ABOUT TO COME TO LIFE. AS I SAID, THE FIRST ROUND WAS ONLY PRACTICE.

YOU'LL BE DEALING WITH ME NOW. α

Ben smiled. Someone had been paying attention. He wasn't alone. There was someone else like him.

"Who wrote the letter, Ben?" Mick asked. "Was it you?"

Ben raised his eyes from the paper and looked at Mick, a slight smirk on his face. "It wasn't me," he said. "I didn't write this."

"What about that other shithead that's in here with you?" Richie asked. "The other letter freak, Carmine Lemon. Do you know if he's been writing any love letters recently?"

"I never see Carmine," Ben replied. "He's in gen pop."

"Tell us who could've written this, kid." Mick pleaded. "Don't let this happen again."

"I honestly don't know who this could be," Ben responded.

"This fucking kid is wasting our time," Richie said, throwing his hand up and slamming it on the table.

"Well, what about the 'K' he mentions in the letter?" Mick asked. "Any idea who he might be after? Was there someone in The Letter Group you thought should be next?"

Ben shook his head while maintaining eye contact, "Nobody comes to mind."

Mick took a deep breath, staring disappointedly at Ben. "You're not going to give us anything, are you?" he said.

"I told you," Richie remarked. "A waste of our fucking time."

Ben's glare shifted back and forth between the two officers. He looked back at the words written in the letter, studying the hidden meaning behind them, then placed it with the envelope on the table and slid them back to Mick.

"Sorry, I can't help you."

"Yeah, I'm sorry too, kid," Mick replied.

Richie slapped Mick on the arm while rising from his chair, "Let's get out of here. Leave this asshole to rot in peace."

Mick folded the letter and placed it back in the envelope, keeping his stare fixed on Ben while he did. Ben didn't flinch. The officer stood up, joining his partner, continuing to look at Ben as if waiting for the young man to provide them with information. It never came.

Turning in frustration, the officers were escorted out of the small room, momentarily leaving Ben to ponder the implications of what he had just read. And as the Correctional Officer grabbed his arm and pulled him from his seated position to escort him back to his cell, a sinister smirk engrossed Ben's face.

He hadn't told Mick the truth. It saddened him to lie to his uncle, but he couldn't give it away; the plan was too great. He didn't know who wrote the letter; that was a mystery to him, but he knew immediately who the "K" had to be. It was all spelled out for him in the letter. "*That bitch of a woman.*" "*The dirtiest 'K' of them all.*" And the fact that Ben "*would be pleased*" was the clincher. He knew exactly who "K" was. K was for Karen, his mother, and he wouldn't dream of stopping what was coming. The smile on Ben's face grew larger, but not only at the thought of his mother getting her just punishment for giving up on him. No, that wasn't the only reason for the excitement he felt. He had noticed how the admirer had signed their name. Ben had used the Greek letter Omega in all of his writings, signifying the end for all those he killed. The writer of the latest letter chose the Greek letter Alpha instead.

This was a new beginning.

THE DARKNESS IS UPON US

SEE WHERE IT ALL BEGAN

SOMETHING SINISTER AWAITS

WITNESS THE RISE OF EVIL

HELL IS FOR CHILDREN

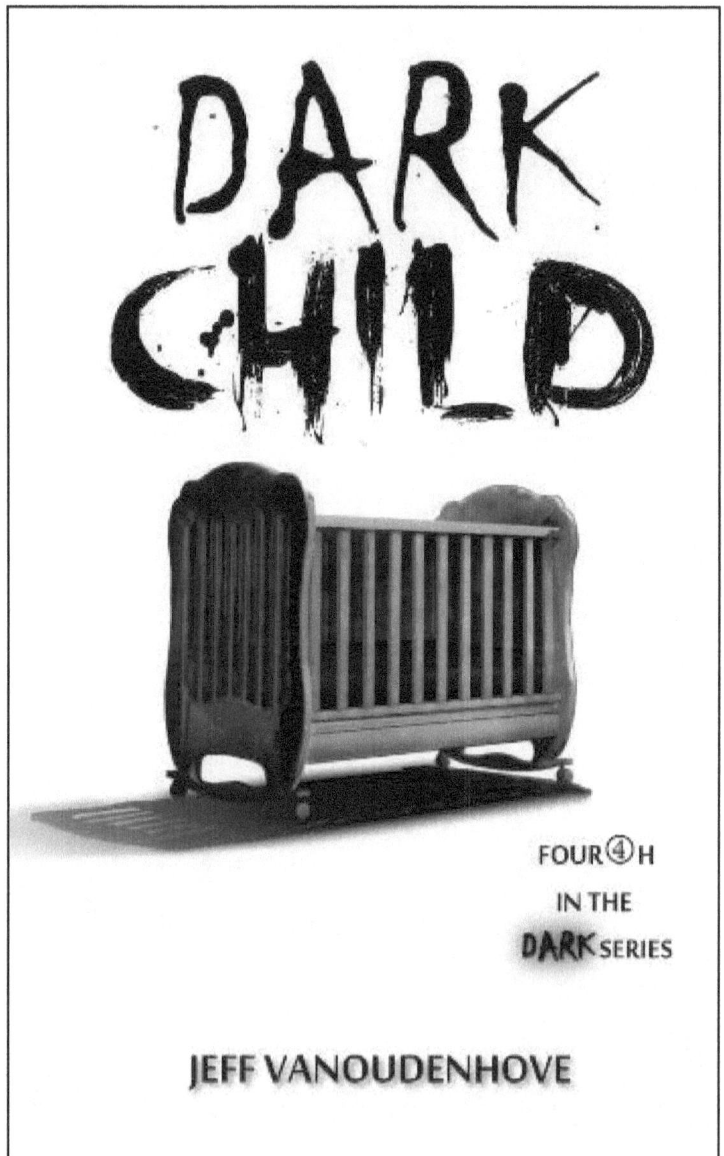

JEFF VANOUDENHOVE

THE END IS NEAR
THE FINAL
DARK
F5FTH
IN THE
DARK SERIES
JEFF VANOUDENHOVE

YOU WILL BE SHOCKED

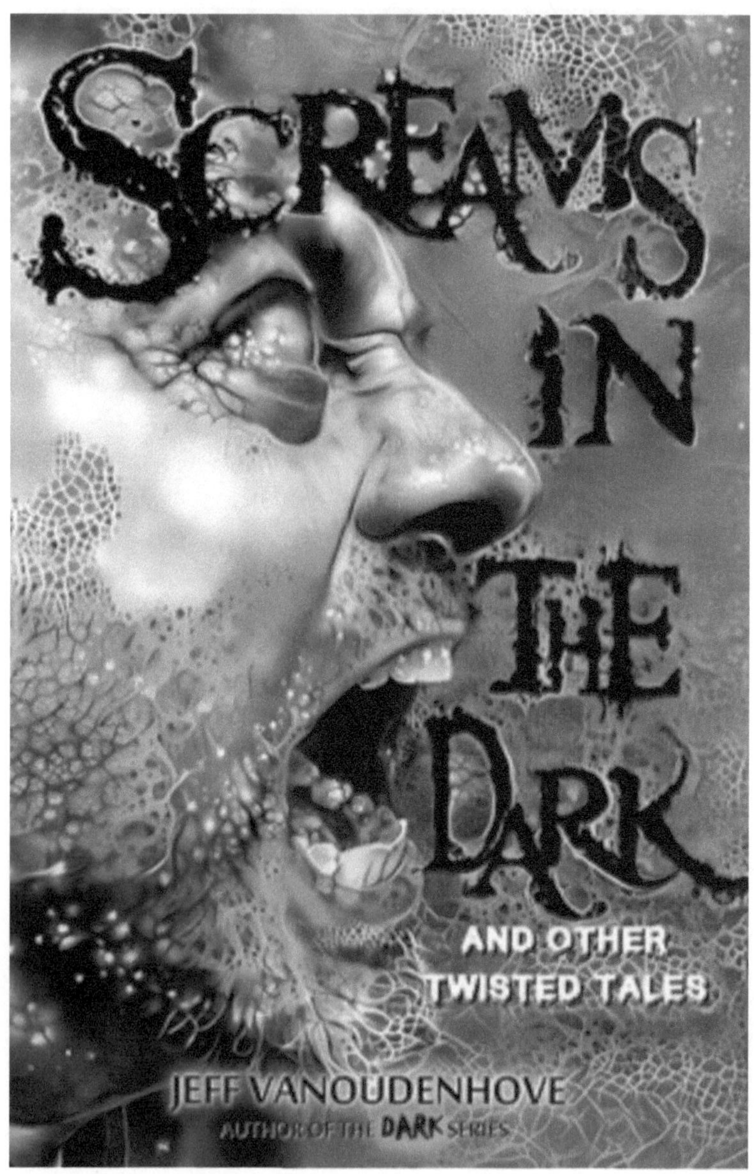

Jeff VanOudenhove has written several novels in the genre of dark fiction, including the psychological suspense series, The Dark Series. His talent for storytelling combines unforgettable characters and dire situations, mixed with astonishing plot twists. The Alphabet Killer is Jeff's seventh book. He lives in Western Massachusetts with his wife.

www.ingramcontent.com/pod-product-compliance
Lightning Source LLC
Chambersburg PA
CBHW030747310726
48969CB00005B/1342